SEDUCING RYAN

The sound of a door opening and closing snapped Angele back to the present.

It was Ryan.

He came in from the parlor, and she saw in the moonlight that he had already stripped off his shirt and was working on his belt buckle. He yawned, and she knew he would not have crossed to her room this night, but she was leaving him little choice now.

She held her breath against a heavy sigh to think what a glorious body he had. His buttocks were high and round and tight. His waist was narrow, and his back was broad and strong. Just to look at his sinewy arms made her tingle with wanting to have them hold her tight.

His thighs provoked a delicious tremor, as well. Firm, muscular.

Her heated gaze moved to between his legs.

He turned toward the bed, and that was when he saw her.

"Angele? What are you doing here?"

Mustering every shred of bravado she possessed, she slowly drew the sheet away so he could see the rest of her . . . see that she was not wearing a gown.

"Do you have to ask?" she said in a voice so husky with desire that she did not recognize it as her own.

"What's this all about?"

"Is it so difficult to figure out?" she purred. "You're my husband, I'm your wife . . . and I want you to make love to me . . ."

very good!

J J

RYAN'S BRIDE

Maggie James

Zebra Books
Kensington Publishing Corp.
http://www.zebrabooks.com

ZEBRA BOOKS are published by

Kensington Publishing Corp.
850 Third Avenue
New York, NY 10022

First Printing: March, 1999
10 9 8 7 6 5 4 3 2 1

Printed in the United States of America

One

Ryan Tremayne's first awareness when he opened his eyes that morning was how his head was pounding like a blacksmith's anvil.

The next thing he noticed was the very naked woman sleeping beside him.

She made a purring noise and snuggled closer but did not open her eyes.

Slowly, through the throbbing pain in his temples, it came back to him—how the evening before, he and his cousin, Corbett, had ventured from the boundaries of Paris to the district of Montparnasse and the many cabarets there. They had gorged themselves with rich French cuisine—*boeuf bourguignon*—casseroled beef with onions and mushrooms cooked in a red Burgundy wine—and *gratin dauphinois*—sliced potatoes baked with cream and grated cheese.

And, of course, they had sampled several varieties of wine, the French national drink. Riesling from the Alsace Valley, Pouilly-Fuissé from the Bordeaux region, and Champagne, perfected by the seventh-century monk, Dom Pérignon.

Somewhere along the way, they had met two lovely *filles de joie* who had topped off the pleasured night like a wickedly irresistible dessert.

Just then the woman's fingers danced across his flat belly to trail downward and between his legs.

Ryan felt a warm stirring in his loins, and, if not for his

headache, would have pleasured her—and himself—one more time. Hell, he couldn't even remember her name but fuzzily recalled that they'd had themselves quite a tumble.

He carefully extricated himself from her caress, and, despite a dizzy lurch, managed to sit up on the side of the bed.

He glanced about at the opulent furnishings of the room he'd not bothered to notice the night before. The bed was set aside in an alcove, like an altar. A white silk rug covered the steps leading up. Four grand columns, entwined with garlands of myrtle and ivy, supported the bed's fancy canopy. The sides were hung with rich silk curtains, embroidered in a design of rose clusters. Elsewhere there seemed endless carvings of doves and cupids amidst the gold, marble, and crystal furnishings.

Ryan took comfort that he and Corbett had, despite how they had been drinking, managed to avoid becoming involved with *les insoumises*—common streetwalkers. It appeared the women had led them to a high-class bordello. No doubt it came with a price to match, but money was one of the few problems Ryan did not have.

He stood uneasily, then, relieved the room did not start spinning, went to the window and drew back the heavy drapes.

Below, all was quiet on the *rue de la Gaite,* which was the center of the district's nightlife. Looking to the west, he calculated by the angle of the sun streaming down upon the tombstones and monuments of the *Cimetière de Montparnasse* that he had slept most of the morning.

It was time for him to be on his way, regardless of how bad he felt. He had not come to France for a holiday. His purpose was to buy coveted French Anglo-Arab horses for breeding at BelleRose, the family plantation in America. To do so, he would have to travel to the province of western France called Touraine. He was looking forward to the trip, for the valley of the Loire River was renowned for its scenic beauty in addition to fine grazing land for horses.

A pitcher, basin, and soap were on a sideboard. While he

bathed, he wondered where Corbett was and hoped he was also awake and getting dressed. Ryan had hired a coach to take them to the town of Chartres, and they were due to leave at noon. If they kept to schedule they would arrive by dark and could spend the next day visiting horse farms.

His clothes had been neatly folded on a chair but reeked of perfume and wine. He would have to change once he got back to the hotel.

After pulling on fawn-colored breeches, Ryan yanked on his white pleated shirt, tucked in the tail, and reached for his coat.

Suddenly long, slender arms reached from behind to wrap about his waist.

"There is no need for you to leave, monsieur."

"I wish I didn't have to." He reached in his pocket, took out his soft roll, and counted out five thousand francs. He couldn't remember whether they had agreed on a price earlier but figured that was more than enough.

She smiled at the amount. She laid it on the sideboard, then pressed against him once more. "Even if you weren't so generous, I would let you stay as long as you want, for free. It was wonderful. *You* were wonderful. It's always just business for me, but with you, it was a pleasure."

Ryan was glad to hear it. He always tried to satisfy the women he bedded. And he owed that to Jessamine Darcy. A Richmond whore, he had gone to her for his first sexual experience when he was only fourteen. She had taken a fancy to him, and for a long time after that, she took him to her bed without charge and taught him everything she knew. And the most important lesson he could learn, she said, was to never be a selfish lover. When a woman was satisfied, Jessamine avowed, there was nothing she wouldn't do for her man—in bed or out.

Reluctantly, he pulled from her twining arms. "I enjoyed it, too, and maybe I'll see you again before I leave Paris." He knew there was little chance of that—not with so many other beautiful women around. He kissed her cheek.

"Now, do you know where I can find the man who was with me last night?"

Her mouth was curved in a disappointed pout to see him go. "The second door on the right. He's with Charmaine."

As Ryan had feared, Corbett wasn't awake. He'd had to pound on the door to get any response from Charmaine. He told her to tell Corbett he'd be waiting for him and to hurry up.

The parlor downstairs was empty. Evidently business was slow before noon on Sundays. Ryan paced about anxiously, paying no attention to the garishness of the decor nor the pretty women passing through ever so often in their revealing negligees.

Maybe he should not have indulged in revelry the night before, but he was not quite thirty years old and enjoyed an adventuresome, albeit sometimes reckless, lifestyle. His father, Roussel Tremayne, was urging him to marry a woman of French birth and settle down. He had warned he would disinherit him otherwise and leave BelleRose to Corbett. Corbett was like a second son and had found additional favor in Roussel's eyes by taking a French wife—Clarice—and producing a son. They all lived in the mansion, which Clarice oversaw ever since Ryan's mother's death some years earlier.

Corbett had assured Ryan he was happy with the way things were. The last thing he wanted, he said, was to see Ryan disinherited. That was why, Corbett emphasized, he and Clarice wanted him to marry Clarice's cousin, Denise. Then they would all be one big, happy family, living under the same roof.

Ryan had never particularly liked sharing the house with Clarice. She could be a witch at times. But Corbett didn't seem to mind.

Ryan believed Denise would look upon sex as her duty and something to be endured in order to have children. He had dared to want more than that in a wife, things like

passion, romance, and excitement, all of which were highly
unlikely with Denise. But he supposed he would do as so
many other men—take a mistress. So, yielding to family
pressure, he had proposed the night before he left for
France.

However, much to his surprise, Denise had said no.

Ryan had been stunned. He wasn't the conceited sort
but had thought she would leap at the chance to marry
him. After all, he was one of the most eligible bachelors
around and also had great family wealth.

At first, he had been downhearted. Corbett tried to
cheer him by saying Denise was only teasing him. Clarice,
who knew her better than anyone, said she was probably
wanting to make Ryan miserable so he would cut his trip
short and return to Richmond to persuade her to change
her mind. Clarice also said she thought Denise was angry
with him for going to a romantic place like Paris without
her. He should have waited and taken her on her honey-
moon. But Ryan had already planned the trip before he
proposed and would have had to delay it longer than he
wanted in order to take her.

He could believe what Clarice said about Denise was
true. She could be quite cunning. But once he reached
Paris, he stopped worrying about it as he began to enjoy
all the pleasures the exciting city had to offer.

Now he fumed to think how he was ready to get down
to the business of buying horses, only Corbett was delaying
things by taking his time leaving a woman's bed. He supposed Corbett felt like a young colt turned out to run in
a pasture, because Clarice kept a tight rein on him back
home. He could not even keep a mistress, because Clarice
watched him like a hawk. It was only occasionally that he
was able to escape for a night of forbidden pleasure, and
then he used Ryan as a cover—much to Ryan's annoyance.

It was almost half an hour before Corbett came running
down the steps, face flushed, shirt unbuttoned, and coat
slung over his arm. He was grinning. "Sorry, but I had a
bit of trouble getting away."

"And we're going to have trouble getting back to the hotel in time. I told you we have to leave by noon if we're to make Chartres by dark."

Corbett yanked on his coat and fastened his shirt buttons as he followed Ryan out the door. "Don't worry. I'm right behind you."

"There are no buggies for hire," Ryan grumbled. "No one wants to work on Sunday."

"It's not a long walk—twenty or thirty minutes. We can make it."

"Oh, *I'm* going to make it." Ryan spoke over his shoulder as he began to take long strides. "And if you don't, you can stay behind."

Corbett snickered. "That might not be a bad idea. Charmaine invited me back, even said she wouldn't charge me her regular price. And she was fantastic, Ryan. Huge breasts and a nice, round ass, and . . ."

Ryan ignored him. He never talked about his women and didn't care to hear about Corbett's. Quickening his pace, Corbett had a hard time keeping up with him while jabbering and soon fell silent.

Actually, there was a lot Ryan didn't like about his cousin, but they seldom had words, and, all in all, got along well. Corbett's father, Lamar, had been Roussel's only brother. When he and his wife were killed in a carriage accident the year Corbett was sixteen, Roussel had taken him in.

Despite the rush and being annoyed, Ryan did not fail to notice the beauty around him. It was spring, and the warmth of the day was sending waves up from the pavement. Tables grew like sudden moss on the rocks of the streets outside the cafes. Lovers, under the spell of the magic season, embraced in passion on benches along the way. Flower vendors quietly offered their perfumed blossoms, and proud parents ventured out with their newborns in buggies.

In the distance, church bells pealed, calling the faithful to worship. That meant it was not quite noon, and Ryan dared hope they could keep on schedule.

"I say let the blasted carriage wait," Corbett called from

behind, gasping. "You're paying him to oblige us, remember?"

"I'm paying him to have us in Chartres by dark, but we won't make it before dark *tomorrow* if you don't hurry up."

"You know, you're not usually so grumpy. It's only been since Denise set you on your ear by turning you down. I say forget Chartres, forget the horses, and let's book passage on the first ship from Le Havre and get you home so you can change her mind. Maybe then you'll be fit company."

But again, Ryan was not listening to him, because something ahead had suddenly caught his eye.

Angele Benet did not like stealing, especially in the shadows of a church, which made it seem even more of a sin. But she was homeless and hungry. Two months earlier, her mother had died. Now Angele was an orphan and struggling to survive by any means necessary.

Neither did she want to rob elderly ladies, but she was afraid to try stronger targets for fear of being overpowered. And jail was the last place she wanted to go. So she preyed on the women on their way to morning mass at the convent chapel of the Abbaye Val-de-Grâce.

Darting out of the thick shrubs lining the walkway, Angele would snatch a reticule, then flee. Her victims never gave pursuit, either too frightened or too frail.

There was never much money. A few francs to buy a loaf of bread and some fruit, enough to keep her from starving.

She had been crouched in her hiding place for nearly a half hour, waiting to catch someone alone. So far the women had walked in pairs or more. She was about to give up, despite how her stomach rumbled with hunger, when she spied a late arrival hurrying along as fast as her feeble legs would carry her.

Angele made ready. She had the act down to a fine art and knew exactly how to snatch the reticule without knocking her victim down. She did not want to hurt anyone and sometimes even apologized for robbing them.

The woman was upon her. Angele leaped forward to grab the small lacework bag, then took off running as the woman screamed in outrage.

Ryan saw the scruffy young boy just as he leaped from the hedging. It was obvious what he was up to, but Ryan was too far away to do anything except yell.

Ryan reached the woman, who stopped screaming when he clutched her shoulders and quickly asked if she were hurt.

She was shaken and angry but said no harm was done.

He ordered Corbett, catching up to him, to stay with her. "I'm going after him."

"It's no use," the woman called as he took off. "He's headed for the catacombs. You'll never find him down there."

Ryan had heard about the city's network of tunnels below ground. Once the site of Roman stone quarries, they were now haven for the homeless . . . as well as the thieves and scalawags of Paris. But he had never been the sort to give up, and kept on going, undaunted.

He could see the boy in the distance, rounding the corner of the Place Denfert-Rochereau. He was not very tall and dressed in rags. He was also holding his tattered knit cap on his head as though it was his most prized possession. Then he reached the entrance to the catacombs and disappeared inside.

Ryan was right behind but skidded to a stop as two burly-looking men stepped from the shadows to block his way. One held a knife and the other, a big stick.

Ryan's wild streak had landed him in the middle of a few brawls in the past. He knew how to fight, and, with no time to waste, reacted quickly. A chopping blow to the throat of the one holding the knife made him drop the weapon and fall to his knees gasping for breath. Snatching the stick from the other, Ryan rendered a blow across his chest that sent him also crumpling to the ground.

The fight gone out of them, the men began scrambling

toward the bushes and escape, but Ryan let them go as he plunged into the catacombs.

He could hear the boy running in the distance and cursed to think he might lose him. There were probably tunnels going in every direction, and if he weren't careful, he could wind up lost in the bowels of the earth. But the boy was probably as familiar with the catacombs as the rats that skittered across his feet.

Finally, Ryan knew he had to turn back. He was running in pitch darkness, bumping into rock walls as the path twisted and turned.

Then he heard a splashing sound and a yelp. Rushing ahead, he nearly stumbled over the boy, who had slipped and fallen in the slimy water. "I've got you, damn you." He groped for, and found, the nape of his neck and jerked him to his feet. "You're coming with me, and you better not give me any trouble."

Angele was not about to surrender. She swung at the man holding her and connected her fist to his jaw, but the blow was glancing. He easily caught her arm to pin it behind her back with a painful twist. She bit her lip against the pain as he began shoving her along.

"I ought to wring your scrawny neck," Ryan muttered as he headed for the light in the distance. "You've made me good and late, damn you. And I'll have to throw these clothes away. They're ruined."

Angele did not speak. She was biding her time. Her arm was hurting terribly because of the way he was holding her, but she was not about to give him the satisfaction of knowing it. As for his clothes, it served him right. He should have to sleep in the catacombs and go days without eating, and then he would know what true misery was.

Once they stepped outside, she came alive. Catching him off guard, she tore from his grasp and bolted for the shrubs. But Ryan was quick and sprang after her. They both stumbled and fell to the ground in a heap. "You just won't learn, will you? I've a mind to—"

Ryan froze. He had rolled on top to grasp the front of

the boy's shirt to give him a sound shake to set his teeth rattling, only it was not a boy's chest he felt. His hands were closed about *breasts*—small but firm breasts that had been concealed under bulky clothing.

He was holding a woman.

His gaze crept upward. Her cap had fallen off, and when she gave her long, thick mane of coal-black hair an arrogant toss, he was suddenly, strangely, reminded of the same spunk he had seen in wild, untamed colts. No matter she was no longer free. Her spirit was yet unbridled.

She glared up at him with eyes the color of warm cognac, aflame with her rage. Her coat had fallen open, and her bosom was heaving. His palms rested against her nipples, and despite the bizarre circumstances, Ryan felt himself becoming aroused.

To avoid embarrassment, he rolled to one side but slid his hands down, grasping her waist to keep her from getting away. "Why, you're nothing but a girl. What the hell are you doing robbing old ladies?"

"I was hungry," she said in French. "Something you would never understand." She gave her hair another insolent toss, then nodded to the stolen reticule on the ground nearby. "I haven't opened it. Take it and let me go."

She was not pleading. Ryan sensed it was not her nature to do so. That was probably what had driven her to steal rather than beg like other paupers—pride, as well as stubbornness.

"And if I do, what then? Will you keep on robbing old ladies?"

Her laugh was bitter. "Which do you prefer—that I steal a few francs or starve to death? But maybe you think I should walk the streets instead."

It was Ryan's turn to laugh. "From what I felt, I think you're more suitable for a rich man's courtesan."

"Like you?" She eyed him with contempt. She could see he was well-to-do despite his rumpled appearance and smelly clothes. "What I am or what I become is no concern of yours. Now let me go."

"Why are you dressed as a boy?" he asked in the French he knew so well—which was fortunate, he thought, since the girl clearly would know no English.

"You think I could survive as a woman? Living in the catacombs? The streets? I wouldn't last a day. Bad things happen to homeless women. Now will you take your hands off me?" She wriggled in his grasp.

Ryan wondered what could have driven a young woman to become a thief and live among the dregs of humanity. Despite her dirt-streaked face, he could tell she would be quite pretty if she were cleaned up. He made his voice gentle. "Why do you live this way?"

She looked at him as though he were daft. "I told you—because I don't want to starve. So I live as a man and steal to survive."

"Don't you have family?"

"No. But that is none of your business."

"But surely—"

She gritted her teeth and clenched her fists. "You wouldn't understand anything about me or my kind. And if you don't let me go, I'll be sent to prison, and I'd rather die."

He saw a glimmer of tears in her eyes but also noted how she bit down on her lip—hard—to hold them back.

A shrill whistle cut into the silence that hung between them.

A gendarme was running toward them. Ryan found himself wishing he had longer to think about whether he should let her go.

"I will take over now," the gendarme said when he reached them. "It's not often we're able to catch these wily bastards."

The gendarme's brows lifted as he realized it was a woman in Ryan's grasp but surprise quickly turned to a scowl. "A woman thief. It always disgusts me." Grabbing her arm, he jerked her roughly to her feet.

"I don't think it's necessary to be so rough with her," Ryan said as he stood.

He yanked Angele's wrists behind her back and tied them with a thin rope that had been looped around his belt. "If these thieves want to pretend they're men, then that's how they'll be treated."

The gendarme spotted the reticule on the ground and bent to pick it up. Then, grasping Angele's arm tightly, he steered her toward the street.

Ryan kept up with them. "Where will you take her?"

Angele turned to look at him coldly. "What do you care?"

The gendarme gave her a sharp smack on the back of her head. "Be quiet. People are in church. They don't want to hear the likes of gutter trash like you." Curtly, he told Ryan, "Jail. For a long, long time. She won't get mercy because she's a woman, believe me."

Rounding the corner to the Place Denfert-Rochereau, Corbett came running to meet them, then slowed, wide-eyed, to see the angry-faced young woman, her hands tied behind her back. "You . . . you mean the thief was actually a woman?"

Ryan stared after the gendarme and the girl as they kept on going. "Yes," he said quietly, sadly, "I'm afraid so."

He watched them till they were out of sight, needled to wonder why he felt so deeply moved.

Perhaps it was the spirit mirrored in her eyes.

And the strange, smoldering desire he felt to try to tame it.

Two

Angele fought to keep track of time, but it was difficult. She could not distinguish night from day, because there were no windows. The only light came through the small square in the door when one of the guards walked by holding a lantern.

Twice a day a bowl of thick, sour-smelling gruel was pushed through the opening. But since the food was always the same, she could not tell the difference between morning and evening meals.

Once a day a guard would briefly open the door to exchange buckets of water for drinking and personal needs, but that, too, didn't occur on any kind of schedule.

At first, she had tried to talk to the guards. She wanted to know when she would go before a judge, and she asked what day it was . . . what time it was. But no one ever answered.

The day she was arrested, she had been puzzled when she was not taken to the central jail in Paris. Instead, she was led along streets and alleys and finally down steps to a dark, narrow hall lined with cells.

Sometimes she could hear the other prisoners, and they all sounded like women. Maybe that meant the city jail was full of men, and the women were kept elsewhere. But then she did not know about such things as jails and prisons and wouldn't be learning now if not for the meddling stranger.

Thinking about him made her stomach churn with fury.

Why had he been so determined to catch her? Most people would have minded their own business rather than chance entering the catacombs. He had obviously fought off Bruno, and Felix, too, which was quite a feat. She had passed them on her way in and called out that someone was after her. They had said to keep on running, that they would take care of it.

She had noticed the stranger spoke French with a foreign accent. American, probably. If she had not fallen, she would have escaped. And he would have eventually got turned around and lost and never found his way out.

And it would have served him right, too, she thought with a fresh wave of anger. Thanks to him, she might be sent to prison for years and be an old woman when she got out.

"Damn him," she whispered in the stillness. "And damn Uncle Henry all the way to hell."

Uncle Henry.

The name rolled like hot bile over her tongue.

He was her father's brother and the reason that her life—her whole world—had been ripped to pieces. If not for him, her father would still be alive, for he'd had him accused and convicted of a crime he did not commit.

Stripped of everything he owned, the shame and humiliation had driven her father to take his own life, and she and her mother were left alone and poverty-stricken.

The reason Henry Mooring hated his brother Cecil and wanted to destroy him was quite clear. In the past, Henry had caused their father much grief with his gambling and drinking, which resulted in his being disinherited. Cecil was bequeathed everything. He offered to share with Henry, but Henry was furious and said he didn't want his charity, vowing revenge. It had been a long time coming, but when it did, Cecil never had a chance against Henry's carefully planned scheme.

But Henry hadn't stopped with taking over the family property and all the wealth and position that went with it. He also wanted Angele and said it did not matter that she was his niece. When she rebuked him, he had brutally raped her and vowed if she did not marry him he would see her in prison, just like her father.

When her mother found out about it, they had fled England and gone to France, her mother's native country. There they used her mother's maiden name of Benet, because they learned word had spread across the Channel that Henry Mooring was offering a huge reward for their return. They were forced to hide, but it was not long before her mother died without warning in her sleep. Angele suspected she had just grieved herself to death.

So Angele was left alone to fend for herself, which was not easy after the way she had been raised. Surrounded by maids, she'd never had to do a thing for herself and spent her time riding the horses she adored over the countryside she loved.

But her mother had also seen to it that she learned everything a well-bred young lady should know. As a result, Angele was just as comfortable among nobility and royalty as she was with the groomsmen who tended the horses and the gardeners who cared for the estate's lush gardens.

It had been a happy life, and though Angele was in no hurry to marry, she enjoyed the attention of would-be suitors. One day, when the time was right, she intended to take a husband and have children. She was confident of continuing the lifestyle she was accustomed to, never dreaming what fate so cruelly held in store. The thought of winding up orphaned, homeless, and starving was inconceivable.

Now, to make matters worse, her uncle's threat had, ironically, come true: she was in prison. And all because of the interfering stranger.

She had thought of little else since that day, playing over and over in her mind all the details. And she had concluded that there was a moment when he'd been about to let her go. A few more seconds, and she was sure he would have shown mercy. There had just been something in his eyes once he discovered she wasn't a boy. He had kept on holding her, and she had seen how the anger and disgust faded to the slightest glimmer of compassion.

She had sensed something else as well, and that was how he had continued to hold her after he knew she was a woman. His fingers had caressed her breasts ever so slightly. Then came another staggering awareness, one that flamed her cheeks to recall. He had been lying on top of her, and while it might have been her imagination when she felt the sudden hardness pressed against her, she didn't think so. Such thoughts were not invented in her mind, especially after her uncle's brutal attack. And in a way, it had brought the terror washing back.

He had teased her about how she could be a courtesan, his wit fascinating at such a time. He was probably a very pleasant person under normal circumstances. He certainly had a nice smile, warm as spring sunshine.

He was strong, she could tell. Yet, as he continued to hold her, his grip lightened a bit, as though he were afraid he might be hurting her. That was why she was so sure that, given a little more time, he would have let her go. He seemed to care. Otherwise, why would he have told the gendarme not to be so rough with her or asked where she was being taken?

She told herself she was being silly. The whole thing had happened so fast, and he probably hadn't given her a second thought once it was over.

Still, there in the damp darkness, Angele preferred to dwell on the stranger rather than her miserable past or precarious future. She also felt a bizarre kind of comfort to remember his touch. It had made her feel that as long as he held her, she was insulated against all harm. And that was an emotion she'd not known in a long, long time.

Tears welled in her eyes, and Angele furiously blinked them away. Her uncle had tried to make her cry the night he raped her, so he would know she felt the pain he intended to inflict again and again until she agreed to marry him. Then he would be gentle, he said. He would not take her so roughly. But Angele had refused and promised herself to be so strong in the future that nothing—no one—would ever make her shed a tear.

To take her mind from the nightmare of the past, she again thought about the stranger, wondering what kind of life he led. He probably had a wife, a family. And he looked like a man of position and wealth, even if his clothes were rumpled and dirty from chasing her.

Then she made herself think of good times, like riding her horse Vertus, her hair blowing about her face as they galloped across the lush, green valleys, wild and free. It was a memory she would forever cherish, for it would likely never be again. Her uncle had taken Vertus, like everything else, and she was no longer free and likely would not be for a long time—if ever.

She felt a little stirring in the pit of her stomach and knew it was not hunger that gnawed but will—the will to survive, no matter what.

"I will not let them beat me down," she said aloud.

"I will not let them beat me down," she repeated, and with each word an inner strength surged. She could feel it winding about her heart, warm and caressing. There had to be a way. There had to be.

And she said it again, even louder, because it felt so good, better than anything had made her feel in too long to remember.

Screams of protests exploded around her from the other prisoners.

"*Shut up, you bitch.*"

"*We ain't listenin' to your caterwauling.*"

"*Hey, I'm tryin' to sleep. Shut that hole in your face.*"

A few seconds later, footsteps sounded outside her door, and Angele cringed. She'd let herself get carried away, and the guard had heard, and there was no telling what he might do. She'd heard the other prisoners yelling back and forth, talking about the torture called The Grave. A wooden box buried in the ground, it was where rebellious prisoners were laid out like corpses and covered up with barely enough air to breathe. They were left there, buried alive, until they were almost dead. And oh, God, she prayed it would not happen to her.

A key turned in the lock.

She had been sitting on the floor, leaning back against the cold wall, but straightened in apprehension.

The door opened. A lantern was held up, and in its glow, she could see the guard called Leon. He was scowling as he swung the lantern about, searching the shadows. Then he saw her and growled, "All right. Get your thievin' ass over here and don't give me no trouble. The commandant wants to see you."

Angele cringed. "Please. I meant no harm. I was just talking to myself. Maybe I was too loud, but I didn't mean to be. I'll be quiet. I promise."

His scowl deepened as he walked to where she was crouched. Reaching down, he twined his fingers in her hair and gave a hard yank. "Don't argue with me, you little bitch, or I'll tear it out by the roots."

Angele managed to stand. He shoved her toward the door, and she nearly fell but righted herself in time.

"Walk ahead of me." He pulled a leather baton from his belt. "And if you try anything, I'll lay your head open with this."

Angele had no doubt he would. She had heard him do it to another prisoner and had peered out the opening in the door to see the blood streaming down her head. She had been dragged out and never brought back. Angele wondered if she had died in The Grave.

After climbing steps that seemed to go on forever, she was taken to a small office where a man sat behind a desk. He had dark, mean eyes, bushy brows, and a hawk nose. His mouth twitched with either pleasure or annoyance. She could not tell which.

He stared at her in silence for a few seconds, then stood and waved Leon from the room and told him to close the door after him.

"My name is Captain Duclos," he said, rising. Then, hands splayed on his hips, he began to circle her as his gaze flicked up and down in scrutiny. "Skinny," he murmured. "But you should still bring a good price."

He took her by surprise when his hand clamped about her throat to jerk her face close to his. "Open your mouth."

She did so, dizzily recalling how her father had always looked at a horse's teeth before buying the animal.

She fought to keep standing despite how her knees knocked together. He had said she would bring a good price and frantically wondered what he meant. She wasn't a slave to be sold at auction. She was a prisoner, and there was a difference. Dear Lord, there had to be.

He released her, and she coughed a few times before she was able to ask, "When will I go before a judge? I've been here—"

His hand closed around her throat again. "You will not speak unless I ask you a question. Is that understood?"

She struggled to nod.

He went back to his desk and sat down. "This is not the city jail," he said, as though she did not have sense enough to figure that out for herself. "We take prisoners here when they don't have room there. But we are getting crowded here, as well. I have to make room. Some of you have to leave."

Angele wanted to ask where she would be taken, but he looked as though he was hoping she would so he'd have an excuse to choke her again. She swallowed her curiosity.

"You are a thief. You will go to prison for a long time. You may even die there. How do you feel about that?"

It was her cue to speak, and she quickly did so. "I . . . I feel badly," she said, wanting to sound contrite when it was all she could do to keep from springing across the desk and raking her nails down his arrogant face. But she had to play by the rules if she were to survive, and that meant she had to appear whipped, beaten. "If you will let me go," she dared add, "I promise I will never steal again."

"Really?" He smiled and leaned back to stare at her through templed fingers.

"Yes. I swear it."

"And why were you stealing in the first place?"

"I was hungry."

"And what will you do when you get hungry again?"

"I'll find work."

"Doing what?"

She had no idea. She had tried everything, from mending clothes to scrubbing floors. But she couldn't let him know that. "I'm not sure. There must be something—"

"Of course there is. And it's the only way you can stay out of prison."

Apprehension was a snake, curling about her spine. "What do you mean?"

He did not meet her querulous eyes. "Don't worry about it. You'll be well taken care of. A man will be coming in a few hours to pick you up. Leon will see to it you get a bath and clean clothes." He wrinkled his nose. "You smell to high heaven. All you wenches smell."

He shoved a piece of paper across the desk along with a pen. "Here. Sign this."

His hand was positioned so that she could not read what was written. "What is it?"

"It merely says that you agree to be released to this man's custody in exchange for his paying your fine to get you out of jail and making sure you won't go back to being a thief.

"Not that anyone really cares what happens to you," he added with a smirk. "You told the police you have no family, that you're all alone in the world. But it's a formality, just in case."

"But I don't know this man," Angele protested. "And I don't know what kind of work he offers. Maybe I'm not suitable. And if I'm brought back, it will look terrible, and the judge might give me a harsher sentence."

Threat was a thundercloud in his eyes as he slammed his fists on the desk. "It doesn't matter that you don't know him. And you'll be suitable once he fattens you up a little. And don't worry about a judge giving you a harsher sentence if you come back. I'll make sure you stay in your cell till you die. Now, sign this if you want to live." He tapped the paper with the pen.

An image flashed before her eyes—her uncle stripping her naked, grunting and panting as he forced her legs apart to thrust himself inside her. She was no fool. She knew what he meant for her to do. She would be forced to work in a bordello.

She shook her head wildly from side to side and stepped back from the paper as though it were a spider about to spring and bite. Panic was a choking knot in her throat, and she had to speak around it. "No, I won't do it. You're afraid one day you might have to account for me—what happened to me—so you want it to look as though I went willingly."

Rage spread across his face like a crimson tide. "You refuse? You dare to cooperate? You refuse a chance at freedom?"

"It isn't freedom. It's slavery."

"You little fool. This man is willing to take responsibility for you and pay your fine."

She was too angry to watch her tongue. "It's not a fine, and you know it. The money would go in your pocket. I'll wager there's not a word on that paper about any fine. You just want it to appear that I agreed to go with him."

"I'm offering you a chance at a new life."

Snatching up the paper, she tore it in pieces and threw them in his face.

Enraged, he shouted, "Leon!"

The door opened quickly, as though Leon had been leaning against it, waiting for his cue to enter.

"Take her to The Grave. Leave her there till she comes to her senses."

Angele could only pray she had the strength to resist. Maybe if Captain Duclos realized she had no intention of giving in, he would just let her rot peacefully in her cell. She preferred that to the fate he wanted her to accept.

Leon seemed to enjoy putting her in The Grave. It was situated at the far end of the hall. He hung a lantern on a peg in the wall, then stooped to lift the rectangular board that covered it.

There was no coffin. Just raw dirt. She could see several holes had been bored in the lid Leon held. They would keep her alive—if she did not die of madness.

"Get down there. And you better get comfortable, 'cause there's no room to turn around."

When she hesitated, he kicked her behind her knees, buckling them. She pitched forward into the hole but quickly rolled over, not about to be buried on her face. Then she would surely suffocate, unable to press her nose to the air holes.

"Once a day, I'll raise the lid and give you a cup of gruel and water. Other than that, you stay there till you do what the commandant wants."

He slammed the lid in place and fastened it. His voice coming through the holes was muted, but Angele could hear and listened in dread.

"It usually takes a day or two to make a woman give in. A few die right away, though. They just can't take it. Maybe you can last longer. You're younger than most of 'em. Maybe smarter, too. When the man comes for you, I'll see if you've wised up yet."

He left her, and the silence afterward became a great roaring in her ears. She felt as though her temples were being squeezed and would cause her head to explode. Her fingertips ached to rub them, but she could not bend her arms. Then her nose began to itch, and she wriggled it furiously to try to bring relief.

She imagined she felt something crawling up her legs, then realized it was needles of stiffness creeping along her flesh. First, her feet, then her calves. Her fingers felt numb. Her wrists began to twitch. Lord, if only she could bend her knees, lift her head.

With the numbness of her flesh came panic to her soul, which made her gasp. Then she realized that if she were to get sufficient air, she had to take small, shallow breaths.

Her heart beat like steady thunder, and she imagined she could feel her heaving chest brushing the coffin lid.

Sleep, she commanded herself. Sleep away the misery and terror. And when Leon came back in a few hours, he would see that she was not like the others. She would not be hysterical. She could take whatever hell they put her in, damn them. And he would tell Captain Duclos, who would realize he had a strong woman on his hands and give up. She'd be taken back to her cell, and sooner or later they would have to let her go.

Wouldn't they?

They couldn't just let her die there . . . *could they?*

It was all just a big bluff . . . *wasn't it?*

Despite all resolve, a tear slipped from the corner of her eye. It trickled down her cheek and into her ear. Reminding herself of the vow she'd made to survive, she tried to concentrate on blotting everything out of her mind so sleep would come.

But the effort failed. She was far too terrified to relax. Time dragged by in the black stillness. She estimated an hour. Maybe two. There was no way of knowing. Her throat was parched and dry, and she longed for water. She would need to relieve herself soon. What then? Was she to be further tormented by having to lie in her own waste? But what did it matter? They expected her to die.

When she first heard the sound, she thought it must be a rat, scraping along the corridor. Then, with a rush of hope, she realized it was someone walking toward her.

"Leon . . ." Her dry lips seemed to crack with the effort to speak.

The lid was yanked away.

It was him. He stared down at her, hands on his hips, his evil face spread in a wide grin.

"You're still alive. Figured you would be. It's only been six hours."

Six hours. And it had seemed like no more than two, at the most. Was that what it was like to be buried alive? she wondered in a panic. To think days passed when actually it was weeks? Or maybe she would not die. Maybe they would give her just enough nourishment to keep her alive for years while she begged and pleaded to end her tortured life.

"I guess you can't get out by yourself. None of them ever can." He stooped to lift her by her shoulders.

She swayed, legs weak and numb, but he held her up and began to guide her slowly toward the steps. Her knees buckled, but he put a beefy arm around her waist for support.

"He's come to see you. It's bad you're looking like you are, but that's your fault. He might take one look at you and decide you're too scruffy. Then it's back to The Grave for you till the commandant decides what to do with you."

Right then, Angele had only one thing on her mind. "Water. Give me water, please."

Leon liked to think he was not truly a bad person. Sure, he was a guard. A tough one, too. But it was just a job. He was paid to be cruel, if need be. So he paused by her cell and helped her inside to drink from her bucket. "It might help if you washed your face." He was glad the commandant couldn't hear him. He'd accuse him of weakening and maybe see that he lost his job.

She drank slowly. She didn't care how she looked . . . did not care what the man waiting for her thought, because she had no intention of signing the paper and going with him.

Leon prodded her with his baton. "Come on. I'm going to be in trouble if I don't get you up there."

They continued on. As they approached the commandant's office, Angele wondered how long she could delay going back. If she could keep the man who wanted to take her at bay, make him think she would eventually sign and cooperate, she could buy a little more time. Pretend to give in. Make it seem she had learned her lesson and would do anything to get out of jail, and—

She froze.

Leon had opened the door and shoved her inside.

And Angele suddenly found herself face-to-face with the meddling stranger.

Three

The trip to Touraine had turned out to be a waste of time, because Ryan could not concentrate on buying horses for thinking about the girl.

Corbett had accused him of pining for Denise. Ryan let him think that, not about to confide the truth.

When they had returned to Paris, he had gone to the city jail and was surprised to learn there was no record of anyone being arrested on the date he asked about. Not for stealing outside the Abbaye Val-de-Grâce or anywhere else in Paris. It had been a very quiet day, and the desk clerk Ryan spoke with said he had been working then and remembered.

Ryan almost gave up. The girl had probably succeeded in persuading the officer into letting her go as she had tried to do with him. And many times since, he wished he had. But, being desperate, she would go back to stealing and eventually be caught again.

Asking around, he learned that authorities were trying to rid the streets of the dart-and-run thieves, pickpockets, and the like. Those caught were being given unusually harsh sentences, and it bothered him deeply to imagine someone so young being imprisoned because hunger had driven her to steal.

And something else besides compassion began to needle as he thought about how it had aroused him to hold her in his arms as she wrestled to free herself. Beneath the bulky clothing, he had discovered a luscious body. Also, if she were cleaned up, dressed up, he knew she'd be quite fetching. So for her to wind up in prison was a waste in more ways than one.

He wasn't sure exactly when the idea took hold. Maybe it had been there all along. But one day, while he walked the tree-lined streets of Paris, drinking the perfume of the spring air, it dawned that all his troubles would be over if he married the girl. She was French, and though she was not cultured and refined, he was confident she could be taught everything she needed to know—just like a wild colt.

As for Denise, he felt no guilt. She had refused him. Maybe she had been playing a coquettish little game like Corbett said. It made no difference. Ryan didn't like women who used guile to get what they wanted, regardless of how it was disguised.

As for Corbett and Clarice being disappointed, he figured it was none of their business. And all his father cared about was having him take a French wife. Besides, he'd never know the circumstances of how they'd met.

His mind made up, Ryan set out to find the young thief. First, he went to the catacombs. He questioned derelicts and drunks, but if they knew anything about a young boy living among them—and Ryan assumed she would go back to pretending to be a boy—they weren't telling. He even tried bribery, but they were a loyal bunch and would not divulge anything.

Next, he went to the Abbaye Val-de-Grâce and asked each and every old woman he saw if they knew the names of the gendarmes in the area. If he could find the one who had made the arrest, then he might be able to learn something that would lead him to the girl.

Finally, thanks to the very woman whose purse had been snatched that day, Ryan tracked down officer Jon LaPrade.

At first, he was defensive and denied remembering anything. But Ryan persisted by bluffing that he knew important people in Paris. He said he hated to go so far and cause the man trouble but would do so if necessary.

As Ryan had hoped, the threat brought LaPrade's memory back like a boomerang. He said he had taken the girl to an overflow jail, because regular facilities were full. Ryan knew that was not likely from what the officer at the city jail had told him.

Impatient, Ryan had whipped the soft roll from his pocket and peeled off several thousand francs. He told LaPrade he was in a hurry and wanted to be taken to the so-called overflow jail, promising not to mention he had steered him there.

LaPrade's eyes had widened to see so much money, and he quickly agreed to cooperate. He even confided to Ryan that the overflow facility was also a place where men could buy young, homeless girls and train them to work in bordellos. The best thing for Ryan to do, LaPrade suggested, was to go there and pretend to be a buyer and ask for a prisoner named Angele Benet. He could say that he had been trying to persuade her to work for him before she got arrested. That way, the commandant would not become suspicious that he knew the truth.

And it had worked. Ryan had told the commandant his story and offered to pay any amount to claim her.

So now Angele Benet stood before Ryan but was anything but glad to see him.

"You!" She spat the word in French like a bitter pill. "What do you want?"

The commandant had left earlier, warning Ryan she was stubborn and might refuse to sign an agreement to be released to his custody. By then, Ryan well understood the situation. If authorities ever did investigate how things were run, the commandant could say he had released first-time prisoners to people agreeing to take responsibility for them and have signed documents to prove the women had gone willingly.

But there was also the matter of a so-called fine to be paid that would not be recorded. It would cost Ryan twenty-five thousand francs if Angele agreed to be released to him, and he knew every bit of it would go in the commandant's pocket. However, at the moment, she didn't look as though she wanted to do anything except claw his eyes out.

"I came to get you out of here." He again was thankful for his ability to communicate with her in French, obviously her native language, and the only one she spoke.

She gave her hair the proud toss that he'd found so delightfully spirited. "Did you now? To work in your bordello, I suppose."

"I don't have a bordello."

"Then what do you want of me?"

He decided to get right to the point to keep her from jumping to a lot of conclusions and wasting time. "Actually, I've come to ask you to be my wife."

Angele's hand flew to her throat, then anger overcame surprise. "What kind of fool do you take me for? Do you honestly think you can trick me into being your whore? That is the most absurd thing I've ever heard of, and—"

"I mean it." He took a step toward her but paused when she held up her hands to fend him off. "If you'll just hear me out—"

"No. You're wasting your breath. The commandant said you'd be here, and I told him then as I tell you now—I will never sign to be released to you."

"He couldn't have known I was coming. I didn't know it myself. I had to track down the officer who arrested you that day, and that's when I found out about this place. I had to pay him to tell me and show me the way. They had no record of you at the city jail, and . . ." He shook his head. "Look, we're not getting anywhere. I'm sincere when I say I want you to marry me."

"And I say you think me a fool."

Actually, he found her to be quite the opposite and was curious as to how she had wound up in poverty on the streets. But there would be time for that later—to learn everything about the woman he wanted for his wife, the mother of his children. Right then, however, he wanted her out of that wretched place. She looked worse than the last time he had seen her. And *filthy*. Good God, she looked like she'd been wallowing in dirt.

He started toward her again.

She had pressed back against the desk and was suddenly afraid of him. No matter that he was elegantly dressed in a fashionable carrick—a double pleat-folded cape that fell to his knees, tight, elasticized breeches of buff-colored wool, and fine leather pointed-toe boots. He had to be mad, trifling with her, and any moment he might attack, and—

He paused within an arm's reach. "I'll bargain with you. If you hear me out and then want to refuse me, I promise I will pay your fine and then set you free."

She regarded him warily. "How do I know I can believe you?"

"You'll have to trust me."

She raised her chin. "I trust no man."

"I think you should ask yourself what you've got to lose by listening to what I have to say."

She supposed that much was true. She also recalled her plan to stall. A few more minutes out of The Grave to breathe and stand and stretch her limbs was ambrosia for the spirit. But she was confused. He said the commandant had not been expecting him, and he sounded as though he was telling the truth. Maybe, by listening, she could figure out exactly what was going on. "Go ahead. Let's hear your lies."

"My name is Ryan Tremayne. I live in America on my family's estate. It's called a plantation. We grow crops there—cotton, tobacco. And we raise horses. That's why I came to France—to buy horses."

She could not resist sarcasm. "And instead you want to buy a wife."

"That was not my intention. I came to buy horses, like I said, but then I met you and decided you'd make the perfect wife." He then went on to explain about his father's edict that the woman he married be French. "And if she isn't, or if I don't get married by the time he dies, then he'll disinherit me. I'll lose my birthright."

Angele mused how he actually sounded as though he were telling the truth. Besides, she reasoned, what other motive would he have to propose to someone like her? "I'm almost tempted to believe you."

"I'm telling the truth, I swear. And we can help each other. You'll have a good life and never want for anything. I'm a wealthy man—or will be one day. You'll live in a mansion and have servants at your beck and call."

"And what do you expect in return?" she challenged.

He shrugged, as though it were all quite simple. "To be my wife, bear my children . . . everything a man can expect from his wife."

Once Angele could grasp the fact that he was quite serious, she thought he was truly out of his mind. Then she allowed that a lot of marriages were arranged for reasons other than love. But there were things he had apparently not considered, and she pointed them out to him. "What will your father think about how we met?"

"There's no reason for him to know. And by the time I get through buying you the finest wardrobe Paris has to offer, he'll think I married royalty. And on the ship on the way over, I'll try to teach you everything you need to know to fit right into society."

Angele truly had a hard time to keep from bursting into laughter. Her parents had seen to it that she attended the best finishing school in Europe. And while she might not be royalty, she was certainly at ease with those who were. Her father had been an important man, which was why his fall from grace had been so devastating. So while she imagined she could actually teach Monsieur Ryan Tremayne a thing or two about society, she decided it was to her advantage not to do so. If she continued to appear to be bourgeoisie, then he would be more tolerant. She might even enjoy the charade.

Then it dawned that she was actually considering accepting his offer. Perhaps she had lost *her* mind. He was a stranger. Besides that, he wanted her to cross the ocean and live in America. "I'll have to think about it," she said uneasily.

"Well, you don't have much time. I'm scheduled to leave in two weeks, and I still haven't found the horses I came to buy. I went to Touraine, but"—he waved a hand of dismissal—"never mind. I'll find the Anglo-Arabs I want if I have to search night and day."

"You won't find them in Touraine."

"And where would you suggest?" he asked, obviously amused.

"You need to go to Blois. There's a man there by the name of François DeNeux. He raises the finest breeding stock of Anglo-Arabs in all of France."

"And how would you know?"

She was tempted to tell him that her own horse, Vertus, came from there. Her father had been an expert about such things. Vertus was the most high-blooded horse available in the country at that time, and he had been determined to buy the best.

"I hear things," she hedged. "People talk."

"And that's probably all it is—talk. Now we really need to get going. We don't have a lot of time to waste."

She gave an unladylike snort. "You seem to forget I haven't said I would."

"I don't know what else I can do to convince you."

She thought how, if it were a trick and she signed the paper, she would be at his mercy. But if she refused, she would be returned to The Grave. And no matter how strong her resolve to survive, she would probably die there. She would never be taken before a judge. No one knew she existed on the outside. No one cared what happened to her.

Except for the stranger.

"What's your decision?" he prodded. "I can understand your reluctance, but I promise I'm serious about wanting to marry you."

She suddenly felt the need to ask, "Would you have let me go if the gendarme hadn't come when he did?"

There was the slightest twist of a smile on his lips. "You know, to be honest, I've thought about that myself. I like to think I would've, because I don't mind telling you it's worried the hell out of me thinking about you in jail. You're too young, and I think you steal because you're desperate—like you said."

"It's worse than jail," she snapped. "It's a living hell."

"Then come with me. What do you have to lose? What reason do you have to stay? You said you have no family."

"I don't."

"You have no home."

"That's true."

"Then why—"

She cut him off. "Because I don't know that I can trust you."

"So what do you think is going to become of you if you stay here?"

Just then the door opened, and Captain Duclos walked in. Having heard Ryan's question, he smirked at Angele and said, "She knows what will happen to her. She's going back to her grave."

Ryan was staggered. "Her *what*?"

Angele locked unflinching eyes with Captain Duclos. "Just what he said, Monsieur Tremayne. My grave. It's a coffin, buried in the ground. He buried me in it to try and make me sign his damned paper."

Ryan's eyes were like ice as he turned on Duclos. "You did that? You actually buried her alive?"

Duclos retreated to behind his desk before explaining, "It's nothing to concern yourself. It's just a place where we put uncooperative prisoners."

"That's barbaric!" Ryan cried.

Duclos shrugged. "We do what we have to do. The jails are crowded. If a prisoner isn't willing to work in order to be freed, then they must face the consequences."

Ryan whirled on Angele. "Sign the paper, and let's get you out of here. If you don't want to accept my offer, so be it. I'll set you free and give you some money to live on till you find work. I can't leave you in a place like this."

Angele had quickly thought it over. She had always yearned to taste everything life had to offer and decided that the idea of going to America was exciting. As for becoming a stranger's wife, well, that would take some getting used to, and she could only hope he would be patient. But what finally convinced her was facing the reality that she had no options. She would get hungry again, steal again, and sooner or later be arrested. Next time, the commandant would see she was sold into a bordello—or worse.

"All right. I'll sign."

Duclos shoved the paper and a pen across the desk. "Do it and then get out. I'm sick of you."

Quickly, she scrawled her name, then angrily threw the pen down. It bounced off the desk, spattering ink on the front of Duclos's uniform. He leaped up, but Ryan held out a hand in warning. "It's over. Let's not have any trouble." He took Angele's arm and rushed her out of the office.

Once they were on the street, he said, eyes twinkling, "If I were you, I'd try real hard not to get arrested around here again."

She smiled up at him. "I won't. And if I get arrested in America, they won't send me back to Paris to jail, anyway."

He looked at her uncertainly.

She didn't keep him in suspense, her eyes also sparkling. "I really doubt I'll have to steal to keep from starving over there. You did say you were rich, didn't you? And if I'm your wife, I shouldn't have to go hungry, should I?"

They had stopped walking, and when he did not immediately respond, she shifted her feet nervously and wondered if this was it—the time when he admitted it really was a trick to get her to sign, after all. She thought about trying to run away and began darting quick glances around.

Finally, he spoke, and it was as though he'd had to come to some kind of final resolution within himself. "Yes, I am wealthy, and, no, you won't be hungry ever again."

He held out his hand to her, and she took it, praying all the while she had not made a mistake . . . and wondering if he were doing the same.

Four

Ryan took Angele to the nearest restaurant. When she realized where he was going, she resisted. "I can't go in there like this."

"Nonsense. You look like you're ready to collapse. You've got to eat."

He drew the horrified maître d' aside. "I know the lady isn't properly dressed, but I'm not asking that you seat us in the dining room. A corner of the kitchen will be fine. But she has to have something to eat. She's been ill." He hoped that might help, but the maître d' continued to stare, aghast, from him to Angele. "I'll make it worth your while," Ryan added, reaching in his pocket.

The maître d' sighed. "Very well. Come with me. I'll take you to the back where the workers eat."

He led them to a room behind the kitchen. The smell of cooking food made Angele sway, and Ryan quickly slipped his arm around her, afraid she would faint.

The maître d' explained he would have to find a waiter, because that area was not staffed.

Ryan had spotted a pot of chicken soup cooking on the stove as they passed through the kitchen. "That won't be necessary. If you can just bring her a bowl of soup, some bread and wine." He looked at Angele. "Do you have a preference?"

Actually, she did but remembered to let him think she had no knowledge of such things—not yet, anyway. "I'm afraid the only difference I know in wine is white from red," she fibbed.

He ordered Chablis, and when they were alone, asked if she were feeling any better.

"Much, thank you. I'm just so relieved to be out of that place."

"You'll feel stronger after you've eaten. Then we'll buy you some clothes and have you fitted for a complete wardrobe. You'll be the envy of every woman in Richmond."

"You really intend to take me home with you, don't you?"

"Of course. Why won't you believe me?"

"There's still a chance it was a trick, so you can take me to your bordello."

He threw back his head and laughed. "I'm going to start thinking that's what you actually want—"

She gasped. "Oh, no, monsieur. Please don't think that. I only meant—"

He quickly reached across the table to cover her trembling hands, then, seeing how it startled her, drew back as he apologized. "I'm sorry. I was only teasing. I just have a lot to learn about you, Angele. And please, call me Ryan."

"Anything you wish."

"I *am* going to take you home, and I *am* going to marry you. But are you sure there's no one you need to contact to let them know you're leaving France? Family? Friends?"

"No one."

"All right, then. I'll make the arrangements. First, we'll see to your wardrobe. I saw a dressmaker's sign in a window across the street. I have some business I need to tend to, but I'll give you some money and come back for you later. You can choose anything you like."

"Aren't you afraid I'll take your money and run away?"

He had thought about the possibility but knew he could not watch her every minute. Besides, he might not know anything about her past but could tell she wasn't stupid. He was giving her the opportunity of a lifetime, and she knew it. "I can't stop you if that's what you want to do, so

I'm not going to worry about it. I hope you won't, though. I think we can have a good life together."

A waiter brought the soup. Seeing how she ate so ravenously, he asked how long since she'd had anything.

She swallowed a mouthful of buttered bread and sipped her wine before admitting, "I'm not sure. And what I did have wasn't fit for pigs. I can't even remember how long I was there. I tried to keep up with the days, but I'm afraid I lost track."

"A week and a day. Yesterday I managed to find the lady you robbed. She was coming out of the abbey after mass and was able to give me the name of the officer who arrested you," he explained. "Otherwise, I'd never have been able to find you."

"I thank God that you did."

"So do I."

She had just bitten down on another piece of bread but paused. "You know, I'm still shocked by all of this. It's happening so quickly and doesn't seem real. I mean, a man of your wealth and position shouldn't have any trouble finding a wife."

He unbuttoned the front of his carrick and shook it from his shoulders.

Angele's gaze dropped to his chest. His ruffled shirt had come open, and she could see a mat of dark-blond hair. She glanced away, hoping he didn't notice how her breath had caught in her throat.

He leaned back to hook one arm over the side of his chair. "There aren't that many Frenchwomen where I live, and I rarely travel. I prefer to stay home and work with my horses." He remembered what she'd said earlier and asked, "By the way, how is it you know so much about Anglo-Arabs? And I believe you said I should look for them in Blois."

"That's right. François DeNeux is one of France's best horse breeders."

He persisted, "And how do you know that?"

"I told you. I hear things."

"Do you ride?"

"Me? Why, no." She laughed loudly, remembering it was to her advantage to seem unrefined. Otherwise, he would never stop asking questions, and it might come out who she was. After all, she and her mother had been further humiliated when word had spread to Paris from England about the downfall of Cecil Mooring. And if Ryan found out, he might want nothing to do with her. Then what was to become of her? She'd been given a miracle and was not about to lose it.

"Tell me something about yourself. Where were you born? How did your father earn his living?"

Just then she smelled fish cooking and blurted, "He was a fisherman, and I was born in a little fishing village near Brittany, to the south of France." She had never been there but knew her geography.

"And that was where you heard about François DeNeux? In Brittany? That's a long way from Blois."

"As I keep telling you—people talk. I listen."

"And you also heard them talking about Anglo-Arabs? What did they say?"

"Only that they are nice horses," she lied again. Actually, she probably knew as much about the breed as he did, but it would seem far too bizarre that a fisherman's daughter would be knowledgeable about such expensive horses. Only the wealthiest could afford them, and they were not found around fishing villages.

She maneuvered to change the subject. "That's all there is to tell about me. As I said before, I'm an orphan, and I have no family. So can we talk about the trip to America? What will it be like?"

"We'll be sailing on the Black Ball Line from Le Havre. It's a steam packet called the *Victory*, the same one my cousin and I came over on."

"And what's a packet?" She knew, but again wanted to appear ignorant of such things.

"A packet carries mail, goods, and passengers. It's comfortable. I think you'll like it. I'll go by the Black Ball office this afternoon to see if I can get a cabin for us. My cousin and I slept in berths in a dormitory coming over. Ladies had a separate room. I'll see what other accommodations are available."

She felt her cheeks warm to think about sharing a room with him and ducked her head to eat her soup.

"The crossing should take around three weeks, a bit faster than the trip over."

"And why is that?"

"Owing to westerly winds, the eastward trip is usually made in shorter time than the westward. We should have good weather, too, so you probably won't get sick."

She felt a twinge of worry. "Why would I?"

"I thought you said you were raised in a fishing village. Surely you know how the roll of the sea can make you nauseated."

She took a gulp of wine, because she could feel herself tensing, afraid to say the wrong thing. "I never went out in a boat. I don't like the water."

He grinned. "But as you keep reminding me, you hear people talk."

She shook her head and forced a smile, then gulped her wine again. "No. Sorry. I just hope I don't get sick and become a nuisance to you."

"You should be fine. I didn't have any trouble coming over, and neither did my cousin."

"Was he the man with you the day you caught me?"

"Yes. His name is Corbett. I hope the two of you will get along. He and his wife live in the house with my father and me."

Angele wondered how big the house was. The manor where she had grown up had over a hundred rooms. She could never remember exactly.

"They have a son," Ryan went on. "He's a bit spoiled, but then so is Clarice—that's Corbett's wife. But don't worry, she's also French, so the two of you should get along quite well."

Angele certainly hoped so. She didn't want any problems.

Ryan Tremayne was offering her a whole new life, and while she still couldn't quite grasp the reality of it all, she knew she wanted it more than anything. He seemed kind and good and generous, and she dared believe they might be happy. She certainly intended to do her part to make it happen.

Ryan nodded to the empty soup bowl, bread plate, and wineglass. "Would you like more?"

"No, but it was all wonderful. Thank you."

"Well, we'll see to it you get something more substantial for dinner. I just didn't want to shock your stomach right now by letting you eat too much."

He left her to find the waiter and pay the bill, remembering his promise of generosity to the maître d'. When he returned, Angele was asleep, her head resting on the table. He gently touched her shoulder.

She bolted upright, embarrassed. "I'm sorry. I didn't mean to do that. I guess it was the wine."

"No need to apologize." They went outside, and he suggested, "Maybe I should take you to my hotel and let you get some rest. I can have a boutique send over something suitable for you to wear for dinner. I think I can guess your size."

"I don't know," she said uncertainly. "I mean, to go to your hotel . . ."

"Don't worry. I'll get your own room for you. I do that for all the girls at my bordello."

Angele laughed, confident he was only teasing.

They began walking, and she tucked her hand in the crook of his arm, carefully avoiding the curious stares from those they passed.

The desk clerk's brows crawled into his hairline when Ryan asked for a room. "Sir, I don't think—"

But Ryan cut him off. He hadn't liked the stares, either, and was tired of all the scrutiny. "The young lady needs accommodation, and since I'm staying in one of your most expensive rooms, I would appreciate your taking care of her."

The clerk pursed his lips. Ryan had made his point. As one of the house's best-paying guests, his demands were not to be questioned. "As you wish, sir, but at the moment I have nothing. However, I do have a couple checking out of a room just down the hall from you, but they've asked to be allowed to stay until six o'clock."

"Fine. I won't be back before then. She can stay in my room. Have someone take her there. I'm in a bit of a hurry." He turned to Angele. "Get some rest. We'll talk more tonight . . . get to know each other better."

He turned to go, but Angele called to him. "I just want to say thank you . . . for everything. You won't regret any of this."

He smiled and kept on going.

The afternoon was passing quickly and Ryan had much to do. First, he went to the nearest boutique and told the proprietor what he wanted—a gown fit for a princess to be sent to Mademoiselle Angele Benet at the Le Pierre Hotel. He didn't care what it cost. He left a large deposit and said he would pay the balance the next day.

His next stop was the office of the Black Ball Line, where he was told there were no cabins available. The agent asked if there was any reason he was dissatisfied with his accommodations on the voyage over.

"No. But circumstances have changed," he revealed. "I'm getting married, and my bride will be traveling with me."

"I understand, but let me explain the situation." The agent took out a diagram of the ship and unrolled it on the counter. "As you can see, the *Victory* only has dormitories. No cabins. Now I can put you on the *James Munroe*. It's about four hundred tons, one hundred feet in length. It has six cabins that will hold two passengers each and room for a dozen men and women in steerage dormitories. There's also a smoking salon for cabin passengers—which we consider first class, a sewing room for the ladies, and a nice dining room. I think you and your bride would be quite comfortable.

"The only thing is," he continued, "you will have to leave a week later."

That was no problem. He needed the extra time to go to Blois and find François DeNeux. If he went home without the horses, his father would be upset, and he didn't want that, not when he was bringing home a wife. "All right. Change my reservation to the *James Munroe* and book two cabins—one for me and one for my cousin, Corbett Tremayne."

The agent leafed through his book and frowned. "I'm sorry, I only have one left, but I can put your cousin in steerage."

Ryan groaned to think of how Corbett would react to that. Then the thought struck that maybe he would want to go back as scheduled, which would be much better. Having him around Angele might prove awkward. "Reserve the cabin on the *James Munroe,* but hold back on changing my cousin's ticket from the *Victory* till you hear from me."

As soon as Ryan left, he wasted no time in getting to the office of the commandant général, the person he knew to be in charge of the city jails. The hour was growing late, and he did not want the sun to set on another day in the hellish prison run by Captain Duclos.

He told the story about how a *friend* of his had endured unspeakable horror at Duclos's jail, as well as being coerced into agreeing to sell herself into prostitution in order to be freed. The commandant général was not only appalled—he was furious. He assured Ryan he had not known what was going on and that Duclos would be dealt with severely. It would never happen again. Apologies were offered. Ryan said it was not necessary. He just wanted to make sure that no woman would ever suffer again as his *friend* had.

As he walked back toward the hotel in the gathering dusk, Ryan thought of the word he had used to describe Angele—*friend.* It was a very important word, perhaps even the key to a good marriage. They had to become friends. Maybe they would never love each other, but they had to make people think they did, otherwise there would be gossip and speculation, which he did not want. That meant he would have to talk to Corbett and see that he kept his mouth shut. But there was a chance Corbett might not even recognize her once she was cleaned up . . . dressed up, especially if he made up a story about having met her when Corbett wasn't around. He would think of something. He *had* to.

And, if Corbett sailed a week earlier, it would really be a blessing.

Ryan quickened his pace as the idea of keeping Angele's true identity a secret took hold. He would not take her out to dinner that night as planned, because Corbett would see her. Instead, he would have a tray sent to her room, then move her to another hotel first thing in the morning. She could spend the next two weeks being fitted for her wardrobe while he went to Blois. And when he arrived in Richmond with her later, dressed in her finest and tutored in the finer graces as much as possible during the crossing, Corbett would never recognize her as the thief from the catacombs.

He passed a clock as it struck half past six and breathed a sigh of relief. Angele would be in her own room by now, and Corbett would be in the hotel smoking parlor, passing time till dinner.

There was nothing to worry about.

Corbett stood outside Ryan's door, reeling a bit from side to side. He knew he'd had too much to drink, but the stuffy old fart he'd been talking to in the bar was willing to pay for his drinks as long as he listened to his stories. They were as stale as the cigar he smoked, but Corbett didn't care. He never turned down free whiskey, because he seldom had money to buy his own. That irked him deeply, because whenever he needed anything, he had to go to his uncle Roussel and ask, which he felt was humiliating. He should have an allowance, damn it.

But all that would change, he was sure, once Ryan married Denise. She and Clarice would run things like they wanted and see to it that he had money.

Corbett pounded on the door. It was time, by damn, for Ryan to go home and make wedding plans. He had been acting strange lately, and Corbett had thought he was missing Denise. But when he'd said something about her, Ryan had blinked like he didn't know who he was talking about. So something was gnawing at him, and the sooner they left Paris, the better.

He knocked again, louder. Ryan was probably sleeping. He hadn't seen him all day. In fact, he had been keeping to himself since they had returned from Touraine. But he always joined him for dinner, and tonight Corbett planned for them to have a serious talk. He had passed a jewelry store down the street, and there was a dazzling diamond necklace in the window. He intended to convince Ryan to buy it for Denise as an engagement present and propose again as soon as he got home. Corbett was sure she'd say yes this time.

"It's all quite simple," he chuckled to himself as he knocked harder, making the door rattle in the frame. "Just let Cousin Corbett take care of things, and it will all work out . . ."

He fell silent as the door opened and he saw the girl standing there, Ryan's silk robe wrapped about her. Then he came alive to bellow, "Who the hell are you and what are you doing here?"

Angele clutched the robe to her neck with trembling fingers. "He . . . Mr. Tremayne . . . he sent me here."

"Like hell he did." Corbett looked her up and down. Then, despite the webs of whiskey lacing his brain, comprehension dawned.

"You," he whispered, reeling. "You're the girl from the sewer."

Five

Angele tried to close the door but wasn't fast enough. Corbett threw his shoulder against it and shoved, knocking her to the floor. He yanked her up, and the delicate silk of the robe tore, revealing she was naked underneath.

Pulling the robe around her, she backed into the room, angry but also fearful. "I don't know who you are, but I'm warning you to get out of here this instant."

Following her, he kicked the door shut. He was able to speak French, because Clarice had taught him. "Not till you tell me what the hell you're doing in my cousin's room."

Angele's eyes went wide. *Cousin.* So *that* was how he knew who she was. Ryan had said his cousin had been at the *abbaye* that day. "You'll have to ask him," she retorted hotly, figuring it wasn't her place to explain anything.

He towered over her. "Well, I'm asking *you,* and you're going to tell me if I have to shake it out of you." His hands clamped down on her shoulders and squeezed.

Angele ground her teeth against the pain. She was not about to let him know he was hurting her. "You've no right to ask me anything."

"I've got every goddamn right." He began to push her, his palms slapping her shoulders, as she stumbled backward. "You're nothing but a common thief. You live in the sewers, and you steal from old ladies."

"That shows how much you know. They're called catacombs—not sewers. Now get out of here, or I'm going to scream."

He snickered, giving her another hard shove that nearly sent her to the floor again as she struggled to keep from falling. "Go ahead. Scream. I'm going to call for the police anyway. You belong in jail. But first I want to know how you got in here and what you stole from my cousin."

She knew he would not believe anything she said, and if he sent for the police, she would be taken right back to jail, and this time there'd be no getting out. She thought fast. She had to keep him talking, asking questions, distract him, then lunge for the door. But she had to have her clothes. She had gratefully peeled out of her dirty, tattered boy's attire and tossed everything into a corner. She would have to try to snatch it all up on the way out, because she couldn't go running out of the hotel wearing nothing but a silk robe that was practically hanging in shreds.

Suddenly she bolted to run around the bed, putting it between them.

Corbett began moving slowly around it. "You're a whore, aren't you? You're too scruffy to be anything else."

Angele knew she did look wretched. Too weary to bathe, she had decided to take a nap first, only she had fallen dead to the world. She had intended to try to make herself look nice for Ryan. She would put on the gown he was to have delivered, and he would be proud to take her to dinner, and—

She glanced about wildly. There was no gown, but how could there be? A hotel employee or messenger would likely not have pounded on the door as though he was driving a nail as Ryan's cousin had done.

He was creeping closer. "Stay away!" she warned. He was between her and the door.

He kept coming. "I don't know how you got in here, but I intend to find out. I can't believe Ryan would have anything to do with the likes of you."

"He said I could stay here. My room wasn't ready yet, and—"

"Your room?" he echoed, incredulous. "A fine hotel like this wouldn't let you eat out of the garbage cans, you little liar. You'll have to come up with a better story than that, and you will—even if I have to beat it out of you."

He lunged, and so did Angele. She tried to make it across the bed, planning to run out the door even if she didn't have time to grab up her clothes. But he was faster. He caught her by her ankle and yanked her back. Flipping her over, he landed on top of her to pin her wrists above her head.

She squirmed wildly, but he held her tight. The robe fell open. His gaze fastened upon her breasts, his breath momentarily catching in his throat. "Maybe Ryan doesn't mind the dirt and grime. Maybe you've got something that makes him overlook everything else."

Fastening wet, greedy lips on one nipple, his hand dove downward to force her legs apart.

Like the waving of a magic wand, Angele turned into a madwoman, fighting, twisting, heaving from side to side to get him off her. The last time a man had groped between her legs, she'd not been able to fend him off. But she had vowed that it would never happen again, that she would die before enduring such anguish and humiliation.

The fierceness of her struggle caught Corbett off guard. Instinctively, he raised from her and fell slightly to the side. Not much, but enough that Angele could take advantage of the opportunity to slam her foot into his crotch, then again to his stomach.

With a yelp of pain, he rolled to his side, clutching himself in agony.

Angele sprang to her feet and began snatching up her tattered clothing to quickly dress. "Damn you to hell," she muttered, furious. "Who do you think you are barging in here and thinking you can have your way with me? I told you the truth. Monsieur Tremayne told me to stay here. He's taking me to dinner tonight."

"Why . . . why would he do that?" Corbett was gasping,

rocking gently from side to side as he continued to hold himself. "I don't . . . understand . . . any of this."

She stepped into the trousers, then pulled them tight around her tiny waist and tied them with the frayed rope to keep them from falling. She'd lost weight in the jail. Her hips were sharp blades, cutting into the already frayed material of the trousers.

Maybe it had all been some kind of cruel joke, and Ryan Tremayne wasn't coming back. No gown was to be delivered. There would be no elegant dinner. He had probably left her to his cousin to do whatever he wanted with her, then take her to their bordello. Marriage. Sailing to America. It was all part of the ruse.

Dressed, her hand on the doorknob, she threw a hating glare at the man who had tried to rape her. He was still balled up on the bed, holding himself and groaning. "Tell your cousin that his scheme didn't work, but I'm sure he'll find other girls stupid enough to work in his whorehouse."

Corbett was lying on his side, head toward the door, and he craned his neck to look at her in bewilderment. "What the hell are you talking about?"

"Don't act innocent with me. You probably help him run it. But I have to say it was a clever plan—making me think he wanted to marry me."

"Marry?" With great effort, Corbett pulled himself up to sit on the side of the bed so he could look at her without straining. "You really are crazy. Ryan would never—"

"Now who's lying? He even said we were going to America to live . . . in a place called Virginia. He really went to a lot of trouble to make me believe him. You two must have a hard time recruiting your whores."

He held up a hand in gesture for her not to go. "Wait. Now I really am confused. Ryan said he was taking you to Virginia?"

"It was all part of the plan—as you know."

"Well, I don't know, and something isn't making sense here. Where did he find you, anyway? I thought you were taken to jail."

"I was. He had me released to his custody, and now I'm getting out of here, because when he finds out I know what he's up to, he'll try to take me back to jail, and I don't intend to let that happen."

She had not finished buttoning her shirt but opened the door, anxious to leave.

A young man was standing there, about to knock. He was wearing a blue cotton coat with matching trousers. He blanched to see Angele's open shirt, the line of her bare breasts beneath. Backing away, he murmured, "Sorry. I must have the wrong room."

He was holding a rectangular-shaped box. A blue satin ribbon was tied around it with a big bow on top.

"I guess I'm going to be in trouble," he said, edging away. "I've been knocking on the wrong door all afternoon."

"Whose room are you looking for?"

"Uh, it's . . . it's all right," he stammered. "I'll find it. I apologize for bothering you."

Corbett, still sitting on the side of the bed, called, "Are you looking for Monsieur Tremayne's room?" He looked past Angele and nodded.

Angele quickly asked, "Are you supposed to deliver a package? To someone named Angele Benet?"

He looked her up and down with uncertainty. "Yes, that's the name on the box. It was delivered to the hotel earlier and I was told to take it to Monsieur Tremayne's room—number 208."

Angele pointed to the numerals painted on the door behind her. "This is 208, and I am Mademoiselle Benet." She practically yanked the package from him. "I'll take it. Thank you."

"Wait a minute . . ." Corbett started to rise. "I think you'd better wait around till he gets here . . ."

But the young man turned on his heel and rushed down the hall to disappear around the corner. Trouble was brewing, and he was not about to get involved.

Angele stared at the box, unsure what to do. The fact that Ryan had kept his promise to buy her a dress meant nothing. It might be part of the plan. But she wanted to see just how nice it was. Perhaps she could sell it for enough money to sustain herself for a little while, anyway.

She glanced at the man sitting on the bed. He only had one hand pressed against his crotch now, and he was sitting up straight, his face no longer twisted with pain. "You're Corbett, aren't you?" She walked back into the room and placed the box on the marble-topped table to the left of the door.

"How did you know that?"

She tugged at the bow. "Monsieur Tremayne told me. He said he hoped we would get along."

Corbett drew his hand from his crotch, the pain lessening. He leaned forward, elbows on his knees. "Why would he say that?"

"Because we were to all live together at BelleRose." She hated sounding so wistful. She was a fool to think he had meant it. He had probably laughed all the way to the dress shop to select the gown she would wear while he wined her and dined her and tried to make her believe how good life could be if she agreed to work for him.

"_Live . . . together?_" Corbett was sputtering, unwilling to grasp the implication of her words. "You . . . mean he was taking you to . . . to Virginia to be his mistress?"

"Mistress. Courtesan. Whore. Who knows? When you get down to it, it's all the same, isn't it?" Opening the box, she gasped, long and loud. The gown was exquisite. Fashioned of emerald-green taffeta, it had a low V in both front and back. The sleeves had several graduated puffs to the wrist, and the skirt was full and gored.

Still making soft, adoring sounds under her breath, Angele gingerly lifted it from the box. And there were other things, as well. Forgetting about Corbett as she laid the dress out on the bed, she hurried to see what else Ryan had sent.

She had to giggle over the corset. Her mother had worn one, but Angele's undergarments had been quilted and heavily starched cotton petticoats attached to the bodice with wide shoulder straps. Things like nipped-in corsets would come later, her very proper mother had assured.

There was also a pair of green satin slippers with rounded toes, a lace shawl, and a pearl necklace with matching earbobs. Then she squealed with delight to discover at the very bottom of the box a prettily wrapped bottle of perfume.

She pulled out the stopper and held the bottle to her nose and breathed deeply. It was sweet but subtle, reminding her of wet rain on the first roses of spring. "Your cousin has good taste," she absently said to Corbett.

"And he's obviously lost his mind."

She paused in her pleasure to glare at him. "You don't have to worry about me. I realize now it was all pretense. He never would have married me."

Corbett hooted. "You're damn right he wouldn't. And I think you're making all this up, anyway. I don't know why he sent the dress. Maybe he thought he owed it to you after bedding you, and—"

"He never bedded me!" she snapped, pushing the stopper back in the perfume bottle with a vengeance.

"You were here, sleeping naked in his bed."

"He wasn't with me." She began stuffing everything back into the box. It would all fetch a good price, and she felt she had it coming to her after Ryan had played her for such a fool.

"He's obviously been here. He had to have let you in."

"The concierge let me in."

"Likely story."

She slammed the lid down on the box and sloppily tied the ribbon around it to hold it together. "I don't care whether you believe me or not."

"I don't. You can be sure of that. I just wish I could understand what this is all about—you in his room, all those things he bought. It's insane. *He's* insane. I still can't believe he would have anything to do with a dredge of society like you."

Angele decided she had taken enough of his abuse. She

tucked the box under her arm. "No, monsieur. I am the one who is insane—to have believed he wanted to marry me."

Corbett flashed an arrogant smile. "Especially when he's going to marry my wife's cousin."

His barbed arrow hit its target. Angele was hurt even deeper to think that Ryan had so glibly lied to her when he was betrothed to someone else. And she thought he should be ashamed for making up such lies about his father, too, claiming he was threatening to disinherit him.

Corbett felt uneasiness creeping. Now that the first shock had subsided, he had to reason that the only way the girl could have got in the room was through Ryan. The concierge would never have let her in otherwise. But, if that were the case, what the hell was he thinking? And he had, apparently, also arranged for her to get out of jail.

Slowly the possibility began to dawn that perhaps she was telling the truth, and for whatever bizarre reason, Ryan had actually asked her to marry him. Maybe he was doing it to take home a French bride to please his father and ensure his inheritance. And, if that was the case, then Corbett was smart enough to realize that he would be a fool to alienate her—at least until he learned the whole story.

She had already walked out, but he sprang to rush to the door. "Wait, please," he called. "Come back so we can talk. I . . ." He paused, hating to say the words that were not inherent to his vocabulary. "I think I'm wrong and I owe you an apology."

Ryan took the steps from the street two at a time. A doorman in a resplendent red velvet coat was ready to open the glass doors as soon as he reached the top.

"*Bonsoir*, Monsieur Tremayne." He gave a slight bow.

"*Bonsoir*," Ryan responded automatically as he rushed by him and on into the lobby. The time was later than he had planned, but at least he had accomplished all he had set out to do. A coach would arrive to take him to Blois at noon tomorrow. He had made arrangements for Angele to be fitted for her wardrobe and had the promise of the seamstress that everything would be ready when they set sail for New York.

He passed through the lobby with its marble floors gleaming in the lights of the candled chandeliers above. Vases of fresh flowers scented the air, and he wondered if Angele liked the perfume he'd selected for her, as well as everything else he had chosen.

He was about to start up the curving stairs but remembered he had no idea which room Angele was in. He turned and went to the desk.

He had not seen the man who was on duty before and introduced himself. "I'm Ryan Tremayne. A guest here. Room 208. The clerk on duty earlier was to assign a room to a lady friend of mine—Mademoiselle Benet. Can you give me the number please."

The man ran his finger down the names on the register and found her name. "Room 320, but she is not there, sir."

Ryan frowned. "What do you mean?"

The clerk gestured toward the rows of tiny boxes on the wall behind him, then pointed to the one marked 320. "The key is still there. When I came on duty the concierge said when he knocked on your door to tell her that her room was ready, she did not answer."

"Did you see her go out?"

"No. And the concierge said he hadn't seen her since he took her up there. He thought perhaps she was sleeping and didn't hear him."

"That's likely. What about the package that was to be delivered to her? If you'll give it to me, I'll take it up to her myself."

"Actually, we've been trying to deliver it to her all afternoon. In fact, one of the hotel's errand boys was just sent upstairs with it to try again."

"Thank you." Ryan turned away but out of the corner of his eye saw the door to the service stairway opening. It was an errand boy. He recognized the blue coat and trousers they wore and smiled to see he wasn't carrying anything. "I see you were able to awaken Mademoiselle Benet and give her the package. Did you show her to her room?"

The boy looked nervously at the clerk, who prodded, annoyed by his silence, "Well? Answer the gentleman."

"No, sir, I didn't," he mumbled.

"Well, come on upstairs with me so you can."

"If you don't mind, I'd rather not, sir."

The clerk gave an exasperated sigh. "Sidney, what is wrong with you this evening? You are not being cooperative with our guest."

Sidney stared at his feet. "I'm sorry. I just don't want to go."

Voice steely, Ryan said, "I think you'd better tell me why."

Sidney shifted his weight from one foot to the other.

"Answer him," the clerk ordered, "or you can look for another job."

"I just don't want to get involved in case there's trouble up there," Sidney blurted. "That man and all . . ."

Ryan felt an invisible rod jam straight down his spine. He grabbed the boy by his shoulders and gave him a shake that sent his head bobbing to and fro. "What are you saying?"

Sidney twisted away, leaping out of Ryan's reach. "She was with somebody—a man. I heard yelling, and . . ." He shook his head wildly from side to side. "Monsieur, I have said too much already. I am sorry, but I cannot help you. I want no trouble."

He turned and ran back into the stairwell, the door banging shut behind him.

"Monsieur Tremayne, I will have the concierge go with you," the desk clerk offered.

But Ryan had already crossed the lobby and was on his way upstairs.

Six

Corbett had chased after Angele and begged her to go back with him to Ryan's room and give him a chance to explain how sorry he was for the way he had behaved. He swore it wasn't like him, and he wanted her to understand he'd been drinking and also shocked to see her.

Reluctantly, Angele agreed, but she refused to let him carry the package. If it was another trick just to get everything back for Ryan, he was going to have a fight on his hands.

When they entered the room, she told him to leave the door open, and he obliged.

He gestured to one of the tall-backed brocade chairs positioned before the white tile fireplace. "Sit down, please. Can I get you a glass of wine? I'm sure Ryan has a carafe around here somewhere."

She gave a curt nod to the mahogany sideboard and the crystal decanters and glasses arranged there. "He does. But I don't care for any, thank you." Her arms were wrapped around the box, which she held tight against her chest. "And I'll just stand, because I don't intend to be here long."

Corbett ran nervous fingers through his curly red hair. He started to pace about, then slumped in one of the chairs. "Please start from the beginning and tell me everything."

"No. *You* tell *me* everything."

"I—" He threw up his hands in surrender. "I told you—

I want to apologize. I realize you couldn't have got in here without Ryan's permission, but as I said, I'd been drinking and wasn't thinking clearly. Now I see there must be some substance to your explanation, and I'd like to hear it again, if you don't mind."

She regarded him coldly. "Well, I *do* mind. You tried to . . . to *rape* me." She hated the feel of the word in her mouth and uttered it quickly, harshly.

"I know my drinking isn't an excuse, but it's a reason, and . . . please . . ." He stood, and she moved closer to the open door. "If what you say is true, then I'm the world's biggest idiot, and I apologize. And you have to believe me when I say that Ryan does not own a bordello. And if he asked you to marry him, he must have meant it."

"You said he's supposed to marry someone else."

"Not officially. And I was apt to say anything, the state I was in, but this has been very sobering, believe me."

Angele had smelled hard liquor on his breath, and she allowed that it had to be difficult for anyone to believe Ryan would want to marry her, looking as she did. But if his cousin was telling the truth, then she could start to believe once more that Ryan's intentions were real.

As for his cousin, she would try very, very hard to give him the benefit of the doubt. He had naturally believed the worst, but it was important to get along with Ryan's family.

"Could we just start over?" Corbett asked with a nervous smile.

Her nod of consent was anything but enthusiastic, yet it was enough for Corbett. The little twit was too stupid to realize he would never be her friend, but he had to make her believe otherwise. Because, if what she claimed was true—as he had begun to fear—then her days were sadly numbered. He was not about to risk losing his good life at BelleRose.

Angele was regarding him warily. "What do you mean when you say Ryan was not *officially* supposed to marry someone else?"

If Ryan married her, Corbett knew she would eventually

hear about Denise. Then she would be angry with him for lying, and it was best to gain her confidence till he figured out a way to get rid of her. "Well, it's a situation where everyone thought they would marry one day." He saw no reason to divulge that Denise had turned Ryan down. That was none of her business, and Denise hadn't meant it, anyway.

Angele relaxed a little. She recalled Ryan saying Corbett's wife was French. That meant her cousin probably was also, and maybe that was why Ryan had been interested in her.

Still, she was nagged by uneasiness, and, deciding there was nothing else to be discussed, she wanted to get away from him. "My room should be ready by now, and I need to start dressing for dinner. Ryan should be back soon."

"Do you know where he went? I haven't seen him all day."

"He just said he had some business to take care of."

"Well, I can go find out about your room."

Angele was grateful. After all, she did not relish walking into the lobby still looking like gutter trash. "That would be nice, thank you."

He turned and slammed right into Ryan.

"Corbett, what are you doing here?"

Corbett looked to Angele, wondering if she was going to start screaming about what he had done, then breathed a sigh of relief when she spoke up. "He was looking for you, and it's a good thing he knocked when he did. Otherwise, I'd still be sleeping. I guess I was more tired than I realized."

"Yes, she was dead to the world, Ryan," Corbett eagerly confirmed. "I had to practically knock the door down. We've just been talking, that's all. Getting acquainted."

"She told you why she was here?" Ryan's mouth was a thin line.

"Yes, and I have to say it came as quite a surprise."

"I'm sorry," Angele leaped to say. "I know you probably wanted to tell him yourself, but I had to explain myself."

"Yes, I suppose you did."

"And I told him how grateful I am for your getting me out of jail."

Ryan looked as though he wanted the earth to open up and swallow him whole.

Corbett's eyes were gleaming. "Yes, that was real nice of you."

Ryan's soft groan went unheard as the concierge rushed up to ask, out of breath, "Is everything all right, sir? The desk clerk was worried and asked me to come up and see."

Ryan absently waved a hand in front of his eyes. "Yes, everything is fine."

"What could be wrong?" Corbett asked innocently.

"The boy who brought the package was confused to find a man in my room," Ryan murmured. "That's all. It's nothing."

Corbett seized the opportunity to point out, "Well, if he was confused over me, imagine how surprised I was when I saw her, and—"

Ryan cut him off to ask the concierge to show Angele to her room.

The concierge nodded stiffly, unable to take his eyes off Angele as he tried to contain his disgust over her appearance.

"Have hot water sent up for her bath," Ryan continued, "and also a *coiffeur*." He turned to Angele. "I will meet you in the lobby in two hours, and we'll have dinner."

The minute the door closed behind them, Corbett exploded. "Have you lost all your senses? The very idea—taking that—that trollop out of jail, telling her you'll marry her. I can't believe any of this." He threw his hands up in the air.

"It's none of your concern," Ryan responded tightly as he took off his coat. He threw it on a chair, then went to the chiffonier and took out a fresh shirt. He'd had to buy new clothes for the trip to France in order to be stylish— something Clarice had insisted upon for both him and Corbett. He did not like at all the lines of costume that he felt produced a womanish figure—sloping shoulders, coat collars rolled high across the back of the neck. He much preferred the comfortable riding clothes and Wellington boots he wore at home.

He got disgusted with himself at times for how he let her tell him what to do, but it was easier than arguing. At least when he got married, she would stay out of his business, and he sure wasn't worried about Angele trying to mother him. Especially when it came to clothes. No doubt the reason she was reluctant to talk about her background was shame over having been raised poor.

He stripped off the shirt he was wearing.

Corbett gave an exaggerated sigh. "We need to talk about this."

"No, we don't."

"Yes, we do. Please tell me you aren't seriously considering marrying that girl."

Ryan pulled on the new white shirt with pleated front. "No, I'm not *considering* it. I'm *going* to. And my mind is made up, so there's no point discussing it."

Corbett went to the sideboard. A crystal decanter filled with whiskey sat next to the wine. He yanked out the stopper and filled a glass, then downed it in one long gulp. Wiping his mouth with the back of his hand, he took several deep breaths, then said, "Damn it, man. You have lost your mind. She's a thief—"

"She said she stole because she was hungry," Ryan said matter-of-factly. "And I believe her."

"And you're a fool. You know nothing about her."

"I know all I need to know. She's an orphan. She has no home. She's grateful to me for giving her one. She'll be obedient. She'll make a good wife."

Corbett poured himself another drink but did not gulp it down as he had the other. He sipped, chest heaving as he appeared to be struggling for composure. Beads of perspiration dotted his forehead. Finally, he emptied the glass and slammed it down with a loud thud. "Have you thought about Denise and how this is going to hurt her?"

"She refused me, remember?"

"But she was only trifling with you . . . playing a little joke."

"I don't joke about things like marriage, Corbett."

Corbett threw back his head and laughed. "I'd say what you're planning to do is the biggest joke I've ever heard in my whole life. You want to marry a thief you found in the sewers—*catacombs*"—he corrected in deference to Angele's earlier reminder—"and take her to BelleRose to be mistress of the house."

Ryan's glance was sharp. "I've no intention of taking anything away from Clarice, so don't start getting any notion like that. Angele knows nothing about running a household. She'll be busy enough just learning feminine graces—which I will expect her to do. Clarice can help."

"Clarice might not want to," Corbett was quick to point out. "She's not going to like this. There could be problems."

"Corbett, the mansion is large enough for two women. I think they can learn to get along with each other." He tucked his shirt into his trousers. He didn't mind them so much. They were ankle-length and fit loosely. Clarice had tried to persuade him to wear the style that was full at the top and tight from the knee downward, with buttons to fasten on each side, but he'd balked at that.

"What about your father?"

"What about him?"

"Do you think he'll accept her just because she's French when he hears about her background? How she was locked up for snatching an old lady's reticule?"

Ryan was putting on the chestnut-colored waistcoat he had selected for the evening. He paused and turned to face Corbett as his eyes hooded with anger. "And just how would he hear about it?"

Corbett turned to pour himself another drink.

Ryan reached around him to snatch the decanter from his hand. "I think you've had enough. And I asked you a question." If Corbett was going to make things difficult, it was best to know now.

"I don't suppose he will find out. I certainly won't say anything."

Ryan looked him straight in the eye. "I'm going to count on that."

"Well, he's going to be suspicious. He'll see right away that she isn't our kind."

"Maybe, but she seems intelligent. She'll learn."

"And how will you explain bringing a bride home?"

"By saying I fell in love with her. My father will just be happy that she's French."

"He'd hoped you'd marry Denise," Corbett said, almost petulantly.

"He doesn't really care, just so his precious French bloodline will continue."

"I should think it would mean something to you, too."

"Not really. I consider myself an American."

Corbett, a panicked look on his face, suddenly cried, "Ryan, listen! You don't have to do this. It doesn't matter if your father leaves BelleRose to me instead of you. It will still be yours."

"Yes, I know that, and I appreciate your feeling that way, but BelleRose is mine by rights, and I don't want anyone to have to hand it to me in defiance of my father's wishes. If it has to be earned, so be it."

"But to marry that girl—"

"It's what I want. Don't you see? I think she'll make a fine wife."

"But so would Denise."

Ryan laughed. "That's debatable. You know as well as I do that she's spoiled and willful and can be quite trying. We've had our arguments, believe me. And I don't want a wife that I have to constantly spar with. With a plantation as large as BelleRose to run, I won't have time."

"So you take a mistress."

"I may well do that," Ryan assured. "But that doesn't mean I want to be miserable when I'm with my wife."

"You're being impulsive, because you're angry and hurt with Denise for saying no, even though you won't admit it," Corbett argued. "I remember how you were on the crossing over here. You hardly said a word. You drank more than usual. And the first few days after we got to Paris, you didn't want to go to the cabarets at night. All you wanted to do was brood. That means you care about her."

"I thought so, too—at first. Now I realize I was just stunned that anyone could be so frivolous about something as serious as marriage."

Corbett could not resist sniping, "As *you* are doing to even think about marrying Angele Benet?"

"I'm not being frivolous," Ryan corrected. "I'm quite serious. And whether you believe me or not, I gave this a lot of thought before I decided to do it."

"It's only been a little over a week since she was arrested. That's not enough time. But I did notice when we were in Touraine your mind wasn't on buying horses."

"That's only partially true. The horses weren't as good as we were told, and you know it. But we're going to Blois tomorrow to look there."

Corbett wasn't concerned with buying horses, continuing to focus on Angele. "And how do you even know there's room for her on the ship? We're sailing in two weeks."

"No, *you're* leaving then, as planned, but Angele and I will be going a week later on the *James Munroe*. There were no cabins available on the *Victory*. I've already made our arrangements."

Corbett sneered and shook his head. "Well, you can just make mine, too. You aren't going to send me ahead to break the news to Denise and Clarice that you're bringing a wife home. You're going to be the one to do that."

"You won't like the accommodations on the *James Munroe*. I booked the last cabin."

Corbett was adamant. "I don't care. There is no way I will go back without you."

Ryan thought it would have been nice if Corbett could have smoothed the way. Denise would get over it, but Clarice might take a while. After all, she might consider Angele a threat to her authority but would soon realize she had nothing to worry about. The last thing Angele was qualified to do was take over a household, see that the servants did their job, plan menus for dinner parties, teas, balls, and all the other things that went with the Tremayne social life. His father enjoyed entertaining so those were extensive.

"All right," he conceded, "but don't say I didn't warn you."

"Anything is better than facing those women without you. Now, about dinner—"

Ryan had not intended to invite Corbett to join him and Angele but saw no way out. They had dined together every night they had been in Paris, and he didn't want to hurt his feelings. And what difference did it make, anyway, now that he knew everything. "You can join us if you like, but you'll need to freshen up a bit. I'm taking her to Au Petit Moulin. I've heard it's very nice, and the food is good."

"I saw the gown you bought her," Corbett said, almost accusingly.

"Did she like it?"

"Oh, yes. She was going to take it with her when she was about to run away, but I talked her into staying."

Ryan had been in the process of pouring himself a glass of wine but froze. "What do you mean she was about to run away?"

Corbett thought fast. "When I started asking questions about who she was and what she was doing in your room, she got upset and snatched up the box and ran out the door." Seeing Ryan's eyes flash with concern, Corbett embellished, "I ran after her and convinced her to come back so we could talk. That's when she accused you of trying to trick her into working in your bordello." Corbett pasted a concerned, worried look on his face. "Do you know what she meant by that, or is she just crazy?"

"No, she's not crazy, and thank you for bringing her back."

Corbett smiled, pleased with himself.

"As for the bit about the bordello, I thought we had

settled all that." He explained about the commandant's immoral and unscrupulous dealings with the female prisoners. "But I took care of that. It won't happen again to anyone else."

"Then I can see why she was upset."

"Yes, when she saw you and realized how late it was, she was probably afraid I wasn't coming back—that it was a trick. Thanks again for keeping her here."

Corbett turned toward the door so Ryan couldn't see him scowl to think he probably should have let her go regardless of the consequences. "I'll be glad to join you for dinner. I'll go change."

"Corbett . . ."

He turned.

"I'm going to trust you not to say anything to anyone— not even Clarice—about how I met Angele. I expect you to corroborate my story that she's an orphan but her family was well respected and prominent in France. I plan to buy her a stylish wardrobe and some nice jewelry, because I want everyone to think her family had money."

Corbett quirked a brow. "You're going to that much trouble?"

"Yes. Because I know Clarice, and I know my father. If they find out the truth, they'll judge her before they get to know her, and that's not fair to her, them, or me. Now, do I have your word?"

With a curt nod, Corbett left to dress for dinner.

Ryan hoped he could trust him. Otherwise, there might be problems he did not need.

Just before seven o'clock, Corbett joined Ryan in the hotel's smoking salon for a sherry. Angele was not mentioned. Instead, Ryan told about François DeNeux and how he had heard he was one of France's best horse breeders. He did not confide that Angele was the one who had told him.

"We should be able to find some good stallions, as well

as a few mares. And there's time to get them to the dock before sailing date."

Corbett chuckled. "Yes, it would be nice to return home with what you came to get instead of something you didn't."

Ryan let the remark pass. He was used to Corbett's bent toward sarcasm and had learned to accept it . . . although he didn't like it.

"Monsieur Tremayne?"

He glanced up to see the concierge. "Yes? What is it?"

"It's the lady. She told the desk clerk she was to meet you. He didn't think you wanted him to send her in here."

"Of course not. Please tell her I'll be right there." Ryan was puzzled as to why he looked so shaken.

So was Corbett, who remarked as soon as the concierge walked away, "Did you see how nervous he was? What do you suppose is wrong? Maybe the gown didn't fit, and she's wearing that godawful outfit she had on this afternoon."

"I doubt that," Ryan said tightly. He tossed some money on the table and hurried out, annoyed that Corbett was right on his heels. He wished now he hadn't invited him along even if it had hurt his feelings. He might make Angele more ill at ease than she probably already was.

Rounding the corner from the smoking salon, Ryan could see a woman standing at the desk but knew it could not be her . . .

But it was.

She turned, and his heart slammed into his chest.

She was, beyond doubt, the most beautiful woman he had ever seen.

Seven

In the near two weeks since Ryan had made his offer, Angele hadn't seen him. He had gone to Blois, leaving Corbett behind to help her get ready for the voyage. She had been trying to slip away from him and finally succeeded the day Ryan was due to return. And now she knelt by her mother's grave in the paupers' section in the rear of the Père Lachaise cemetery.

In the distance, the great double towers of the Cathedral of Notre-Dame, tricolors flying in the blue sky of France, could be seen. They were a startling white, framed by green chestnuts and oaks, guarding Paris with their brotherly strength.

Looping north and west in great bends flowed the sleepy Seine River, spanned by bridges.

It was a portrait of serenity, and Angele thought it a peaceful place for her mother's eternal rest. Her deepest regret, however, had been that there was no marker on the grave. She'd had no money to buy one, and the city did not provide anything. The mound of dirt would eventually level out beneath the summer rains, and grass and weeds would grow to hide any evidence of a grave. It would almost be as though her mother had never lived, and Angele felt that a real tragedy. Her mother *had* lived, indeed, and a wonderful life it had been. She and Angele's father had adored each other, and . . .

Angele pressed her fingertips against her eyes, holding back tears.

She loved her parents so much. And though she would probably never again visit either of their graves, she had found a way to buy a simple marker for her mother—even though it was, in a way, stealing. Ryan had given her money to buy trunks in which to pack her lavish new wardrobe, but she had bought cheap ones and had money left over.

Actually, she felt little guilt. Ryan did not seem to care about money. He had not only bought her expensive clothes but jewelry as well. One pair of diamond earbobs, she knew, would probably have provided her with food and shelter for years.

She was glad he had gone away, because she wanted time to think about what lay ahead. She knew she would have to submit to him as his wife, and, remembering how it had been with her uncle, her hands trembled as she reached to pluck a dandelion from the grave.

After it happened, she and her mother had never talked about it. She would have liked to. She wanted, needed, re-assurance that her uncle was different from other men. She couldn't imagine her father being so brutal, but even if a man were gentle, would there still be pain? She didn't know but would soon find out, and fear crept like the ivy twining about the trees that lined the path through the cemetery.

She hadn't meant for her mother to find out what her uncle had done. Shamed, humiliated, and terrified, she had hidden in the cellar. A servant going down to get wine for dinner heard her crying and told her mother. When her mother came, she made her tell what had happened. And that night they had fled together in the dark with only the clothes on their backs.

Eventually, after finding food and shelter wherever they could, they made their way to Paris. Her mother had to sell the earbobs she had been wearing when they ran away to pay for their passage.

Angele rocked back on her heels now, her new striped gingham skirt bunched about her ankles. The bow of the plumed poke bonnet tickled her neck, and she tugged at it to loosen. It was a cool day, and she had draped a fine cashmere shawl over her shoulders.

She had been in such a hurry that morning it was surprising she had managed to make herself presentable. But she'd had to rush in order to get away from Corbett. She still did not trust him and wondered if she ever would, because something about the way he looked at her sometimes made her flesh crawl. And try though she might, she had not been able to put his crude behavior that first day out of her mind.

She hoped that once she became Ryan's wife and moved into the mansion at BelleRose, she might feel differently. She wanted everyone to accept her, and planned to do everything she could to make them. After all, once she left, there would be no turning back. Her future depended on Ryan, and though she didn't love him, she planned to dig in her heels and stay, no matter what.

As she mused, a man carrying a shovel came walking up the trail to the paupers' section. He saw a woman bent over a grave and squinted against the sun to see her better. Even from a distance, he could tell she was dressed in fine clothes. Probably rich. So what was she doing kneeling at a pauper's grave? Surely anyone of means would not have kith or kin buried in such a place.

He continued on. He had another grave to dig for someone else too poor to be buried anywhere else.

Angele did not notice the man as he passed by. She did, however, hear the approaching carriage.

"Mademoiselle Benet?" The man holding the reins over a splendid black horse removed his top hat and smiled uncertainly.

She straightened and lifted the hem of her skirt above her ankles to keep it from dragging in the tall grass as she walked toward him. "*Oui.* I am so pleased you could meet me, monsieur. I was afraid you wouldn't receive my note in time." She had only been able to get away from Corbett long enough the day before to slip a messenger a few francs to deliver the envelope to the stone cutter.

"I am Wilfrin Montague." He got down from the carriage. "I brought some sketches of my work. Do you see anything you like?"

She leafed through them and quickly seized upon the drawing of an angel, carved into a modest stone. "This one." She gave him a slip of paper on which she had written her mother's name and the date of her birth and death.

"Very good." He put the paper with his others. "It should take me a few weeks, and I will put it in place myself."

He told her the price, and as she counted out the money, he remarked, "It is so good of you to want to put a stone here. Few people do in this section, you know."

Angele knew, all right, and if she had the means and the time would have had her mother moved. But she had neither, nor would she ever see the marker. She trusted the stone cutter, however. Besides, he had no way of knowing she was leaving France, never to return, so he would keep his promise.

He cast a glance up at the dark clouds gathering. "It looks like it might rain. Would you like to ride out with me? It's a long walk back to the gates."

She said she would be pleased. He helped her up into the carriage, and she cast one last glance of good-bye at her mother's grave.

She didn't see the man peering out from behind a tree perhaps fifty feet away.

Corbett wished he knew what Angele was doing. The sneaky bitch had almost got away from him, but he had been too smart for her. The day before, he had seen her slipping back up the stairs from the lobby. She was supposed to be in her room, claiming she had a headache. He had no idea what she had been up to and couldn't find out. The desk clerk and concierge were no help. So Corbett vowed she'd not sneak off from him again.

He was watching her like a hawk soaring above a mouse, waiting for the right moment to strike. Ryan expected him to accept her and be nice to her, and Corbett knew it wouldn't do for him to say anything against her that he couldn't prove.

She had refused to go to dinner with him the night before, claiming her head still hurt, and he had arranged for soup, fruit, and baguettes to be delivered to her room. But he had hired one of the hotel's baggage boys to keep vigil during the night, lest she try to leave.

This morning, when he had knocked on her door to ask whether she was ready to have breakfast and begin their final day of shopping for her luggage, she had again complained of a headache. Calling through the door, she said since Ryan was due back later in the day, she would go with him to buy the trunks if she felt better. If not, he could go get them without her.

Suspicious, Corbett had hidden outside a doorway just down the street from the hotel.

He didn't have to wait long.

She came out and began walking hurriedly, purposefully, along the Canal St.-Martin. He followed, keeping a safe distance lest she look over her shoulder and see him.

He was puzzled when she turned through the massive wrought-iron gates of the Père Lachaise cemetery. She passed the area of the well-to-do, buried in mausoleums resembling miniature mansions made of rock, or with tall, sky-reaching stones to mark their place of eternal rest. He assumed she was visiting a relative's grave, but when she continued on, he began to think perhaps she was going to exit through a rear gate—till he saw that she was actually heading for what could only be the burial section for the poor. Few markers, sunken, untended graves, it was a very dreary place.

He stopped to get a rock out of his shoe, then stepped into a hole and twisted his ankle. Cursing softly, he stumbled into a stone grotto where there was a bench. He sat down to massage his ankle and allow the pain to subside, then followed in the direction Angele had gone.

By the time he found her, she was kneeling beside a grave, and he darted behind a tree to watch. Then the man in the carriage came, and Corbett silently cursed because he could not hear what they were saying. They didn't talk long before the man took her arm and helped her into the carriage.

Excitement mounting, Corbett ignored his aching ankle and hurried as fast as he could after the carriage.

Not only had Angele met a man in the most remote part of the cemetery—a perfect trysting place—but she had also left with him. He felt a thrilling rush to think of what Ryan's reaction would be when he told him. She was exactly as Corbett had suspected—a conniver, a schemer. She was obviously after the Tremayne money, and the man she'd just met might be in on it.

Maybe, he thought, imagination running wild, they planned to rob Ryan and then kill him. There was no telling what she was capable of doing. He might even be in danger himself.

But when would they strike? They were due to leave for Le Havre in the morning, and—

He had reached the gates and slowed in wonder.

She was walking briskly along, and it appeared she was headed toward Montparnesse. The man and the carriage were nowhere in sight, so what the hell was she up to?

She continued on, and he struggled to keep up. His ankle was throbbing. It was also starting to rain. They were going to be soaked, but she kept on going, seemingly oblivious to the weather.

The Abbaye Val-de-Grâce loomed ahead with its two-tier façade and dome modeled after St. Peter's in Rome. Angele was, Corbett realized with a start, returning to where she had been caught stealing reticules. Then it dawned she was actually headed for the catacombs. Rounding the corner of Place Denfert-Rochereau, she lifted her skirts and plunged right into the woods and the embankment leading to the underground stone quarries.

The skies opened and the rain poured down. Corbett uttered an oath which was received with a frown by two nuns leaving the abbey. He ducked his head in apology and darted by them. It was dry inside, and he could wait there until Angele came out. He damn well had no intentions of following her any farther. She could call them catacombs or whatever she wanted, but as far as he was concerned they were sewers, and she was nothing but a sewer rat. And the sooner Ryan realized that, the better. There was still time to stop the madness . . . time to keep him from making a terrible mistake. Denise was the wife for him—and also Corbett's assurance of continuing to live at BelleRose.

Angele needed no light to show her the way. This time, however, she was not being chased and could pick her way along carefully so she wouldn't fall in a puddle. Still, she tried to walk quickly. No longer disguised as a boy, it was dangerous for her to be there. But there was one more thing she had to do before she left Paris.

She took the first tunnel to the left, where the old people lived.

A fire was burning, casting wild shadows against the cold, gray walls.

A man and woman were huddled together near the flames for warmth. Worn, frayed woolen shawls hung about their bony shoulders. Their heads were bowed, and their gnarled, veined hands were intertwined.

They did not hear Angele approach. Their hearing had faded along with their hope for a better life in old age.

She knelt before them, and they gave a startled cry in unison.

"Dear Lord . . ." the old man whispered in a paper-thin voice. "What do you want of us . . ." Milky eyes blinked in terror.

The woman made soft moaning sounds as she pressed closer to him.

Angele did not have time to explain how once they had befriended a bedraggled boy—or someone they believed to be a boy. They had shared what little food they had. They asked no questions. They knew the boy grieved because his mother had died. And they had wrapped their arms around him in comfort.

Angele had shared the tiny cavern within the catacombs with the couple. She knew they had a hard time, for they could not move about like the younger folk.

She took the rest of the money she had not spent from her reticule and folded the old man's fingers about it. "Take this," she whispered. "It will help you for a while, at least."

His mouth fell open when he saw how much it was.

"I wish it could be more." She pressed her lips to their foreheads in turn while they stared at her in bewilderment, then she left as quickly as she had come.

Ryan paced anxiously about in the lobby. The clerk behind the desk peered at him over his glasses, then sighed as he started toward him again.

Splaying his fingers on the counter, Ryan asked for not the first time, "Are you sure you don't know where they went? It's getting late, and—"

"No, monsieur," the clerk repeated with forced politeness and patience. "I have no knowledge of either the lady or the gentleman."

"And you say you've been here since morning?"

"*Oui*. It is almost time for me to leave." He sounded as though he were glad.

Ryan had been at the hotel since noon. He had told Corbett when to expect him. There was a lot to be done to get ready to leave for Le Havre at first light the next morning. In addition, he and Angele needed to fill out some papers so the ship's captain could perform their mar-

riage ceremony. Time was growing short, and Ryan was
getting worried.

He had the concierge open the door to Angele's room,
worrying she might be in bed sick. He had seen the trunks
she had bought and had delivered. They were cheap, and
he was disappointed, but it was too late to do anything
about it now. But why hadn't Corbett helped her make
the selection? He knew about such things, and Angele
couldn't be expected to, what with her background.

Ryan didn't know where to start looking and began to
imagine all kinds of things that might have happened.
Maybe they had both been in some kind of accident.
Worse, what if Corbett had had too much to drink as he
sometimes did? Angele would be terrified.

Damn it, he fumed, he never should have gone off and
left her. If his father got angry because he came home
without the horses, so be it.

As he paced about, he thought again how he knew so
little about the woman he was going to marry. True, she
was lovely, and he looked forward to their wedding night
with heated anticipation, but there was a remoteness about
her, a coldness, that bothered him. He had not tried to
kiss her. Had not even put his arm about her, really. Yet,
if he made to touch her, she winced, as though she found
his closeness revolting. He only hoped that once they were
married things would be different. Probably she was only
shy, afraid, as any virgin would be. Then, too, she had been
suddenly thrust into a world she'd never known before,
and that had to be frightening.

He tried to get his mind on something else. She had
been right about François DeNeux. He had excellent Anglo-Arabs, and Ryan had bought three mares and three
stallions, spending more than he'd planned—but money
was never a consideration when it came to horses. He intended to have the finest in all of Virginia, maybe the entire South.

The situation at hand crept back into his mind once

again. They had to be all right. Corbett would not dare do anything foolish.

Ryan turned toward the stairs, thinking he should go wait in his room. Evidently the clerk had told some of the other employees he was upset, because they were starting to look at him strangely as they passed. Besides, he had whiskey in his room, and he could use a drink.

He was halfway up to the first-floor landing when the clerk called sharply, "Monsieur Tremayne. The lady you have been waiting for is here."

Ryan turned to see Angele walking across the lobby. She hesitated as the clerk spoke, then glanced up at Ryan with anxious eyes and flushed cheeks. Her hair was wild about her face, and the gingham dress she was wearing was spattered with mud.

He rushed to meet her, keeping his voice low as he caught her arm. "Where have you been? Is anything wrong?"

Instinctively, she resisted a man's touch and pulled from his grasp. "No, of course not. I just had some things I wanted to do before we left."

"Where's Corbett? Why isn't he with you?"

"I felt like being alone today."

She started by him, but he firmly took her hand and led her up the stairs.

Angele tensed. She could tell he was annoyed, but when Corbett told how she had sneaked out—as undoubtedly he would—he was really going to be mad.

When they reached the landing and turned, and the staff could not longer see, Ryan quietly said, "I don't like this, Angele. Corbett didn't want to go with me to Blois, and I agreed with the understanding he would keep you company. I don't want you out alone."

Angele was swept with indignity. He was not her keeper, for heaven's sake! "You seem to forget," she reminded stiffly, "that before you met me I was quite alone."

"That was different. You passed for a boy. Now you're a lady."

"I can take care of myself." She looked up at him and saw how his blue eyes were troubled. "Really. You don't have to worry about me."

He returned her stare. "I said I didn't want you out by yourself, Angele, and that's the end of it."

She bit back an angry retort, not about to jeopardize her position. Let him think she would be subservient. Once they were married, he would quickly discover she had a mind of her own and was not about to be treated as chattel.

Pretending acquiescence, she nodded, then, making her tone pleasant, inquired as to whether his trip to Blois had been successful.

"Very much so. I bought some fine horses, and they're being rushed to Le Havre to be boarded on the ship." They had reached the door to her room. "I'll tell you about them at dinner."

Angele looked beyond him to see Corbett coming down the hall. "I don't want to go to dinner. I have a headache. I plan to retire early."

Before Ryan could respond, Corbett reached his side. "I'm sorry to hear that, Angele," he said to her. "If you're sick, maybe we should have a doctor come take a look at you."

Angele pulled her hand from Ryan's. "I'm not sick. I just don't feel well. I'll be fine by tomorrow morning."

Ryan agreed with Corbett. "I'll ask the concierge if he can find a doctor. We can't have you start the trip sick."

"You are both making a fuss for nothing. I'm going to bed, and if anyone knocks on my door, I won't answer." She stepped inside her room, closed the door behind her, and locked it.

Ryan stood there a moment, then whirled on Corbett. "Why did you let her go off by herself this morning? I told you to keep an eye on her."

Corbett started walking away. Ryan was right behind

him, asking again why he had not followed his orders. Corbett waited till they were a good distance from Angele's room. Probably the little conniver had her ear pressed to the door, wanting to hear what he had to say about her, and there was no way he was going to let her know he had followed her. He could tell she was wary of him, but he had to put on a genial front. After all, Ryan could be quite stubborn, and if he insisted on marrying her after what he had to tell him, he couldn't make it look as though he were trying to make trouble. If that happened, Ryan would be prone not to believe him in the future.

"Damn it, Corbett. I'm tired from the trip, and I've got a lot to do to be ready to leave tomorrow. I don't need to be worrying about Angele. Now, I asked you—why didn't you keep an eye on her?"

Corbett clenched his teeth to keep from grinning as he responded to pique his cousin's interest, "And what makes you think I didn't?"

Eight

Angele knew Ryan was still angry, because he was quiet and brooding on the ride to Le Havre. Corbett, however, seemed to be trying to make up for how Ryan was acting, talking constantly and going out of his way to be nice to her.

It was a gorgeous day. A gentle breeze blew puffy fingers of snowy-white clouds across a tinted cobalt sky, and the sun was a teasing peach-and-golden orb, sending warmth in peekaboo waves.

They stopped for lunch at a tiny cafe. Ryan declined food but had several glasses of wine. Angele wondered fearfully if he might be having second thoughts about marrying her. That birthed worries of what she would do if he decided to abandon her in Le Havre. She had no money. He would probably strip her of her jewels so she'd have nothing to sell to keep from starving. But she told herself she was being silly. He was just angry. He was probably also tired from the trip to Blois. Besides, he had spent a lot of money on her and wasn't likely to throw it away by changing his mind.

At one of the rest stops, he stayed in the coach. Angele walked around in the perfumed air to stretch a bit, and Corbett went with her. She took the opportunity to try to find out just how upset Ryan was. "He's hardly spoken to me all day," she confided to Ryan's cousin. "He must have been furious when you told him how I slipped away from you yesterday."

"I didn't tell him that you did," Corbett said smoothly.

Her eyes widened. "You didn't? Then what—"

"I told him you'd said you wanted to have your last day in Paris all to yourself, and that I understood. So it's me he's angry with for letting you go. Not you."

"But why did you take the blame? It was all my doing."

"Because I didn't want him upset with you right before your wedding. Besides, he's been angry with me before, and I don't let it bother me. He'll be all right once we're on the ship and on our way. Don't worry about it."

"But I do," she protested. "It's not fair, because it wasn't your fault."

He shrugged and smiled. "I don't mind. Besides, maybe it will help make up for the awful way I acted that day when I found you in his room. I'm really very, very sorry about everything I said and did, Angele.

"And," he continued with an admiring glance, "that night I saw you in the hotel lobby all dressed up, I realized then and there why Ryan wanted to marry you. He could see you are a truly beautiful woman."

Angele blushed and murmured a thank-you, then, because she really did want to forget the bad encounter between them, she urged, "Let's just pretend it never happened and never mention it again."

He gave a sigh of relief. "I'm glad you feel that way. I want us all to be one big happy family."

"That's nice of you. And I hope your wife will feel the same way. You did say everyone thought Ryan was going to marry her cousin."

She didn't notice how his face tightened, or how his eyes suddenly gleamed with his resentment. And it was only with a concerted effort that he was able to keep his tone light and warm as he lied, "Clarice won't care. She's always stayed out of Ryan's business." He quickly changed the subject. "You really had me worried yesterday, though. I was afraid something would happen to you."

They were walking along a path bordered by primroses. Angele stumbled on a rock she didn't see, and he caught her arm. "Like now," he laughed. "What if you'd been hurt? I'd never have forgiven myself when I was supposed to be looking out for you. And that's why Ryan is so angry with me—I didn't do what I was supposed to."

"He only thinks that," she corrected. "And I'm going to let him know different. I'll tell him what really happened."

He tensed. "I wish you wouldn't. He'll think I said something to you about it. Really, I'd prefer you didn't."

She was hesitant to agree, but Corbett sounded quite adamant. In fact, she noticed that he almost seemed scared. Well, he knew Ryan better than she did, so maybe it was best to let it alone.

He paused and put his hand on her shoulder. "But I would appreciate your doing me one favor, if you will."

Angele never promised anything blindly. "You'll have to tell me what you want first."

"Why didn't you want me to go with you yesterday?"

"Because I wanted to be alone."

"Where exactly did you go?"

She decided he was being too nosy but didn't want to offend him by saying so when they had started getting along so well. She continued walking, and he fell in step beside her. "I just wandered around the city. That's all. Since I may never return, there were a few places I wanted to visit."

And men you wanted to see, you lying strumpet, Corbett thought, careful to keep his expression pleasant and compassionate. Last night, he had made Ryan pry everything out of him.

Yes, he had assured him, he *had* kept an eye on Angele, secretly following her when he realized what she was up to. Ryan, then, of course, had insisted on knowing exactly where she had gone. Corbett had let him stew a while, pretending to resist, murmuring how he hated to tattle. Finally, he had told him about seeing her meet a man and leave with him in a carriage. He did not mention it was in a cemetery.

Ryan had clenched his fists and scowled and uttered an oath. He wanted to know where they went, and Corbett said he had no idea, because he could not keep up on foot. He decided not to say anything about her going to the catacombs. It was more important for Ryan to focus on the fact that she had met a man and think she had gone off with him.

Gingerly, Corbett had asked if he were going to proceed with his plans to marry her. To his surprise—and disgust— Ryan had assured him that he most certainly was. After all, he had pointed out with a smile that was almost menacing, you didn't shoot a colt just because he was hard to break.

No, Corbett had bitten his tongue to keep from saying, *but sometimes you have to take a whip to them.* Ryan wouldn't have appreciated such a remark. He did not believe in beating animals into submission.

So Corbett had kept his silence. And now it was time to come up with another plan. No doubt, Ryan felt he had an investment in her due to all the money he had spent. He was probably also confident that once they were married he could control her—break her like a high-spirited colt. But Corbett could not take a chance on that happening and knew he had to find a way to get rid of her. He only hoped the man he had hired to find out who was buried in the grave Angele had visited would write to him with interesting news soon. He also hoped he might be able to learn something about the man she had met, even though that was unlikely. Still, the more he could find out about the devious little bitch, the sooner he could turn Ryan against her.

But Corbett didn't intend to waste any other opportunities that might come his way—such as maybe getting rid of her *before* they reached New York.

And he had no qualms about the method he might have to use.

* * *

Lulled by the warm breeze and the swaying of the carriage, Angele felt herself getting drowsy. Ryan was already asleep on her left, while Corbett slumped against the door on the other side.

She turned toward Ryan and pretended to close her eyes as she watched him and wondered what kind of man he really was. She knew so little about him, only that he liked horses and needed a French wife to keep from being disinherited. He seemed kind, but there was a forbidding air about him that warned he was not a man to be reckoned with.

Had he had many women? she wondered. He was certainly attractive. And what of the one everyone thought he was going to marry? Was she pretty? Well bred? And what was his family going to think of him for bringing home a total stranger, someone they knew nothing about?

Her body rocked in unison with the motion of the carriage, and finally she fell asleep—only to awaken some time later to realize with a start that her head was resting on Ryan's shoulder.

And, at the same instant, dread washed like a spring rain to see that her hand had fallen between his legs.

She started to snatch it away, then something—curiosity, she supposed—made her hesitate. Beneath and to the right of the buttoned closing of his trousers she could feel a slight bulge, and her cheeks flamed to know she was actually touching a man in his most private of places.

She could hear Corbett snoring. He was unaware of what was going on, thank heavens.

Closing her eyes, she waited a moment, then opened one eye to make sure Ryan was still asleep. She thought she saw the tiniest flicker at the corner of his mouth, as though he might be about to smile, but he remained still, no doubt dreaming.

Opening both eyes then, her gaze lowered to his thighs, and she felt a strange shiver to think how the muscles of them seemed to strain against his trousers. He was a strong man, she could tell, well built and muscular, and she prayed that when he did claim his husbandly rights he would not make her scream with pain.

Pushing aside memories of the anguish inflicted by her uncle, Angele recalled whispered, giggled conversations in the night among the girls at Miss Appleton's finishing school. She had listened shyly as they talked of stolen kisses when they could escape the watchful eye of nannies and governesses.

One of them had been bolder than the rest. Leticia Wainscot had confided that she had actually let a boy feel her breasts, and she described in detail how it had felt to have his fingertips tweak her nipples. They had swollen tight as cherry pits, she'd said, beneath his touch. And Angele had gasped along with the others when Leticia further admitted he had put his mouth on her, suckling like a babe, and how she had experienced a tingling *down there* . . .

Would Ryan do the same? Angele wondered, then told herself the only thing she should be concerned about was that he didn't hurt her. After all, Miss Appleton had said the purpose of a man having his way with a woman was only supposed to be for the purpose of creating life.

When each girl began to have her monthly time, Miss Appleton would call them into her office for a private talk. Angele well remembered her meeting. Miss Appleton hadn't looked at her, staring down instead at her hands, which were folded in her lap. She had whispered as though the words were too shameful to be spoken, and Angele had trouble hearing her. But the message had been clear— mating with a man was painful and dirty, something to be done in the dark quickly, and only to make babies. A wife should also never let her husband see her without her clothes, because it would arouse him and make him want to do the *nasty thing*.

The other girls had cornered Angele and made her repeat everything Miss Appleton had said, word for word, to make sure she'd given the same lecture. Then they had laughed and ridiculed the woman and agreed it was no wonder she was an old maid.

Angele had giggled along with them, not understanding but wanting the camaraderie. However, after her uncle's attack, she was glad she'd not had to be around the girls again, for she'd have told them Miss Appleton was quite right. It had been everything she'd said it was, and Angele prayed she would never again know such pain and degradation.

But now she was only hours away from perhaps reliving the nightmare, and she was terrified.

For a few moments, Angele had been lost in thought, oblivious to the present. She was quickly yanked back, however, when she realized her hand was moving . . . moving because—to her horror—what she had been touching was *growing.*

With a soft gasp, she withdrew and twisted away. Fearing her touch had awakened him, she expected him to berate her for being so unladylike. After a few seconds, however, she realized by his even breathing that he was still asleep.

Slowly, she turned back toward him to peek from beneath lowered lashes. She swallowed a great, shuddering gasp to see the bulge in his trousers and was grateful he didn't know that she had touched him. He might think—God forbid—that she was depraved, and that would never do.

She squeezed her eyes tightly shut, determined not to open them again until they reached Le Havre.

Ryan also peeked from beneath lowered lashes. He saw how her brow was furrowed, and the way she was squeezing her hands against her bosom so tight her knuckles were white.

She had touched him by accident. He had not been sleeping and knew when she moved. His erection had been by accident, however. It had been a long time since he'd had a woman. Trying to keep from bursting out laughing, though, had taken a lot of effort.

She was such an enigma. One moment, he thought she was all innocence and without guile. The next, he sensed a hardness, a shell about her that was impenetrable.

He frowned to think of Corbett's recounting of her actions when she had sneaked away from him. Who was the man she had met? Had she actually been living two lives—one as a boy thief and the other as a whore? But if that were true, why, after he had turned her into the true beauty she was, had she gone off with a man? Certainly not for money. She didn't want for anything now. In fact, he had been surprised to find she was not extravagant and had opted to buy cheaper luggage than he had suggested. He hadn't asked her to return the money she had saved, so she was certainly not without funds. She could also have taken the jewelry he had given her and run away alone, or with the man she had met, if she had wanted.

Ryan scoffed at such a thought. Angele Benet was not stupid. She wanted everything he had to offer. But one thing he would not tolerate was an unfaithful wife.

Corbett had not wanted to tell what he had seen but was finally coaxed into it. Ryan was impressed at his reluctance. Evidently, Corbett had accepted his decision to marry Angele, having realized nothing would change for him and his family. Clarice might be upset for a while, because she had hoped her cousin would also become her sister-in-law, but everything would work out for the best.

At least, that's how Ryan hoped it would be.

Angele awoke when Corbett let out a loud yawn and said, "Well, thank God we're here. If I don't soon have a whiskey to wash this dust from my throat, I think I'll choke."

She turned toward Corbett, not Ryan, unable to look at him just yet for fear she might blush. The memory was still quite vivid.

She had never been to Le Havre and was disappointed to find the port city dirty and depressing. The streets were dark and dingy, crowded by people more wretched and

destitute than any she had ever seen in the catacombs.
Women with babies suckling at their breasts sat on slimy
street corners, each with a hand outstretched, begging for
money. Drunken men stumbled in alleyways or passed out
in doorways. Ragged, dirty children roamed about, begging for food more than money.

The harbor, however, was completely different. Sea gulls
darted and sang in their endless search for food, and a
sharp yet sweet wind blew in from the water. There were
boats bobbing in the distance, others at anchor close to
shore.

Rounding a bend in the road, she marveled at the sight
of a huge ship.

"So that's the *James Munroe*. It doesn't look any bigger
than the *Victory*," Corbett said, unimpressed.

"It's adequate," Ryan all but snapped.

When they reached the pier, Ryan made to get out of
the carriage but paused to remind Corbett, "You know
you could have sailed a week ago on the *Victory*."

Angele was startled to hear how irritably he spoke.

"And we both know why I didn't." Corbett matched his
cousin's coldness as he alighted on the other side. He held
out his hand to Angele, since Ryan was ignoring her.

She sensed the tension between them, but it passed
quickly in the preparations to board.

The dock was crowded, and she was aware of the admiring stares of the men and envious glances from the women.
Ryan had chosen her traveling ensemble—a fitted coat of
blue taffeta with a white flounced skirt. He also selected
her hat, which she didn't care for. It was called a poke
bonnet and had plumes and ribbon bows. She thought it
a bit frivolous, but Ryan said it was the latest style, and he
wanted her to learn to dress fashionably. How she wished
she could tell him that such things were taught at her finishing school, and she didn't need him or anyone else to
tell her how she should dress.

But one day, she promised herself, she would let him
know he had not married out of his class, after all. In fact,

he might have married *above* it, for she'd not seen his
home or the measure of his wealth and social prestige. For
the time being, however, it was important for him to believe her helpless and vulnerable, ignorant of all social
graces until she was comfortably established in her new
life. And no doubt it made Ryan feel magnanimous to
raise her from the dredges of her previous existence.

But despite how he was behaving—pouting, almost—
Angele was tingling with excitement over the voyage and
the future—albeit uncertain—that awaited.

Stiffly, woodenly, Ryan escorted her up the gangplank.
She was anxious to explore her surroundings, but he
turned her over to a polite steward with instructions to
take her to their cabin. "I have to see the captain about
performing the ceremony," he said without enthusiasm.

Corbett came up behind them and set his valise down
with a deliberate thud. "Why the hell won't anyone carry
this damn bag for me?" he demanded of the steward.

Ryan had walked away, and though Angele knew he
could hear Corbett complaining, he kept on going.

The steward held out his hand. "May I see your papers,
sir?"

Corbett fished in his coat pocket. "What kind of ship
are you people running that you make your passengers
carry their own luggage on board? I almost didn't get my
trunks loaded, and if my cousin hadn't intervened they'd
still be sitting on the goddamn pier."

The steward admonished him with a sweeping glance.
"Monsieur, please. The ladies."

"Just have someone take this bag to wherever I'm supposed to be." Corbett gave him the papers.

The steward looked at them and frowned. "You do not
have a cabin, monsieur. You are in steerage. And steerage
carries their own bags."

"*Steerage?* Are you out of your mind? I know all the cabins
are taken, but surely you have something between them
and *steerage,* for God's sake. A dormitory on the same deck
as the cabins. Anything."

Ignoring him, the steward continued. "You should not even be boarding at this gangplank. I must ask you to go back to the pier and find your way to where cargo is being loaded. Steerage goes on board there. It's the bottom deck."

"I . . . I'll do no such damn thing," Corbett stammered, rage choking him.

Angele was embarrassed for him, because everyone around was staring. Instinctively, she backed away a few steps. The steward saw her discomfort and warned Corbett, "Monsieur, I must ask you to leave or you will force me to have you physically removed."

Corbett was fast losing control. "I'd like to see you try, you pompous son of a bitch. Now, you listen to me. My cousin booked our passage, and I know he got the last available cabin. And if you think I'm going to be treated like scum just because there's no more room in the upper-class sections, you're sadly mistaken."

Angele was afraid of what might happen next and breathed a sigh of relief that Ryan had finally turned around and was walking briskly toward them. She could see he was quite angry.

But it wasn't the steward who was the target of Ryan's wrath. Instead, he caught Corbett by his arm and said something in his ear that no one else could hear. Corbett nodded, tight-lipped, but continued to glower at the steward.

Then Ryan murmured something to the steward, who immediately smiled, then signaled to one of the deckhands to take Corbett's luggage.

Ryan gave Corbett a pat on the back. "You might have to sleep in steerage, but you'll have access to everything else up here. If you have any more problems, let me know. It's going to be all right."

Angele saw that Corbett seemed appeased as he followed the deckhand carrying his luggage.

The steward turned to her. "This way, mademoiselle."

She followed him down a short corridor. There were

four thick wood doors on either side. At the very end, he opened one and stood back for her to enter.

Her eyes went to the bed. It seemed to dominate the room, folding out from the wall like a giant tray, secured by chains. It hardly looked big enough for one person, much less two, and thoughts of sharing it with Ryan made her cringe.

There was a small table and two chairs. An oil lamp hung from the ceiling. A chamber pot sat in one corner, and she was relieved to see a privacy screen. She would not have to undress in front of Ryan.

The steward gestured toward a ceiling-to-floor cabinet. "That's where you can put your clothes. The dining room is all the way forward. Breakfast is at seven, lunch at twelve, and dinner is served at six."

She thanked him and walked to the porthole. It was the ocean side, and all she could see was dark blue water fading into the horizon. "It will take us several weeks to reach America, won't it?"

"Yes, mademoiselle, and the ladies gather to sew during the day, or they read. You shouldn't be bored."

Angele didn't intend to join them. Ladies asked questions, and she didn't want to be evading answers continuously. Skirting Ryan's subtle queries was difficult enough.

He left her, saying her luggage would be along shortly.

Alone, Angele stared at the bed. It seemed to be growing . . . filling the room. She could almost feel it start to press against her, backing her against the wall, and suddenly she couldn't stand it any longer. She had to get away from it and the horror of thinking about what was going to happen when night came.

Bolting for the door, she yanked it open and slammed right into Ryan as he was about to knock.

He saw that her face was flushed and her eyes were wild. "Angele, for God's sake, what's wrong?"

She reeled slightly and put a hand on the doorframe to steady herself. "Nothing," she murmured. "I was just going out on deck to get some air. It's stuffy in here. I think

I'm getting seasick." If he thought that, it might give her a reprieve for a few nights, anyway.

"I doubt that. The ship hasn't left port yet. We aren't moving."

"Then maybe it's something I ate."

"You ate the same food Corbett did, and he's not sick. You're just nervous. Let's go."

She drew back as he held out his hand to her. "Go where?"

"To be married. The captain is waiting to perform the ceremony. We need to get it over with before we sail."

Get it over with, she mused dismally as he slipped his fingers around hers. That was not how she had envisioned her wedding day—as merely something to be done with.

But then nothing about her life, of late, had been anything like she ever dreamed it would be.

Nine

The marriage ceremony was quick and perfunctory. The captain had wasted no time. Busy with preparations for sailing, he was not pleased with having to perform a wedding. As soon as it was over, he had murmured hasty congratulations and rushed back to his duties.

They were standing toward the bow. Ryan and Angele just looked at each other, both feeling a bit awkward.

Corbett stepped forward to give Angele a quick kiss on each cheek and welcome her to the family.

She was grateful and said so.

Ryan thanked him also, and Angele noticed he seemed startled by what Corbett had done. Actually, she thought he should be embarrassed. After all, he could have said something—anything—instead of just standing there with that same, grim expression he'd worn since leaving Paris.

Corbett shook his hand. "Congratulations. It's a shame the rest of the family and everybody else couldn't be here, but I'm sure Clarice will make up for it and have a big party so everybody can meet your bride."

"I'm sure she will," Ryan said without enthusiasm.

"And now I think I'll go have another drink in toast. Care to join me?"

Ryan shook his head. "I want to talk to Angele."

She tensed, hoping he wasn't planning on taking her to the cabin right then. Surely, he would wait till dark.

"Then I'll see you at dinner." Corbett smiled but not

with his eyes. "At least I can leave steerage to eat with my own class."

"You can leave steerage anytime you want," Ryan corrected. "It certainly cost me enough to bribe the steward to let you have the run of the ship."

Corbett kept on going.

Angele stared after him. "I'm sorry he has to sleep in steerage. I've heard it's terrible." Actually, she knew it for a fact from her own experience. She and her mother had steerage accommodations when they had crossed the Channel from England to France. Though they were grateful for escape and willing to use any means to do so, the trip had been almost as dismal as living in the catacombs. Food was hardly palatable, and people slept in a common room on hammocks or pads on the floor. She couldn't imagine a man like Corbett having to put up with such misery.

"He'll be fine." Ryan took her arm. "Let's stroll around a bit and meet some of the other passengers. We've got plenty of time before dinner."

"I don't think I'm going to feel like eating tonight."

Ryan flashed her a look. "Nonsense."

"I'm afraid I'll get seasick."

"No, you won't."

"Well, I'm not feeling well now." Because of the apprehension over the night ahead, her head felt heavy and her stomach was churning. "I really want to go to the cabin and lie down for a while."

He ignored her protest. "The fresh air will be good for you."

Rather than argue, she decided to let him have his way for the time being.

They met a couple who were also from Paris. When introductions were made, Angele was relieved when Ryan didn't let on how they had just got married. People tended to fawn over newlyweds, and it would only mean more questions as to how they had met, and so forth. And, when the woman, Madame Annette Marceau, asked where they were from, Ryan gave the impression they were *both* from

Virginia. He went on to proudly boast that it was one of the thirteen original states of America.

Madame Marceau then looked to Angele, who had not said anything, as though expecting her to contribute to the conversation. Nervous, Angele blurted without thinking, "Virginia was also the tenth state to ratify the Constitution—in 1788."

The instant she spoke, she was sorry she had, for Ryan drew a sharp breath of surprise that she had known that.

The couple chatted a while longer, but Angele was afraid to say anything else. When Ryan finally steered her away, he remarked, "You know, I was under the impression that you've had no formal schooling."

"I haven't," she lied.

"Then how do you know Virginia was the tenth state to ratify the Constitution? You even know the correct year."

She shrugged. "I hear things."

"That's what you said about François DeNeux."

"And I was right, wasn't I? You said yesterday that you bought some fine horses."

"You were, and I did, and I'm going to go see about them in a little while."

Anxious to get his mind on something else, she cried, "Let's see to it now! We need to know if they're being cared for like they should be."

He laughed. "And how would you know? Or have you also heard about that, too?"

It would have been so easy to remove the mocking sneer from his face by telling him she had grown up around stables and probably knew more about raising horses than he did. She could also brag that she had been the best rider at Miss Appleton's school and could outjump any man for miles around her father's estate. "No," she said instead, "but I'd like to see them, anyway."

"The cargo area is no place for a lady. You can see them when we get home. I might even teach you how to ride."

And that, she thought, suppressing a smile, *would be an experience he would not soon forget.*

She drew her hand from his and folded her arms across her bosom as though to ward off a chill. "It's getting cool. I think I'll go to the cabin now. I don't want to walk anymore."

"Later. Right now we need to talk. It's the first time we've been alone since you ran off yesterday."

They had reached the stern. The ship was starting to slowly move away from the pier, and everyone else had gathered at the bow. It was a quiet area, and, due to the way the deck curved behind the bulkhead of the stairway leading below, no one could see them. Angele liked the privacy and thought how it might be a good place for her to hide away with her thoughts during the voyage when she felt the need.

Crisply, she informed him, "I didn't run away." Corbett said he had fibbed for her, and she believed him. Ryan was just venting his anger on her for a change. "And I don't feel like talking," she added coldly.

"You don't seem to feel like doing a lot of things, and I'm sorry, but I want to know where you went yesterday and why."

"How many times must I tell you? I wanted to say goodbye to Paris in my own way."

"Did you meet anybody—a man, perhaps?"

Her skin prickled. There was no way he could have found out. "Of course not."

"Are you sure?"

She whirled on him, masking guilt with indignity. "I don't think this is a fitting conversation on our wedding day."

"You're my wife, and I've a right to know where you go and what you do. I also have the right to know everything about you. So far you've told me nothing except that you're an orphan. You've said nothing about your family. You say you were raised in a fishing village, yet you seem to know a lot about unusual things for a girl of your background—like horses and history—subjects not exactly taught in the home of a fisherman."

"I told you—I hear things. I listen to people when they

talk. It's how I learn. You should try it sometime," she added huffily, "instead of asking so many questions." She turned her face toward the water, the stiff breeze blowing her hair about her face. Again, she attempted to get his mind on other things. "The sea is so beautiful. I can't believe I'm actually sailing all the way to America."

He snorted. "You're obviously more excited over that than getting married."

"It's not exactly an orthodox marriage, you know. You needed to take a French wife, and I needed to get out of jail. It's that simple. Besides, I don't know you yet. I'll have to wait and see if I made the right decision."

"And so will I."

She seized the opportunity to ask a question of her own, one that had been burning inside since the day he made his proposition. Whipping about to face him, she challenged, "And what if you find you didn't make the right decision? What if you ultimately feel that you made a terrible mistake? We haven't discussed that possibility, and we should, because I need to know what's to become of me if you do."

"Do as you're told, Angele, and that won't happen."

"No," she fired back. "That's not good enough. And besides, I've a will of my own, and I won't always agree with you. What then? Will you make me leave?"

"I want you to have my baby as soon as possible. After that, I would never ask you to leave."

"Good." She nodded with satisfaction and even managed a small smile, despite the dark way he was staring down at her. She would not have to worry—*as long as she produced a child.*

"But . . ."

She stiffened. His tone was foreboding.

"If you don't have a baby, and we ultimately decide we can't stand each other, then I suppose we could come to some kind of financial settlement so you could go your own way."

Angele brought up another possibility. "And what about

your inheritance if the marriage ends before we have a baby? Wouldn't you be faced with having to find another French wife?"

"Maybe. But I would hope my father wouldn't hold it against me that it didn't last. After all, I did do what he asked by marrying a pure Frenchwoman. If it doesn't work out . . ." He shrugged.

Pure Frenchwoman. That was another reason Angele knew she had to keep her past a secret. He couldn't find out she was only *half* French. He might hide it from his father, but he would hate her for having deceived him.

"I intend to do my part," she said. "We should get along well."

"I'm glad you feel that way. And don't worry—I'll teach you as much as I can about etiquette and so on before we get home. After that, Clarice can take over."

"Fine." Angele suppressed another smile to think how she could probably teach Clarice a thing or two about social graces.

It nettled that he continued to look at her so intensely. "Is something wrong?"

"Have you told me all you want to about yesterday?"

She threw her hands up, pretending to be disgusted. "There is nothing to tell. I walked around to take one last look at Paris. I can't understand why you're making such an issue of this."

"Have you ever been with a man, Angele . . ."

She blinked, at first not understanding what he meant, but then it dawned just as he made it clear by lowering his voice to add, ". . . *intimately?*"

Taken aback, jolted to the tips of her toes, she all but shouted, "No, I haven't!" And it was not altogether a lie. Her uncle had been intimate with *her.* She'd not been intimate with *him.* And she had fought him tooth and nail till he slapped her to dizziness and submission.

"Why do you ask me this?" she demanded.

"A man has a right to know."

"Well, you asked me, and I've told you, and now I am going to the cabin. Don't try to stop me."

She turned on her heel and all but broke into a run to get away from him. Nothing had been resolved, she thought, frustrated. He was still curious about her past. Worse, he had confirmed her fears that the marriage would end if he wasn't pleased with her. And she couldn't let that happen—no matter what.

Because, sadly, life offered her no other option.

Ryan started to go after her but thought better of it. She was angry, but she would get over it. Hell, he was angry, too, because she had looked him straight in the eye and lied to him. She *had* met a man in Paris, and, according to Corbett, had got in his carriage and ridden off with him for the better part of the afternoon. As for her saying she had never been intimate with a man, he would soon know if she had lied about that, as well.

He told himself it should make no difference, but he knew it did. Despite the circumstances of how they'd met, despite her lack of upbringing and everything negative there was about her, he couldn't deny being drawn to her. And he wanted her, damn it.

Ryan was well aware of how Angele caught the eye of every man in the dining room when they entered. She was wearing a pale-pink gown. The bodice was edged in black lace and pearls, scooped only low enough to show the barest swell of her generous bosom. She had coiffed her own hair in an upswept pouf, capped by the pearl-and-diamond comb he had given her along with many other fine pieces of jewelry. She was truly a lovely sight, and it was obvious everyone who saw her thought so, too.

He continued to be amazed by the wardrobe she'd selected. He had told the dressmaker not to spare any expense but discreetly let her know that due to Angele's upbringing, she would need guidance. The dressmaker had reported, however, that Angele had demonstrated a keen sense of fashion and needed no help.

She was beautiful and mysterious, and he was delighted she was his bride. But it bothered him that when they had talked on deck earlier she had brought up the possibility of their marriage failing. He didn't want that to happen. She was going to make a good wife, and he would make sure everything worked out as he planned.

Once she gained a little weight and got over her experiences of living in the catacombs and being in jail, she would be in good health and able to have fine children. In addition, he would see to it that she learned everything necessary to function in and be a part of Richmond society. She would eventually take charge of the household. As the wife of the plantation master, it was only right that she do so. Clarice might not like it, but she would have to accept it.

Dinner passed in a blur of banal conversation with others seated at their table, food Ryan hardly tasted, and too much wine to try to quell anticipation of the night ahead.

Corbett also had too much to drink, and Ryan saw how it appeared to make Angele uncomfortable when he held his champagne glass up in toast to the *newlyweds*. She looked as though she wanted to sink from her chair and crawl beneath the table.

Not long after that, she excused herself, declining dessert and tea with the ladies while the men went to their salon for cigars and brandy.

Walking with the other men, Corbett caught up to Ryan and whispered, "I can't believe you're wasting time like this on your wedding night. Why do you want to smoke cigars and drink when you can be in bed with your bride?"

"And sometimes I can't believe how uncouth you can be, Corbett," Ryan snapped. He turned from the direction of the smoking salon and went instead out on deck.

Corbett was right behind him. "I didn't mean to make you angry. I just don't understand why you aren't in your cabin."

"I'm giving my wife time to herself."

"Your *wife.*" Corbett snickered. "You know, I still find all of this hard to believe."

"Well, it's not important that you do. But at least you've had the good manners to make her think you approve."

"Whether you believe me or not, I have nothing against Angele personally, and I hope you know I hated telling you about her going off with that man, because I don't want to be involved in any of this. But I have to say I'm surprised you went ahead and married her after you heard about it."

Actually, Ryan had thought about saying to hell with it, but he had a lot invested in her . . . and he also wanted her. "I don't think it's anything to worry about."

"Did you ask her about it?"

"Not directly. I don't want her thinking you followed her. We're married now, Corbett, and there has to be peace. She'd resent you if she knew you told me, and I don't want that."

"I don't, either. And if you're not worried, then neither am I. There's probably a logical explanation." He slapped Ryan on the back. "And now that you've done it, you know I wish you well."

"Thanks. Now, why don't you go join the men? I'd like to be alone."

"Sure. Sure. I'll see you at breakfast—if you can get up that early." With a wink, Corbett went back inside.

Ryan waited a few moments, then decided it was time to go to the cabin. He had given Angele ample time to prepare herself.

He was ready—and eager—to claim his bride.

Angele wished she hadn't drunk so much. Wine always made her sleepy. Combined with the champagne, she had hardly been able to keep her eyes open, but at least she was relaxed—on the surface, anyway. Her heart had stopped threatening to leap right out of her chest and her hands had quit shaking. But she had not trusted herself to contribute to dinner-table conversation. She had left that to Ryan and Corbett and the two couples seated with them, afraid she would stammer or stutter if she tried to join in.

Once, when Ryan had leaned back laughing at something someone said, his legs had spread slightly, causing his thigh to press against her. She had glanced down, to where her hand had lain earlier, but quickly looked away. *What was wrong with her, for heaven's sake?* She was acting like a strumpet. At least she thought she was, even though she had no idea how a strumpet behaved. But ladies weren't supposed to enjoy looking at a man's privates, and, despite things that had happened in her past, Angele considered herself a lady.

It was the wine, she had told herself, and had pushed her empty glass away. Then Corbett signaled to the waiter to have it refilled, and, because the butterflies were starting to swarm in her tummy again, she drank it.

She had been grateful when it was all over. And it was only with much effort that she was able to walk back to the cabin without stumbling. Her head was spinning and starting to ache, and, dear Lord, she was so drowsy.

She had undressed quickly, not bothering to hang up her gown. Tossing it on the floor, she grabbed up the nightdress she had bought. Plain, unshaped, and made of muslin, it had a falling collar with a frill that continued down the front opening as a border. The sleeves were long, gathered into a cuff, and fastened by a handmade button. Ryan had told the dressmaker in Paris they were to be married, and she had suggested something more revealing in silk or satin, but Angele had refused.

She knew the steward had been to the cabin, because the lantern was burning when she entered and the bed covers had been turned back. Angele crawled beneath them, pulling a blanket all the way to her nose. Tears stung her eyes as she prayed Ryan would be gentle and do it quickly.

She also prayed to stay awake, but that prayer quickly went unanswered as the wine carried her away to a deep, deep sleep.

She was hiding in the stables, beneath a pile of straw. If only her mother would return, she would be safe. Her uncle would not dare touch her then. But he had sent her to the village on an errand, and Angele knew it was because he wanted her to be alone . . . and helpless. For weeks he had warned he would have his way with her and she would be wise to stop rebuking him. So she had run away from the manse, intending to hide for as long as necessary.

They were both at his mercy, he taunted, forced to look to him for every bite that went into their mouths.

Cecil Mooring had shamed his family, Uncle Henry delighted to remind, and the only thing that stood between them and poverty was his charity—which they would not enjoy much longer if Angele didn't agree to marry him. And if she refused, he swore he would ultimately have her, anyway.

Angele could not bring herself to give in and had not let her mother know what he was up to. The poor soul had been through enough and was sickly. So Angele fought to keep her uncle at bay and hide everything from her mother.

Suddenly thick strong fingers wrapped about her ankles, and Angele screamed as she was yanked, facedown, from the straw. He yelled at her to shut up, and when she continued to scream, he slapped her till she was nearly unconscious.

He pinned her wrists above her head, holding with one hand while he used his other to roughly tear off her clothing. She squeezed her eyes shut against the hot, stabbing pain, and . . .

She screamed, long and loud, because the nightmare was real. He was there, beside her, drawing up her nightdress as his hot, moist lips trailed across her cheeks.

"Angele, stop it!" Ryan clamped his hand over her mouth. She was twisting and writhing from side to side as she fought, and a nail raked the corner of his eye. He was finally able to grasp her wrists, folding her arms across her chest as he gave her a vicious shake. "Stop it, I say. What is wrong with you? I'm your husband now. I have a right to touch you . . ."

She became still, staring up at him in the lantern's mellow glow. He was not her uncle. He was her husband, as he said, and she knew where she was and why she was there and realized she had been having the nightmare again.

As she seemed to wilt beneath him, Ryan slowly relaxed his hold, then rolled to the side to look at her, bewildered. "My God, what made you do that?"

"I . . . I was asleep," she managed to say, still trembling. "You . . . you startled me."

"I'm sorry. I didn't mean to. I was just going to crawl into bed with you and kiss you awake, like this . . ."

His mouth closed over hers, gentle yet demanding. She didn't respond and lay like a statue in his arms. He had released her hands, but she still held them to her bosom.

He slipped his tongue between her lips to part them, but she drew back.

He began to pull her nightdress up, warm fingers dancing up her legs. Angele's spine went so rigid she feared it would snap. He was naked, and she could feel the hard swelling against her bare thigh. He spread her legs and used his knee to keep them apart.

"No, wait . . ." she begged. "I . . . I can't do this . . ."

"Of course you can," he murmured, his tongue licking her neck. "I'll be easy, and I'll make it good for you. Just relax."

"No, please, don't . . ." She pushed against his chest, but it was like pushing at stone. "Don't touch me."

She bucked against him as he slipped his hand between her legs and began to stroke.

He slipped a finger inside her, and despite her terror, a warm sweetness began to spread upward, and she felt a sweet hot shudder as he began to massage her pearly nub. "Tell me you like it," he commanded. "Tell me it makes you want more . . ."

Her legs went straight, toes pointing, and she tried harder to push him away, but he held her tightly, pressing his arm across her chest as he continued the tender assault of her cleft. "You have to like it," he said throatily, as his own desire was swelling to bursting.

"No, leave me alone!" she cried, bucking from side to side.

He was determined to give her pleasure quickly before he lost control and spilled outside her. He dove his middle finger deep and up as his thumb took over the near-frenzied assault of the nucleus of her sex.

He felt her coming against his finger, but instead of moaning with delight, she was sobbing as though he were hurting her. He knew he wasn't. Not yet, anyway, and he didn't want to but had to have her then and there.

As the last shudders subsided, he entered her, slowly at first but then hard and furious to feel no resistance, no tearing of her maidenhead. And as he took himself to glory, the awareness screamed at him above the ecstasy of climax that she was not a virgin.

She had lied.

As soon as he finished, he pulled from her and stood beside the bed to glower down at her. "Why in hell did you fight me? Why did you act like you were scared to death? You weren't a virgin. You lied, Angele." He reached to snatch the sheet away that she had pulled to her chin in terror as he blazed out at her. "See?" He pointed accusingly between her legs. "There's no blood. And I felt nothing holding me back."

She continued to stare up at him, tongue clamped between her teeth to keep from crying. She tasted blood.

"Why did you lie to me? You should have known I'd find out the truth."

She swallowed hard, lifted her chin, and reminded herself she would not fear him. Not ever. To fear was to be weak, and she had promised herself never to surrender to weakness again. "I owe you nothing but submission," she said defiantly.

"Remember that," he warned. "And I warn you—never resist me again. You are my wife now, and I'll have you any time I want, any way I want. I don't care how many men you've had in the past, but don't pretend virtue with me. And from this day forward, you will be faithful—or else."

He dressed quickly and stormed out of the cabin.

Angele could only watch in pained silence, wondering if perhaps she had, tragically, chosen the wrong path to her destiny.

Ten

It had been a long time since Ryan had left the cabin. Angele worried he would drink too much, because he was so upset with her.

After tossing and turning and knowing she wouldn't get any sleep, she decided it would probably be best if she went somewhere and hid till morning. It would be better to face his wrath when he was sober. Maybe then she could find a way to make him see she wasn't immoral, like he thought.

Snatching up the gown she'd worn to dinner, she put it on and wrapped a warm shawl around her shoulders. It would be chilly on deck, and that was the only place she could think of to go. She remembered it had been private on the stern, thanks to the bulkhead. No one would see her there.

Stepping outside, she pulled the shawl tighter against the biting ocean wind.

She turned to the rear of the ship but hadn't gone far when she heard music and the sounds of revelry. It came from below, in steerage.

Walking slowly, she pressed close to the interior walls, not wanting to venture too far out on the deck until she made sure the way was clear and none of the steerage people had drunkenly found their way upstairs. The last thing she needed was a confrontation with rowdies and no one about to come to her aid if needed.

She wished she had admitted to Ryan she wasn't a virgin. Without going into detail, she could have let him know it was not by her choice. But she had tried so hard to put it from her mind, to pretend it hadn't happened, that the lie had slipped easily from her lips. To tell the truth would have brought the horror crashing down again, but now he thought the worst.

And what had made him ask if she'd met a man in Paris? There was no way anyone could know. And now she wondered if maybe she should have told him about that, as well. Surely he would not have been angry over her wanting to have a marker put on her mother's grave. But, feeling so insecure and desperate, she'd been afraid to take any chances.

So here she was, somewhere in the Atlantic Ocean, married to a man who doubtless wished he'd never laid eyes on her. She was just going to have to try to please him, no matter how it sickened her. He wanted more than submission, and she shuddered to wonder what that meant. Now she wished she had dared to ask intimate questions of the girls at school who seemed to know more than they should. Then she would know what her husband expected of her but doubted even then she would be able to perform to his satisfaction.

She was almost to the stern when two men came stumbling along. From the glow of a boxed lantern hanging nearby, she saw they were sharing a bottle of whiskey, passing it back and forth between them. She tried to shrink back in the shadows, but one of them spotted her.

"Eh. Leon." He spoke in French to his companion. "What do we have here?"

The one named Leon squinted. "A lady," he said. "A pretty little lady in a pretty little dress." He hiccupped. "Something tells me we're not in steerage. Something tells me, Benny, my friend, that we have strayed into the forbidden territory of the rich, and, my, my, aren't they lovely?"

They laughed together and staggered toward her.

Angele mustered all her bravado. "That's right. You *are*

somewhere you don't belong, and if you don't leave this instant, I'm going to scream. Then you'll be caught and beaten and put in a dungeon." She had no idea if that were true, but the men believed it. They exchanged frantic looks, then turned and ran back the way they'd come.

She moved faster, wanting to reach the bulkhead before she ran into anyone else. Maybe there, shielded from the wind, she could sit down and fall asleep. In the morning, everything would be better.

Or so she hoped.

Corbett had suspected something was wrong when Ryan appeared in the smoking salon. After growling that he wanted to be left alone, he had gone to a table in a far corner and sipped moodily on a glass of brandy.

Finally, curiosity gnawing, Corbett decided to pay Angele a visit. By pretending to be concerned because Ryan was upset, maybe he could find out from her what had happened. She probably wouldn't tell him about anything so personal, but there was always the chance she might need a shoulder to cry on. And, if she and Ryan were seriously at odds with each other, maybe then Ryan would be ready to admit he'd made a big mistake. They were due to dock at the port of Cherbourg the next day, and Ryan could put her off there. As for the legality of the marriage, Corbett reasoned Ryan could go on as though it had never happened. He could tear up the papers, and no one would ever know. Simple. Easy. And when they got home, he could propose to Denise. She would accept. And they would have a lavish wedding and live happily ever after.

Corbett chuckled. Maybe not *happily*, but what difference did it make? He wasn't really happy with Clarice, but she served a purpose.

And another reason he would like to see Ryan get rid of Angele was so he could share the cabin with his cousin the rest of the way. It didn't matter if he did have the run of the ship. He still had to sleep in steerage.

He rounded a corner just in time to see Angele leaving her cabin. She didn't notice him as she turned in the opposite direction. He decided to let her go and follow to see where she was going. Maybe she had a man on board she was off to rendezvous with. Nothing she did would surprise him.

When she had encountered the steerage rowdies on deck, Corbett hung back in the shadows to watch. Maliciously, he was hoping they would throw her overboard, which would solve everything. Ryan, noble bastard that he could be sometimes, wouldn't have to feel guilty over sending her back. She just disappeared at sea, that was all. Life would go on according to plan—*his* plan.

But Corbett was stunned to see how she had stood up to the men. They slunk away like scolded puppies, and he realized she had more spunk than he'd thought. She might even be able to stand up to Clarice—or anyone else who got in the way of her good fortune in marrying well. She could cause all kinds of trouble, and he realized he might just have a formidable foe on his hands.

He moved slowly. The wind was really too strong to be out on deck. He saw how Angele reached out to steady herself, sometimes staggering backward a few steps. For her to be out meant she was also upset over whatever had happened between her and Ryan.

Corbett was not sure exactly when the idea struck. Perhaps it had been there all the time, or maybe it had germinated when he'd had the wild hope the two rowdies would take care of the problem for him. But suddenly it blossomed and rapidly bloomed.

He would push her overboard.

And it looked as though she were going to make it very easy for him to do.

As she drew closer to the stern, she fought the wind to cross the deck to the railing. Sliding her hands along it, Corbett could see she was heading for the bulkhead. It was probably her plan to hide there, unseen, and worry everybody. Well, he would just help her along with wanting to cause distress . . . *all the way to the bottom of the ocean.*

Ryan told the waiter he didn't want another drink. Sometimes he did imbibe too much when he was worried about something, but not when it was important. Like tonight. He wanted a clear head so he could try to figure out what had gone wrong and how he might make it right.

It would be so easy to just say to hell with her, he mused not for the first time. She was a liar, a sneak, a thief, and maybe immoral, to boot. And though she didn't want to talk about her past, it was obvious she was uneducated and had no culture and little refinement. So why in hell, then, did he think he could take her home to Virginia and pass her off as a well-born, well-bred French lady, worthy of having offspring to carry on the respected name of Tremayne? He had to be the world's biggest fool.

He could have bought Denise an expensive gift, proposed to her when he got home, and she would have said yes this time. But now, thanks to a moment of temporary insanity, he felt he had the weight of the world on his shoulders and didn't know what in hell to do about it.

But there was one harsh fact he had to accept—Angele was his wife now. Regardless of her past, she was his responsibility. He had no one to blame for his predicament but himself, and it was up to him to make the best of it. For starters, he needed to resolve to be more patient and tolerant, as well as apologize to her for the way he'd acted earlier and give her a chance to explain herself.

The smoking salon was almost empty. A glance at the clock on the wall told him why. It was nearly one A.M. He paid for his brandy and left, wondering where Corbett had disappeared to. It wouldn't have surprised him if he had bedded down in the salon to keep from sleeping in steerage.

All was quiet and still as he walked toward the cabin. If Angele were asleep, he would not wake her up. They could talk in the morning. He would bed down in a chair with a blanket. He didn't want to chance frightening her again by crawling in bed with her.

The steward had given them two keys, and he and Angele each had one. He just hoped she hadn't thrown the bolt inside or he would have to wake her whether he wanted to or not. But the key turned, and the door opened easily. Stepping inside, he moved to close it, then did a quick double take.

The bed was empty.

With rising panic, Ryan rushed out, looking right and left as though expecting to see her innocently appear from a night stroll on deck.

The ship gave a sudden, sharp lurch, and he caught the hand railing to steady himself. It was too rough for her to be out, and he cursed himself for having left her when she was so upset.

He thought about sounding an alarm but decided to take one quick look on deck to see if he could find her himself.

Pushing against the heavy door to the outside, he saw that the wind was much worse than he'd thought. He remembered her comment about the stern being a perfect place to go if somebody wanted to be alone, and, no doubt, that's where he would find her. But if he didn't, he would wake the whole damn ship to help search for her.

Reminding himself once more that she was his responsibility, he brushed aside the thought that his concern might be motivated by another reason—that he cared for her more than he wanted to admit.

He ducked his head against the heavy gusts and was swallowed up by the night.

Angele could hear waves washing behind the ship as it cut through the water. Staring down, she was looking into a black abyss and could see nothing but imagined she was gazing into the past she seemed unable to escape.

She would have to put it all behind her, she vowed for probably the hundredth time. Her future was as bright as the dawn that would eventually rip away the night. She would make it happen by trying very, very hard—to please her husband, to make her new family like her. And she wanted children. Lord, yes, she wanted to be a mother, to love and be loved in return. Ryan would make a good father. She sensed that somehow. And everything was going to turn out all right, because she would not allow it to be any other way.

First, she would settle down by the bulkhead and try to sleep. Then, when she awoke, she would return to the cabin and tell Ryan as much as she dared—taking the money she had saved on the luggage to pay for her mother's marker, meeting Mr. Montague—all of it. And she would also manage to offer some kind of explanation as to why she was not the virgin he had obviously hoped she would be.

Now, she needed to rest, so she could think clearly, frame her words for the best possible understanding, and she was so terribly, terribly tired . . .

Corbett could barely make her out as she stood at the railing, a dark figure against a blackened sky.

He knew it was now or never.

Lunging from the shadows, he ran at her, placed his palms flat on her back and shoved.

She screamed and toppled over but managed to hook her arm about the middle rail and fight to hold on.

A loud voice rang out from somewhere close by. "What's wrong? Who's that screaming?"

Corbett's blood ran cold.

It was Ryan.

"Angele, was that you? Where are you? Answer me, damn it . . ."

Corbett thought fast. He saw that Angele was hanging on, but there was no time to make her let go and fall to her death as he wanted. Neither was there time for him to escape without Ryan seeing him. There was only one thing to do, and he did it.

Grabbing her, he pulled her up as he cried, "Thank God I was nearby and saw those rowdies bump into somebody. I didn't know it was you." He set her on her feet, his voice all kind, all caring. "Goodness, Angele, are you all right? Did they hurt you?"

"No, I—"

But her words were cut off by Ryan whipping around the bulkhead. "Who's there? I can't see—"

"It's Angele," Corbett was quick to tell him, appearing properly upset. "Some rowdies from steerage bumped into her, nearly knocked her overboard. I got worried about her when I saw you in the salon and went to check on her. When she didn't answer my knock I went looking for her. That's when I saw them and heard her scream. I'm going after them! They went that way." He pointed. "You see to her. I don't think she's hurt."

Thrusting her into Ryan's arms, he hurried away as though chasing the men responsible for the evil deed. Actually, he was heading back to steerage to find the bottle he had stashed under his bunk, because he had never needed a drink more in his life than he did right then.

Ryan gripped Angele's shoulders, trying to see her in the dark. "Are you hurt? What happened?"

"I'm fine, just scared. And I don't know what happened. Someone bumped into me, and I fell over the railing. I didn't hear a sound. If not for Corbett, I'd be . . . ." Her voice trailed off as she shuddered with horror.

"It must have been one of the two men I frightened away earlier," she added.

"What are you talking about?"

She told him about the brief encounter, remarking that she hadn't thought she made them angry enough to want to harm her.

"You never know when men are drunk what they're thinking, or what they'll do. But you're safe, and that's all that matters. Now, let's get you inside. You're cold."

* * *

Back in the cabin, over her protests, he rang for the steward and asked him to bring a glass of warm cognac. "It will help you relax," he told her. "You've had a bad experience."

She undressed behind the screen, put on her nightgown, and got into bed.

When the cognac arrived, she sipped it propped against the pillows. "You were right. It is relaxing me. Thank you for being so thoughtful."

Pulling up a chair, he sat beside the bed and looked at her thoughtfully for a few moments. "I'm sorry," he said. "I shouldn't have treated you like I did. I had no right to expect—"

"Yes, you did," she disputed. "Especially after I lied to you. But I couldn't help it. Something happened to me once that I'd rather not talk about. I know you probably don't believe me, and I can't blame you, but that's how it is. I'm not immoral. I never have been and never will be."

He so wanted to believe her. "Well, you don't have to talk about it. And now I'm just grateful Corbett was there to save you."

"He said he was looking for me."

"Yes. He got worried when I went into the smoking salon looking like I could bite a nail in two and figured we had a problem. He was trying to help."

"I'm certainly indebted to him. A few more seconds, and I'd have had to let go."

"I'm glad you didn't."

She stared up at him in the dimness of the room, his face soft in the lantern's glow. He sounded—looked—as though he really meant it. Then, cynically, she thought that of course he didn't want her to fall overboard. Not after he had spent so much money, gone to so much trouble. He didn't want his bride to die on their wedding day, for goodness' sake.

"It's not what you think."

She cocked her head, not understanding.

"I've got an idea what you're thinking, and you're wrong. I don't care about the money I've spent. It's you—I don't want anything to happen to you. I still think we can have a good marriage, Angele."

She stared at him over the rim of her glass, then took another sip before responding. "I'm going to try, I promise. And there's something else I have to tell you. You asked if I met a man yesterday, and I did. His name is Mr. Montague, and he's a stone cutter. I wanted him to make a monument for my mother's grave.

"And there's more," she rushed to say before she lost her nerve. "I used the money I saved by buying cheaper trunks to pay him."

"That's all right. And if you had asked me for the money, I would have given it to you. I'd also have been glad to go with you to help make the arrangements."

She set the empty glass aside, then absently, nervously, fingered the sheet. "I'm sorry. I should've said something."

Slowly, he pulled the sheet from her and drew it down to her waist. She was wearing a fresh nightdress. The one he had torn lay crumpled in the corner. "I'll buy you a new one," he murmured.

"It doesn't matter," she whispered nervously, seeing the heat in his eyes.

Gently, he cupped her breasts and began to softly caress them. "I'll buy you anything you want, Angele. Just be good to me, that's all I ask."

Angele breathed deeply and closed her eyes as he began to take his clothes off. Then he slid the nightdress up over her head and tossed it aside. "I want to look at you—all of you. And I want you to look at me. You've nothing to be afraid of. I won't hurt you. And this time, if you tell me to stop, I will. Now, open your eyes."

She did so, staring up at him as he stretched out beside her. His eyes locked with hers as his fingertips began to squeeze her nipples.

She didn't flinch or pull away. This time her back arched not in terror but instead yielded to pleasure as hot fingers of longing wrapped around her spine. In wonder, she found herself wanting to curl into him, to press herself yet tighter.

But it was he who moved closer, so that she could feel his hardness pulsating against her thigh. He slipped a hand down to her bottom and began to knead the firm flesh, and she marveled at the unfamiliar sensation.

Taking turns with her nipples, suckling and leaving them hot and moist, he raised his lips to hers, soft at first, then possessive and probing. He tasted of warm cognac, and she wanted his tongue and leaned into him, deepening the kiss. As she did so, her breasts rubbed against his chest, the mat of hair deliciously tickling her skin. His tongue moved deeper, and her own danced around it, tasting, wanting more, dreamily thinking how she had never known such ecstasy could exist.

She was startled to realize how her breasts were actually throbbing, and, as he touched his penis to her thigh, her legs parted as though with a will of their own. Her hips began to undulate, only a little, but enough to find the hard ridge of his penis as she rocked against him with primitive instincts he had magically awakened.

She was not afraid, nor was she reluctant. It was as though his body was sending secret messages to hers that assured her he would not harm her, would not leave scars upon her soul . . . only memories of joy nonpareil.

He found her hand and pulled it to his penis. "Touch me. Feel me."

Her fingers were paralyzed. "No. I . . . I can't," she all but whimpered in her protest.

"Maybe it's too soon," he murmured. And then he mounted her, slipping her legs about his waist. As he entered her, she stiffened and held her breath. His body pressed her down onto the bed as he gave a hard, steady jab, sheathing him firmly, deeply.

She cried out. He was hard, thick, and impossibly large,

yet she took all of him and felt herself writhing uncontrollably around him.

He pulled back, but only a little, watching her intently as he did so. "Am I hurting you?"

She realized then that she was making crying noises due to the wondrous sensation, the pleasure that was close to sweet torture. Her heart was thudding, and she shook her head wildly and clung to him tightly, jolted by a strange, inner warning that something fierce yet wonderful was about to rip her apart.

His whispered words of masculine reassurance couldn't be heard over the roaring in her ears. She continued to hold tightly, her nails digging into his back as he went deeper, harder. The bed moved up and down, creaking, straining, as he relentlessly pushed in and out.

She felt it coming. A dark, honeyed emotion that spread slowly at first, then crept into her belly and squeezed tight like a clenching fist. He rode her harder, as her climax spread like the waves in the windblown sea. She held her legs wider apart, convulsing and arching, and he had no mercy as he drove yet deeper and she wanted none. She craved only him, as much as he could give her.

She whimpered, shuddered, but on he drove. When he climaxed, his strong body bucked, and she struggled to breathe from the impact of his final thrust.

He was heavy on her, and she felt his heart thundering in unison with her own. He was damp with sweat, and so was she. She turned her face into his neck, embarrassed by how she had responded, the wanton, wild way she had behaved.

"It's going to be all right, Angele," he murmured sleepily as he continued to hold her. "We'll *make* it all right."

Angele knew she would be awake a long, long time.

She had just discovered what it really meant to be a woman, and she would savor the joy . . . as she wondered what it would ultimately mean.

* * *

The beds were no more than thick, canvas hammocks, hanging by ropes from the ceiling in stacks of three. Corbett had been the last to claim one and had to take the least coveted, which was on top.

The men on each side of him, and beneath him, snored and grunted. Unpleasant odors assaulted his nostrils, and he knew he had never been so miserable in his entire life. And now he would have to put up with it for weeks, because he'd failed in his attempt to get rid of Angele.

Irritably, he yanked the worn, rough sheet over his head to try to shut out the noises and smells. It was hot, but he didn't care if it worked.

He had failed, but somehow he would find a way. Clarice would help, and, together, they would succeed in driving the little fortune-seeker from BelleRose.

And they would also make her wish she had never set foot on American soil.

Eleven

Angele was awakened by the rocking of the ship. Everything in the cabin that was not fastened to the floor was sliding back and forth.

She sat up but had to grab the chain holding the bed to keep from tumbling to the floor as the ship gave a sharp lurch to the side.

Still groggy, she managed to scramble to the porthole as the ship dipped in that direction . . . and what she saw made her stomach tilt along with the room.

The sky was dark, black almost, and the ocean was foaming with huge, choppy waves. It was a terrible storm, and the rain beating against the porthole sounded like rocks were being thrown against it.

The floor tilted the other way. She fell back on the bed and held on to the chain with one hand, the other covering her mouth. She knew she was going to be sick, and when the ship stilled for the very briefest of moments, she managed to reach the chamber pot.

There was a knock at the door.

"Go away." She hoped it wasn't Ryan. She didn't want him to see her retching. In fact, she didn't want to see him at all. She was too embarrassed over last night. Miss Appleton had said men didn't respect women who didn't act like ladies, and *ladies* didn't enjoy the terrible thing their husbands did to make babies. But she *had* enjoyed it, so what must he think of her now?

"Madame, are you all right?"

It was the steward, and she called feebly, "Yes. Just leave me alone."

The floor moved again, and she and the chamber pot along with it.

He persisted. "Madame, your husband sent me to tell you he would like for you to join him for lunch."

"Lunch?" Was it really that late? "No. I don't feel like eating. I may never eat again."

"Ah, you are seasick."

He sounded amused.

"I'm afraid a lot of the passengers are," he called, "but it's just a squall. It will be over soon."

"Not soon enough for me." She managed to crawl back to the bed.

"I will tell your husband that you aren't feeling well."

"Don't you dare!" she all but screamed.

When he didn't respond, she knew he had left.

She closed her eyes. Never could she remember being so sick, and the more the ship rocked, the worse she felt.

Her head began to ache, and her throat was burning. Worse, she began to worry that the ship would turn over and they would sink. Suddenly life in the catacombs and the guilt over robbing little old ladies seemed like paradise compared to what she was going through now.

She didn't hear Ryan when he came in. She was curled into a ball, her face pressed into the pillow to stifle the moans she couldn't hold back.

Warm hands touched her shoulder to gently roll her onto her back. She was too weak to protest.

"Angele, I had no idea you were sick."

"Leave me alone. I think I'm dying."

He chuckled. "No, you aren't, and according to the captain, we'll be out of this soon. It's just a little squall."

"I don't care how little it is, it's enough to make me *want* to die."

"Nonsense." He sat down on the side of the bed, bracing his feet against the floor as it tilted again. "The steward said he was bringing some ginger water for you to drink. It's supposed to help settle your stomach. Is there anything I can do for you?"

"Yes," she whispered. "Go away and leave me alone."

He laughed again. "No, I'm not going to do that. You're my wife, and it's my duty to take care of you."

Duty. Angele disliked the word and didn't know why. After all, it was the most she could expect from him.

"I can see you're really sick. If it were last night, I'd think you were faking."

Her eyes were closed, because she was too embarrassed to look at him, but hearing the amusement in his tone made her angry. He seemed to be enjoying her misery. Eyes flashing open, she glared up at him. "I'm glad you think this is all funny. I wish it were you instead of me."

"I don't get seasick. I'm surprised you do. Didn't you ever go out with your father in a boat?"

"No." She closed her eyes again and folded her arms across her face. "I hate water. I told you that."

"Yes, I remember, because that's one of the few things you *have* told me about yourself."

Grumpily, she retorted, "Well, I don't know anything about you, either."

Just then the steward knocked and called that he had the ginger water. He also gave him a message from the captain that they were moving out of the squall.

"Thank you." Ryan could already feel the sea calming a bit, because the ship wasn't tilting quite as bad.

He returned to Angele. Slipping his hand behind her neck, he gently raised her head so she could drink the ginger water.

"I'm afraid it will only make me sicker."

"You have to try. Take small sips."

It didn't taste bad, and, after a few swallows, her stomach felt less queasy. She finally managed to drink all of it, and her headache seemed better.

Ryan set the empty glass aside. "Well, I'm glad to see

that. As stubborn as you are, I figured I'd have to pour it down you.''

"*I'm* stubborn?'' She looked at him, aghast.

"That's right. Look what a hard time I had last night making you enjoy yourself. You were so damned determined not to.''

Mortified, she turned her face toward the wall. "That's not a nice thing for a man to say to his wife.''

"My God, do you really think that?''

"Please, Ryan, I don't feel like talking about this.''

"All right.'' He stood. "Maybe later. I want things to be good between us, Angele, and they can be if you'll stop being afraid of me. I'm not going to hurt you, but there are a few things I expect from you.''

She didn't respond, and he went to the door. "I'll leave you now, but I'll be back to check on you later. If you're up to it, I'd like for you to join the ladies.''

"I don't want to.'' She turned over and sat up. The ship wasn't lurching anymore, and the ginger water had quelled her nausea, but she had no intentions of sewing with the women. She hated sewing, tatting, knitting—anything that kept her indoors. It had been a bone of contention with her mother, as well as Miss Appleton. She much preferred being outside riding or hiking—anything to keep her in nature, because she loved it.

He closed the door and walked back to the bed to tower over her. "I didn't ask if you wanted to, I said it was what *I* wanted. If I'm going to present you to my family and friends as a well-bred lady, you're going to have to learn a few things. Sewing is one of them. You can also learn how to carry on a conversation. I've noticed when we're around other people you won't talk because you're so insecure.''

Insecure. She wished the word were a club so she could beat him over the head with it. "I don't like to waste my time with silly things like sewing, and the reason I don't talk is because I'm not interested in anything anybody is saying.''

"But if you understood the subjects they were discussing, you would be."

"I doubt that. The women gossip about other women. They make fun of their hats, their gowns—everything about them. And the men talk politics. No one wants to talk about anything I'm interested in."

"Like what?" He leaned closer, for she had his full attention.

"Like . . ." She floundered, not wanting to go too far, and quickly made up a story, which was becoming easier and easier to do. "Like animals. I knew a man who had a farm, and he let me help take care of all his animals." That was not altogether a lie. There had been a lot of animals on their estate in England—sheep, cows, goats, pigs. And she had loved being around them, much to her mother's dismay. Her father hadn't cared, because he had always wanted a son, anyway, and didn't care if she sometimes behaved like a tomboy.

Ryan shook his head as though he hadn't heard her right. "You *like* taking care of animals?"

"That's right."

He slapped his palm against his forehead. "We've got more work to do than I thought if we're going to turn you into a lady by the time we reach New York. Stay in bed the rest of the day, but bright and early tomorrow, my dear wife, your lessons begin."

After he left, Angele glared at the closed door as though she could still see him standing there giving orders. She would cooperate but only because she had to.

And, she thought with a mischievous smile, if he thought it would take a lot of work to turn her into a lady, then far be it for her to prove him wrong.

She managed to appear sick on into the next day, thus postponing the dreaded time when she would have to join the ladies. Worse, Ryan had taken it on himself to tell Annette Marceau that Angele didn't know the first thing about sewing. And, of course, Mrs. Piermont said she'd be delighted to teach her.

That night, Angele decided to go to dinner. She was tired of warm broth and tea and wanted real food. She was also bored with staying in the cabin.

She dressed in one of her favorite gowns among those she'd had made. Fashioned of peach silk and satin, an embroidered lace bib draped from the scoop neckline, with matching lace sleeves to her wrists. It was very delicate, much more suitable for a ball instead of a ship, and she almost changed her mind about wearing it. Then Ryan came to escort her to the dining room, and there was no time.

"You are stunning, Angele," he said, his gaze sweeping her from head to toe. "Absolutely stunning."

Feeling a bit shy, she murmured, "Thank you," and took the arm he held out to her.

When they entered the dining room, once again heads turned at the sight of her.

"I'm glad you're feeling better," Annette Marceau beamed up at her when they reached their table. "And your gown is so pretty, my dear."

Angele thanked her for the compliment as the men politely stood. A waiter held her chair for her.

There was a tray of small loaves of bread on the table, and she felt like throwing one at Ryan when he said to Annette, "My wife can't wait for her sewing lessons to begin. What time should she meet you and the other ladies tomorrow?"

Annette was pleased. "Ten o'clock will be fine. And she'll probably want to join us after lunch for our literary group. Nanette Lanierre is going to talk about Jane Austen's *Northanger Abbey.*"

"Wonderful," Ryan said. "I'm sure she'll enjoy that."

Angele fumed over how they discussed her like she wasn't there. And the thought of having to discuss *Northanger Abbey* made her want to run for the chamber pot again. She'd had to read the book in her English literature class at Miss Appleton's school and had been bored silly. She would much rather discuss Austen's *Emma* but would, of course, have to pretend ignorance of such cultured topics as authors and books.

Concentrating on eating solid food for the first time in two days, she mostly ignored the conversation going on around her. But she took notice when she heard Corbett ask Ryan how one of the Anglo-Arab mares was doing.

"Her leg is still bothering her," Ryan said. "Unfortunately, none of the crew down there know how to do anything except toss hay and rake out a stall. I'm afraid it will have to wait till we get home so Jasper can see to it." He swept everyone with an apologetic look. "I'm not much good at doctoring horses. I've always depended on my stableman to do that."

"What exactly is wrong with her leg?" Angele tried not to sound too concerned, although she was.

His glance told her he was annoyed she had asked so specific a question. "She has a sore, and it isn't something to be discussed while we're eating."

"But she doesn't know that," Corbett said, lips twitching. "And she likes horses. Don't you, Angele?"

Ryan glowered at him.

"Sorry," Corbett murmured, although he wasn't. He had made his point as to her lack of manners, and Ryan knew it.

The rest of the meal passed in a blur. Angele forgot her hunger as she worried about the mare. If no one on board knew what to do for her, there might be serious consequences.

The captain stopped by the table to tell them they would be docking in Cherbourg in a few hours, explaining, "We're way off schedule because of the squall. It blew us a bit off course."

"Then why stop there at all?" someone asked.

"We have to take on passengers and some cargo."

Annette gave a haughty sniff. "More steerage passengers? From the sounds of their revelry last night, there's too many of them already."

"No," the captain said. "Haven't you noticed an empty cabin in your class? But don't worry. It shouldn't take long, and then we'll be on our way. If you're asleep by the time we get there, you won't even know we're stopping." He gave them a little salute and moved on to the next table.

Angele had decided she had to do something about the horse. Pressing her fingertips to her temples, she swayed a teeny bit, as though she felt dizzy.

Corbett, seated directly across from her, was the first to notice. "Is anything wrong?"

Everyone at the table turned to look at her as she answered, "Yes. I'm afraid I still feel a bit weak, and if I may be excused, I'd like to go back to my cabin."

Annette made clucking noises of sympathy. "You poor dear. I do hope you're better by tomorrow."

Angele managed a smile. "I should be all right by then. I just need some more rest."

She made to get up, pushing back her chair, but Ryan quickly moved to assist her. "I'll walk you back."

The other men rose politely once again, despite her telling them it wasn't necessary.

Ryan took her arm and led her out. "Maybe you ate too much. Do you want me to stay with you?"

"No, no, of course not. I'll be fine. I just overdid it a bit. A good night's sleep is all I need."

He saw her to the door and said he would be back after a brandy and cigar with the men. She told him not to hurry.

She waited till she thought he would be back in the dining room. Then she left the cabin, hurrying toward the stairs at the end of the hall she had seen the steward and some of the crew use. It was dark, and she didn't have much time. Ryan might be worried about her and not tarry in the men's salon over a half hour or so, and in that scant amount of time she had to find the area where the horses were and try to help the mare with the injured leg.

Her gown caught on a splintered step. She wished she'd had time to change into something less fragile. Maybe it was good she would be sewing with the ladies. She could get her hands on a needle and thread and try to repair the tear before Ryan noticed and asked how it happened.

Two decks down she heard the sound of music and singing and knew she had reached steerage. The cargo and horses had to be at the opposite end of that level.

At the bottom of the steps, there were two doors. She opened the one opposite the noise and knew at once from the damp, loamy smell that she was in the right place.

Several lanterns were burning, and she saw a boy, not yet twenty, lazily tossing hay over one of the railings.

"Excuse me, but are these Monsieur Tremayne's horses?"

He jumped, startled, for he'd not heard her approach and was surprised to see a woman. "They . . . they are," he said uncertainly. "He . . . he's the only one who brought horses on board this time. They're all his."

"And which one has the injured leg? I'd like to see her."

He looked at her uncertainly.

"Please," she begged. "I don't have much time."

"But you aren't supposed to be here. I mean, ladies don't come here, and I'll get in trouble."

"No one will know if you hurry."

It was obvious she meant to have her way, so he reached for a lantern and motioned her to follow him to a nearby stall. "It's some kind of sore. It keeps getting bigger. I don't know what's wrong with it. She hasn't put her weight on it since yesterday, so it must be hurting worse."

Angele stepped up on the bottom rung of the stall. "Hold the lantern up so I can see her."

The mare was favoring her right foreleg. It barely touched the floor.

"I'm going in there. Keep holding the lantern up."

He moved to block her. "You can't. If you get hurt, they'll throw me to the sharks."

Angele stepped around him. "Nonsense. I told you—no

one will know, and if they do find out, I'll say you tried to stop me."

Unlatching the gate, she stepped inside, careful to move slowly. Her father had taught her that even the most gentle horses could be spooked and become dangerous.

She had coiffed her hair in ringlets which were held back from her face with a comb. But when her head scraped a low beam, the comb tore free and her hair tumbled down around her face.

"Easy, girl." She made her voice soft. "I'm not going to hurt you. I just want to take a look at that leg of yours."

The mare tossed her head and stomped back a few paces.

"Lady, be careful," the boy shouted.

"Please be quiet," she hissed. "We don't want anyone to know I'm here, remember?"

She reached out and began to rub the mare's neck, and she didn't move away anymore. "See? I told you I wouldn't hurt you. Now let me see . . ."

She motioned to the boy to lower the lantern. He was hanging over the railing. Because she still couldn't see well, she took it from him and set it on the floor.

"No." He scrambled over the railing. "You can't do that. If she prances around and knocks it over, the whole place will go up in flames."

"Then hold it," Angele said, picking it up and handing it to him. "I can't understand why you're so scared."

"It's not my job to take care of these animals. But there was nobody else, and they made me do it, and I got kicked by a horse once and nearly broke my leg, and I'm not getting any closer than I have to."

"Just stand there and don't get in my way, and everything will be fine." She knelt and heard the boy suck in his breath as she gingerly lifted the mare's hoof. She could see the swelling and oozing. "I was afraid of this—it's beginning to get infected, and if something isn't done, gangrene will set in and kill her."

"Monsieur Tremayne looked at it this afternoon and said it's just a sore—that there's no injury he can see."

"It isn't a sore." Angele had probed with her finger and found what she had suspected—something hard and sharp embedded in the flesh. "Do you have a needle?"

"No. What do you want one for?"

"She's been stung by one of those huge bees that Blois is known to have, thanks to all the vineyards in the area. The stinger is still in there, and that's what is causing the sore and infection. I have to get it out."

"That horse will never let you dig into her with a needle."

"She let me find the bee's stinger. I think she knows I'm trying to help her."

As if to confirm it, the mare dropped her head and nuzzled Angele's hair. Laughing, she said, "All right, we understand each other, don't we, girl?"

Straightening, she told the boy she was going to find a needle. "And you go to the kitchen—galley—whatever it's called, and find some vinegar. I'll be back as soon as I can."

Giving the mare another pat, Angele made her way back upstairs.

After the men left the dining room for their brandy and cigars, the women usually lingered over dessert and coffee or tea. Tucking her hair back up as best she could, and pausing to wash her hands, Angele was relieved to find them still there.

As she crossed to Annette, their stares told her she hadn't succeeded in making herself completely presentable.

"Angele, my dear," Annette murmured. "I thought you had gone to bed."

"I'm feeling much better, and I thought if you'd loan me a needle and thread, I'd practice some stitching tonight."

"A good idea. I have both, I'm sure. A lady must always be prepared, you know." She opened her purse, fished about, and brought out a needle wrapped in a piece of cloth. "And here's some thread, too." Her gaze dropped to Angele's torn hem. "I suppose you're going to practice on yourself?"

The other women exchanged amused glances.

"Yes, yes, I am. Thank you." Angele all but snatched the items from her hand. "I'll see you all in the morning. Good night." She flashed a smile and forced herself to walk away slowly.

The boy had vinegar waiting. "What do you want it for?"

"I'll show you in a minute." She told him how to hold the lantern again, then sat down next to the mare, who watched with trusting eyes.

Angele rubbed her leg. "Wouldn't it be wonderful if you could be my horse when we get to BelleRose? I think we'd get along well, you and me. Now be very still, and I'll try not to hurt you and get this over with as quickly as I can."

After a few tense moments, she announced in triumph, "I've got it. Now, hand me the vinegar so I can pour it into the wound to draw out the poison left by the bee. Then I'll wrap a clean rag around it to keep it moist. In a day or two, she should be as good as new."

The boy watched with interest, but when Angele asked for the rag, he said he didn't have one. "Just the shirt I'm wearing, and since it's the only one I've got, you'll forgive me for not giving it to you."

She knew there was only one thing to do and reached to tear off a strip of silk from her hem. It was no trouble. It was practically in tatters, anyway, and, no doubt, Annette and the ladies had noticed and that's what they thought was so funny. She wondered if her face was smudged. She hadn't thought to look in a mirror.

"There," she said finally. "All done. See?" She patted the mare. "I told you I wouldn't hurt you."

Then she turned on the boy and warned, "Don't say anything about this, understand? No one is to know."

He looked at her as though he thought she were out of her mind. "And what do I tell the monsieur when he comes down here tomorrow and wants to know who wrapped a piece of silk around his horse's leg?"

"You will find something else by morning and change it. Soak it again in vinegar. If he asked who did it, fib and say a passenger from steerage wandered through who knew something about horses, saw her, and wanted to help. You are not, under any circumstances, to say it was a woman, understand?"

"You don't have to worry," he assured her. "I'm only too happy to pretend you were never here."

Back in the cabin, Angele leaned against the closed door and only then breathed a sigh of relief. No one had seen her coming upstairs. No one but the boy would ever know she'd taken care of the horse, and he wouldn't tell. Her secret was safe.

She took off her dress and held it out to see how much damage was done—and groaned. There were dark smudges, and the hem was ragged and raw. She would never be able to mend it or clean it. There were even bloodstains she'd not noticed before. It was ruined.

There was only one thing to do—ball it up and throw it out the porthole. If Ryan were to see it, she'd be hard-pressed to come up with a plausible explanation.

In her hurry to get rid of the gown, she didn't bother putting on her nightdress.

Naked, she stood on tiptoe and tried to reach the port-hole but couldn't quite do so. Dragging the chair over, she climbed up, and, after much struggling, succeeded in opening the round window and pushed it open.

She tried to shove the gown through, and her heart tripped when part of it caught on something. She couldn't just let it hang there for someone to see when they got to Cherbourg. It would be traced to her cabin—and her.

The porthole was not very wide but big enough that she could poke her head through, along with one arm. Gripping the bottom of it, she hoisted herself up and leaned out as far as possible.

The gown was caught on a splinter. She stretched farther. Then, just as she had it and gave a yank to send it floating away into the night, she heard a loud noise as the chair tipped over and hit the floor with a bang.

She grimaced to think how she was going to have to drop to the floor, and hoped she wouldn't sprain her ankle—or worse.

Taking a deep breath, she braced herself and prepared to push backward.

Suddenly firm hands clamped her buttocks at the same instant she heard Ryan's angry voice.

"Angele, would you mind telling me just what the hell you're doing hanging out the porthole naked?"

Twelve

"Now, will you please explain yourself?"

Ryan had pulled Angele down from the porthole and set her on her feet.

She groped for a believable answer. "I . . . I needed fresh air."

"Then why didn't you put your clothes on and go outside?" He couldn't hold back a grin. "Even though I must say your hanging there naked was quite a sight."

Naked.

Angele stared down at herself in horror. Then, peering up at him through lowered lashes, she saw the look in his eyes and knew she had broken one of Miss Appleton's most important rules.

She yanked the sheet from the bed.

Ryan snatched it from her and playfully said, "I've never seen you naked."

And you aren't likely to again, Angele thought as she tried to cover herself with her arms.

He pulled them away. "Don't. You're beautiful. Why don't you want me to see you? It'd suit me if you walked around naked in here all the time."

"That . . . that would be rather cold, don't you think?"

She made to step backward, but he put his hands on her waist and pulled her to him. "Why are you scared of me, Angele? Haven't you realized by now I'm not going to hurt you?"

Sliding his fingers into her hair, he tilted her head back, then lowered his mouth to hers. He kissed her long and hard.

Angele didn't respond. She was perfectly still, her neck stiff, spine rigid.

He used the technique Jessamine Darcy had taught him and sensuously made love to her mouth. Slowly he dipped his tongue in, then withdrew it. He repeated it, again and again, teasing, tantalizing, all the while running his hands up and down her bare arms as he continued to hold her.

She raised her hands and made tiny fists and shook them as he continued his honeyed assault, but still she didn't react.

He could feel her heat against him.

He moved to cup her head in his hands and tilted her farther back, sliding his lips from hers to nuzzle her throat, then trailed to her ear.

"No, please, don't . . ." she whimpered as his tongue began to circle inside her ear. "I . . . I don't want you to do this . . ."

"Yes, you do. You like it. Say it, Angele—say you want more . . ."

She tried to shake her head but his long fingers held her in a viselike grip.

He returned to her mouth and kissed her again and felt his own lust rising, deepening to a churning urgency. His moan of desire came from deep in his throat. He wanted her, but this was one time he would make her want him so desperately she would toss aside her fear and inhibitions.

He dropped a hand to her bottom and pulled her against him so that his erection burrowed into her cleft. Gently, he pushed to and fro, rubbing her pearly nub, and she whimpered but still remained rigid.

His other hand went to her full, firm breast. Flicking his thumb over her nipple, he was pleased to find it already hard. He knew then, despite how she was fighting against it, she was aroused. He dipped his head and flicked his tongue across it, then, lips fastened to her breast, grasped her waist to lift her and lower her to the bed.

He was still suckling at her breast as he laid her down.

And she was still not moving.

He raised his head to see that her eyes were tightly closed, her fists still clenched. "Tell me you want me, Angele."

"I . . . I don't," she lied.

"I'll make you," he growled, although he wasn't angry. Actually, though his loins threatened to burst with need, he was enjoying the torment.

He spread her legs and began to massage between them. She bit down on her lip and arched her back. He plunged his finger inside and worked it around, and, uncontrollably, her hips began to undulate.

"Say it," he commanded.

"No."

"Say it," he repeated, louder, almost harshly.

"Never . . ."

He parted her, trailing a fingertip up and down to torture, tease, then lowered his face.

She tried to rise from the bed, her fingers diving into his hair to grasp and try to pull him from her. "No, please . . ."

"*Yes*, please," he murmured, his breath hot against the heart of her. "Yes, I *do* please . . ."

He began to circle her hot little bud with his tongue, then nibbled between his teeth, ever so gently, licking back and forth. Then he plunged deep inside, grasping her hips and holding her firm. In and out, around and around, and he felt her shuddering, knew her climax was near.

Abruptly, he withdrew.

Her lashes flickered, and then she was looking at him with glazed eyes of wonder. Her hips continued to move, ever so slightly, and he slipped his finger inside her again to feel the gentle squeezing in signal that she was about to explode.

"Tell me you want me, Angele."

"I . . ." She could not say it.

"Beg me, damn it, or I'll leave you this way, so help me."

He mounted her, spreading her legs wider and probed against her so she could feel his hardness, feel him pulsating against her, ready to enter.

Her whispered plea was barely audible, but it was enough.

"Please . . . take me . . . please . . ."

And he did so, driving inside her. Deep. Hard. She wrapped her legs around him and dug her heels into his buttocks to spur him onward.

She pushed against him, lifting from the bed, wanting all he had to give.

He felt her shudders become tremors.

Her nails dug into his back, but it was a delicious pain, and he welcomed it.

She gasped and moaned and cried out, and he felt her explode into a million pieces around him as he drove himself home, deep . . . deep . . . deeper.

They lay very still, and their flesh was wet and slick. He knew he was too heavy on her and, after kissing her one more time, raised himself and moved away.

"Why did you do that?" she asked in a thin voice that rang with humiliation.

"I meant for you to enjoy it, too, and the only way was to make you admit to yourself that you did."

"It . . . it wasn't necessary."

"I think it was."

She was silent for a moment, and he could feel her eyes on him as he put his clothes back on. Then she said, "It isn't necessary, you know."

He quirked a brow at her as he fastened his trousers. "What are you talking about?"

"To . . . to make a baby, you don't have to make me want you."

He burst into laughter, but seeing the hurt look on her face was instantly sorry he had. He quickly sat down on the bed beside her and tried to take her in his arms, but she shrank away from him. She had the sheet wrapped tightly around her again, but he wasn't about to take it. "I'm sorry, Angele, but I don't think you understand."

She shook her head that she didn't.

"We don't do this just to make a baby." He was trying to keep from laughing again. She was so incredibly naive that he knew losing her virginity couldn't have been by anything other than force, and he'd like to strangle the bastard responsible. "We do it," he went on to explain, "because we enjoy it. Not just me, but you, as well. I want you to. And I'll teach you. Now, I know it's new to you, and you're shy about it, but you're my wife and you'll learn."

She seemed to relax a little, and he decided to give her time to think about it. He patted her cheek. "Get some sleep. I'll be back in a little while. I only came to check on you because Annette Marceau told her husband about your coming back to the dining room to get a needle and thread. She said she thought you wanted it to sew up your gown, because it looked as though you had ripped it. When he told me, I wanted to find out how you did it. I was afraid you might have fallen somehow and hurt yourself." He glanced about the cabin. "Where is the dress, anyway?"

"Uh, it's nothing. I've already mended it and put it away."

"Good. Then maybe you'll catch on quickly when you start your sewing lessons tomorrow. Now go to sleep. I'll try not to wake you when I come back. We're about to dock in Cherbourg, and Corbett and I are going to stroll around a bit."

"What time is it?"

He took out his pocket watch. "Almost midnight. Sweet dreams."

After he left, Angele sat up and hugged her knees against her chest.

She was still shaken by what he had just done . . . how glorious he made her feel. Even more so than before. But what he'd said about doing it even when they weren't trying to make a baby bothered her. It provoked fears she'd hoped never to have to face when she married. Miss Appleton had said some men were like that, though, and to pray she never got one for her husband. Then she recalled again how some of the girls laughed about it. So maybe it was Miss Appleton who was wrong. After all, she'd never been married, so how could she know?

With a deep sigh, Angele lay back on the pillow, arms propped behind her head as she stared dreamily up at the ceiling. Maybe she didn't know much about things like that, but whatever Ryan had done was wonderful, and though she dared not let him know it, she had enjoyed every minute. Just thinking about it made her feel a warm rush between her legs.

She touched her nipples, still hard from his velvet tongue. She had liked that, too.

Maybe it wasn't wrong to enjoy it. Ryan certainly didn't think so. And it was just between them. No one would ever know. As long as he was pleased, satisfied, nothing else mattered.

She felt secure and comfortable for the first time in a long while.

The evening had gone well.

She had taken care of the mare's wound and managed to get rid of the spoiled gown.

Her secret was still safe.

Snuggling down, she wickedly didn't get up and put on her nightdress.

Perhaps Ryan would be pleased to find her still naked when he returned.

With a smile on her lips, she fell asleep.

Ryan was worried about the mare and decided to check on her before meeting Corbett at the gangplank. When he got home, by damn, he was going to have Jasper teach him about such things. He might be the best in the valley at breaking a colt and training a horse, but he'd always left doctoring to Jasper. That had to change. It was all part of his new life, and it was called responsibility for everything at BelleRose. Before, he hadn't really worried about anything except having fun. But now, with a wife, he was ready to settle down.

He just felt good about everything all of a sudden. He had worried Angele couldn't be trusted after Corbett told him what she had done in Paris. And making it worse was how she had so calmly lied when he confronted her. But now that he understood, he would not worry about her being deceitful.

Like Simone.

It still made him feel like a fool to remember the green-eyed beauty he had fancied himself in love with when he was several years from twenty. She was the daughter of old friends of his parents' who had settled way south in Atlanta. She had come with her mother to spend the summer, and Ryan fell for her on sight.

They made love in the gazebo, and her passion had rocked him to his very soul. She was not a virgin and didn't apologize. She told him she loved him, too, and wanted to marry him, and that's all that mattered to him.

Till he caught her with somebody else.

It had been by accident, but looking back, Ryan knew it was blessed fate that showed him what a treacherous little bitch she really was.

He'd had to go with his father to Philadelphia on business. They were supposed to be gone two weeks but finished early. His father pretended to be annoyed over how Ryan was in such a hurry to get home but was secretly pleased. Nothing would have made him happier than for Ryan to marry Simone. She was French. Her family was close to theirs. It was the ideal match.

They had arrived at BelleRose just after dark. Ryan had raced into the house to look for Simone, but she was nowhere to be found. Her mother said she had gone for a walk.

Thinking she would be at the gazebo, missing him and

dreaming about the wonderful times they'd shared there, he decided to sneak up and surprise her.

But *he* had been the one surprised.

They were hidden by the thick honeysuckle vines that almost covered the gazebo.

He could hear the sounds of their frenzied lovemaking as he approached.

At first, he couldn't believe it. But then he heard her cry out the name of the man taking her to glory—Lehman Trotter, son of the man who owned a neighboring plantation. Lehman had a reputation as a womanizer, and Ryan had seen him flirting with Simone at a barbecue his father had hosted before they left for Philadelphia.

His first instinct had been to tear through the vines and rip the lovers apart, beat Lehman senseless, and then shame Simone before both their families.

But pride kept him from doing it. In the foolishness of his youth, he had bragged to everyone that he and Simone were going to be married, and he couldn't bear the thought of being humiliated.

He had gone back to the house and went to bed, heartsick. And the next morning when Simone danced into the breakfast room to shower his face with kisses and chide him for not waiting up for her to return from her walk the night before, he was glad they were alone.

He had leaped from his chair to grab her wrists and squeeze so hard she cried that he was hurting her.

"As you hurt me last night." He had flung her away from him and told her he knew what she'd done with Lehman, and he wanted nothing more to do with her.

That very day, Simone pretended homesickness, and she and her mother left for Atlanta. He never heard from her again.

As for Lehman, Ryan reasoned that he must have known he and Simone were found out, because ever since that fateful summer, he had carefully kept his distance from BelleRose.

So Ryan was glad he had married a woman he felt he

could trust, even if she didn't want to talk about her life before they'd met. It was the future that was important, which seemed to be looking brighter all the time.

He was also optimistic that sooner or later she would not be afraid to show she wanted him. He longed for that day, because then he'd have what he'd always hoped for in a wife. He wouldn't need a mistress like so many other men. He'd find complete and total satisfaction in his own bed.

The stall area was dark, but a softly burning lantern hung outside the door. Ryan used it to light his way to the small room where the boy who tended the horses slept.

He was just about to knock on the door when it opened and the boy rushed out. When he saw Ryan, he paled and staggered back a few steps.

"Sorry. I didn't mean to startle you. I know it's late, but I'm worried about the mare, and you said you'd ask around and see if any of the crew knew how to make a poultice that might help. I was wondering if you did."

As he was talking, Ryan noted that the boy looked scared, and he was stammering. "Uh . . . no. I . . . I mean yes. Someone did do something to her that might be helping. But . . ." he tried to edge by, heading for the ladder the crew used to get to the loading area, "I haven't had time to see. We're in port now, and they just signaled for all hands to help load cargo."

Ryan was sure the call to report to work had nothing to do with how the boy was acting. "I think you'd better come along with me to see about her."

"But I can't, sir. I'll be in terrible trouble if I don't get topside right away. And I promise, as soon as we're done, I'll go have a look at your horse."

He ducked around Ryan before he could stop him and scrambled up the ladder and disappeared above.

Mumbling an oath, Ryan went back to the stalls. If anybody had put a poultice on the mare, he needed to make sure it looked like they knew what they were doing. The boy's behavior bothered him, and if anything had been done to make her leg worse than it was, there'd be hell to pay.

He stepped up on the lower rung of the stall and held the lantern high so he could see. Sure enough, there was a bandage around the mare's foreleg.

He noticed a strange odor. Was it vinegar? Mammy Lou, the old Negro who'd been the cook at BelleRose since before he was born, made the sour liquid from apples and used it to spice up collards and turnip greens. She had also used it on him the few times he recalled being stung by bees. But why was he smelling it now in a horse stall?

Being very careful with the lantern, he entered the stall. The odor was stronger. The mare seemed calm, not fidgety with pain as the last time he'd seen her.

Kneeling, he touched the bandage.

It was wet.

He put his fingers under his nose and sniffed.

It was vinegar, all right.

Then he noticed something else and held the lantern as close as he dared. He didn't want to scare the mare or she'd start prancing around, which could prove dangerous in such a small place and with him holding a burning light.

"Well, I will be damned," he whispered as he saw the bandage was peach colored and made of silk with a bit of lace at the edge. It was the same material as the gown Angele had worn earlier, had torn, and which she claimed to have mended.

He left and climbed up the ladder and found the boy working with the other deckhands.

Seeing Ryan, the boy backed away again, his face turning much paler than before.

Ryan motioned to him. "Come with me. We need to talk, and I think you know why."

One of the men, a big, brawny sort with the look of one in authority, called, "Is something wrong, sir?"

"I just need to talk to this boy for a minute."

The man frowned. "Go with him, Gerard. And you'd better not be in trouble over not tending those horses like you're supposed to. I'll have you thrown overboard, you little slacker."

Doggedly, Gerard followed Ryan. When they reached the mare's stall, Ryan pointed at the bandage. "I want to know who's responsible for that."

"One of the hands. I'm not sure of his name."

Ryan clamped a hand on his shoulder, because he had started to fidget and he was afraid he'd run away again. "I think you do know. Tell me his name so I can find him. I want to know about the vinegar."

"Uh . . ." He was floundering again. "He said it was a bee sting. He got the stinger out and then put the vinegar on it to draw the poison. And see?" he added brightly. "The mare's a lot better, isn't she? So now I have to get back."

"It wasn't a man who did it, Gerard. It was a woman. And that bandage was made from the gown she was wearing. Now don't lie to me."

The boy swallowed hard, looking everywhere but at Ryan. "I . . . I think it might've been. Yes, sir. But I wasn't supposed to tell. I was supposed to change it, but I fell asleep, and then I heard the signal to get up top."

Ryan chewed on his lip thoughtfully. Angele had diagnosed the problem and dealt with it. She obviously knew how to treat horses, but what puzzled him was why she wanted to keep it a secret. What was she hiding? But, more than that, she had lied. And he didn't like that. Not one bit.

"You won't say anything, will you, sir?" The boy was squirming again and looked as though he wanted to cry. "I could get in real bad trouble. And if they find out while we're in port, they'll put me off here. I didn't mean no harm, and I swear to you I tried to stop her, but she wouldn't listen."

"It appears my wife is a very headstrong young lady," Ryan remarked, more to himself than the boy.

"But she certainly has a way with horses. The mare didn't give her a bit of trouble . . . just stood still as could

be, like she understood she was trying to help her. And
see? She puts weight on that leg now. She's definitely a lot
better."

Ryan's hand dropped from his shoulder. It was true. The
mare was on the mend. Jasper couldn't have done better
himself. "We won't say anything about this to anyone,
agreed? I don't want it known that my wife was down
here."

Gerard nodded furiously. "Oh, no, sir. You don't have
to worry. I won't tell a soul, and I appreciate your keeping
me out of trouble."

"It wasn't your fault. Just be sure you change the bandage as soon as you can."

Ryan didn't want anyone to wonder about silk and lace
being used on his horse.

Corbett would be waiting, but Ryan didn't want to postpone confrontation with Angele. He was furious and
wanted to know how much of *anything* she had told him
was true.

And, as much as he hated to admit it, it appeared he
had stupidly done the one thing he had promised himself
he would never do again—get involved with another deceitful woman.

Only this time it was worse.

He was married to her.

He slowed.

Maybe it would be best, after all, to just go ahead and
meet Corbett and go ashore. It would give him time to
calm down, because already gratitude was beginning to
overshadow his anger. Maybe she *was* keeping something
from him, although so far, he could find no fault with her
intentions.

Besides, blowing up and ranting and raving wouldn't
help the situation. She was probably already asleep, anyway. It could wait till morning.

He went on up to the main deck. Corbett spotted him

and came running, waving his arms and calling, "Wait, Ryan! Stay there. I have to tell you something. Don't come out here."

Puzzled, Ryan looked past him to where a crowd was gathered at the railing. They were staring down and pointing, babbling excitedly.

"What's going on?" He started toward them.

"There's been an accident. Don't go over there."

"Why not? I want to see." He tried to sidestep around Corbett, but he quickly moved to block him. Ryan scowled, annoyed. "What is wrong with you?"

Corbett put his hands on Ryan's shoulders.

He was having a very hard time not dancing a jig across the deck.

In fact, he had to speak through clenched teeth to keep from grinning from ear to ear.

"It's Angele." He made his voice quiver. "She's fallen overboard, Ryan. I'm afraid she's dead."

Thirteen

Ryan's legs felt as though they were made of wood as he walked toward the railing.

Imperiously, Corbett shouted, "Get out of the way! Let him through. That's his wife down there."

A chorus of gasps erupted as people leaped back to watch Ryan in sympathy. They were also curious as to how he would react to seeing his wife floating facedown in the water.

Ryan froze, thinking it couldn't be happening. He had left her only a little while ago. It had to be a mistake.

Corbett touched his arm. "Come on. Let's go back inside. You don't need to see her like that."

Ryan's chest was heaving. "How come they haven't pulled her out? How come they're leaving her down there for everybody to stare at?"

"They just found her a few minutes before you came out on deck. One of the hands saw her when he was on the pier, tying up the ship. He started yelling, and everybody waiting to go ashore went running over there. Me, included. Nobody knew who she was, but then I saw the dress she was wearing."

Hope was a rosebud, about to burst forth into radiant blossom. "Which dress are you talking about? When was she wearing it?"

"At dinner tonight. The peach gown . . ." Corbett's

words were lost in the thunder of Ryan's footsteps as he ran to the railing.

Gripping it tightly, he looked down into the cold black water. The only light came from the men on the pier holding lanterns. But it was enough. And he knew then why Angele had been leaning out the porthole when he went back to the cabin. She was getting rid of the gown so he wouldn't see how she'd ruined it taking care of the mare.

Ryan started laughing.

Corbett tried to pull him back from the railing and leaned very close to whisper, "Listen, I know it's a shock, seeing her like that, but you have to tell yourself it might be for the best. I mean, we both know you were impulsive, but we can forget it ever happened . . . forget you ever met her, much less married her. Denise won't know. I won't even tell Clarice. We'll just forget it. Now come on. You're scaring everybody by how you're laughing."

Ryan shook his head from side to side and slapped his hands up and down on the railing as though he were beating a drum. He continued to chuckle as he watched Angele's gown bobbing up and down. In the scant light, it did look like a body, head and limbs shadowed and dangling below the surface. It was easy to understand why, at first horrified glance, Corbett had thought it was her.

"Sir, I think you'd better let your friend take you back to your cabin."

Ryan felt another hand on his other arm. It was the captain, grim-faced and stern.

"We'll get her out, and when you feel like it, you can go ashore and make whatever arrangements you'd like." He looked at Corbett. "Or we can bury her at sea. But we can talk about that after he's had a chance to get hold of himself."

Ryan thought about just letting them find out for themselves when they fished a soaked—and very empty—gown from the water. But there was no need to prolong the unpleasant situation. "I'm laughing because that's not my wife down there."

The captain leaned over the railing to take another look. "But your cousin identified her by her clothing."

Ryan explained. "That's just it. That's only her gown floating down there. Not her. Look closer, and you'll see."

The captain, believing Ryan didn't want to accept the reality of the tragedy, yelled down to the man on the pier, "What's taking so long? Can't you get a dock hook out there and pull her in? This poor man up here is losing his mind while everybody stands around watching his wife float, for God's sake."

The crewman set the lantern down as someone handed him a long pole with a hook on the end. Holding on to a piling with one hand, he stretched until he was able to snag the gown. Immediately, he yelped, "Well, I'll be boiled in rum, it's not a body. Just a gown spread out in the water looking like one."

Ryan simultaneously slapped his hands on the captain's and Corbett's backs. "Close your mouths, gentlemen, before a flying fish sails right in. I told you it wasn't my wife down there."

As soon as Ryan and Corbett stepped off the gangplank, Corbett declared that he needed a drink. He also offered an apology in case Ryan thought he'd been callous when he said that Angele's drowning might have been for the best.

Ryan told him not to worry about it. "You were just trying to help me cope. I know you still have your misgivings about me marrying her, but I appreciate how you've accepted her. And I'll always be grateful for how you saved her life last night."

Corbett said he was glad he had been there to do it, then added to further smooth things between them, "To tell the truth, when I saw that gown down there, I thought the rowdies had probably been waiting for the chance to finish what they started."

"I don't think we have to worry about them, anymore, but I still don't want her out at night by herself."

"Have you told her that?"

"Yes, I have."

Corbett snorted. "Like you told her I'd be taking her about in Paris? A lot of good that did. She sneaked off to meet a man and spent the better part of the day with him. I still can't get over—"

Ryan cut him off. "There was nothing to it. The man was a stone cutter. She met him to discuss having a marker made for her mother's grave.

"You didn't tell me that she met him in a cemetery," he ended on a slightly accusing note.

So, Corbett thought, it was her mother's grave. And when the investigator he had hired discovered that, he would gather other information about her, as well. Hopefully, it would be terrible enough that Ryan would have second thoughts about her daughter bearing his children.

Corbett had used what money he had left to pay the investigator, so he had not bought Clarice a gift in Paris. But he didn't think she would care, because when she found out about Ryan getting married, she was going to be so angry nothing else would matter.

Cherbourg was a busy seaport, and Ryan enjoyed looking around even if Corbett seemed preoccupied. He figured he was either tired, still worried over what had happened—or both. So after a few drinks at a waterfront bar frequented by sun-wrinkled old fishermen, Corbett looked relieved when Ryan said they might as well return to the ship.

Corbett headed for his accommodations in steerage that he constantly complained about, but Ryan lingered on deck to watch the new passengers come on board. They looked harried, as though they'd had to rush to get there.

He stepped forward to introduce himself, speaking French.

The woman looked at her husband with such dismay it was as though she were wondering what else could happen to make her miserable. "I told you no one would speak English on this dreadful boat. That's why I wanted to sail from Southampton."

The man had a long, thin nose, and he stared down it in censure. His accent was deeply British, like hers. "You were the one who insisted we spend spring in Paris and then visit your sister in Cherbourg. I wasn't about to go all the way back to England to take another line, and this isn't a boat, by the way. It's a ship, and I wish you'd remember that and not embarrass yourself."

They were surprised when Ryan spoke next in his native tongue. "Well, you'll have two people on board you can talk to. My cousin is traveling with me, and he's American."

"Thank heavens." The woman seemed to melt with relief. "This has been such an ordeal. We were supposed to leave days ago, and then they wake us at an ungodly hour to tell us that if we're still going we have to dress and be at the dock in minutes.

"Forgive me," she added, embarrassed. "My name is Ramona Wright, and this is my husband, Nicholas."

The two men shook hands, and Ryan offered to show them the way to their cabin. "I know where it is, because my cousin has been lusting after it. The ship was full, and he's in steerage and hates it."

Ramona cooed sympathetically, "What a shame. The poor man. But tell me, can we dine together? I can't stand the thought of being around a bunch of foreigners all the way."

Nicholas gave a sigh of disgust. *"They* aren't foreigners, my dear. *We* are. And you must be tolerant."

She waved a gloved hand in dismissal. "The only thing I *must* do is get some sleep." She told Ryan she would probably sleep all day and would look forward to seeing him at dinner.

Ryan thought it would be nice to converse in English for a change. It might also be good for Angele. It bothered him that she seemed so shy around other people, but if she really felt left out due to not understanding what was being said, then she might talk more to the Marceaus, since they only spoke French.

She was asleep when he entered the cabin. He stood looking down at her face, bathed in the lantern's glow, and thought again how beautiful she truly was. Her ebony hair fanned the pillow, and her long, silky lashes seemed dusted with flecks of gold as they brushed her cheeks.

The sheet had slipped from her shoulder, and as he pulled it back up, his breath caught in his throat to see that she was still naked. Probably she'd been too tired to put on a nightgown.

He felt himself grow hard but would not force himself on her again tonight.

Force.

He shook his head to think of it that way. The only thing he had done—or *tried* to do—was make her accept the fact she was a woman, and that it was perfectly all right for her to enjoy her body, and his, as well.

He stripped off his clothes, then spread a blanket on the floor. He was not about to get in bed with her and startle her as he had before.

He was uncomfortable as hell, but there wasn't much left of the night, anyway, and, after a long time tossing and turning, he fell asleep.

Angele opened first one eye, then the other, saw Ryan lying on the floor, and promptly sat up in bed. "What are you doing down there?" The sheet fell away, and she snatched it back.

He shook himself awake. "I didn't want to scare you by getting in bed. I was afraid you'd start screaming again."

She could have told him that would not have happened, because the nightmare hadn't returned. In fact, she had slept quite well.

"Besides," he went on to say, "you did a good job of scaring everybody last night yourself."

She saw something in his gaze. What? Anger? Amusement? She couldn't be sure. "What did I do?"

He yawned and stretched. "You fell overboard."

"I did *what?*" He wasn't making sense. Maybe he wasn't fully awake yet.

He had rolled himself up in the blanket, and when he pushed it away, she saw he was naked.

She also saw that he was erect and quickly turned her head.

"It's all right for you to see me this way, Angele," he said with a touch of annoyance as he got to his feet and reached for his trousers.

"I . . . I'm still not used to . . . to any of this," she managed to say.

"Back to what I said . . ."

She nodded but didn't look at him. "Go on. I don't think I heard you right."

"You were throwing the gown you tore out the porthole when I came in last night, weren't you?"

She gulped, glad she had an excuse not to have to face him. "Why, no." She managed a nervous giggle, as though it were the silliest thing she'd ever heard. "Why on earth would I do that?"

"Because it was torn and dirty. You didn't want me to see it."

She felt a ripple of panic. How on earth could he know? It must have floated instead of sinking. They hadn't been out at sea. The ship had been coming into port at Cherbourg. Someone had probably recognized it as being the gown she'd had on at dinner. Why hadn't she just stuffed it in the bottom of her trunk?

Finally, she offered the lie, "I fibbed when I said I mended it. The truth is—I don't know the first thing about sewing, and I was ashamed for you to find out. But I wanted to try, and when I failed, I was embarrassed and wanted to get rid of it."

Once he had his trousers on and fastened, he walked over to the bed. "How did you tear it?"

"It snagged on something. That's all."

"Where?"

"I don't remember."

"Yes, you do. You went down to the horse pens and took a bee stinger out of the mare. Then you tore a strip of cloth off your gown, soaked it in vinegar, and wrapped it around her leg. You probably got filthy down there and didn't want to have to explain to me why, so you decided to just get rid of the dress. Only it didn't sink. It was so light it floated right up to the pier. Corbett saw it, and since it was too dark to tell there wasn't a body in it, he came screaming to me that you were dead."

Angele couldn't help it.

She giggled.

"I don't think it's funny."

She knew he did, because he had a faint twitch at the corner of his mouth. "Corbett shouldn't have been so quick to jump to conclusions."

"It's easy to see why he did. Everybody was upset and excited. But that's beside the point. What I want to know is how you knew what was wrong with the mare."

"I just guessed."

"You just guessed," he repeated dully.

"That's right. I've heard about bees stinging horses around vineyards. Blois has a lot of vineyards. So I just assumed that's what it was, and I was right."

Sarcastically, he said, "And, naturally, you knew exactly what to do for it, because, once upon a time, you heard somebody talking about it."

She nodded in affirmation. The explanation sounded good to her.

He sat down on the side of the bed and reached to cup her chin in his hand, forcing her to look at him. "Why is it that I get the feeling you're lying?"

She didn't like being so close to him. His bare chest brought back heated memories of how the thick mat of

hair had deliciously tickled her breasts. And as he shifted
to turn and face her, his shoulder muscles rippled, and
she flamed to see the marks left by her nails as she had
raked his back in the throes of passion.

"I . . . I don't know," she managed to say finally, squirming beneath his touch. "I don't know what else to tell you."

He let his hand drop. "You might try the truth."

She blinked as though she had no idea what he meant.
"About what?"

"Your past. All of it. Look—" He made to touch her
again, but she shrank back against the pillows. He sighed
and ran his hands through his hair, then shook his head
in frustration. "Don't you understand that regardless of
the circumstances of how we met, I'd like for this marriage
to be a good one? And it would help if you weren't so
damned mysterious about your past . . . your family."

Angele supposed it would do no harm to confide a little—tell him how she'd been raped, since he knew she
wasn't a virgin. And she could also tell him something
about her mother. Just a little. Enough so that he wouldn't
feel she was hiding something. The rest, about her father
being British, and how she'd lived in England and was only
half French, well, she would have to think long and hard
about that.

"Well?" he prodded.

She needed time to think about it and decide exactly
what she wanted to confide and what had to be left for
later. And she had to be careful not to say the wrong thing,
which might whet his curiosity all the more.

She also wanted a more appropriate setting, when both
of them were fully clothed.

Finally, she conceded. "Maybe we can talk tonight after
dinner. You can ask me questions, and I'll try my best to
answer." Maybe by then, she would have her thoughts
sorted out.

"Besides . . ." She gave him a gentle push, "I'm
starved."

"We both missed breakfast. And it's time for you to meet

the ladies for your sewing lessons. I'd say after having to throw away an expensive gown, you need them, too." Blue eyes turned to stone. "As for our talk, we'll have it tonight, for sure."

She hated the thought of having to sit with the women and endure mindless chatter till lunch but saw no way out.

"And another thing . . ."

She saw he still wore a stern expression.

"You are not to go back to the horse pens. It's not a fitting place for a lady."

"Then see to it that the mare is properly taken care of, and I won't have to."

They locked gazes in challenge. Angele was determined not to be the first to look away, no matter how harshly he glared.

But Ryan solved the problem by appearing to make it a draw. Surprising her with a quick kiss, he bolted to his feet, ending the tense moment.

He finished dressing, then paused on his way out to cut her a sideways glance and warn, "There's something you need to know about me, Angele. I despise scheming women. So don't ever let me catch you in a lie again. Now, you'd better hurry up and get dressed. You're late."

Wanting to end the discussion on a light note, he smiled to add, "The ladies probably think you actually *did* drown."

After he left, she stared at the closed door and thought how, from their first meeting, she had sensed there was a dark, dangerous side to Ryan Tremayne. She knew she should tread softly, but it had never been her nature to do so when she felt strongly about something.

So he would learn, sooner or later, that he had a wife with mettle.

And then she would worry about that dark, dangerous, side of him.

Corbett tensed as Ryan walked into the men's smoking room. Damn it, he looked happy, and that was the last thing he wanted him to be till he got rid of the sewer rat. He greeted him by asking, "Well, did you find out why your bride threw her gown in the ocean?"

"I sure did." He told him the whole story.

Corbett was shocked that Ryan seemed to find it all so amusing. "Well, by damn, if it were me, I don't know which I'd be the angriest over—her throwing away an expensive gown or going down to the horse pens after she'd been told not to."

"I can't be angry over either when I think about it. I mean, she did help the mare. For all I know she might have kept her from going permanently lame. I've never had a horse become infected by a bee sting before. Besides, Angele is different from other women, Corbett. She's spirited, and she thinks for herself. That's one of the things that attracted me to her."

Corbett snickered. "It could prove to be a very *bad* thing, Ryan. Do I have to keep reminding you that she's not like us even if she is French? She has absolutely no class. And you could have some serious problems in the future, because I don't think she'll ever fit in. Richmond society will never accept her."

"But I thought *you* had accepted her," Ryan said pointedly. "You don't sound like it now."

Corbett was quick to amend, "Oh, I have. Really. But it's different with me. I'm your family. Your blood. I'll stick by you, no matter what. Other people won't have to."

"Aren't you forgetting one little thing?" Ryan asked with a smile that bordered on being sinister. "The Tremaynes have always been one of the most prominent families in Virginia. Invitations to balls, parties, and barbecues at BelleRose are as coveted as the highest bid for cotton. People won't dare snub my wife."

The way he said it, Corbett knew he meant it, and he wouldn't have dared to contradict him, anyway.

Ryan slapped him on the shoulder. "I want you to know I appreciate how nice you've been to Angele, and I'm sure I can count on Clarice to do the same."

"Of course, of course."

He watched as Ryan went to talk to the new passenger from England.

He could count on him and Clarice, all right.

They would be more than glad to take care of his problem.

Fourteen

At dinner, Ryan made the introductions, explaining that Nicholas and Ramona Wright didn't speak French, then inquired, "Does anyone know English besides me and my cousin?"

"I'm afraid we don't." Annette Marceau answered for her husband, as well. "But don't mind us. We can talk with your wife."

"Good," he said, relieved. "By the way, Angele didn't have much to say about her sewing today. How did she do?"

Annette smiled indulgently. "All thumbs, I'm afraid. I don't think the poor child has ever been around a needle in her life."

Ryan gave Angele a wink no one else saw. "I think she has."

Annette reached across the table to pat Angele's hand. "Don't worry, dear. You're coming along nicely, and by the time the trip is over, you'll be able to tat and crochet like the rest of us. You'll need to keep practicing, of course."

Ryan said she would have all the time she needed. "She won't have anything else to do."

Inwardly, Angele groaned. The last thing she wanted to do with the rest of her life was sit around all day sewing. Ryan was going to learn she had a mind and a will of her own—and soon.

Annette continued. "It's a shame you dropped your dress overboard, dear."

Ryan gave Angele a sharp look, and she quickly repeated the story she'd told to the ladies that morning. "I explained how I had fallen and got the gown dirty and was trying to shake it out the porthole to get some of the dirt off, but the wind tore it from my hands."

"I see." He turned to the Wrights and began speaking in English.

Angele tried to listen, pretending, of course, not to understand what was being said. Annette tried to get a conversation going with her, but soon gave up, used to Angele not having much to say.

"What's this about her dropping her gown?" Ramona wanted to know.

Corbett spoke before Ryan had a chance. "Well, that's what she says happened, and I can tell you, it gave everybody a fright. The gown floated, and it was dark, and when I saw it I recognized it as being Angele's and thought she'd fallen overboard and drowned. I told Ryan and it gave him quite a scare till we all realized no one was *in* the dress. But it was hard to tell in the dark water."

Ramona cast a querulous glance at Angele. "But wasn't it quite late? Didn't you wonder why she would have been out on deck at such an hour?"

Angele could tell by how the nerves tensed in Ryan's jaw that he was annoyed with Corbett for revealing so much. "Sometimes Angele enjoys taking walks by herself late at night."

Corbett further exasperated Ryan by bragging, "I had to save her life the first night we sailed. Some drunken rowdies from steerage shoved her, and she fell over the railing but managed to hang on till I got there and pulled her up."

Ramona looked at Angele again, this time in wonder, then gushed to Corbett, "Well, that's wonderful. Thank heavens you were nearby."

Angele saw how Corbett's chest puffed out a little as he proudly exclaimed, "I have to say it feels good to know I actually saved a life."

Saved a life.

After getting over the shock, Angele had found herself wondering, more than once, if the incident had actually happened as Corbett claimed. She hadn't heard anyone walking either toward her or away from her. And she hadn't been aware of anyone being around her at all till she felt hands on her back, lifting . . . shoving . . . pushing. Then she heard Ryan shout, and suddenly Corbett was there to pull her up and declare he had saved her life. But she refused to dwell on it, because surely Corbett wouldn't have tried to kill her.

Would he?

She lifted her glass of wine to take a sip as Corbett asked Nicholas Wright where they lived in England.

And when she heard his reply, her hands trembled uncontrollably and she was barely able to set her glass down to keep the contents from sloshing over.

"Grayton. It's south of London."

She noticed Annette was looking at her and she swallowed hard, forced a smile in her direction, then busied herself slathering butter on a roll as her blood turned to ice.

Grayton was where *she* had lived . . . and where Uncle Henry still did.

Nicholas went on to explain, "Actually, we've only been there a little over a month. We barely had time to move in before we were to leave on this trip, and since we'd planned it for some time, we decided to go ahead with it."

Ramona spoke up. "But it was long enough to know we are going to love it there. The region is quite popular for hunting and raising horses. We'll probably get involved, ourselves, when we return."

"Ryan raises horses on his plantation," Corbett interjected.

"Really?" She smiled at Ryan. "And how large is your plantation?"

"A thousand acres, more or less."

She seemed impressed and turned to her husband.

"Lord Mooring said that was the size of his estate, remember, dear?"

Angele felt her heart stop, then start to beat so fast and furious she feared it would burst from her chest.

Ramona addressed Ryan again. "Lord Mooring is one of the wealthiest and most respected men in the Grayton region," she explained. "His estate is called Foxwood, and his manor house is enormous and quite impressive. He was kind enough to invite us to a fox hunt the weekend before we left."

Angele bit her tongue so hard she tasted blood.

Ramona Wright was wrong.

Foxwood was much larger than the thousand acres Ryan claimed for BelleRose. It was over two thousand, her father had told her.

And how was Uncle Henry able to claim the title of *Lord*? Her father had been the rightful Lord Mooring. It was a title bestowed upon the original landowner, handed down from eldest son to eldest son. Her uncle had no right, even after he took over the land when her father had been stripped of it and sent to prison. The title was not something that could merely be asserted.

Annette noticed how Angele had paled and reached across the table to pat her hand again. "Are you all right, dear? You don't look well."

"I'm fine," she murmured, aware that Ryan had heard Annette and was watching—but only momentarily. He immediately turned back to the Wrights, apparently enjoying chatting in his native language, as well as interested to hear about their life in south England.

"So how was the fox hunt?" Corbett wanted to know. "I've always wanted to go on one."

"Marvelous," Nicholas said. "Lord Mooring has splendid horses. Dogs, too. His pack of fox terriers are extraordinary."

Of course they are, Angele thought angrily, bitterly. *My father trained them himself, because he was extraordinary.*

Suddenly she knew she couldn't bear to hear any more

and was about to excuse herself when Ramona's next words were like ice water in her face. She tried to pretend she hadn't heard, because she wasn't supposed to be able to understand English. She reached for her water glass and took a big swallow to busy herself, giving thanks that Annette was busy talking to her husband and didn't notice her unease.

"Poor Lord Mooring, he's been through so much grief of late. His brother was convicted of some dastardly deed and took his own life to escape the humiliation. Lord Mooring had to step in and take over Foxwood, and it's said that even though he was devastated, he was determined to look after his sister-in-law and her child. But something terrible happened. They disappeared."

Angele forgot to breathe.

"Disappeared?" Corbett echoed.

"Yes. He thinks his sister-in-law ran away because she was so ashamed of what her husband had done."

Corbett, ever curious, wanted to know, "Whatever *did* he do?"

"We don't know," Nicholas Wright volunteered. "Evidently it was something so terrible no one was willing to talk about it. But Lord Mooring is beside himself over his sister-in-law and his niece. He's offered rewards all over England for their return. He says he's duty-bound to see they're cared for."

"He thinks they might have even gone to France," Ramona added. "That's where his sister-in-law was born. When we were in Cherbourg, my sister had even heard about the reward."

Ryan commented that it was all very sad and he hoped they were found. Corbett expressed the same sentiment. Then the subject changed, and Angele was relieved, because she was having a very hard time pretending she didn't know what was being said.

A reward.

All over England.

And France, as well.

Dear God, she had escaped just in time. But one thing was certain—she couldn't tell Ryan anything. Not for a long, long time.

Somehow she made it through the rest of dinner. She declined coffee and dessert, anxious to go back to the cabin where she could be alone. She excused herself, but Ryan surprised her by also getting up and saying good night to everyone.

"I noticed you didn't seem to be enjoying yourself at dinner," he said as they walked along. "So I didn't want to leave you by yourself."

She didn't want him thinking she'd been upset, and tried to be humorous. "Are you afraid I will actually fall overboard this time?"

"No. But you seemed worried about something. You hardly touched your food."

"I wasn't hungry."

"You never are."

She shrugged. "Maybe it's the food."

"But it's delicious," he argued. "I think the chef does a good job."

"Does he also cook for the steerage passengers?"

He laughed. "Corbett walked through the room where they eat just as they were sitting down to lunch today and said he'd starve before he'd take a bite of any of it. I think he's exaggerating because he's not happy about having to sleep down there. The captain told me they have the same food as the crew, and you know the crew wouldn't have it too bad."

"I guess Corbett blames me for being there. If I weren't along, he'd be sharing the cabin with you."

"If you weren't along, we wouldn't even be on this ship. Remember? We'd have returned on the same one we came over on, and both of us would have slept in a dormitory for men. It's not as nice as this, but it's certainly better than steerage."

They had reached the cabin door. Angele used her key to open it, then urged, "Why don't you join your friends now? I'm not going back out tonight. I'm tired, and I want to go to bed."

His voice was as warm and caressing as cashmere. "I want to go to bed, too—but not because I'm tired."

She tensed. Engaging in a sexual episode was the last thing she felt like doing at the moment. The Wrights had ignited all the old memories, and she needed to deal with them. "I'm really, really tired," she emphasized.

"You just think you are." He pushed the door open and motioned her inside, then closed it.

He had just taken off his coat when there was a knock.

"Monsieur Tremayne," the steward called softly. "I have the champagne you ordered."

Ryan looked at Angele, who was still standing in the middle of the room and making no move to begin undressing. "This will put you in the mood," he whispered huskily.

He opened the door and took the champagne.

Angele shook her head. "I . . . I don't feel like drinking."

"You'll love this bottle. It's the finest they have on board. It came from the captain's personal stock. He let me have it as a favor."

"Maybe some other night."

She turned away and began to fiddle with the ribbons on her bodice.

He put his hands on her bare shoulders and spun her around. "Come on. Let's sip champagne and have that talk."

"Not tonight," she said, too loudly.

His brows rose.

She rushed to finish before she lost her nerve. "The past doesn't matter. We're married, and that's the only thing that does. And quite frankly, I'm tired of your questions. My goodness, Ryan, you met me when I was a thief. You took me out of jail. Do you actually think there's anything more horrible I can tell you about myself?"

"Actually, I was hoping you could tell me something good."

She saw annoyance flash in his eyes but didn't care. "Suffice to say that everything you learn about me from now on *will* be."

"So far, it hasn't been."

She cocked her head and reached to grab his hands and fling them from her shoulders. "What is that supposed to mean?"

"Only that you've lied to me on several occasions, and I've told you that if there's one thing I can't stand, it's a deceiving woman."

"And since you've told me that, I haven't done it again."

He reached for her with heat-glazed eyes. "Maybe it doesn't matter. Maybe this is all that does . . ."

His hot, hard mouth captured hers in a deep kiss and then he abruptly let her go to command, "Take your clothes off or I'll rip them off."

She stepped behind the screen, her pulse pounding.

Through the screen's webbing, she could see him as he stripped. A little gasp escaped her lips when she saw that he was already aroused.

When she was naked, she called to him to please turn down the lantern.

"No" came his abrupt response. "I want to see you."

She knew arguing would be in vain.

She stepped from behind the screen.

And it was his turn to gasp.

"I've never seen you this way. My God, you are truly everything a man could want . . ."

He crossed to pull her into his arms. Her face pressed against his granite chest, as always, the mat of hair tickling deliciously.

Closing her eyes, she breathed deeply of his masculine scent.

His hands dropped to her buttocks, and he began to knead the tender flesh, pressing her into him. "Stand on your toes."

Bemused, she whispered, "Why do you—"

"Just do it," he said gruffly, raising her up.

And then she knew why he wanted it, because his hard penis slid between her thighs, then her cleft.

He bent and again kissed her, this time more forcefully, his mouth almost brutal as his tongue devoured her.

He moved himself to and fro, massaging the hot nub of her center with the tip of his organ. Angele's toes went stiff, and her fingers dug into his shoulders to hang on tight, because the sensation as he rubbed against her was so divine she wanted it to last forever.

His mouth stayed fused with hers as he backed her toward the wall. Her nipples hardened, and he felt them and moved his chest ever slowly from side to side, rubbing against her.

Angele clung to him even tighter, stunned by the unbelievable pleasure he was evoking in two places at once.

Her heart was leaping, and her head was whirling furiously. She felt as though she were drowning in his kiss as he sucked her tongue into his mouth and nibbled it ever so softly.

Her back was pressed against the wall. He continued to push himself in and out of her cleft with maddening rhythm.

He raised his lips to murmur, "Stay on your toes and spread your legs."

She didn't understand, and he showed her. Lowering his hands a few inches, he grasped her thighs and pulled them open. Then he held her by her waist and lifted her up till she was on the very tips of her toes.

"Now when I push inside you, wrap your legs around me."

Again she didn't know what he meant, and there was no time to ask, because the next thing she knew, he had impaled her.

All at once she understood, because it seemed only natural to leap upon him, her legs scissoring about his back, and she wrapped her arms yet tighter and held on.

He shoved harder, and her hips bounced against the wall, but she didn't care. Her teeth sank into his shoulder as she tried to muffle her cries of rapture.

It was as though she could feel him all the way into her belly, and she delighted with each hard thrust he gave.

His hips undulated, grinding to set an even more delightfully torturous cadence.

Somehow he managed to lower his head to one of her breasts as he held her. He sucked as much as he could into his mouth, his tongue flicking to and fro over her nipple.

Angele's hands went to his thick blond hair and, unconsciously, she began to kiss his neck, licking the perspiration away.

Her lips found his earlobe, and she sucked and chewed, breath ragged, panting.

She felt the explosion coming and began to shake her hips against him, wanting more, deeper, harder.

He felt it, too, and drove into her mercilessly.

It began as a tiny spark, in the very core of her, and then it spread upward into her loins like a great, all-consuming fire.

It roared all the way to her breasts, her nipples, and then to her heart and back down again.

The feeling didn't end but went on and on, and Angele thought she would surely die and didn't care in that crystalized moment in time if she did.

Ryan was moaning in his throat and suddenly cursed and said, "I want to be deep inside you . . ."

In one fluid motion, he stepped from the wall and then gave her a forward thrust that sent her back arching downward.

Her hair touched the floor, and she stretched her arms to cling to him, but he wasn't about to let her fall. He held her buttocks firmly as he rammed into her, again and again.

Then, with a guttural cry, he gave one last push and spilled into her.

He held her that way for a second, then helped her to

rise up against him. Her arms twined around his neck, and he rained kisses over her face.

He set her on her feet, then bent to lick a drop of sweat that had rolled from her neck to her breast.

"Delicious," he whispered. "Like all of you."

Angele was rocked with awe. Never had she imagined such ecstasy existed.

The girls at school had been right, she thought with a secret smile.

Miss Appleton really hadn't known what she was talking about.

Fifteen

For the remainder of the voyage, Angele busied herself pretending to learn how to sew. Every morning she met with all the ladies except for Ramona Wright. Due to the language barrier, Ramona and her husband kept to themselves except at mealtimes, when they could converse with Ryan and Corbett.

Though she didn't return to where the horses were penned, Angele knew that the mare was healing nicely, because Ryan thoughtfully kept her informed.

She hinted that since she had helped the horse, perhaps it could be hers once they got to Virginia. Ryan hadn't been at all receptive, pointing out that she didn't know how to ride. When she said she was anxious to learn, he countered by bluntly reminding her he hoped she'd get pregnant right away and then, of course, she couldn't do anything as strenuous as ride a horse.

Angele didn't argue. Everything in its own good time, she reasoned. For the present, she was pleased they were getting on so well. In fact, she had begun to secretly look forward to their lovemaking. And even though he let her know that he'd like her to be more adventuresome in bed, all she could bring herself to do was yield to whatever he wanted. She instigated nothing.

As for Corbett, Angele avoided him as much as possible. Since he did so many things she disapproved of. He drank too much, and swore, and she noticed he was quite a flirt with the ladies when their husbands weren't around. He was handsome, and he knew it. He had curly red hair, and his spicy brown eyes were fringed by lashes too long for a man.

Another thing that annoyed her was how not a day went by that he didn't find a subtle little way to remind that he had saved her life. Even Ryan had remarked once or twice that Corbett was so proud of himself he'd probably never let her forget what he'd done. She longed to tell Ryan how it gnawed at her that she wasn't at all sure anyone else but Corbett was around that night. But to do so would make it appear she was accusing him of pushing her overboard, and, without proof, she didn't dare say anything. After all, Corbett and Ryan were kin. And what was the old saying about blood being thicker than water?

Every time she was around Ramona Wright, she longed to ask about Foxwood, how it looked now, and did she hear of a horse named Vertus when she and her husband had spent a weekend there.

Finally, they reached the bustling seaport of New York. Angele rushed out on deck as soon as she heard they were sailing in and was glad when Ryan joined her at the railing to share the excitement.

As they stood together, he casually put an arm around her shoulders. Instinctively, she pressed closer. It was a good moment, the two of them standing side by side as they arrived in America to begin their life as husband and wife.

She stole a glance at him from the corner of her eye. He was a very attractive man. He treated her well, and, so far, she felt like the luckiest woman on earth.

He turned to smile at her. "Happy?"

"Very. But I have to admit I'm nervous."

"About meeting the rest of my family, I suppose. That's only natural, Angele, but don't worry. Give them time, and they'll accept you. They have to. You're my wife."

She didn't want them to accept her merely because they

had to. She wanted them to like her for herself but supposed that was asking too much. But that wasn't her only concern. "It's all so new and different. I just hope I won't disappoint you."

"You won't. And don't worry. Clarice will teach you everything you need to know about what goes on around the house, and I'll hire a tutor to come in and give you lessons in other things."

She frowned. "Like what?" She hated pretending to be ignorant.

"You need to learn to speak English. And you need to learn how to read and write. Unfortunately, the South is behind in education compared to the North. There are fewer schools and even fewer girls attending. But BelleRose women have always been literate, and so will you. Besides, you won't have anything else to do but study."

That didn't exactly set her afire with enthusiasm. She had always been active. Even when her parents sent her away to school, she'd spent the afternoons riding or hiking. "I'm sure I'll find lots to do," she said. "I'm not the sort to stay indoors."

"You'll learn to be a lady, and ladies stay indoors a lot," he said pleasantly . . . but firmly.

Just then, Corbett joined them, and the cozy time ended—for Angele, anyway. He positioned himself on the other side of her and commenced to monopolize the conversation.

She lapsed into silence, and soon Ryan was talking to Corbett about the horses and how anxious he was to get them to BelleRose. He seemed to forget she was even there, and she wondered if that was how it was going to be in the future . . . if he would have any time for her at all.

After disembarking and saying good-bye to their fellow passengers, Ryan told Angele to wait for him on the pier. "I want to watch when they unload the horses. Then I need to make arrangements to get them to Richmond."

"How are you going to do that?" He hadn't even told her what *their* mode of transportation would be.

"I'll hire wagons. I'm sure not going to drive them like cattle. And once they're taken care of, I know of a nice inn where we can get a good meal and spend the night."

"Ah, we're going back to Mrs. Dudley's." Corbett walked up to where they were standing. Angele had noticed him spending an unusual amount of time saying farewell to one of the female steerage passengers.

"That's where we spent the night before we left for Paris," Ryan explained to Angele. "Mrs. Dudley is a widow and rents out rooms."

"Well, at least the food is good." Corbett smiled at the girl again and waved, then turned back to Angele and Ryan. "I'm afraid I can't say the same for the beds. It was like sleeping on a sack of rocks. But after spending these last weeks in steerage, I won't complain if she puts me out in the barn. And don't forget there's a tavern just across the street."

Ryan was brusque. "I'm not interested. Now, look after Angele while I see to the horses."

She felt like telling him she might be safer on her own, but that kind of thinking could only lead to trouble.

"So," Corbett said, folding his arms across his chest and rocking back on his heels. "How do you like New York?"

She shrugged. "It looks big. Lots of construction going on, from what I can see. Buildings. Houses. I can tell there's a diversity of people, and that's interesting. Actually, I wish we could spend a few days here."

"Ryan is chomping at the bit to get back to BelleRose. You could never get him to stay."

"Well, maybe one day." She hoped it wouldn't take Ryan long to see to the horses, so he would join them again.

"A lot of planters come north during the summer months, you know."

That caught her interest. "Really? Maybe Ryan and I can do that."

"Don't count on it. I think once we get home you're

going to see a whole new side to him. You're in for some surprises, I'm afraid."

"In what way?" she asked stiffly.

"Well, for one thing, you've had him all to yourself on the ship. And that's good, because you just got married. But when he gets to BelleRose, he has a lot of responsibilities, so don't expect him to spend much time with you. He'll be much too busy. I know Ryan."

"Maybe it will be different now that he's married."

"I doubt it. After all, we both know why he married you, Angele."

She had turned away from him, as though to shut him out, but at that, she whirled about. She felt her ire rising and fought to keep it down. The last thing she wanted was to lose her temper, but he had her dander up with his last remark. "And just what do you mean by that?"

"He didn't propose because he was in love with you. You're just chattel—like his slaves. And I'm sorry if it bothers you for me to say all this, but I just think you ought to know what you're in for."

She could kick herself for even bothering to debate with him but had to say, "Well, I don't think it's going to be that way at all."

He shook his head in wonder that she could be so naive. "If you expect more, you're going to be terribly, terribly disappointed. Listen . . ." He reached to touch her arm, but she drew back, "I'm your friend, and I want you to remember that, no matter what. If you have problems, even with my wife, I want you to come to me. Understand?"

Angele understood only that, despite all his efforts, she still didn't trust Corbett.

Maybe it was because of what happened in Ryan's hotel room that day in Paris.

Or perhaps it had to do with how he tended to drink so much and her suspicions that he might be unfaithful to his wife.

But there was something else she didn't like to think about and that was how she couldn't help comparing him to her uncle. Never once had Uncle Henry given any hint that he was anything but loyal to her father and devoted to him as his only brother. She even remembered how her father had said, over and over, how deeply he respected Henry for accepting that he didn't inherit any of Foxwood. He also vowed that Henry would never want for anything. He would always have a home there.

And all the while Uncle Henry had been scheming to destroy her father and take everything.

Since the situation with Ryan and Corbett was somewhat similar, Angele couldn't help but think about it.

She also recalled Corbett saying his wife's cousin was the one everyone thought Ryan would marry. It was only natural Corbett would have preferred that he had, because then he would never have had to worry about being asked to leave BelleRose.

And it could also be his motive if he had, indeed, been the one who tried to push her overboard.

Corbett, eyes hooded with concern, prodded, "You do understand I want to be your friend, don't you?"

"Yes, but I'm curious about something. What makes you think I might have problems with your wife?"

"Nothing specific. She can just be a bit hard to get along with sometimes. That's all. You come to me, and I'll take care of it."

Coolly she informed him, "I doubt that will be necessary. I try to handle my problems in my own way. But thank you for your concern, although I have to say I don't like being compared to chattel."

He shrugged. "That's how it is."

Something else had needled her. "You said chattel . . . *like his slaves.*"

"That's right."

"He mentioned having servants, not slaves."

Corbett shrugged again. "Servants. Slaves. What difference does it make?"

"A lot if what I've heard is true about the way slaves are treated. And besides, servants are paid. I know, because"—

she paused, about to say that her father had servants at Foxwood—"I have heard how it is done in France. People are paid to work. And they can come and go as they wish."

"Well, it's different here. Slaves are bought, sold, and traded. Planters have to have them to work the crops."

She felt tension at the back of her neck, and her pulse began to pound as indignant anger surged. "Then they should have to pay them."

At that, Corbett's face darkened. "You should watch making remarks like that."

They locked gazes for a long, steely moment, then Corbett softened his tone. "I hate to seem harsh, Angele, but it's for your own good."

Over his shoulder, she could see Ryan approaching. "You're probably right," she said to pacify him and end the tension. Regardless of her suspicions, nothing would be gained by making an enemy of Corbett.

That night, as she lay in Ryan's arms after he had made love to her, she asked him to describe to her in detail everything about BelleRose.

He did so, and she could tell he was extremely proud. But when he mentioned having over two hundred field hands and how Clarice was always complaining about having only eight servants in the house, Angele seized the opportunity to bring up the subject of slavery.

"I suppose it costs a lot to hire that many people," she said carefully.

"They aren't paid, Angele," he said quietly. "They're slaves. I call them field hands, or servants, but that's what they are—slaves. And some of them have been at BelleRose since before I was born. Like Mammy Lou. She took care of me when I was a baby, and her mother took care of my father when he was little. She has a granddaughter—Selma—and I've already decided she'll be mammy to our children. But till they're born, I'll see to it she's your personal servant. You'll like her. She's every bit as likable as Mammy Lou."

Angele had had her own maid at Foxwood. So had her

mother. But they had received money for their services. The idea of slavery was appalling, and she said as much, explaining she had heard how they were mistreated . . . beaten. "I could never stand for that."

He had been lying on his back but quickly turned on his side to face her. "Slaves aren't beaten at BelleRose. They never have been, and they never will be. They're treated well. Not like on some plantations. You don't have to worry."

"But if they're slaves, then they're held against their will."

His mouth tightened. "It's a way of life. They don't know any other . . . and neither do we. Corbett told me you two had a discussion about this and that he warned you to keep your opinions to yourself. I agree, because it wouldn't do for my wife to go around saying she's against slavery. There's a lot of debate over it. People are taking sides. Some folks even think it might lead to a war between the North and South one day. I hope not. And I want to stay out of the controversy. Life will go on at BelleRose like it always has, and you'll be expected to accept things the way they are without comment. Do you understand?"

He looked grim.

He also looked on the verge of anger.

"I understand," she whispered.

Even though she didn't.

Ryan took note of Angele's discomfort, which she tried to hide. "I'm sorry it's been such an uncomfortable ride," he apologized, "but till steamboat travel is available all the way to Richmond, this is the only way to get there except on horseback."

"I'd prefer that," she said as the stage wagon hit a rock and threw her up to bump her head.

"This is a lot nicer than the old freight wagons with boxes built on top for passengers. They had to sit on back-less benches, all facing forward, and enter from the front by scrambling all over the seats. At least we've got a door on the side, and we can face each other."

Corbett, sitting opposite them, said, "And don't forget we have room in here for nine passengers on three seats, and I guarantee before we're a quarter of the way to Richmond we'll be full and all squeezed against each other. But don't worry," he teased Angele. "You can always sit outside with the driver on the box if it gets too crowded. Of course, it might rain and you'll get wet, and then there might be bandits. You could get shot."

"Corbett, that's enough," Ryan snapped.

"I'm only joking."

"You're scaring her."

"No, he's not," Angele protested.

"Well, I'm tired of his nonsense," Ryan grumbled.

"Then maybe I'll sit out there so I won't bother you." Corbett slouched down in his seat, pulled his hat over his face, and lapsed into an angry silence.

Angele found it upsetting that Ryan and Corbett were so often at odds with each other. And while Ryan seemed to dismiss each incident, she could tell that Corbett held on to it for a while, pouting and brooding. It was not a good sign and did nothing to dissuade her from worrying that he might be as jealous of Ryan as her uncle had been of her father.

They stopped for the night at inns along the way, where there was always a hot meal waiting and a place to sleep.

As Corbett had predicted, they did take on other passengers, and soon the stage wagon was filled to capacity. Still pretending only to speak French, she was spared having to make conversation and was grateful, because even Ryan found the three men and four women annoying. The women talked incessantly, and the men seemed to compete to see who could speak the loudest to be heard over the women. Corbett gladly sat outside with the driver and took the weather as it came, while Ryan pretended to sleep all the time.

The top half of the body of the coach was open framework, covered by thin leather curtains that buttoned down to solid panels below. It gave everyone a good, albeit dusty, view of the passing landscape. But when it rained and blew in, the curtains had to be closed, which made it unbearably warm, as well as dark.

Angele had grown used to feeling as though she were being playfully tossed about in a sheet, thrown to the ceiling to flatten her bonnet, then slammed back down to the seat. The other women, however, screamed and carried on, crying they were hurt—which only made Ryan pretend to sleep all the more.

Several times, when they approached a steep hill, the driver asked the men to get out and walk in order to lighten the load for the horses. When Angele hopped down, anxious to breathe truly fresh air, Ryan made her get back inside, chastising her for wanting to do something so unladylike.

Wearily, she mused again over how much he had to learn about her and her ways.

But only when the time was right, which would not be until she had dug her heels in good and deep . . . and couldn't be pried loose.

Sixteen

Angele fell in love with Richmond at first sight.

The cobblestone streets were bordered by tall, shading oak trees.

Sweeping front porches of whitewashed houses were draped in fragrant honeysuckle vines.

Ladies in pastel-colored dresses twirled parasols over their heads as they strolled along the boardwalks.

And men lifted their top hats politely as the stage wagon rolled by.

She also found the downtown area delightful. The buildings were made of bright red brick. Painted letters on the big glass windows proclaimed Dry Goods and Hardware stores, banks, undertakers, printers, feed stores, and apothecaries.

The stage driver reined in the horses in front of a livery stable.

At the last rest station, Ryan had selected a pink taffeta dress from one of Angele's trunks and asked her to wear it for the final leg of the journey. It had a high collar, pouffed sleeves, and a huge skirt that required starched, stiff petticoats beneath. It was terribly hot and uncomfortable, and she also didn't like the ruffled bonnet that complemented the dress. But, as he helped her down from the wagon, she glanced about to see that her outfit was similar to what other women were wearing. Actually, it was the only one Ryan, himself, had chosen, and the French stylist had wrinkled her nose and said it was outdated. But he had liked it and bought it.

She tugged at the lace-edged collar, which was scratching her neck. Ryan was busy talking with someone on the street, and Corbett, standing beside her, whispered, "Stop fidgeting, Angele. Ladies don't do that."

"They do when they itch," she said, then walked away. Since leaving New York, he had taken it upon himself to tell her what she should and should not do. It had become quite annoying, especially since Ryan allowed him to do it.

She walked about, looking in store windows. Sometimes people murmured a "good afternoon" in passing, and she was careful to respond in French. More and more lately she found herself wishing she could have found a way to let Ryan know she spoke his language, but she had been so hell-bent to hide the fact she was anything except pure French. Still, had she given it more thought, she might have come up with a believable explanation. Now she couldn't communicate with anyone, and that would be a problem until she pretended to learn English.

The web of deceit in which she found herself entrapped reminded her of words of Sir Walter Scott she'd had to memorize in school: *"O, what a tangled web we weave, when first we practice to deceive."* She had tangled herself up, all right, and only hoped she could continue to maintain her ruse. She had come too far to ruin everything now.

She saw Ryan coming toward her and felt a tiny little rush and chided herself. It didn't matter that their lovemaking had become more and more passionate and enjoyable. That was only instinct—lust—and had nothing to do with caring anything about each other. Ryan was also a careful, considerate lover, and he constantly took her to pyramids of joy that left her breathless and shaken with wonder. Still, she had to keep reminding herself of Corbett's warning—that she was nothing more than chattel.

"What do you think of Richmond so far?" he asked.

"It's beautiful, and the people are friendly. I just wish I could talk to them," she was careful to add.

"You'll learn. And don't worry about telling the servants what you want. Clarice speaks French fluently, and she can translate for you when I'm not around."

"What about your father? Does he speak English?"

He laughed. "Only when he has to."

He took her arm, and they began walking toward the carriage he had hired to take them the rest of the way.

"I just hope he'll like me," she said.

"Don't worry. Everything is going to be fine. Corbett has promised not to even tell Clarice the truth about how we met. Everyone will believe you come from a wealthy, prominent family."

Resentment flared, and she fought against it, managing to keep her voice even. "Is that so important? I thought your father's only requirement was that your wife be French."

"True. But he would naturally hope I'd marry someone from a good background."

"That sounds terribly snobbish."

"Maybe, but it's only logical in our family. The Tremaynes have always been proud, and marriages have usually been arranged, but my father knew I'd never allow him to hand-pick my bride. He settled instead for his ultimatum of her being French, and I had no choice but to go along with that."

"I think even that is dictatorial and unfair."

"By your way of thinking, maybe so."

"But what if you had fallen in love with someone who wasn't French?" she persisted. "What then? Would you have walked away because of what your father wanted?"

"I can't say, because it didn't happen."

"But if it had—"

He cut her off. "It didn't, so there's no point in discussing it."

But she was still bothered, because even though she was fighting it, there was no denying she was attracted to him. That made her think about what might have happened had they met under different circumstances. Would he have been drawn to her even though she was a poor runaway? And if he had fallen in love with her, would he have defied his father and married her?

She would probably never know but would always wonder.

Angele was awed by the breathtaking scenery they passed. "And I thought the countryside of France was the most beautiful in all the world. Everything is so fresh and green, and the lakes are crystal clear. I can even smell perfume in the air."

"Honeysuckle, wild roses, and gardenias," Ryan said, obviously pleased she was so impressed. "Maybe one day I'll take you on a trip to the Shenandoah Valley, and then you'll think you've gone to heaven."

"I feel like I'm already there."

He smiled and patted her arm.

Corbett had lapsed into a moody silence and sat with his head flopped back against the seat and his eyes closed.

Angele wondered if he was angry with her but decided she didn't care even if he was. She certainly intended to do her best to get along with everyone, but there was a limit to how much nagging she could endure from him or anyone else.

They traveled south of Richmond, then along the James River. Ryan explained the river eventually reached the Atlantic Ocean.

"So why didn't we just sail in?" she asked innocently.

Corbett gave an amused snort but didn't open his eyes.

Patiently, Ryan said there was not a seaport for big ships. "We could have gone into Philadelphia, which would have been closer, but the Black Ball Line didn't go there."

"Is BelleRose close to the water?"

"BelleRose isn't close to anything," Corbett said dryly.

Ryan threw him an annoyed glance that he didn't see because he still had his eyes closed. To Angele, he said, "We own a lot of land and much of it does front the river, but the house was built back a ways. I think my ancestors were afraid of flooding."

They left the river and turned up a winding road. Then they reached open fields on either side, and she could see Negroes working their way through long rows of some kind of green plant covered in what looked like popcorn. They dragged big sacks behind them.

"Cotton," Ryan said, knowing she had no idea about any of the crops.

A white man on horseback and carrying a rifle appeared to be standing guard over the workers. When he saw the carriage approaching, he dug his heels into the horse's flanks and galloped toward them. He let go of the reins to hang on to the rifle and still have a free hand to yank off his hat and wave it frantically over his head. "Sakes alive," he yelled. "Welcome home . . ."

"Who is that?" Angele asked, wondering if it could be Roussel Tremayne, though this man looked much too young and agile.

"Roscoe Fordham. He's my overseer," Ryan explained, then told the carriage driver to stop, and as soon as he did, he and Corbett quickly got out.

Roscoe reined in and leaped to the ground with a hand outstretched to Ryan. "Welcome home. It's good to see you. How was the trip . . ." His voice trailed as he saw Angele.

Ryan responded, "Wonderful, Roscoe, wonderful. And just wait till you see the Anglo-Arabs I was able to buy. Good blood. I've got the makings of the finest herd in all of Virginia now."

Roscoe continued to stare at Angele.

Ryan noticed and casually said, "This is the new Mrs. Tremayne."

Roscoe had put his hat back on but immediately swept it from his head. "Pleased to meet you, ma'am."

Angele nodded.

"She doesn't speak English."

"Well, tell her welcome for me."

Ryan didn't take the time. He was too anxious to ask what had gone on during his absence.

Roscoe said there had been little rain and the cotton was drying out in the field so he had ordered picking to start earlier than usual. Tobacco plants were being suckered, which meant the flowering tops were being broken off the leaves. Corn was coming along nicely, as well as all the other crops.

Angele listened but pretended not to when Roscoe's face turned mean as he told about how three slaves had run away from a neighboring plantation. "Dogs got one of 'em, but the other two got away. So all the planters up and down the river are worrying there's some kind of underground railroad goin' on, so they're taking turns sending men out to patrol the riverbanks at night to keep an eye on things. Last night was our turn, so I took some boys and went."

Angele was amazed at how quick Ryan flashed with anger.

"Damn it, that's the last time you or anybody else goes from BelleRose!" he all but shouted.

Roscoe looked from Ryan to Corbett, who was standing behind Ryan. Angele noticed how Corbett rolled his eyes. Then Roscoe argued, "How come? This is a problem we've all got. If some nosy Yankee is comin' down here and helpin' slaves run away up North, we need to know it so we can hang the bastard."

Ryan didn't mince words. "Slaves don't run away from BelleRose, because they're treated well. We don't have any problems, so there's no need to get involved in those of other people. That's final, Roscoe. We mind our own business."

"Well, yes, boss, whatever you say." Roscoe had put away his gun and was rolling his hat around in his hands.

Angele looked Roscoe Fordham up and down. He was a huge man, with wide, hulking shoulders. His shirt was unbuttoned, displaying a barreled chest and a stomach that hung over his belt. He had beefy arms and big hands and hairy knuckles. His skin was the color and texture of leather.

"We'd best get on up to the house," Ryan said finally. He turned toward the carriage, but Corbett hung back, and he prodded, "Come on. The horses will be here soon, and I want to alert the stablehands."

Corbett shook his head. "I need to talk to Roscoe some more. You go on ahead. I'll walk."

"As you wish." Ryan signaled to the driver.

"Why didn't he come with us?" Angele asked as soon as the driver popped the whip and they were rolling down the road once again. "Is he afraid to be there when you introduce me?"

"No. He just wants to talk to Roscoe some more."

He had told her Corbett oversaw the fields, while he looked after the horses and livestock. It was their arrangement, and she supposed it was only logical Corbett would want to talk to his overseer at length after having been away for so long. Still, she couldn't help wondering if he feared an ugly scene.

She worried, too, about the slaves running away, as Roscoe had revealed. She wondered why, and also where they went when they did. Even though she'd been warned to stay out of anything to do with them, she couldn't help thinking about it.

After they passed the fields, they rounded a curve where split rail fencing began that bordered lush green lawns on each side of the road. Then the house came into view, and she gasped, "My God . . ."

Ryan beamed with pride. "It was built by my grandfather and passed on to my father, because he was oldest son, and one day I'll pass it along to mine."

"It . . . it's like something out of a fairy tale. And I thought the estates in England were extraordinary."

The instant the words were out of her mouth she felt a wave of panic.

"England? You lived in England?"

"No," she managed to say calmly. "But I visited there once."

"When . . ."

"Please," she urged, squeezing his arm. "Tell me about the house." *Anything to get him to stop asking questions.*

The mansion stood four stories high and had a chimney at each corner. Made of gray fieldstone, the windows were long, narrow, and arched at the tops and composed of many small panes of glass. There was a low wall around the edge of the roof, and Ryan told her it was a walkway that circled the whole house.

"There are six separate gardens," he pointed out as they drew closer. "And they're all laid out in different patterns."

Regal oaks and maples stretched to the sky and bordered the sculptured areas as far as she could see.

Finally, the carriage turned into the long, circular driveway.

A winding terrace joined the house to a narrow stairway made of pink marble that rose from the cobblestone driveway. Neatly trimmed shrubs hugged the base of the house and were interspersed with thick rosebushes.

There were two front doors, large and arched like the windows, and as Ryan helped her alight from the carriage, one of them opened.

An old Negro man stepped out on the porch, his hair the color of the cotton Angele had seen in the fields. His whole face lit up with his smile as he carefully came down the steps, his body slightly bent to one side by rheumatism.

"Praise the Lord, Mastah Ryan. You're home safe and sound. We've missed you so much."

He held his arms open wide, and Ryan stepped into them, returning his hug with gusto. "Willard, I missed you." He quickly told Angele, in French, of course, "I've known Willard my whole life. He's our butler, but he's also a good friend."

Willard blinked, confused over who she was and why she was there.

Ryan didn't keep him wondering for long. "This is my wife, Willard. Her name is Angele, and she's from France and doesn't speak English yet, but she'll learn quick. Till then, Clarice or I will interpret for her."

"Yes, sir." Willard's head bobbed up and down. "Tell her I said Welcome to BelleRose."

Ryan translated, and Angele nodded and smiled. Willard seemed like such a nice man. She longed to be able to tell him she hoped they would become friends and regretted, once again, the extent of her charade.

Ryan motioned Angele up the stairs as he asked Willard, "How is my father? Mr. Fordham said he was doing fine."

"Well, Doctor Pardee seems to think he's gettin' along all right, but he still won't leave his room. He sho has missed you. Every day he tells me to be sure and let him know if I see you comin' down the road, but you surprised me. I was in the back, polishin' silver, and one of the youn-guns came runnin' from the yard to tell me."

"Polishing silver, eh? Has Clarice had a party while we were away?"

"No, but she's been plannin' to have one as soon as you get back. Now she'll have a big reason—to introduce your new bride to everybody."

Angele groaned inwardly at the thought. The last thing she wanted was a party before she pretended to quickly learn how to speak English. Otherwise, there would be more awkward moments than she cared to think about.

But her worries instantly faded as she began to turn around and around in the huge, circular foyer to look at the velvet-draped portraits of Tremayne ancestors. A crystal chandelier hung from the ceiling high above, and a curving stairway wrapped about the wall, which was covered in brilliant gold satin.

There was a parlor on one side, filled with furniture in brocade and cherrywood and mahogany. On the other, there was a huge ballroom. "You must really entertain a lot," she remarked.

"Yes, we enjoy it, and we have a lot of friends."

She already felt lost in the spaciousness of the house and asked how many rooms there were.

"As best I can recall without walking around counting, there are two dining rooms—one large for formal dinners, and then a small one for the family. Besides the ballroom, there are three parlors. This one"—he gestured to the one beside them—"and one that belonged to my mother, and one intended for any other Tremayne wife in the house—such as you."

Angele knew that meant Clarice had taken over his mother's parlor, but she didn't care. She didn't intend to spend her time sitting around in parlors, anyway.

"There's also a library, sewing room, sun porch, and a couple of rooms where food is put after it's brought in from the kitchen, which is outside. The family quarters are at each end of the second floor, and the third floor is for guests. Sometimes they travel a long way and spend the night after a party, and sometimes we invite people to stay the weekend, or longer.

"The fourth floor," he continued, "is where Willard and Mammy Lou and some of the household servants sleep so they'll be close by if they're needed during the night."

He walked toward the curving stairway and beckoned her to follow. "Now I'll take you up to meet my father."

"He's asleep, Mastah Ryan," Willard interjected. "I looked in on him a little while ago. He had a bad night, so I thought it'd be good for him to take a longer nap, but if you want me to, I'll go wake him up."

"No, no," Ryan said quickly. "Let him sleep, and when he rings for you, let me know. Meanwhile, I'll show Mrs. Tremayne around before I go out to meet the horses."

"You found the horses you went to fetch," Willard said. "I'm so glad."

"And they're beauties."

Angele continued to look from one to the other, pretending not to understand.

Ryan held out his hand to her, started into the ballroom, but paused to ask Willard, "Where is Clarice, by the way?"

"I'm right here."

Angele's gaze snapped to the stairway, along with Ryan's. Willard, she noted, went down the back hallway as fast as his rheumatism would allow.

Clarice Tremayne's frosty blue eyes were squinched at the corners, and her forehead was knit in a frown. She was dressed elegantly in a soft pink taffeta dress, the bodice edged in lace and the sleeves tapering to points at her wrists. Pearls and matching earbobs complemented the dress, and her hair was sleekly drawn from her face and held by a snood.

"Welcome home, Ryan," she said in perfectly enunciated French, all the while her gaze locked on Angele. "And who is your guest?"

"She's not a guest," Ryan said quietly. "She's my wife."

Clarice's hand lifted slightly from the gleaming mahogany banister, as though about to clutch her throat in horror. Instead, she managed to maintain her composure, and, cocking her head to one side, asked, "What did you say?"

Ryan clasped Angele's hand to pull her forward. "I want you to meet my wife, Angele Benet Tremayne. We met in Paris, and it didn't take long to realize we wanted to spend the rest of our lives together, so we were married on board the ship when we sailed from Le Havre."

Clarice stood perfectly still.

Ryan led Angele back across the foyer to wait for her to come down.

"I'm pleased to meet you, Clarice," Angele offered.

For a moment, she thought Clarice was going to turn around and go back up the stairs without a word. It was hard to tell what she was thinking by the stunned look on her face.

"I know it has to be a big shock for you and everybody else," Ryan said when the silence became awkward, "but Angele is going to make a fine wife, and I know the two of you will be good friends."

Angele cringed inside as Clarice suddenly continued on down the stairs.

"Yes," Clarice said with cool demeanor, mouth barely curved in a smile. "I'm sure we will." She placed her fingertips on Angele's shoulders in a stiff caress. "Welcome to our family, dear."

When she kissed her cheek, it was all Angele could do to keep from shivering, for her lips were as cold as her eyes.

Ryan looked pleased.

"You are French?" Clarice asked tonelessly.

Ryan answered for her. "Yes, she is. She comes from a wonderful family. Very prominent. Very wealthy. Good blood. Our children will carry the Tremayne lineage proudly."

Angele gritted her teeth to think how he sounded like he was talking about a brood mare.

He steered them into the parlor as he continued talking to Clarice. "I'm going to depend on you to teach her what she needs to know about plantation life, living in America . . . everything. I'm going to hire a tutor to teach her to speak English, but you can help with that, as well—"

Clarice froze. "You mean she can't speak English? But all well-bred European girls these days speak fluent English."

"Not all of them," Ryan defended.

Angele was having a very hard time listening to them talk about her as though she weren't even there, but, afraid she might say the wrong thing, kept out of it.

Clarice swept Angele with doubtful eyes. "And you say she comes from a prominent, wealthy family?"

Ryan slipped his arm around Angele's waist, and in a voice laced with tension, declared, "She satisfies everything I ever wanted in a wife."

Clarice gave a curt nod. "Very well. And you can rest assured I'll do everything I can to help her adjust to her new life."

Clarice went to a long, tasseled rope and gave it a yank. Within seconds, a round-faced and smiling Negro woman appeared in the doorway. She wore a plain gray muslin dress and had a bandanna tied around her head. As she stood expectantly with her hands folded across her round tummy, Angele smiled to think how she looked like a fat, happy apple.

"This is Mammy Lou," Ryan told Angele, then explained to Mammy Lou that Angele was his new wife.

For an instant, Angele thought she was going to run across the room and hug her like Willard had Ryan. Instead, her smile spread to a grin that displayed the whitest teeth Angele had ever seen.

She began talking to her, saying how glad she was to meet her and how she hoped she would be happy, but Clarice crisply informed her that Angele didn't understand what she was saying. "Now, bring us some lemonade. Ryan and his bride are probably thirsty after their ride."

Angele seized on the opportunity to add to the conversation. "Actually, it wasn't so long. I enjoyed it. The scenery was beautiful."

Clarice settled on a lavender divan and fluffed her skirt about her. "Tell me about yourself," she said bluntly.

Angele and Ryan took chairs side by side. "There's really nothing to tell," she began. "I was an only child. My parents doted on me and kept me home to be with them. I had tutors, but there wasn't one who knew English, and—"

Ryan cut in, "That doesn't matter. We're going to take care of that."

Clarice persisted with the inquisition that Angele had anticipated and dreaded. "And your father? Tell me about him. Where was his estate? Who were some of your people? I might have heard of them. I was in Paris a few years ago."

She hesitated, unsure of what to say, and couldn't help stealing another glance at Ryan, who once more came to her rescue.

"Angele is an orphan. She still grieves for her parents and doesn't like to talk about them."

"I see." Clarice pursed her lips.

Angele told herself it was only natural that Clarice would ask questions. Besides, it was good preparation for the encounter yet to come with Roussel Tremayne. Still, her first impression of Clarice was that she was not all pleased with the situation.

She was grateful when Ryan changed the subject. "I'll

be glad when Father wakes up. I'm anxious for him to
meet Angele."

Tonelessly, Clarice said, "Well, it's best to let him get his
rest. I like him to stay as quiet as possible. I just hope this
isn't too big a shock for him."

"He has to know," Ryan said with a shrug.

Mammy Lou brought the lemonade, but just then Willard came to say that Master Roussel was awake.

"I haven't told him about your bride, sir, but I did tell
him you're home. He said for you to come right up. I've
got him dressed and in his chair."

Ryan stood, grabbed Angele's hand, and pulled her with
him. "Let's go. I've got to hurry so I can get to the stables.
After you meet him, Clarice can show you to your room."

They were almost out the door when Clarice called,
"And where would that be, Ryan? Do you want Corbett
and me to move out of the north wing?"

He looked apologetic. "Actually, I think that would only
be proper. The north wing is meant for the next heir to
BelleRose, and I only gave it over to you and Corbett after
Danny was born so you'd have more room. Do you mind?"

She said she didn't, but Angele sensed that she actually
did and quickly protested, "No, don't ask them to move,
Ryan. Anywhere is fine with me. I don't need a whole wing."

Ryan squeezed her hand. "Don't worry. It's tradition,
and Clarice knows that as well as anybody. Now, let's go."

She looked over her shoulder, wanting to somehow con-
vey to Clarice how truly sorry she was, but she had busied
herself pouring lemonade.

Angele saw that her hands were trembling.

Roussel Tremayne sat in his favorite chair by the window.
From there he could see the south lawns with their intri-
cate patterns made by different shades of grass. He also
had a view of the road leading up to the house, and he
sat there as majestically as any king had ever surveyed a
kingdom.

He barked out a command to enter when Ryan knocked on the door. His lips parted in greeting, but then his eyes fell on Angele.

Ryan didn't give him a chance to ask who she was. He led her straight to him. "This is my wife. Her name is Angele."

Roussel stared her up and down.

His expression was impassive. Angele couldn't tell if he were shocked or angry, but she refused to glance away when his eyes boldly met hers as though in challenge. She even lifted her chin ever so slightly in the hope he could tell she was not afraid of him or anyone else . . . even though she felt as if she had swallowed butterflies and they were fluttering about in her stomach.

She wished Ryan would say something else, but he was obviously waiting for his father to make the next move. It was not long in coming.

"You're beautiful," Roussel said matter-of-factly. "I can see why my son married you. Are you French?"

"I was born in Paris," she lied.

"Are you educated?"

At last, Ryan interceded. "Not as much as I would like. Her parents loved her so much they wouldn't let her go away to school. But she's intelligent. She'll learn fast. And she has the necessary social graces."

Angele bit back a chuckle. Ryan was probably patting himself on the back for that, because he had coached her all the way across the Atlantic. Actually, it had been harder for her to pretend ignorance than learning had ever been.

Roussel leaned back in his chair, his hands gripping the arms as he continued to rake her with almost insolent eyes.

Angele still didn't glance away, for she was doing some perusing of her own. He had a stern face, and though his eyes were piercing, alert, there was a kindness in their rheumy blue depths. His hair was white but still thick. No baldness among the Tremayne men. He had wide shoulders like Ryan, though they were stooped with age. She could tell he had probably been quite handsome once, and even now he was appealing in a mature sort of way.

But she couldn't yet determine whether she would come to like Roussel Tremayne, for something told her he was a man who would not be easy to know.

"How did you meet?" he asked curtly, coldly.

Ryan started to speak, but Roussel waved him to silence. "Let her speak, goddamn it."

Without thinking of the consequences, Angele cried, "Sir, there is no need to be profane."

She heard Ryan's soft groan and saw how the old man's eyes narrowed. But she faced him, undaunted.

Suddenly he threw back his head and laughed, long and loud, then looked Ryan straight in the eye and said, "I like her. Hell, yes, I like her. She's got pepper in her blood, like Tremayne women are supposed to have. By damn"—he slapped his knee—"you can keep her . . . with my blessings."

And in that moment, as Angele saw the twinkle in his eye and basked in his genuine grin of welcome, her reservations faded and she knew that she would come to like this man a lot.

"Why do you even care if he got married?" Roscoe asked Corbett. "You knew he would sooner or later."

"Yes, you idiot," Corbett snapped, "but I'd planned for him to marry Clarice's cousin, remember? Then I wouldn't have anything to worry about."

"What makes you think you have to now? Ryan isn't going to let her take over and run you off once the old man is gone."

"Don't be so sure. She might get rid of you, too."

Roscoe's brows snapped together. "I sure as hell hope not. I make more money here than I could anywhere else. Besides that, I like my job."

"If it's up to me, you'll keep it, but the new Mrs. Tremayne might have other ideas. It just so happens that she's against slavery. If she had her way, they'd all be paid for their work and come and go as they please."

Roscoe stared at him incredulously. "You don't mean it."

"I *do* mean it. I've already had to warn her to keep her mouth shut."

Roscoe's frown deepened. "That could lead to trouble, but I don't know what you can do about it. After all, he loved her enough to marry her. All we can do is hope for the best. Maybe if you try to get along with her—"

"Don't be a ninny. Of course I get along with her. But as for Ryan loving her, that's a laugh."

Roscoe was looking even more perplexed. "I just don't understand any of this."

Corbett put an arm around his shoulders. "You will, my friend, after you hear what I have to tell you about *Ryan's bride.*"

Seventeen

"I can't stand her, I tell you. How could you have let this happen?"

Corbett watched Clarice stomp about the room. Two weeks had passed since he and Ryan had returned from France, and she was still ranting about Angele. "You were there. You could have stopped him. Do you realize what this means? When your uncle dies, we'll be homeless. That little tart will see to it Ryan kicks us out. Just you wait and see."

He scowled at the thought. "I've told you a hundred times, we're going to find a way to get rid of her. Ryan didn't marry her because he loved her, for heaven's sake, so it won't take much to make him see he made a mistake."

"Don't count on it. Have you seen how she fawns over him? It's sickening."

"She's just buttering him up because now that she's seen BelleRose, she's going to do everything she can to hang on to him."

Clarice whirled about and threw herself in a chair. She hated the rooms on the third floor. She was not a guest. She was matriarch of BelleRose and would fight tooth and nail to remain so. "I still can't believe he'd marry a common thief. There's no telling what she's capable of doing. I'm afraid to leave my good jewelry lying around, or anything else that might be valuable. She's liable to steal all she can and then run away."

"I'm afraid we won't be that lucky. But maybe I'll soon hear from that man I told you about—the one I hired in Paris to see what he could find out about her. Maybe he'll have something that will make Ryan want to run her off."

"I doubt that. If taking her out of prison didn't make any difference, nothing will."

"Stop being so dramatic," he snapped. "And stop nagging about it and try to get along with her."

"That"—she pointed a finger at him, cheeks blazing—"will never happen. I am not going to patronize her. And aren't you forgetting about Denise? She's my cousin, Corbett, and her heart is breaking because you weren't smart enough to stop *your* cousin from marrying a strumpet."

He gave a sarcastic snort. "The only thing that could ever bother Denise would be not finding a man to take to bed whenever she feels like it. And from what I hear, that hasn't been a problem so far."

Clarice was aghast. "How dare you say such a thing?"

"It's true, and you know it. I'm surprised Ryan never found out."

"We have to get them back together."

"I know, but we've also got to be careful. If he gets suspicious, he won't believe anything we say against Angele."

"I still say you shouldn't have let him marry her in the first place."

"When have you ever known him to listen to me?" Corbett challenged. "The only reason I get along with him, anyway, is because I'm always buttering him up, and I'm tired of that, too. I'm also sick of having to ask for money when I want something. Hell, the artisans are treated better than I am. They do get paid a little for their work, but that's only one step above slavery."

Clarice laughed. "Now who's being dramatic?"

Ignoring her, he mused out loud, "I wonder how it would be if we both tried to get along with her? If she wound up liking us, she'd let us stay when the old man is gone."

Clarice was quick to nip that notion in the bud. "Don't you dare start thinking that way, Corbett. There's only one woman who's going to run this house, and that's me. Denise agreed with it, too. She said she had no interest in taking over my duties, but I thrive on them, and you know it."

"Yes, yes, I know." He waved a hand in front of his face, wishing he could wave her out of his sight. He was worn out from her constant harangue over Angele. "But I think we should concentrate on figuring out a solution to the problem instead of whining about it, and—"

There was a knock on the door, and a soft, hesitant voice called, "Miz Clarice? It's me—Mammy Lou. I have something to tell you."

Clarice walked to the door and yanked it open. "Well, what is it? You know I don't like to be disturbed when I'm resting."

Lou bowed her head contritely. "Yes'm. I know that. But you also told me to let you know if Miz Angele got to messin' around in your tea kitchen."

Clarice frowned. The tea kitchen was where light refreshments were prepared for her drop-in guests or when Uncle Roussel wanted an afternoon snack. Special fine china had been imported from England, crystal from Ireland, and a silver coffee service from Spain. Everything was kept polished and gleaming. Even the linens were rare, brought from Belgium and starched and pressed to perfection. It was not a room where she wanted someone of questionable background to be.

"So? What is she doing there?" Clarice asked waspishly.

"She said Mastah Roussel invited her to have tea with him this afternoon, and she wanted to fix it herself.

"They sure are gettin' along good." Mammy Lou smiled, but the smile instantly faded when she saw the look on her mistress's face.

Clarice didn't like how Roussel had taken a fancy to Angele. He even wanted a ball held in her honor as soon as the arrangements could be made.

"She's been spending a lot of time with him, hasn't she?" Corbett remarked.

Clarice ignored him, because a plan was starting to take

shape. Tapping her chin with her forefinger, she walked to the window to stare out at nothing in particular as she asked her, "Has she already finished?"

"No, ma'am. She got the tea to brewin' and went to the kitchen out back to wait for the cookies I was makin' to get done. They're takin' a long time, though. I can't get the oven hot enough 'cause there ain't no firewood. All the menfolk have been called to the fields 'cause the cotton is ripenin' so early. There ain't nobody to chop wood."

Corbett bounded to his feet as he said to Clarice, "I'll go tell Roscoe to see that it's taken care of."

Clarice raised a hand. "Stay where you are."

He sat back down.

She turned to Mammy Lou. "I've just decided I want some fried apple pies for dessert tonight, with fresh whipped cream. You'll need to go to the root cellar to get some dried apples. Forget about Miss Angele for the time being."

Mammy Lou knew not to question orders given, no matter how odd they might seem, and she hurried to obey.

When she was gone, Corbett demanded, "Just what the hell are you up to?"

"I'm going to teach Angele a lesson about meddling in my tea kitchen, and I'm also going to show Ryan what a nuisance she is."

"Good. Just be careful. I think the old man really does like her. I heard her reading to him last night before he went to sleep."

"If my plan works, that was the last time she does it, because he won't want anything to do with her. And I'm going to see to it she stays busy from now on, anyway. Until now I've tried to avoid her, because I don't want anything to do with her, but that has to change. I intend to make her as miserable as possible so when Ryan finally does come to his senses, she'll be glad to leave."

She left him and hurried downstairs.

The tea Angele had made was brewed to perfection. Clarice could tell by the aroma.

There was a certain cabinet in the little tea kitchen where special herbs and spices were kept, some specifically to treat Roussel's various ailments. The jars were all similar to the ones used to store tea leaves. Anyone not familiar with the contents of the cabinet—*anyone meddling where they shouldn't be*—could easily pick up the wrong bottle.

She took down a jar of chopped pigeonberry leaves and put them in the teapot. In the past, Dr. Pardee had prescribed a special pigeonberry brew for Roussel to drink when he was constipated, emphasizing the exact amount to be used so as not to cause severe diarrhea.

She used three times that amount.

To keep the berries from being tasted, Clarice also added a bit of honey to sweeten the brew.

After a few moments, she scooped out the leaves. Then, hearing someone coming up the back porch steps, she slipped out of the tea kitchen, unseen.

Angele carried the tray to Uncle Roussel's room.

He had told her to just call him Roussel, but she didn't think that was proper. Worse would be to call him *Father*—something she resisted out of respect for the memory of her own. So he had finally told her to just address him as Uncle, like Corbett and Clarice did, and that suited her fine.

He was sitting in his favorite place by the window, and she put the tray on the table beside him. "I'm sorry it took so long, but I'm afraid they're having trouble with the oven. Something about not enough firewood because all the men are picking cotton."

He grunted. "When I was able, we got the damn cotton picked and kept plenty of firewood, to boot. The trouble is, Corbett doesn't know what he's doing. He leaves everything to Roscoe, and Roscoe's interested in one thing—the crops. It doesn't make a tinker's damn to him if there's firewood for the kitchen stove or not.

"And I can't depend on Ryan," he raged on as he took

the cup of tea Angele handed him, "because all he cares about is his horses. It's even worse since he brought back those Anglo-Arabs."

Silently, sadly, she agreed with him. Ryan hadn't even come in to supper the night before, and it was so late when he finally came to bed he hadn't reached for her—the first time since they were married. And that bothered her, because if he ceased to want her, and she didn't get pregnant, there was no telling what might happen. He might ask her to leave, and in just the short time she had been at BelleRose she had come to love it and wanted to stay.

And she had also stopped fighting the reality that she was, helplessly, falling in love with her husband. She found herself living for the moments when he kissed her and only wished she could return his bold caresses. But she held back, afraid to touch him in the way she longed to.

"One of these days," Roussel said around a cookie, "I'm going to get out of this goddamn room and go out in the yard, and—"

Angele had sat in a chair nearby but leaped to her feet. There were times when she used curse words herself, but never, ever, was she profane. Her father had always said that was the epitome of blasphemy. "Uncle Roussel, I've told you I won't stand for that kind of talk in my presence, so if you'll excuse me—"

He waved the cookie in the air, showering the floor with crumbs. "No, I won't excuse *you,* but you excuse *me.* All right? I forget sometimes how it offends you."

She sat back down. "And I will continue to remind you."

The tea was warm, and Roussel had been thirsty and had gulped down a whole cup at once. He held it out for a refill before Angele had a chance to pour her own. "I hate these damn tiny cups Clarice insists on using. They aren't for men. They're for little old ladies with bony fingers. I've got my own cups somewhere in this infernal house. Mammy Lou will know where they are. I'd appreciate it if you'd get me one so you can pour me more than a swallow.

"It's good tea, too," he complimented. "Real sweet, just like I like it. Much better than what Clarice makes."

Angele was glad to oblige, but before she had even left the room, he was already pouring more tea into his tiny cup.

She liked the peppery old man and had decided the reason he cursed was to sound tough and in control of his dominion. But despite that, she enjoyed being around him. He didn't ask questions about her past. He accepted the fact she was French and contented himself with proudly telling her about his ancestors. He was a good storyteller, too, animated and interesting. She much preferred to be with him than Clarice, and with Ryan not around all day, she escaped to Uncle Roussel's room whenever she could.

"So you're the one who's been meddling in my tea kitchen."

Clarice was standing by the door, hands on her hips, face pinched with anger.

Angele wondered why she was so upset. "I'm sorry, but Uncle Roussel asked me to make his tea. I thought it would be all right."

"All right?" Clarice swept her with a glare of contempt. "How dare you barge in here and try to take over? No one comes into my tea kitchen unless I say so. Do you understand me?"

Angele backed away. "I didn't hurt anything."

"That's not the point. Now, what are you doing back? What do you want this time?"

"I was looking for Mammy Lou so she could tell me where to find Uncle Roussel's favorite cups. He says the one he has is too small." She hated having caused trouble, but, dear Lord, she hadn't known. And Clarice was making too much of it, anyway, but she didn't dare say so. The last thing she wanted was confrontation.

"Well, that's what you get for trying to take over. Mammy Lou knows to take him the large cups and so do I."

"But I meant no harm. I just wanted to do something nice for him."

She watched as Clarice's lips twisted in a sardonic smile. "Well, you *did* do harm. You've probably made him sick, because you stupidly put pigeonberry tea in the pot, and if he drinks too much, it will make him deathly ill." She picked up the jar from the counter and shook it at her. "I found this next to the teapot. It's what you used. Now get up there and stop him from drinking any more. I'm going to send for Doctor Pardee."

"Dear God." Angele turned around and ran down the hall and up the stairs, skipping steps, lifting her skirt above her ankles.

She charged into the room only to stop and gasp to see Uncle Roussel doubled over in his chair. His hands clutched his stomach as he lifted anguished eyes to her and moaned, "I'm sick . . . so sick. Get Willard . . . quick . . ."

Willard bounded into the room right behind her, having been summoned by Clarice. Believing Angele didn't understand English, he grabbed her arm and steered her toward the door as he said to Roussel, "I'll take care of you, mastah. Don't worry. The mistress, she already sent for the doctor."

When he turned away, Angele raced back across the room to snatch up the teapot, lift the lid, and look inside.

It was empty.

He had drunk it all.

With heavy heart, she then allowed Willard to escort her out once again.

Dr. Pardee walked into the parlor. He was carrying his worn leather bag and set it on a table just inside the door, then opened it and began rummaging inside.

Ryan had been sitting in a chair next to the marble fireplace but quickly rose. "How is he?"

"He's going to be all right, but he's got a bad case of diarrhea, thanks to that infernal poisoned tea."

"I can't believe she did something so stupid," Clarice

wailed. She was dabbing at her eyes with a handkerchief. It was a hot, sultry evening, and a little Negro girl stood over her, solemnly waving a palm leaf fan to cool her.

Angele hung back in a far corner, embarrassed and feeling terrible.

Dr. Pardee took out a bottle containing a white liquid. "Give him two tablespoons in a big glass of water every two hours till his stomach settles down."

Ryan was worried. "This could be serious if he doesn't get over it right away. We all know he's not in good health."

Dr. Pardee patted his shoulder. "Your father is a very strong-willed man. I've always told him he wouldn't die till he was ready, and, believe me, he's not ready. And you don't have to trust my word . . ." He winked. "I think Parson Barnes would agree with me."

Angele saw the tense muscles in Ryan's face relax. If the doctor could make jokes, then it had to mean his father really was going to be all right. She, however, was having a difficult time trying to pretend she didn't understand a word that was being said.

Clarice half rose, then fell back against Corbett as though the effort was too great. "Doctor, I beg you not to say anything to anyone about this. It wasn't intentional by any means. Angele didn't try to murder Uncle Roussel, and—"

"Clarice, no one even remotely thought she did." The words flew out of Ryan's mouth on the crest of a horrified gasp. "There's no need to say something like that to Doctor Pardee. He knows it was an accident. Angele didn't know what she was doing and made a mistake, that's all."

Doctor Pardee agreed. "Yes, it was a mistake, and we all make them, so there's no need to dwell on it. And you don't have to worry. I'm not one to carry tales, and you all know it. But if I did, there'd be a lot of nervous folks around Richmond." He rolled his eyes, evoking a smile from only Ryan, as Clarice and Corbett were grim-faced.

Angele bit down on her lip to keep from smiling, too— the first time she'd felt like it since the nightmare began.

Dr. Pardee snapped his bag shut with a sigh. "But Ryan,

you do need to tell your wife to be careful with pigeon-berries. A stronger brew would likely have killed him."

Clarice threw an angry look at Angele. "Don't worry. It won't happen again. That was the first time she used my tea kitchen, and it will be the last."

Ryan waited until Willard had shown Dr. Pardee out before informing Clarice in no uncertain terms, "No, it won't be the last time. You're going to do as I asked you when we first got home—show Angele around so she won't make mistakes. I want her to learn about the tea kitchen, and all the herbs, spices, and medicines at BelleRose."

Clarice had gone pale, stunned that he was speaking to her so sharply.

Corbett was staring up at the ceiling with tight lips and stormy eyes.

Ryan continued in a gentler tone. "I know you've been in charge here for a long time, Clarice, and I'm sure if Angele understood what we were talking about, she'd agree with me when I say that she has no desire to take anything from you. But I do want her to have her rightful place as my wife, and she can't do that till she understands how things are around here."

Angele felt like running across the room and throwing her arms around him for taking up for her but had to continue her pretense.

She also wished she could tell him that she couldn't have made a mistake when she brewed the tea. She knew about such things. Miss Appleton had made sure all her girls could make delicious tea and serve it with grace and charm. She was also aware of the need to sniff the leaves used for freshness. She had done so, and the aroma had been quite different from that in the pot when she had checked it after Uncle Roussel had emptied it. And she intended to say as much when the time was right, but, for the moment, she was savoring how Ryan was defending her.

But at his next words she winced . . . and hoped no one noticed.

"Beginning tomorrow, she's to spend all her time with

you. It's nice that she reads to my father, but I think he'd agree it's more important for her to learn about the workings of the household."

He started for the door, shoulders drooped with weariness. "Now I've got to get back to the stable and check on the mare that's due to foal before long. She doesn't act right, and I'm worried about her."

Angele seized the chance to pretend to be concerned that he was leaving and asked, in French, of course, "Aren't you going to have supper?"

"No. I'll eat something later. Don't wait up for me."

She bit back disappointment.

It would be the second night he hadn't made love to her.

He continued walking out of the room, but Clarice's words made him spin around.

"I thought you said you were going to hire a tutor. You can't expect me to take time out from my responsibilities to teach your wife what she should have known when you married her. And don't forget Uncle Roussel insists on having a party for her, and I have a lot of planning to do for that."

"I'm going into Richmond in a couple of days," he said. "I have some business to take care of, and I'll try to find one while I'm there. Till then you can surely find time to help her, all right?"

Clarice said nothing more, and the moment the door closed behind Ryan she turned on Angele with a vengeance and said in French, "You'll do as I say and not give me a moment's worry or you'll be sorry."

Angele was stunned. "I don't intend to, Clarice. I've told you—I'd like for us to be friends."

"Hmph," Clarice snorted. "You think I want to be friends with a murderer?"

Corbett spoke for the first time. "Now, Clarice, there's no need for that. It was a mistake."

"But not one that *I* made," Angele was quick to declare. "I know how to make tea. I didn't put pigeonberry leaves in the pot. I don't know how they got there, but it was not by my doing."

Corbett put his hand on Clarice's arm. "Maybe they were already in there," he gently said. "Maybe the pot hadn't been washed properly. Sometimes Mammy Lou and the other servants get lazy and don't clean as well as they should. You need to say something to all of them about it.

"Now then . . ." He patted his knees, smiled, and stood. "Let's go in and have supper, shall we? Uncle Roussel is going to be all right, so no real harm was done."

Clarice gaped at him. "I remember when I had diarrhea last winter and thought I was going to die. I *wanted* to die. When I think of how that poor man is suffering all because she didn't know what she was doing, it makes me so angry."

Corbett gave her a warning look but kept the smile plastered on his face. "We've discussed this enough. Now, let's forget it and have a pleasant supper."

"If you'll excuse me, I'm not hungry." Angele headed for the stairs.

"You leave Uncle Roussel alone," Clarice called after her. "He needs his rest."

As soon as she could no longer hear them, Corbett shooed the little girl with the fan out of the room, then furiously turned on Clarice. "Are you crazy? You don't want to alienate her."

"I know what I'm doing."

"Then would you mind telling me?"

"It's quite simple. While we were waiting for Doctor Pardee to come down, I thought of how we should handle the situation." She looked quite proud of herself. "When Ryan is around, I'll be very exasperated as I tell him how I'm trying my best to help her but that she won't cooperate. On the surface, it will seem I'm opening my heart to her, but when we're alone, I don't intend to walk on eggs. I'll make her feel so stupid and useless she'll be ready to swim all the way back to France."

Corbett shook his head. "I've told you before—she's going to hang on like a tick on a hound's ear. She came from a sewer and now she's living like a queen. She isn't going to surrender lightly, my dear. But I know we have to try everything, so you go ahead and do whatever you think will work, and I'll do the same."

She gave him a hug—something she rarely did. "Good. Now, let's go eat."

He caught her wrist. "Do you think it worked?"

Her hand fluttered to her throat and she batted her eyelashes with all innocence. "Whatever are you talking about? You don't think I'd poison his tea, do you?"

He snickered. "I damn well do. I've been expecting you to poison mine for years."

"And one day I might." She tweaked his nose playfully. "I think everything went well. I knew just how much to use to make him good and sick without doing any real harm. It was a wonderful success, too, because now Ryan sees how clumsy Angele can be."

"But he was taking up for her—"

"Only because he felt he had to," Clarice pointed out. "After all, he doesn't want it to appear he made a poor choice in a wife."

Corbett nodded. "That makes sense."

Smugly, she added, "My plan was doubly successful, because now Roussel won't think so highly of his daughter-in-law. As miserable as he's feeling, he won't ever want her to come near him again."

"My dear"—he kissed her cheek—"you are a genius."

"I know," she murmured smugly. "So just leave everything to me."

The north wing consisted of two large bedrooms separated by a parlor. So far, Angele had shared Ryan's bed, but this night she headed for the room on the other side.

Selma, in the process of turning back the covers of the bed, glanced up and saw her. "Wait, missy!" she cried. "I'll fix the bed over there for you if that's where you're gonna sleep tonight." Then she caught herself. Her mistress didn't understand what she was saying, so she hurried to show her what she meant.

Brushing by her, she proceeded to draw back the thick satin coverlet. It was a beautiful bed, Selma's favorite in the whole house. It had a lace canopy overhead, and the matching skirt below the mattress hung all the way to the floor.

Actually, the whole room was Selma's favorite. Pale apricot brocade draperies covered the floor-to-ceiling glass doors that opened to the front balcony. Flowered satin in a deeper shade of apricot covered a pair of matching sofas, and a white marble fireplace was flanked by chairs upholstered in cut velvet.

Selma had got in the habit of speaking her thoughts aloud in front of Angele since it made no difference. "You know, I never did understand why you and Master Ryan didn't take this bed. It's lots softer than that one over yonder with the horsehair mattress. This one's got real goose down. I know 'cause I helped pluck the geese that made it. It's somethin' Miss Clarice wanted, and what she wants, she generally gets."

Angele went to the French doors and drew them open, lifting her face to the welcome breeze. Lightning lit up the darkening sky, and thunder rumbled in the distance.

Selma rambled on. "Miss Clarice was plenty riled when she had to give up these rooms, but that probably ain't nothin' compared to how mad she is over you poisonin' Master Roussel. Mammy Lou said she didn't see how it could be an accident, 'cause the jar with the pigeonberry tea was way up on the shelf in the back of the cabinet. You'd have had to be lookin' for 'em."

She folded the satin coverlet on a special mahogany rack in the corner, then began plumping the pillows. "Now if it was Miss Clarice you wanted to poison, I can't say as I'd blame you 'cause there's been times I wanted to do it, myself. But Master Roussel, now he's a good man. He's cranky as an ol' settin' hen, but he's always been good to me and my people. That's why nobody can understand why you wanted to do away with him."

"I didn't."

Angele turned from the balcony to face Selma.

"And I don't think it was an accident, either, Selma. I think it was done on purpose, and I think Clarice was the one responsible."

Selma dropped the pillow she had been holding and gave a little cry.

Angele had spoken to her in English.

Eighteen

It was the day after Angele had revealed her secret to Selma.

They were on the banks of a rushing creek, where blackberries grew profusely. Angele was supposed to be getting ready to join Clarice and some of her lady friends for tea. But Selma had told her Willard wanted her to gather some blackberry root so Mammy Lou could mix up her own remedy for Master Roussel that she said would work better than the medicine Dr. Pardee had given him. Angele had wanted to go along. It was a wonderful day, with heavy melting clouds in a field of sky, and she didn't want to be indoors. She might be late for tea, but so what? She had been with Clarice all morning, and all Clarice did was find fault with her. What was one more thing for her to fuss about?

Selma, stooping to yank at a root, shook her head. "I swear, Miz Angele," she said, "I just can't get over you bein' able to talk to everybody but not letting nobody know it."

Angele dipped a handful of berries in the cool water to rinse them. "I probably shouldn't have let you know, either, Selma, but as I explained last night—I just couldn't keep still another minute about that tea. But remember, you promised not to tell a soul. Not even Toby." She popped the berries in her mouth and wondered how long it had been since she had delighted in the fresh-picked taste.

"Yes, ma'am, I did, and I won't, but if you let Miz Clarice know, she'd have to quit callin' you stupid."

"I don't care, and when the time is right, I will let her know, but I have my own reasons for wanting to keep it a secret for the time being."

"Well, I want you to know that I like you fine, and I wish you'd go ahead and take over the house. I'd much rather work for you than Miz Clarice." She made a face. "Nobody likes her."

"Selma, I don't think I want to listen to you talk against her. It isn't proper."

Selma ducked her head. "Yes, ma'am. I'm sorry."

Angele could tell she had hurt the woman's feelings, but there had to be propriety. She didn't like Clarice, either, but it wasn't something to be discussed with the servants. She had been taught that the less they knew about the family they served, the better.

To get her mind on something else, she asked again about Roussel. "Willard *did* say he's much better this morning?"

"Yes, ma'am, but he was up most of the night. Kept Willard up, too, of course."

"Did Willard say he was angry with me?"

"If he did, Willard didn't tell me."

Her apron filled with blackberry roots, Selma straightened with a weary sigh. "I reckon I've got enough." Squinting, she looked up at the sun to see how late in the day it was. "We'd best be gettin' back," she decided. "I'd say Miz Clarice's guests ought to be arrivin' right about now."

Angele longed to send Selma on her way, then stretch out on the creek bank, her face to the sky, and dream away the afternoon. But though she might be excused for tardiness, Clarice would have fits if she didn't make an appearance at all.

"Oh, Lordy, Miz Angele, look at your hands and arms."

They were stained with purple-pink blackberry juice, and she went to the creek and dipped them, then rubbed her hands together, but the color barely faded. "It won't come off."

"You're gonna have to scrub with lye soap. You got it all over your face, too," she giggled.

Angele laughed and threw up her hands. "I don't care. This has been the most fun I've had since I got here, and I hope to do it again."

They had reached the blackberry patch by way of a path from the house, but Selma said she knew a shortcut. "We can cross by where I live."

The slave cabins were made of brick and close together in long, twin lines. Each had a window on each side of the front door with a small, flat-roofed porch across the front. Stones were stacked neatly to make steps.

Wide-eyed children stared as Selma and Angele passed. Some of them were naked, and all played in the dirt with toys that looked to have been whittled or carved from sticks or wood.

An elderly, plump-faced woman nodded obediently, and Selma said, "That's Rosa. She tends the young'uns while the women work in the fields. She's too old to get out there and bend her back in the sun. We got a few other old folks, but they help out in other places where it ain't as hot."

"Doing what?" Angele found herself wanting to learn more about how the servants lived and worked.

"They help the artisans." She made it sound like *ar-tee-zuns*. "Makin' bricks, pots, and plates, weavin' cloth, things like that. Some sit in the root cellar puttin' up onions and potatoes for the winter. Everybody stays busy."

Angele smelled something delicious cooking and asked what it was.

"Catfish." Selma licked her lips. "That's somethin' else Rosa does. She tends the cookin' pot durin' the day. That's so's when the women come in, it won't take 'em long to get supper for their menfolk and young'uns. Tonight it's catfish stew, and all the women have to do is get their own pots and have Rosa give 'em their share, then stir up some dumplings and drop 'em in."

"What else do you have to eat?"

"We'll fry some corn pone, and if the kitchen workers had time to bake, there might be a few pies to share."

"Then I suppose everyone goes to bed as soon as it gets dark, because they're so tired."

"No, ma'am. We all like to have some fun. It makes the time we're workin' a whole lot easier, so ol' Barney, he'll play his banjo, and Jed'll bring out his fiddle. The young'uns will dance, and the old folks will sing and clap their hands and stomp their feet, and then after a while we'll turn in."

Angele had sometimes heard music wafting through the French doors of the bedroom during the night and knew it had to come from the servants. It was surprising that they could even attempt to enjoy themselves amidst their woeful lot in life but was glad they did.

"It sounds like fun," she said wistfully. "I wish I could join you sometimes."

Selma laughed nervously. "You could never come down here."

"Why not?"

"It wouldn't be proper."

"I get lonely sometimes, especially after supper. Mr. Tremayne goes back to the stables or for an evening ride, and that's when Clarice spends time with little Danny." *Not that I want to be with her, anyway,* she thought.

Selma couldn't help sneering. "That's the only time she spends with that little boy. She can't stand *young'un noises* as she calls 'em, so she has Ruby—that's Master Danny's mammy—keep him quiet all day and away from around her. But just before his bedtime, she'll read him a story and tuck him in bed."

Angele knew that and thought it very sad. She could count on one hand the number of times she had seen little Danny since coming to BelleRose, and he was adorable. When she had children, she intended to care for them herself, regardless of tradition or what anyone thought.

"You still ought not come down here," Selma said with a worried glance. "That'd make all the white folks mad."

There was a thick row of shrubs bordering the cabins. Beyond that was a wooded area.

Selma turned. "We'll go this way."

Angele saw a path curving around the woods that went toward the barns and chicken pens. She had been there out of curiosity and knew it was off to the side and would take much longer to go that way. "It's closer to keep going straight."

"We can't. That's where Mr. Fordham lives, and he don't allow slaves to go in there unless he sends for 'em."

Angele lifted her chin. "Well, I'm not a slave, and I'm in a hurry, so come along. He won't say anything to you if I'm with you."

She started walking, but Selma leaped in front of her to plead, "Oh, missy, I wish you wouldn't. Come on with me. It won't take long to go the other way."

Angele saw that she looked absolutely terrified. "Selma, what is wrong with you? What are you afraid of?"

"Nothin'. Just come on with me."

"He's not going to hurt either one of us."

Selma shook her head wildly. "I just can't. You go on if you want to, but I can't."

The woods were thick with vines and undergrowth, the sun shielded by leafy oaks. It reminded Angele of every haunted forest she'd ever read about in fairy tales and decided to follow Selma instead.

But she still wondered why the girl was so scared. Slaves were not to be mistreated at BelleRose. Ryan had told her it was an unbreakable rule. So what was there to fear besides a harsh scolding?

As the house came into view, Selma pointed and said, "Look. I can see some carriages in front. Miz Clarice's tea done started. You'd better hurry. I'll take these roots to Mammy Lou, and then I'll be right on up to help you with your bath. We've gotta get them juice stains off of you. I'll fetch some lye soap."

Entering through the back door, Angele turned toward the rear stairs which the servants used. If she could make it to her room without being seen, Clarice would never know she'd been outdoors picking berries with Selma and think instead she had been out walking and lost track of time.

But luck was not with her.

Clarice was standing outside the double mahogany doors that led to the north wing.

"In heaven's name, where have you been? All my guests are here, and they're waiting to meet you. And what is that horrid purple stain you have all over your hands and face? You look dreadful." She threw up her hands. "What am I going to do with you?"

Angele carefully stepped around her. "It's berry juice, and it will wash off. I'm sorry I'm late. I'll hurry and be right down. Please offer my apologies."

Clarice started after her. "Berry picking? What do you mean? You have no business out in the fields. My Lord, hurry up and bathe. I'll make excuses for you."

Angele wondered if she was ever going to do anything right. When Clarice told Ryan—as she surely would do—he wouldn't take up for her this time. She had sneaked away from the house, and he'd be angry about that, for sure.

Selma came with a string of servants behind her, each carrying a bucket of hot water.

Selma scrubbed her with the lye soap and managed to get the stains off, then slathered her with fragrant toilet water. But it seemed to take forever, and Angele feared the ladies would leave before she got downstairs, and that would make Clarice all the more angry with her.

While Selma had scrubbed, Angele silently lectured herself to try harder to get along with Clarice, even if she was mean and nasty when no one else was around.

She brushed her hair out smoothly and let it hang down her back. There was no time to do anything else.

Hurriedly, she took out the first gown she got her hands on. It was a sheer, straight-line drape, caught to her figure only by a narrow high-waisted girdle that supported her breasts. It was cut low and the skirt was slashed to several inches above the thigh. The fabric was a thin silk in a soft melon color, and the only undergarment accompanying the gown was a cotton slip.

The French stylist had insisted it was the latest fashion and predicted the rest of the world would, too, just as soon as windblown ships could carry the new designs across the ocean. Angele wasn't so sure. It seemed a bit more sophisticated than the garments the ladies in Virginia wore, but there was no time to worry about it now. She stepped in matching slippers and rushed out.

She could hear voices coming from the parlor and felt relief that the ladies hadn't yet left. There was still time to make amends. Clarice had already told her none of them spoke French but that she would interpret.

"There you are," Clarice said with an irritable frown when Angele appeared in the doorway.

The ladies raised their brows in unison as their eyes flicked over Angele's gown. She knew then, beyond all doubt, that it really was too sophisticated.

Clarice, blinking against her own reaction of disapproval, coolly said to no one in particular, "This is Ryan's bride, Angele. Smile and nod and make polite noises, but she won't know what you're saying."

They were introduced in turn, and Angele decided they seemed nice enough.

Servants were passing silver trays of sugar cookies, spice cakes, hot tea, and cold lemonade.

Despite the large size of the parlor, Angele found it was charmingly informal and inviting. Three Palladian-style French doors were open to the side terrace, and the air was laced with the delicate fragrance of mimosa and lavender.

Angele politely sat with the ladies and sipped her tea and munched a few cookies while they talked of mundane things that would not have interested her even if she had been able to join in. They gossiped about other women, the stale-as-day-old-bread sermons, as they called them, of Pastor Barnes. They also complained about lazy slaves who had to be watched every minute to make them get their work done.

"Mary Etta, did they ever find those two runaways from your place?" someone asked.

Angele concentrated on picking cookie crumbs off her skirt while carefully listening to the woman bemoan the fact that the two Negroes had disappeared. She said her husband, along with some of the other planters, were suspicious that an underground movement was going on, and they were keeping a closer watch on their slaves in case they thought about running away, too.

"We don't have to worry about that at BelleRose," Clarice said airily, lifting her little finger as she sipped her tea. "Our slaves are so well treated we'd have to run them off."

The ladies shared a laugh, and a few teased Clarice that she might be overconfident.

Afraid her annoyance and boredom might show, Angele quietly drifted out the open doors and onto the terrace.

"Oh, dear, she's leaving," one of the women said. "I guess we weren't very polite."

"Don't worry about it" came Clarice's snickering response. "It's like being around a deaf mute if you can't speak French. Ryan is going to hire a tutor for her when he goes into Richmond in a few days."

"Do you think she can learn enough to carry on a small conversation, at least, by the time you have the ball?" someone else asked.

"I hope so. It's so awkward."

Another woman giggled, "Well, Denise speaks French, and I imagine she's got a lot she'd like to say to her—although I doubt Angele would want to hear it."

Hearing Denise's name, Angele's interest was piqued.

Then came a different voice to say, "Well, from what I hear, everyone thinks Ryan only married her because Denise turned him down. I'll wager he still loves her."

"Of course he does," Clarice agreed, as though stricken that anyone could possibly think otherwise. "He worships her, and, yes, I do think he married impulsively. Men do that sometimes when they've been hurt, and, according to Corbett, Ryan was truly crushed. He was positively sick all the way to France, and when he got there, he lost his head. But"—she gave an exaggerated sigh—"it's too late now. What's done is done. We have to respect the sanctity of marriage. I just hope Angele can make him happy. I adore Ryan, you know. He's like the brother I never had."

Angele was glad her back was turned, because never would she have been able to hide the devastation that was surely mirrored on her face.

Ryan loved Denise.

He had asked her to marry him.

And she had refused.

So he had married *her* instead.

Impulsively.

Foolishly.

And probably wished a hundred times over that he hadn't.

Her arms were folded, nails digging into her elbows. Her knees were trembling, and she managed to make it to a nearby chair and lower herself into it lest her legs give way.

Such a silly fool she was to have let herself fall in love with a man who had only married her to keep from losing his inheritance . . . a man who loved another woman and always would.

Then, slowly, from deep within, the spirit that had once made her want to seize all life had to offer and be willing to face any obstacle to make her dreams come true suddenly began to surface.

Fate had hammered her into the ground, but she had managed to survive and would, by God, continue to do so. As long as Ryan wanted her, she would stay at BelleRose, but if she ever felt that she was a burden, that he honestly and truly regretted having married her, then she would go.

Until then, she was going to fight tooth and nail for what was rightfully hers . . . even if he did love another.

And so what, she asked herself with fiery determination, if he *had* married her because Denise refused him? Had he not chosen her, then it would have been some other woman. Certainly there was no cause to worry or stew over that. Angele knew what she had to concentrate on was making him ultimately glad she was his wife.

And she would start this very night.

She was naked.

She was also in Ryan's bed.

And if Miss Appleton could know, she would probably scream and fall into a dead faint.

It was quite late. Ryan had rushed through supper, then gone back to the stables. He was leaving for Richmond early in the morning and would be gone for two days, so there was a lot he had to take care of.

She was far too nervous to sleep. She lay there staring at the silver webs the glow of a full moon had spun across the ceiling. She had left the French doors open, wanting the hallowed light to creep inside, and also to smell the fragrance of the jasmine twining about the porch railing.

She didn't have to worry about a manservant hovering about waiting for Ryan to come in, because he refused to have one help him dress and undress as Corbett did. Angele smiled to think how Selma had told her he thought it was silly and that he also liked his privacy.

So far, she hadn't regretted letting Selma know they could understand each other. Selma was a talkative sort and liked to gossip, so she had learned a lot in only a short while, most of it quite interesting.

She knew that Corbett and Clarice fought a lot, and that Clarice had sworn she would never have another baby, because having little Danny had hurt so much.

She also knew that Clarice drank more wine and brandy than she wanted people to know about, and that she made Selma sneak the empty bottles out of the house.

And she had also found out, thanks to Selma, that Roussel Tremayne enjoyed music and had been known to visit the

slave cabins once in a while and pick a little banjo himself.
He was a good man, and all the Negroes loved him.

"He never sells a family," Selma had told her. "Once a
man and woman jump the broom, he never lets 'em be
separated."

Jumping the broom, Angele learned, occurred when, after
the ceremony, someone held a broom a few inches off the
floor, then, holding hands, the newlyweds hopped over it
to seal their marriage.

"Actually, he hasn't sold anybody in years," Selma had
explained. And, proudly, she had recited how she knew
America had banned slave trading from Africa and the
West Indies ten years earlier, so Master Roussel had kept
the ones he had, decided to pay the artisans small wages,
and said he regarded all his slaves as part of his family and
would not have them broken up.

"A good man," Selma repeated several times. "A fine,
God-fearin' man. And it scares us to think what'll happen
when he dies, 'cause Mastah Ryan, he's always left things
to Mastah Corbett, and . . ."

She had stopped talking at that point, a fearful gleam
taking hold of her eyes, and no amount of prodding by
Angele could entice her to continue.

The sound of a door opening and closing snapped her
back to the present.

It was Ryan.

He came in from the parlor, and she saw in the moonlight that he had already stripped off his shirt and was
working on his belt buckle.

He yawned, and she knew he would not have crossed to
her room this night, but she was leaving him little choice
now.

He liked to sleep naked, and she liked to look at him
when he did without letting him know it. And she could
watch him now, as well, because he was not yet aware of
her presence.

She held her breath against a heavy sigh to think what
a glorious body he had. His buttocks were high and round

and tight. His waist was narrow, and his back was broad and strong. Just to look at his sinewy arms made her tingle with wanting to have them hold her tight.

His thighs provoked a delicious tremor, as well. Firm, muscular.

Her heated gaze moved to the place between his legs, and she gasped in awe at the size of his manhood even when not aroused.

He turned toward the bed, and that was when he saw her.

"Angele? What are you doing here?"

Mustering every shred of bravado she possessed, she slowly drew the sheet away so he could see the rest of her . . . see that she was not wearing a gown.

"Do you have to ask?" she said in a voice so husky with desire that she didn't recognize it as her own.

He laughed uneasily. "What's this all about?"

"Is it so difficult to figure out?" she purred, stretching lazily, arms above her head so her breasts would lift provocatively. "You're my husband, I'm your wife . . . and I want you to make love to me.

"Come here . . ." she beckoned, boldly reaching to caress his penis, which had quickly grown hard, and tug gently on it.

With a soft groan, he sat on the bed, bending over her. Folding her arms about his neck, she leaned back to offer her breasts to him. He devoured each nipple, then kissed his way on up to her mouth. And when his lips closed over hers, she heard a smothered growl of raw animal desire come from deep within him.

She reached down and cupped him between his legs. "Now," she commanded. "I want you now." She spread her legs wide, inviting.

He surprised her with a gentle laugh. "No, my sweet. This was your idea tonight, so it's up to you to do all the work."

He lay down on the bed, then lifted her up to straddle him and firmly impaled her.

She gave a soft cry, for he went deep, but it didn't hurt. In fact, she gloried in how he filled her.

In the moonglow, she saw how he was looking at her not only with longing but something else. What? Adoration? She dared not think love.

But there was no time to ponder, for he was guiding her up and down on his shaft. "Like this. And wiggle your hips around. Yes, ah, that's it. That's good . . . keep the rhythm . . . harder, yes . . . that's the way . . ."

He closed his eyes in ecstasy, his fingertips pinching her nipples ever so gently. But if her movements slowed, he pinched harder and whispered for her to go faster.

Hot, sweet needles of pleasure rippled through her belly, and soon she needed no coaxing. She was finding her own cadence, her own thrusting speed.

She gave her hair a reckless toss and threw back her head as she made soft, moaning sounds deep in her throat.

She rocked faster, bouncing up and down, almost rising from his shaft before slamming back down and undulating about.

"Now . . ." she cried. "Oh, yes, now . . ."

And after they climaxed together, Angele wasted no time in moving off him to burrow her face in the pillow to stifle any sound she might make in that honeyed moment of glory.

She was afraid she would say that she loved him.

Ryan couldn't fall asleep.

Long after Angele was breathing deeply and evenly, he was wide awake.

To find her waiting in his bed had been shock enough. But add the fact she was naked and then turned into a tigress was enough to keep him up till dawn.

What was wrong with her?

And what was wrong with him?

Hell, he stayed away from her because he couldn't bear

being around her for fear of letting her know he had come to care for her so deeply.

He also hadn't liked how she seemed to submit to him out of duty alone.

And he was damned if another woman would make a fool of him again. Angele had married him for one reason and one reason only: it was the lesser of all the evils she faced.

Also, she knew he was wealthy, and she was no fool. She wanted to live in the lap of luxury and had nothing to lose by accepting his offer.

Only now things were getting complicated, damn it, because he was falling in love with her, which could be a big, big mistake, because she could be planning to leave at any time.

Clarice said she wasn't happy, that she whined and complained all the time. She griped that she was bored, she sassed Clarice when she tried to show her how things were to be done, and when she had shown up at the tea—deliberately late, according to Clarice—she made no attempt to communicate through her to the ladies present.

But he well knew how Clarice exaggerated. He also knew she was not an easy person to get along with, and if the truth be known, he couldn't stand being around her, himself, and wondered how Corbett was able to put up with her.

Then there was the tea incident. There was no way he would ever believe Angele had intentionally tried to harm his father, but he had to agree with Clarice that she was obviously clumsy and irresponsible.

Now there was this new side of her to try to figure out. Seductive, wanton, sexual, sensuous—everything he wanted in a woman . . . a wife.

But why?

What had changed her so suddenly?

Was she pretending to want to make him happy in order to lull him into thinking she was completely content as his wife . . . while all the time planning to leave?

He shook his head in the darkness, brushing against

her. She gave a little sigh of contentment and snuggled even closer.

He felt a stirring in his loins.

God, how he had come to care for her . . . desire her.

Maybe, he decided there in the stillness of the night, it was a good thing he was going to be away for the next few days. He needed time to mull things over. But then he asked himself what good it would do. After all, if she decided to leave, there wasn't anything he could do to stop her.

A gentle breeze wafted through the open doors to set the filmy curtains to dancing in the ribboned moonlight.

Suddenly he was struck with the idea that if she became pregnant, she would not go. She wouldn't dare strike out on her own in such a condition.

He smiled and drew her closer.

Nineteen

Angele had never dreamed she would miss Ryan so much.

He had been gone two days and sent word he would be gone a third. A meeting of horse breeders had lasted longer than expected, but he found it too interesting to abandon.

Clarice kept her promise to keep her busy. Angele let her think she was teaching her basic words in English. She also pretended to practice her tatting and embroidery. Then there were the lessons in table manners, holding tea cups properly, and arranging flowers—all things Angele knew almost better than she did.

And through it all, she endured Clarice's criticism and sarcasm. She was miserable, but Clarice didn't give her a chance to get away from morning till bedtime.

Then one afternoon Danny was crying and not feeling well, and Clarice had to go to him. She left Angele with instructions to continue with her sewing, but the minute she was gone, Angele slipped upstairs to the south wing and knocked on Uncle Roussel's door.

Willard came to the door and grinned. "Miz Angele. How'd you know Mastah Roussel's been sayin' he hoped you'd come to see him?" His hand flew to his mouth. "I'm sorry. I keep forgettin' you don't know a thing I say. Well, come on. At least Mastah Roussel can talk to *you.*"

Roussel was in his bedroom, sitting in his usual spot by the window. At the sight of Angele, he cried with delight,

"I'm so glad to see you. I've been wondering where you've been. Come sit down and tell me everything you've been doing."

"What I've been doing . . ." she said anxiously as she pulled a chair closer and sat down, "is wanting to tell you how sorry I am for what happened. But Clarice didn't want me bothering you, and I was so afraid you might be angry with me."

He grunted. "Hmph. That old bat. Always tending to somebody else's business. Hell, no, I'm not angry. I didn't blame you for anything."

"Thank goodness. And though I don't know how it happened, it certainly wasn't intentional."

He looked shocked. "Who said it was? I sure never thought so. I'm just sorry me being sick kept you from visiting. I've enjoyed our little talks."

"No more than I have. You taught me more about Virginia than I would have known otherwise."

"Nonsense. I can tell you're smart. You'd have learned on your own. But tell me, how are you and Ryan getting along? Are you happy?"

The question took her by surprise. "Well . . . yes . . . I suppose so. I can't answer for him, of course."

"I worry about it, because I like you, and we both know why he married you."

She felt her hair prickle on the back of her neck.

"Don't look so surprised. I'm sure he told you he had to take a French wife or lose BelleRose. I would have arranged a marriage for him, myself, if there'd been any suitable Frenchwomen around, but there weren't—except for Denise, of course. I guess Clarice has seen to it that you know about her."

Angele nodded.

"Well, I don't mind telling anybody how glad I was to hear she turned him down. Hell, she's Clarice's cousin, and just like her, and the two of them in one house would've put me in my grave a damn sight sooner than I'm planning on going." Narrowing his eyes, he apologized. "Sorry. I'm cursing again, and I know you don't like it."

Angele shrugged. "I don't mind the hells and damns. It's blasphemy I can't abide."

"And you're right. You're right. I'm glad you brought that to my attention." He grinned. "Nobody else around here ever dared. Now back to you and Ryan. Marriages arranged by families aren't unusual and you know it, and even though yours was done in a different way, there's no reason you two won't be happy together. My wife and I married because our fathers agreed we would from the time we were babies. I learned to love her, and I believe she loved me."

"I don't suppose it really matters," Angele offered, "as long as we get along well."

"Maybe," he said, almost dreamily, looking over her head as though into the past and smiling at what he saw. "But love makes everything better. I hope that happens to you and my son.

"Now then . . ." He motioned to Willard and spoke to him in English. "We'd like some sherry."

Willard took on a worried look. "Sir, you know the doctor said you're not supposed to drink anything like that till he has a chance to come by and make sure you're all right."

"And you know how much I care what that old goat said," Roussel snapped. "Now get my best bottle of brandy from the cabinet and two glasses." He cut his gaze expectantly to Angele. "You will join me, won't you?"

"Of course." She would never have dreamed of refusing—not because she cared so much about the brandy but because she knew it would make him happy, and that had come to be very important to her.

Willard poured them each a glass, and as they sipped, Roussel gazed wistfully out the window. "I'd give anything to go for a ride. Do you think maybe you could go with me one afternoon? I'd like to show you all around my paradise, because that's what it is to me—paradise."

"Uncle Roussel, I would love to," she said with gusto, and meant it.

"Then it's all settled. Today's Friday. We'll go Sunday afternoon. I'm sure I'll be up to it by then."

They held up their glasses in promise, and Angele's heart warmed to think how she had made a new friend.

Clarice was furious to find Angele had slipped away and nagged about it all through dinner. Afterward, she ordered her to her room with the warning not to come out till morning. "I'll not have you bothering Uncle Roussel, and I'm sure Ryan will agree with me."

Angele didn't care. She would find a way to visit the dear old man.

It was a sultry night but still beautiful. The moon had only begun to wane, and as she stood on the porch outside her bedroom, she breathed in awe to see the gardens below bathed in silver.

It was not a time to be alone, and she wished Ryan were there with her. They hadn't shared such moments since the voyage to America, when they would stand on deck and marvel at how the moonlight made the ocean sparkle as though heaven had sent a shower of diamonds.

She missed him terribly.

The last night they were together, when she had so brazenly offered herself, he had made love to her again as the sun was rising. And it had been wonderful. She felt such a part of him, coveted not as chattel but cherished as something—*someone*—he cared for deeply.

But, of course, it had only been lust on his part, and the magic ended when a servant called through the door that it was the time he had asked to be awakened to get ready for his trip into Richmond.

So now she was fighting the demons within that made her wonder if he would see Denise while he was there. Selma had told her the woman lived right in town in one of the big, two-story brick houses shaded by great oaks and magnolias. She knew because she had gone there several times with Clarice to serve her while she visited for a few days.

The house was richly furnished, Selma had gushed, maybe even more so than BelleRose. Denise's father was also a planter but so rich he didn't want to be bothered with tending the land and hired overseers to do it for him and report back to him in Richmond. He didn't want to farm himself, it was said, and everyone thought Denise probably felt the same way. Not wanting to live out in the country on a plantation was thought to be the reason she had refused to marry Ryan. She liked the busy social life in town, and everyone said Ryan would never leave BelleRose to live there.

Angele wasn't surprised at that, knowing how he loved his home. But that didn't mean Denise refusing him had made him stop loving her—*if,* she reminded herself, he ever had. His interest in her could be only because she was French. Then, too, she was well aware Clarice had wanted them to get married and might have exaggerated. So perhaps there was really nothing to worry about, and she hoped he would come home soon so she could show him once more how much she wanted him.

The sound of banjos drifted to her in the breeze. The Negroes were singing and dancing again, and Angele moved to the end of the porch to hear them better.

She found herself wishing she were having fun along with them, and, suddenly, it struck that there was no one to stop her, no one to know if she went to them. Clarice had retired for the night. Corbett was in Richmond with Ryan. Mammy Lou and the rest of the household servants would be asleep up on the fourth floor.

The trick would be getting out of the house without being seen or heard, if anyone was awake and about.

Her heart began to race with excitement she'd not known since she was a young girl at Miss Appleton's. Sometimes she and some of the other students would climb down a trellis to the ground to play silly games in the dark. Mostly they did it to prove to themselves that they could.

And it just so happened there was a trellis that ran all the way to the ground from her porch. One of the yard workers had cleared it of wisteria vines that hadn't come back after winter. It was good and sturdy, too.

She changed into a plain dress of beige cotton. There were no frills or lace on it, so she wouldn't have to worry about snagging it on anything. She certainly didn't want a repeat of what had happened on board the ship with her very fragile ball gown.

There was scant light, but she felt her way along, careful not to make any noise.

After what seemed forever, she dropped the last few feet to the ground. Losing her balance, she fell backward on her bottom into a camellia bush and whispered an oath. The crushed foliage would be seen in daylight. She could only hope it would be thought an animal was responsible, not someone falling from the trellis.

Dusting off her bottom and brushing camellia petals from her hair, she went around to the rear of the house. In the darkness of the woods, she saw the glow of light. Roscoe Fordham was still up, but she was not about to risk walking by his cabin, anyway. Instead, she went through the chicken pen, which was quiet and empty with all the hens roosting.

The well-worn path to the slave cabins was darkened from moonlight by overhanging trees, but she followed the sound of the music and light from the fires.

Then she saw the Negroes—clapping hands and stomping their feet as they circled around a few couples dancing in the center of the clearing. Children ran about giggling as they chased each other.

The air was rich with the smell of something wonderful cooking in a big, iron cauldron. Jugs were being passed, with everyone taking a big swallow from them. Angele knew it was apple cider, because Selma had told her how they made it every fall, then stored it in their own dug-out root cellar so they could enjoy it year round. Slaves, Selma had pointed out, were not allowed to drink any kind of whiskey or wine, even if they had any.

Sadly, Angele mused how she hadn't had much of a social life since before the trouble came to Foxwood. Until then, her parents had entertained with regularity. And at Miss Appleton's, there were dances sometimes, and boys from a nearby preparatory school had been invited.

It wouldn't be long until the ball at BelleRose, but she wasn't looking forward to it. Having to pretend not to speak English and knowing Clarice would be watching her with a critical eye was not her idea of a gala evening. Her only enjoyment would come if Ryan danced with her, and, since he didn't think she knew how, he probably wouldn't ask and expect her to decline if any of the male guests asked.

Suddenly there was a shout, "Look. Oh, Lordy, look. It's a white lady . . ."

A small boy was pointing at her. The music came to an abrupt halt. The circle broke up as everyone turned to stare, and those sitting on the ground stood.

Silence fell like a shroud.

Angele smiled brightly and gestured for them to continue, saying in French, "Go on with what you were doing, please. I just want to watch."

No one moved.

No one spoke.

And then Selma pushed her way through the crowd.

Grim-faced, she came to her and said, so low no one else could hear, "Please, Miz Angele, you can't come here. Now they think I can speak a little French, 'cause I work up at the house, but not enough to be able to talk to you good, and they're gonna get suspicious. So you go on back, please."

Stubbornly, Angele shook her head. "No. I'm tired of being cooped up in the house all the time. I want to be here, in the sweet night air where there's dancing and singing. Please tell everyone I mean no harm, and no one knows where I am, so they aren't going to find out."

Selma's lips twisted with indecision. Finally, with a ragged sigh, she could only say, "Ma'am, I have to do what you say."

Angele was relieved there would be no more arguing.

"Now tell them to keep on with what they're doing. They won't even know I'm here."

Selma went back to the crowd and relayed her message. There were nervous, exchanged glances, but soon the music started up again. Gradually, they all seemed to relax and began dancing and singing once more, with Angele clapping her hands and stomping her feet right along with them.

She hadn't eaten much supper, so when she was handed a bowl of soup with chunks of sweet turtle meat, boiled eggs, and potatoes, she ate ravenously. There were also biscuits with lots of butter.

Selma huddled close so if anything needed to be said, no one would notice, but Angele was having such a good time conversation was unnecessary.

Then she noticed the crowd began to thin as mothers took their children off to bed. She supposed she should leave soon, herself, and was about to do so when a young Negro man suddenly slipped from the darkness. About to squat in front of Selma, he saw Angele, and his eyes went wide.

"It's all right, Toby," Selma said quickly. "She just wanted to join the fun.

"This here's my husband," she murmured to Angele, then asked Toby what was wrong.

Angele saw how she took his hands and squeezed them because he looked so scared. His upper lip was beaded with sweat, and when she saw blood on the front of his shirt, she instinctively drew away.

"It's Mastah Ryan's mare." He was trembling. "She's foalin', and Jasper, he's down with the rheumatiz and ain't no help. It's all he can do to move around. Nobody knows what to do. Mastah Ryan is gone, and we don't dare go tell Mastah Roussel, 'cause he ain't in no shape to do nothin'."

"No, he isn't." Angele was already on her feet.

Toby rocked back on his heels and looked from her to Selma to say in wonder, "She talks like us."

"I know, I know, but don't tell anybody." Selma glanced

around frantically and was relieved no one was close enough to hear what was going on.

"Let's go, Toby." Angele motioned to him.

Uncertainty veiled his face.

"Please!" she pleaded. "If I'm going to try and save the foal, I'll need your help."

His fear, his reluctance, was maddening.

"Toby, you *have* to help me."

"Go with her," Selma urged.

As they were finally hurrying through the night, Angele wasn't thinking of anything except the life of the mare that meant so much to Ryan, as well as her foal.

"How come you don't let nobody know you can talk?" Toby asked, right beside her.

She laughed. "I can talk."

"I don't mean that."

"I know you don't." She reached to pat his arm in hopes of putting him at ease. He looked frightened enough to leap right out of his skin. "I just like having a secret, Toby. Do you understand? And will you help me keep it?"

"Sure, if that's what you want. It don't matter to me, anyhow. And Selma, she says good things about you. She likes you real fine, she does. Says you're the best thing that's happened at BelleRose in her whole life."

Angele was gratified to know that, but there were more important things on her mind. "Now listen carefully, Toby. I peeked in the kitchen the other day and saw one of the women making biscuits. She was using something thick and white to make them, and it was greasy. I don't know what they call it here. Do you?"

"Yes'm. That's called lard. We make it in the winter when we kill hogs. The women boil the fat off the hog, and—"

"Thank you, Toby, but I'm not particularly interested in hearing the details of how it's made. I want you to get me some and bring it to the stables."

"How much do you need?"

"Not a lot. A bucketful probably."

When they neared the kitchen, Toby took off in that direction while Angele kept on going toward the stable area. Through a window, she could see lanterns burning inside one of the buildings. She went to it and pushed the doors open.

Jasper was bent over with pain as he tried to minister to the mare, who was down on her side on the ground, hind legs thrashing. Two young boys hovered nearby, looking terrified and bewildered.

When Jasper saw Angele, his face twisted with shock. "Lord have mercy, lady, what are you doin' here?" Then, remembering she only spoke French, he nodded sickly to the boys, "She don't know a word I'm sayin'. You all are gonna have to get her out of here right now."

"I do know what you're saying," she said quickly, figuring there would be time later to ask them all to keep her secret, but more and more it seemed not to matter so much.

Crossing the straw-littered floor, she knelt beside him. "And I know a little bit about horses. I was hoping I could help since Toby said your rheumatism is bothering you."

"Botherin' ain't the word." He grimaced. "It's killin' me, that's what it's doin'. And these boys here don't know nothin' about deliverin' colts, and this one don't want to come out . . ."

"We may need to turn it."

"I've been tryin' to, but my hands just aren't strong enough. Toby and the boys are scared to try. Lordy, I wish Mastah Ryan was here."

"What about Mr. Fordham. He—"

"No, ma'am!" he all but shouted. "He wouldn't want to do it."

"Is there anyone else who could help?"

"No, ma'am. Mastah Ryan, he's always let me be in charge, but not too long ago I told him he's gonna have to let me show somebody else 'cause I'm gettin' too old for this."

"He trusts you and hates to turn the responsibility over to anyone else."

Jasper beamed proudly. "I reckon that's so."

The horse let out a loud, pitiful whinny and kicked her legs harder, her belly bucking up off the ground as painful contractions struck that were having no results.

The foal was obviously in the wrong position, and if something wasn't done quickly, both it and the mare were going to die.

The doors opened with a bang as Toby all but fell into the barn beneath the weight of a huge barrel of lard he was carrying.

"Boy, what're you doin' here?" Jasper yelled. "And what you bringin' that for?"

"Miz Angele wanted it," he said, as though that explained everything.

"Set it down here." She rolled up her long sleeves, then began slathering lard up and down her arms. "Haven't you ever greased up like this, Jasper?"

"No, ma'am. Before my hands got all crippled up, I knew how to slip 'em right in and pull a foal out."

"This will make it easier. I saw it done once."

And she had, only no one had known she was watching. She had sneaked back out to the stable after her father had ordered her to bed. One of her favorite mares was birthing, and though the stablehands spoke in low tones around her, she sensed there was trouble. Her father hadn't wanted her to see it, but she had hidden in a hay-filled stall, fascinated as she witnessed the difficult birth. She had never forgotten it and was glad now that she hadn't.

Taking a deep breath, she reached inside the mare, remembering how that night the man delivering her father's mare had explained step by step exactly what he was doing.

Suddenly she fell back as the wet, slick newborn slid from its mother and into the world. And as Jasper and Toby and the two young boys laughed with delight and relief, he struggled to stand on his wobbly legs.

"Would you look at that!" Jasper cried jubilantly. "It's a colt. Mastah Ryan got the colt he was wantin'."

Already he was trying to nuzzle his mother, who had managed to stand.

Angele was almost crying she was so happy. "I don't care what it is, so long as it's all right."

"He sure appears fine to me."

She looked down at herself and made a face. Blood and lard streaked her arms, as well as her dress. Without thinking, she said out loud, "Well, I guess this is another dress I'll have to throw away."

"That's right."

She whipped about to see Ryan standing in the doorway.

His blue eyes burned like hot coals as he started toward her.

"And this time," he said in a voice thick with anger, "you can lie to me about it in my own language."

Twenty

Ryan towered over Angele as she sat in a chair staring up at him, undaunted by his anger.

They were in their parlor, where Ryan had taken her after making sure the mare and colt were all right while she washed up at the water pump outside the stable.

Nostrils flaring and nerves in his jaw pulsing, he slammed his fists together and demanded, "Well? What else haven't you told me? And tell the truth. I'm sick of your lies."

"Nothing," she said with a straight face. "And I never lied about not speaking English. You never asked me if I could. You just assumed I *couldn't*."

He turned away, fingers kneading his forehead in frustration. "This is no time to be capricious."

"And I'm not trying to be. I'm just stating a fact. Besides," she added with a twitch of a smile, "I found out many things by pretending I didn't understand."

"I imagine you did." He might have been amused to think about it had he not been so concerned that her deceit might go much deeper. "So how did you learn?"

She had her explanation ready. "I had distant relatives living in London. I stayed with them a while. They taught me. Actually, I didn't tell you because you were so damned insistent that everything about me be French, I was afraid you'd be resentful."

"That's ridiculous, and you know it. And I thought you didn't like cursing," he added. "Now listen to you!"

"It's blasphemy I can't abide, and I never use profanity unless I'm really annoyed—like now," she said hotly. "You and your entire family are such snobs about your precious French heritage that I was afraid I'd be treated like a leper for even visiting England."

"We aren't snobs, Angele. My father just wants to preserve the lineage. I told you that when I asked you to marry me."

"All I am saying—"

He sighed to interrupt. "I hope you realize that you've made me look like a fool. When a man doesn't know his own wife can speak English . . ." He shook his head in disgust.

Actually, she was relieved the secret was out, and she wasn't worried about him being angry. He would get over it, and to hasten him along, she pointed out, "You know, you haven't even thanked me for saving your colt."

Curtly, he said, "Thank you," then, "Now would you mind telling me how you knew what to do? And don't say you overheard someone talking about it once upon a time."

She shrugged as though it were nothing. "I learned in England. My relatives raised horses. I was around them a lot. They let me help around the stables, and I enjoyed it."

"And I suppose you can ride."

"Of course."

"And you didn't tell me that, either."

"I didn't want to *tell* you," she said petulantly, "I wanted to show you, only you never have time for me. You're at the stables or out riding from daylight till dark, and then you sit in your study and drink with Corbett."

He frowned. "Don't nag, Angele."

She frowned right back. "Then treat me like your wife instead of chattel."

He was tempted to laugh at her unusual show of audacity, but her expression stopped him.

She pressed on. "Now that I've told you I can ride, will you give me a horse and go with me?"

"I don't know." He went to the sideboard. Taking the

stopper from a crystal decanter, he poured himself a brandy. "It's understood I want you to have a baby as soon as possible. If you were pregnant and didn't know it, you could get hurt."

"No, I wouldn't. I happen to be an expert rider, probably even better than you if the truth be known," she added with an airy sniff.

"I doubt that."

"All I want to do is ride, for heaven's sake. I don't enjoy being cooped up in the house all day."

"That's where ladies belong, Angele, and I'm trying my best to turn you into one."

"I don't need your help. I'm very much a lady."

"Being down on your hands and knees delivering a colt isn't exactly ladylike in my opinion."

Their gazes locked.

Angele put her hands on her hips and stood with feet slightly apart. She was not about to be intimidated by either his glare or his harsh tone. "I got the job done, *Master* Tremayne, and I saved the colt, and maybe the mare, too. But you don't care about that. All you *do* care about is what other people think, and as far as I'm concerned, if it comes down to saving an animal's life, they can all go spit."

He blinked, stunned by her outburst, then, slowly, he broke into a wide grin. "My God, woman, you do have grit, don't you?"

She relaxed a little. His anger appeared to be on the wane. "I just like to think for myself, which means I don't like being told what to do every minute of the day."

His grin faded. "There's such a thing as decorum, and you're going to have to learn that. As my wife, certain things are expected of you from society, and delivering colts isn't one of them. You could have told Jasper what to do."

"His hands are crippled with rheumatism, in case you haven't noticed," she snapped. "He couldn't have reached inside and turned the foal."

Anger rolled back. "I've noticed. I notice *everything* about my people."

"Your *people*," she spat the word. "*Slaves*, I believe is the word more commonly used."

He let the remark pass, instead saying, "Toby could have followed your instructions."

"I was in a hurry. It was quicker to do it myself. Now I'm tired, and I'm going to bed."

He tossed down the brandy, and before she got to her door quietly said, "You will sleep in my room tonight."

"No. I won't." She kept on going, head held high, back ramrod straight. He had made her angry, and she was not about to give in to him this night. He would soon learn she was not in servitude like his *people*.

She locked the door, making sure the key clicked loud enough for him to hear.

Actually, she would have liked nothing better than to throw herself in his arms and taste his brandy-sweet kisses and feel him deep, deep inside her. But pride overrode desire. He had chastised her and tried to make her feel ashamed of what she had done, and that she could not abide.

She undressed and put on a nightgown, then got into bed. She left the lamp beside it burning low, because she liked to watch shadows flickering, dancing, on the walls.

Her mind wandered back to the afternoon when Ryan had taken her for a walk along the edge of the cotton fields. It was only a few days after they had arrived at BelleRose. He had told her how cotton was grown, harvested, and then baled and taken to Richmond to be sold.

That day she had felt so close to him, for he had made her feel he truly wanted her to be a part of his world. Since then, however, he had shut her out more and more.

And now, rather than be grateful for what she had done, he was more worried about what people would say when they heard about it.

But she also knew he was chafed over how she had concealed her understanding of English. She blamed herself for not telling him earlier, but somehow the opportunity never came—till tonight—and she was glad it had happened like it had. Otherwise, she might never have had the nerve. Instead, she would have struggled through lessons and been thought a diligent student.

As she lay there, other worries needled, such as whether he had seen Denise while in Richmond and if he regretted not repeating his proposal to see if she would change her mind.

Rolling over, she pounded the pillow with her fists and cursed herself for not going to him when he'd wanted her.

Maybe she couldn't bring herself to use words to let him know how she really felt about him.

But she could use her body.

Only it was too late.

If she went to him now, he would think she was groveling and weak.

Ryan had one more brandy. He knew he was drinking too much lately, but the woman was driving him crazy, and drinking dulled his senses to where he didn't worry about it so much.

He took off his coat and threw it across the room. Likewise he yanked off his shirt and sent it sailing. Then, barechested, he went to the window to stare out into the night, hands on his hips.

Damn it to hell, he had lost his heart to a woman who might not fit into his world after all. Her past was still an enigma. He still worried she would run away once she got her hands on enough money. Yet, he had been amazed at how she had finally responded to his lovemaking, actually being quite bold about it lately.

Had she also, he frowned to think, been hiding the fact that she knew how to please a man?

Just what was in her past that she sought to hide?

Or was there really anything at all—except his imagination?

He never should have let himself care about her, but he had, and now he wanted her to stay. And the only way he could ensure that happening was to make her pregnant. Then she couldn't leave unless she abandoned her own child, because she had sense enough to know he would use all his wealth and power to keep her from taking it with her.

He thought of the last time they had made love, when she had friskily got down on her knees, turning her bottom up to him and inviting him to penetrate her from behind. He had reached around her to put his fingers between her and massage her hot little bud as he had ridden her. When she climaxed, she had bucked like an unbroke pony, and he had laughed out loud with delight . . . then moaned with ecstasy, because never had he climaxed so powerfully. It had left him shaken.

And thinking about it now made him hard.

He wanted her.

And why shouldn't he have her? She was his wife, damn it. Besides, if he allowed her to get away with pouting because he dared chastise her, then she'd never get pregnant.

Unbuckling his belt, he loosened his trousers and took them off.

He went to her door and tried to open it.

It was locked.

"Angele?" he called softly.

There was no response.

He jiggled the handle again. "Unlock this door."

"Go away. I told you I'm tired."

He drew a deep, ragged breath, then drew back his foot and smashed the door in with one mighty kick.

He reached inside and turned the lock, swinging what was left of the door open.

She was sitting up in bed, the sheet pulled to her chin, her face pale with fear.

"You are my wife," he said with a husky growl from deep in his throat, "and when I want you, I'll have you."

As he started toward her, she reached quickly to extinguish the light.

She didn't want him to see how glad she was that he *did* want her.

She intended to show him instead.

Roussel was delighted when he learned that Angele understood English, and summoned her to his quarters the very next day to tell her so.

She gave him the same explanation she had given Ryan, but guilt was a cold knife to her heart when he said all that mattered was that she was pure-blooded French. Dear Lord, she prayed the truth about that would never come out.

They went for a carriage ride that lasted all afternoon. She was thrilled as he showed her all around the plantation, something Ryan had not taken the time to do so extensively.

He had also heard about her delivering the colt and seemed not in the least concerned over what others might say.

She had offered the same contrived explanation she had given Ryan—that she had lived in England around relatives who had horses. She admitted it had been her first delivery.

"Then you have extra reason to be proud," Roussel had praised.

He also had said how much he was looking forward to the festivities planned for the coming weekend. There would be a ball on Saturday night. An orchestra was coming from Richmond to play. Then, on Sunday, a picnic would be held in the yard beneath the shading oaks, and later the men would jump their horses in competition on a track to be set up on the lawn.

"It's something we do at the end of every summer," he had explained. "All the men contribute to buying a fine saddle trimmed in silver, made by one of the best leather craftsmen in Virginia. The winner of the contest gets the saddle."

When she asked if Ryan had ever won, he said no, because Ryan liked to ride for pleasure, not competition.

She had truly enjoyed the outing, and that night Roussel had come downstairs and joined everyone for dinner. It was the first time he had done so in months, and he carried on a running conversation with Angele after asking that she be seated to his right.

She loved talking to him and didn't miss how pleased Ryan looked. Neither did she fail to see how Clarice flashed with annoyance to give up her usual seat next to the master of the house.

The night before the ball, Ryan retired to his study right after dinner. He said he had to go over BelleRose's books and might be up late.

Bored, Angele wandered out to the stable to look at the horses. Just as she was leaving, Roscoe Fordham came around the corner.

Tipping his hat, he said, "Evenin' Miz Tremayne. Your husband's got himself some nice horses. I guess you're proud, too, since the really fine ones came from your country."

He had never spoken to her before the few times she was around him, but then he'd not known she would understand.

"Yes, I certainly am," she responded, impulsively adding, "And I can't wait to ride one of them, especially the mare. I healed her leg from a bee sting, so I can't help feeling she's mine."

He asked what she meant, and she told him, and before long they were chatting like old friends. She decided he wasn't frightening, as she'd thought. Actually, he seemed nice and was certainly friendly and polite.

He said he would be glad to take her riding sometime if Ryan didn't mind. He knew how busy he was.

She thanked him and said she might take him up on his offer. Then they went their separate ways.

It was almost dark. Angele returned to the house but didn't want to go inside. It was a warm evening, but a cool breeze had managed to drift up from the river. She sat in one of the rockers on the porch and thought about the ball. She had selected a white taffeta dress with lots of lace around the bodice and billowing petticoats beneath the pink, ribboned skirt. She thought the color appropriate since her marriage to Ryan was being formally announced on that occasion. It would make her feel like a bride again.

She had told Selma she wanted her hair done in a very conservative style, pulled straight back from her face and twined with a white net snood. Actually, she'd have liked to leave her long black tresses flowing down her back but knew Clarice would say it wasn't dignified enough for a married lady. According to her, only young, unmarried women wore their hair loose.

Angele made a face in the darkness.

If Clarice had her way, she'd dress, act, and look like an old woman—as *she* did.

All was quiet and peaceful.

From somewhere in the distance she heard the mournful call of a whippoorwill.

Lazily, she rocked to and fro, wishing Ryan was beside her in the jasmine-scented air.

Suddenly a window slid open not too far behind her, and she jumped, startled, then got very still as she heard Corbett's voice.

"I don't know how you stand it so hot in here. If you want to talk to me, I've got to have some air . . . and a whiskey, too."

"Help yourself. You know where it is."

Their voices were clear. She did not have to strain to hear every word. She told herself she shouldn't eavesdrop but reasoned she was there first, enjoying the evening. Why should she go back inside the warm house just because Corbett had opened a window? Besides, she liked the sound of Ryan's voice, and if she couldn't be with him, at least she could listen to him.

Corbett sounded annoyed. "What did you want to see me about?"

"I was just going over the roster of field hands, and I see a couple of names have been crossed off," Ryan explained. "Has Roscoe said anything to you about it?"

"Didn't I tell you? There was an accident on the river while we were gone. Roscoe said they were unloading lumber, and a slave fell in. He couldn't swim, and neither could the idiot who tried to save him. Both of them drowned."

Angele felt a pang of sorrow and made a mental note to ask Selma if it was anyone she had been close to.

Sounding more than a little upset, Ryan said, "No, I didn't know, and I'm going to crawl all over Roscoe for not telling me the minute we got home. I want to know exactly what happened, damn it. And if it was carelessness, I want to know who was responsible."

Corbett's tone indicated he couldn't have cared less. "What's two slaves more or less? We can buy more if we get short-handed."

"We don't buy or sell at BelleRose. You know that."

She could tell Ryan was getting angry, and it was obvious Corbett did, too, because he abruptly changed the subject.

"Looks like we've got good weather for this weekend. I'm glad. Uncle Roussel is really looking forward to it."

"So am I." The tension seemed to have been lifted. "It will be nice to entertain again. There's a lot of people I haven't seen in quite a while."

"Like Denise?"

Ryan didn't say anything, and Angele could not resist getting up from the rocker and tiptoeing to stand right beside the window. When he did speak, she didn't want to miss a single word.

"Well?" Corbett prodded. "You haven't seen her since we got back from France, have you?"

"No."

Angele breathed a sigh of relief.

"Clarice has. She says she's mighty upset over your marriage and thinks you did it to spite her."

"She can believe whatever she wants."

"Don't be like that. You two were always close. I still think you're in love with her."

Ryan murmured something Angele couldn't make out, because just then a bullfrog began to croak loudly just off the porch. She wished she had something to throw at him and thought about taking off her shoe, but Ryan and Corbett might hear, and she didn't want them to know she was out there.

From then on she caught only snatches of conversation, but it was enough to know that Denise was coming to the ball, and Corbett wanted Ryan to say something to make her feel better about everything. "After all, she's my wife's cousin."

"I know, I know," Ryan said. "And I suppose for that reason I should have gone to see her so there wouldn't be any tension between us this weekend."

Then Corbett asked a question that made Angele snap to attention.

Washed with dread, she strained to hear how Ryan would respond.

"Are you sorry you married so impulsively?"

Before he could answer, Clarice burst into the room to lash out at Corbett, "Don't think you're going to sit in here and drink all night. This is our time with Danny. Now, get upstairs right now."

"All right," he groaned. "I'll be back later, Ryan."

Angele didn't want to go inside. If she saw Ryan, he might be able to tell she was upset and wonder why.

She decided to go to the slave quarters. She could hear their music from the porch. They were having a good time, and she wanted to join them to get her mind off her worries.

Selma was happy to see her but full of questions to make sure it was safe for her to be there. "Are you all done for the evening? Did you read to Master Roussel? Is he asleep now? Is Miss Clarice bedded down, too, and Master Ryan busy?"

Angele laughed. "Yes to everything. Now, what's that delicious smell?"

"Brown sugar dumplings with cinnamon and butter. Come on. There's plenty."

Angele followed her, waving to everyone, happy and also at peace, because here she was accepted. There was no need to worry about being criticized or having to please anyone. She could be herself and just enjoy living, and she reveled in it.

And she also, for the moment, didn't have to wonder if, had Clarice not interrupted, Ryan would have told Corbett that, yes, he did regret marrying her.

She raved over the dumplings, and then someone offered to show her how to pick chords on the banjo. She eagerly accepted, losing all track of time.

Selma gently reminded her that it was getting late, and she should be getting back.

She didn't seem so friendly all of a sudden, and Angele wondered if she were trying to get rid of her. But her feelings weren't hurt. She was ready to leave, anyway, because the rich dumplings had made her stomach a bit queasy.

"Yes, I guess I should go," Angele said, "but I want to ask you about something first. I heard about the drownings in the river and was wondering if you were close to either of the victims. If so, I wanted to offer my sympathy."

Selma blinked. "I don't know what you mean."

"I'm talking about the two men who drowned while Ryan was in France."

"I ain't heard, and I would've if it happened. The big bell rings a special way when somebody dies, and it ain't rung. They must have been from another plantation, and we haven't been told about it."

Angele was baffled, because she was sure she had heard the conversation right. "Master Ryan asked Master Corbett why two names had been crossed off the roster he keeps," she explained to Selma. "Master Corbett said Mr. Fordham told him there had been an accident at the river while

they were away, and the two names were the men who
drowned as a result."

Angele noted how Selma's face took on a terrified look,
but only for an instant before she began to babble, "Yes'm,
yes'm, the river, the drownin'. Now I know what you mean,
but I didn't know 'em. Sorry. Now you better go."

She walked away before Angele could ask anything else.
It was obvious she didn't want to talk about the accident,
but why had she denied knowing about it in the beginning? It didn't make sense.

As she headed down the path, Angele heard a faint
crashing sound that seemed to come from the woods at
the rear of the slaves' compound. She went back to peek
though some bushes to see what was going on.

A young Negro man stumbled into the clearing. Suddenly his knees buckled, and he pitched forward. The others closed about him.

She was too far away to hear what was being said. With
a cold chill moving up and down her spine, she reasoned
it was probably good that she didn't. Because, if what she
suspected was true . . . if the Negro was, indeed, a runaway
slave, then it was best she didn't know.

When she reached the house, she circled around to
Ryan's study.

Light was coming from the window, and she peered inside to see him sitting on the leather sofa in front of the
fireplace. Corbett was beside him. Evidently he had helped
get little Danny to bed, then returned.

Their feet were propped on a table, and they were sipping wine, obviously enjoying themselves. Angele felt certain they would be there for some time.

So, with Clarice undoubtedly in bed and sound asleep,
Angele decided it would not be necessary to climb back
up the trellis. Instead, she went around to the back door.

Quietly, she opened it and stepped inside.

All she had to do was tiptoe up the back stairs.

Suddenly the door to the tea kitchen opened, and Clarice stepped out. She was holding a lantern. "Well, well," she gloated. "I knew if I waited long enough, I'd catch you sneaking back in."

Startled and upset, Angele floundered for an explanation. She didn't want to get the Negroes in trouble by saying she had been with them. "I went for a walk," she said. "There's nothing wrong with that."

"Liar," Clarice sneered. "I saw you from my window when you went through the barnyard and followed you far enough to know you were going to the slave compound. Now, you come along with me." She grabbed her arm and held tight, nails digging in. "I want Ryan to see once and for all just how *bourgeois* you are."

Angele was tempted to tear away from her and continue on to her room but feared it might look as though she were ashamed—which she wasn't.

Clarice yanked her along to Ryan's study, opened the door, and pushed her inside.

"Now tell him," she commanded harshly as Ryan leaped to his feet, stunned by the intrusion. "Tell him what you were doing in the woods at this hour of night . . . and *who* you were with."

Twenty-one

Ryan's study was one of Angele's favorite rooms in the house. It was so masculine . . . *so like him.*

A huge stone fireplace was at one end, and the walls were adorned with mounted heads of wild boar, deer, and even a black bear. The air was fragrant with the scent of leather and tobacco, and there was a fluffy fur rug made of red fox pelts on the floor.

But Angele wasn't thinking about how cozy the room was just then.

Ryan had known something was wrong when she and Clarice walked in. He immediately got up from the sofa and went to sit behind his desk before coolly asking, "Well? What's this all about? How come you two are still up at this hour?"

Angele saw no reason to try to hide what she had done, especially since Clarice thought she had sneaked off for a clandestine rendezvous with some man. Besides, she was not feeling at all well. The nausea was getting worse. "I don't know why Clarice is so upset," she began. "All I did was walk back to where the Negroes were, because I heard their music."

"Dear God," Clarice moaned. "She was mingling with the slaves . . ." She clutched her chest, and Corbett moved quickly to help her to the sofa.

Stiffly, Angele challenged, "I see nothing wrong with that."

"They should have told you it wasn't proper," Corbett said quietly. He looked at Ryan. "I'll have Roscoe talk to them."

"No, don't do that," Angele protested. "They did tell me I shouldn't be there. It wasn't their fault. I don't want them getting in trouble because of me."

"All that time," Clarice wailed. "You were there all that time. Ryan, I know she was gone at least two hours, if not longer. This is terrible, just terrible. No Tremayne woman has ever done such a thing."

Angele threw up her hands. "This is ridiculous. I did nothing wrong. I just watched them sing and dance, and I ate some dumplings, and—"

Clarice threw her head back on the sofa and wailed, "Merciful heavens, she even *ate* with them. The next thing we know, she'll be inviting them to tea, and then she'll want them to sit at the table with us. This cannot go on. It simply cannot."

Ryan had been sitting with templed fingers, listening to everyone. Finally, he said, "Actually, I don't see anything wrong with it. Before my father got down, he did the same thing. He'd join them when they cooked a catfish stew or killed a hog. I've been known to go back there for barbecue chicken once in a while, myself." He smiled at the memory. "Nobody cooks chicken like Jasper."

Once again, Angele felt like running and throwing her arms around his neck for taking her side but held back. Besides, Clarice had jumped up and run to the desk to lean across and yell that even if he and his father had been back there, no Tremayne woman ever had—till now—and it was wrong and people would think scandalous things of Angele.

Ryan let her rave, and when she finally stopped to catch her breath, he turned to Angele. "I think you'd better stay away from there. Clarice is right. It isn't proper for a woman to go down there, especially after dark, and socialize with them. I know how you feel, but that's how it has to be."

At that, Angele's ire exploded. "This is just more of your family's snobbery, Ryan."

And, with that, she flounced out of the study, curtly closing the door behind her.

The instant she was gone, Clarice demanded of Ryan, "Do you see now what I have to put up with? Insolence. Stubbornness. That girl just doesn't care what people think. I only pray we get through this weekend without her doing something else to embarrass this family. I wish"—she paused to take a ragged breath—"that we weren't even having a social. But your father insisted."

Ryan regarded her coldly. "I know he did. He's told me how he's grown very fond of her, because she has mettle. She reminds him of my mother, because she was also a strong, spirited woman. So having Angele around makes him happy."

"Well, she doesn't make *me* happy." Clarice got up from the sofa and poured herself a sherry, ignoring Corbett's frown of disapproval. "And she's going to be the death of me if you don't see to it she behaves herself and does what I tell her to. Believe me, Ryan, I have tried, really tried, to help her. I like her, and I want to be her friend, but she obviously doesn't feel the same toward me. She doesn't care, and she's not interested in learning anything I can teach her. She even told me she wished she'd never left France. She said if she had it to do over again, she wouldn't have."

"I was worried about that," Corbett said as though he really was. He was also pleased that Clarice lied so well.

"Enough about Angele," Ryan said wearily. "Now, tell me, Clarice—why did you invite Denise this weekend? I know she's your cousin, but didn't you think how awkward it might be?"

Clarice mustered an innocent look. "No, and I don't think it will be. Besides, it would've caused talk to exclude her. After all, she's always been invited to every function we've had at BelleRose for as long as I can remember. I'm sorry if you're upset."

Ryan sighed. "It's too late to do anything about it now. Maybe it will be all right."

"I'm sure it will. Now, I'd better go to bed, and you all should do the same. We all need to be up early."

After she left, Corbett said, "Let's have one more drink before we turn in." He went to the sideboard and poured for both of them, then sat back down. "I'm sorry about Denise. Clarice didn't tell me she was going to invite her, or I'd have said not to."

Ryan was twirling his glass around and around on his desk, staring at the amber liquid. "I've got enough problems without adding another, but I'll manage."

"What do you mean?"

"That I wish sometimes I had listened to you."

Corbett had just taken a sip of his drink and nearly choked. Coughing, sputtering, he finally managed to clear his throat, and, with eyes watering, croaked, "What did you say?"

"I said maybe I should have listened to you."

"You mean you wish now you had proposed to Denise again?"

"No. I'm starting to wish I hadn't married Angele."

Corbett quickly took another swallow of whiskey, afraid if he didn't he was going to be grinning from ear to ear with joy. "But why? I mean, the two of you don't get along? I didn't know . . ."

"It's not that." Ryan gave a long, shuddering sigh. "I've just almost reached the conclusion she's never going to fit into our world and be happy here.

"And it also bothers me," he added, "how she kept it a secret she could speak English."

Corbett wriggled deliciously in his seat, liking what he was hearing. "Then you think she might run away and go back to France?"

"I don't know."

"Maybe you're worrying for nothing. She's probably just having a hard time adjusting. She'll settle down." Corbett was amazed at himself for sounding so sympathetic.

"I hope so," Ryan said quietly, soberly. "Because I don't want her to go."

Corbett felt a twinge of apprehension. "It would be embarrassing, I know, but not for long. After all, some people probably wouldn't be surprised. Clarice says lots of folks think you only married Angele because you were upset over Denise turning you down."

Ryan smirked. "And when have you ever known me to give a damn about gossip?"

Corbett felt a stronger twinge. "Then what are you saying?"

Ryan looked at him dismally. "I'm saying that I love her, Corbett . . . and I don't want her to leave me."

Corbett swallowed hard, fighting to maintain his composure. He hadn't expected this, and it was quite a blow. He needed time to think before he messed up and said the wrong thing. "Everything will work out for the best. Now, maybe we'd better call it a day. We've got a busy weekend ahead of us."

After Corbett left, Ryan had one more drink in the hope it would relax him, then went upstairs.

Entering the parlor, he turned toward his own room. He wanted Angele with every beat of his heart, but he feared his desire might make him weak. He might, God forbid, toss aside all resolve and tell her how much he loved her . . . how much he wanted her to stay with him forever. And, if she was planning to leave, it would only make matters worse.

And he didn't want her pity.

He wanted her love.

He was almost to his door when he heard hers open. It had long since been repaired since the night he had kicked it open.

"Ryan?" she called softly. "Please, I need to speak with you."

He did not turn around. "Can it wait till morning? It's late, and I have to be up early."

"No, it can't." She padded across the floor to stand directly behind him. "I've got something I want to say."

He turned, his breath catching in his throat. She was wearing a white gossamer gown that revealed every curve of her luscious body. Gritting his teeth against his longing to take her in his arms, he managed to sound weary as he said, "All right, what it is?"

"First, I want to know if you're angry with me about going to visit the servants." She shuddered to add, "I can't say the word you and your family use."

He made no comment on that, though he didn't like the word *slave*, either. "No, I'm not angry, but I meant what I said about your not going there again."

"Because of Clarice."

He hedged. "Well, it really isn't proper."

She pressed, "But mostly it's because of Clarice, am I right?"

"Angele—"

She held up a hand. "No. Wait. I want you to be completely frank with me, Ryan. I'm of the opinion that you and your father are very compassionate toward the Negroes. You said you had both been to their compound at different times for barbecues and such, so I think if it weren't for Clarice's objection, you wouldn't care. The Negroes treat me with respect. So it's all because of her, isn't it?"

"Let's talk about this some other time."

She stamped her foot, eyes flashing. "No. I've kept silent too long as it is. I'm sick and tired of the way Clarice treats me, and I want it to stop. She undermines everything I do."

"Undermines?" he echoed. "Angele, all she wants is to help you learn our ways, but you resist at every turn. You sneak off when she's not looking and disappear for hours on end. You're insolent and rude to her—"

"That's a lie!" she cried. "I knew it! Ryan, you have to listen—she's the one who's rude. She talks terribly to me, and—"

"Enough." He caught her arms and gave her a gentle shake. "We've always had peace in this house, and it's going to keep on being that way. Now, after this weekend, you, me, and Clarice are going to sit down and settle things. There's no reason why you two can't live under the same roof and be friends."

Angele yanked from his grasp. "No reason except that she wants you to get rid of me so you can marry her cousin."

"That's not true. She's told me how she's trying very hard to get along, but her patience is wearing thin, because you refuse to cooperate."

Angele decided she had gone too far to hold back any longer and plunged ahead to challenge, "Have you ever thought about why she and Corbett wanted you to marry Denise in the first place?"

He wondered what she was getting at but offered, "Because she's Clarice's cousin, I suppose."

"No," she said with resolve. "They wanted you to marry her so she could manipulate you, and Corbett would eventually take over BelleRose."

It was a serious accusation, but he couldn't help laughing. "That's the most ridiculous thing I've ever heard. Now why on earth would you say that? He's my cousin, for God's sake. He's family. They both are."

"That doesn't matter. My uncle betrayed my father."

Suddenly his interest was piqued. She had always resisted sharing anything to do with her family . . . her past. "Then tell me about it. I'd like to hear it."

She saw no point in doing so. Besides, she would have to be so careful with details he would surely ask about. "I don't like to talk about it. Just believe me when I say you can't trust people just because you're related to them."

Disappointed that she had, again, thrown up a wall between them, it was easy for resentment to surface. "Unless you're willing to substantiate your suspicions and accusations, this conversation is a waste of time. And I think you're just annoyed with Clarice, anyway, because she caught you slipping out to the compound. But there's no need in making trouble. Now, go to bed, and, as I said, the three of us will talk about it later.''

She looked at him for a long, searching moment, then said in defeat, "Why should we? You won't believe anything I say, anyway."

He pondered her words as he got ready for bed.

Maybe she was right, and, if so, it was her fault. She had, after all, given him so many reasons to doubt her.

Yet, despite all that, there was no denying he loved her.

Roscoe grumbled as the pounding on his door grew louder. If it were one of the slaves waking him up in the middle of the night, they goddamn well better have a good reason.

"Wait a damned minute!" he roared over the sleepy buzzing in his head. "And stop that infernal pounding . . ."

He swung his legs over the side of the bed, stood, and started shuffling across the floor in the darkness. It was a nice cabin. The Tremaynes always took care of their head overseer. There was a bedroom in the rear, and a sitting room between it and the office in front.

He didn't do much in his office, because he wrote little and read hardly at all. But it made him look important, and he liked that.

But he didn't like stumping his toe on his boots, which he'd left in the middle of the floor. Cursing, he stumbled the rest of the way to the door and yanked it open. "By damn, you better have a good reason for gettin' me outta bed—"

"I sure as hell do." Corbett pushed him aside as he entered.

Roscoe couldn't see him. "Let me get a lantern going."

"No. I don't want anybody to see a light and know you're up. We can talk in the dark."

"What's so important it can't wait till morning?"

"I want you to start watching Angele all the time. I want

you to follow her everywhere she goes. I want to know who she talks to, who she sees."

Roscoe liked that idea a lot. The new Mrs. Tremayne was real easy on the eyes. "Sure, but how come? You think she's got a lover already? Kinda soon, ain't it?"

"No, of course not," Corbett snapped. "But I want to catch her doing something to make Ryan want to get rid of her. Just tonight Clarice caught her going to the slave compound."

Roscoe was furious to hear that. "She's got no business there."

"No, but don't try to stop her. Ryan told her not to do it again, so if she does, we need to know it."

"And that's all you want me to do—watch her?" Roscoe asked, then pointed out, "This could've waited."

"No, it couldn't, because I want you to get started first thing in the morning making sure you're around her as much as possible without making her suspicious. Make friends with her if you can. See if you can get her to take you into her confidence."

"I offered to take her riding."

"Now what made you do that?" Corbett exploded. "That was impertinent, Roscoe. You're the overseer, damn it. You don't go around offering to take the ladies of the house riding."

Roscoe grinned in the darkness. "Maybe I had in mind riding something besides horses. I mean, she does act kind of restless and bored."

"I am not amused."

"And I'm not trying to be funny," Roscoe said lazily.

"Forget those kinds of notions. I've told you what I want you to do, and if you want to keep your job here, you'd better do it, because if we don't get rid of that little bitch, *she* is going to get rid of *us*."

Roscoe knew that was a distinct possibility and was not about to take any chances. "You don't have to worry. I won't let that happen."

"See that you don't."

Corbett disappeared into the night. And Roscoe decided not to go back to bed.

He had a lot of thinking to do.

Twenty-two

Corbett grumbled because Clarice had given him so much to do. He liked to relax before a big party, not help with preparations. She had also given him the responsibility of keeping an eye on Danny, because his mammy had been recruited to help decorate the ballroom.

But Danny was no trouble, Corbett thought, smiling as his son happily chased a butterfly across the lawn.

He had always wanted a large family, but after Danny was born, Clarice had said she would never endure such anguish again. She had not allowed him in her bed since. Consequently, he took his pleasure with any willing woman he took a fancy to. If Clarice ever suspected, she never said anything.

"Corbett, bring Danny to eat his lunch."

He turned to see Clarice waving from the front porch.

She looked beyond him and pointed. "Somebody's coming up the road."

Sending Danny inside, Corbett went to meet the man on horseback. His beard was gray, and his face was lined with wrinkles. His clothing was old and worn, and he wasn't wearing a gun. Corbett decided he had nothing to fear from the stranger and greeted, "Welcome to BelleRose. What can I do for you?"

The man shifted in the saddle, obviously weary from a long ride. "I'm lookin' for Mr. Tremayne."

"Which one?"

"Mr. Corbett Tremayne. I got a letter for him. The postmaster in Richmond asked me to bring it out. He said Mr. Tremayne's been askin' had it come yet. It's all the way from France."

Excitement surged. "I'm Corbett Tremayne. Give it to me." He held out his hand.

The man just sat there looking down at him. "Well, sir, I didn't ride all the way out here for nothin'. The postmaster, he said you were so anxious to get this here letter that you'd pay me for my trouble."

Impatience made him grind his teeth. "Yes, yes, of course." He fished in his pocket but found no money. Gesturing helplessly he offered, "How about if I pay you the next time I'm in town?"

The man chuckled. "I might not be around, and I need the money now or I wouldn't have agreed to bring it out here. I'll just wait till you go find some."

Exasperated, Corbett snapped, "All right. But can I have the letter now? It's important, and—"

"Afraid not. You might go in that big house of your'n and not come back out, and then what will I do? And I'm hungry, too. I could use a bite to eat."

Afraid if he made the old geezer angry he would just ride away without handing over the letter, Corbett ran all the way to the house.

He found Clarice in the family dining room with Danny. "Who was that man riding up?" she asked.

"I'll tell you later. Give me some money."

"What for?"

Forgetting Danny was sitting there, all ears, Corbett yelled, "Get me the money, goddamnit, and hurry up."

Stunned, she pushed back from the table. "I'll see what I have."

Danny began to bang on his plate with his spoon, chanting, "Money goddamnit—money goddamnit."

"Danny, stop that this instant!" Corbett roared.

"And you stop yelling at him," Clarice snapped as she came back into the room. "It's your fault. He repeats ev-

erything. Here." She thrust some coins into his outstretched hand. "This will have to do, but what's it for?"

"I don't have time to explain." He counted the coins,
hoped they would be enough, then glanced down at the
plate Clarice had just been served. Fried chicken, boiled
corn, hot biscuits, and tomatoes. He snatched it up and
rushed out.

"Where do you think you're going with my lunch?"
Clarice called after him. "You come back here this instant."

He kept on going, rushing across the lawn to where the
man had dismounted and was standing in the shade beneath a sprawling oak.

"Here." He handed him the coins, then the plate. "It's
the best I can do. Now, give me the letter."

"Mind if I sit here and eat?"

Corbett could not risk Ryan seeing him and asking questions. If the letter contained no useful information, then
he didn't want him knowing he had used what money he
had left in Paris to pay someone to send it to him. But if,
on the other hand, there was something he could use
against Angele, he wanted to wait till the right moment to
present it. "Actually, I do mind," he said in as polite a
tone as he could manage in his eagerness to get his hands
on the letter. "We're expecting guests, and it doesn't look
proper for someone to be sitting on the ground eating.
So if you'd just ride on down the road . . ."

The man's eyes narrowed. "What about the plate?
What'll I do with the plate?"

"Leave it on the road. Someone will get it later. It
doesn't matter. *Just give me the letter.*" His voice rose.

The delicious smell of the chicken made the old man
anxious to eat. "All right. Don't be so danged impatient."
He went to his saddlebag, took out a crumpled envelope,
and before he could give it to him, Corbett snatched it
from his hand and hurried away.

He didn't look back to see if the man left, because he
had already dismissed him from his mind.

He waited until he was in his room before reading the

letter, then, with each line, his heart beat faster. By the time he finished, he was trembling from head to toe.

It was exactly what he had hoped for—information that would prove Angele had lied about herself from the very beginning.

He ran to find Clarice. She was still in the dining room. She didn't argue about getting up from the table to go with him, curious over why he was so excited.

At last, when they were alone, he showed her the letter. As she read, he said, "Remember I told you about paying someone to find out who was buried in that grave Angele was visiting in Paris when I was spying on her? And how she later told Ryan it was her mother? Well, this letter is from that man, and what he's got to say is very interesting. Read on."

"I'm trying to," she said, annoyed. "But I can't with you blathering."

Corbett was silent for a moment, then could stand it no longer. "I know who Angele really is. On the ship there was a woman from England, and she told us the same thing that's in that letter, how Angele and her mother had run away. She didn't know their names, but they were the women she was talking about. She said a rich man was offering a reward for anyone who could tell him where they were." He smacked his fists together. "I can't wait to tell Ryan."

Clarice looked at him menacingly. "You aren't going to do that."

He blinked. "And why not? This letter proves she's half English. It explains her understanding the language, knowing about horses, everything. She lied by making him think both her parents were French to get him to marry her. She tricked him. And when he finds out, he'll divorce her and marry Denise. This is what I've been waiting for, hoping for—something to use against her and make Ryan see he's got to get rid of her."

"You idiot." She shook the letter in his face. "Didn't

you wake me up last night to tell me Ryan told you he loves her?"

He had done so after returning from his talk with Roscoe. "Yes, but—"

"Don't you see? If he loves her, it's not going to make any difference. He'll accept that lie just like he's accepted all the others he's caught her in. I wonder if it would even matter to Uncle Roussel, she's got him so bewitched. And if you do tell Ryan about it, he'll be angry with you for interfering."

Corbett looked confused. "Then what do we do? We can't keep it a secret she isn't French."

"Of course we can, because it is not, ultimately, going to matter. Just keep on with your plan to have Roscoe follow her till we find something else that will completely turn Ryan against her. If need be, we'll make him think she's sleeping with Roscoe."

"I still say—"

"Corbett, listen to me. I'm just as upset and angry about this as you are, because it proves what a little conniver she really is. But we have to stay calm and think things through so that when it's all over with and she's gone, Ryan won't blame us for any of it. Understand?"

He nodded reluctantly. He would like nothing better than to march right in to Ryan that very minute and show him the letter.

"Besides," Clarice continued, "we have to wait till after this weekend to do anything, so our guests won't suspect anything is wrong."

"All right. But are you absolutely sure we shouldn't just go ahead and let Ryan know the truth?"

"If you hadn't told me what you did last night, I would say so, but now that he's gone and fallen in love with her, it would take more than finding out her father was English to change how he feels."

Corbett took the letter and scanned it once more, then gloated, "I'll wager they ran away from Angele's uncle because he caught them stealing from him."

"I wouldn't be surprised. Now, I've got to finish my lunch, so I can take a nap before getting dressed for tonight."

She started for the door, then hesitated. "But there is one person I have to take into our confidence."

He knew without having to ask.

Her smile was wicked. "I just can't wait to tell Denise."

Angele stirred and moaned as Selma pulled the cord to open the drapes, flooding the room with light. "Not yet," she pleaded. "Let me sleep a little longer."

"Missy, you can't." Selma plumped the pillows behind her as she groggily sat up. "It's soon gonna be time to start gettin' dressed for the ball. You've slept most of the day away. I fixed you some eggs and toast and tea. You eat while I get your bath ready."

Angele took one look at the plate of scrambled eggs and gagged. "Just tea and toast," she said. "My stomach is still upset from the dumplings last night. All that butter and brown sugar didn't agree with me."

Selma wasn't listening. "What are you gonna wear tonight? I'll get everything ready. You've got to hurry. Miz Denise is already here."

Angele's hand, on the way to her mouth with a piece of toast, froze in midair. "Already? Why is she so early?"

"She's stayin' the weekend and needs to get settled in. They're unloadin' her trunks now."

Angele pushed the tray away and swung her legs over the side of the bed. "Did you say she's going to be here all weekend?"

"Yes'm. I heard Miz Clarice tell Mammy Lou to get one of the guest rooms ready for her 'cause she's gonna be here for a few days."

Angele felt a wave of nausea and wondered if it was her upset stomach or vexation. Whatever the cause, she was determined to get through the festivities with head held high.

After she finished her bath, Selma coiffed her hair in

ringlets. Held at her crown by a glittering diamond-and-ruby comb, the ringlets brushed her shoulders, a few stray curls saucily wisping about her face.

Angele was still bothered by what she had seen the night before, and, as Selma worked, she mentioned again the incident of the reported drowning. "Are you sure you didn't hear about it? I distinctly understood that—"

"No, ma'am," Selma cut her off. "If it happened, I don't know about it."

The conversation reached a dead end, and Angele gave up. Something was wrong, but Selma wasn't going to talk about it.

When she was finished, Selma stepped back to admire what she had done. "You're gonna be the most beautiful lady at the ball. Now, I'll help you with your dress."

Looking at the gown she had planned to wear that Selma had laid on the bed, Angele declared, "I've changed my mind." She went to her wardrobe and moved hangers aside till she found what she was looking for. "I'm wearing this instead."

Selma's eyes rounded. "It's red as blood, Miz Angele, but it sure is pretty. I've never seen one like it."

"Red has always been my favorite color. Ryan hasn't seen this gown. I've been saving it for a special occasion."

Selma helped her into it, commenting on how the velvet material clung to her every curve. "And you don't even have to wear those new-type corsets Mammy Lou told me about that Miz Clarice bought in Richmond. It looks like it was made with you wearing it."

Angele turned in front of the full-length, gilt-edged mirror. Actually, she had almost been sewn into it, because the dressmaker in Paris had made it fit like a glove. The bodice, however, seemed tighter than when she had tried it on months ago. Her breasts were all but pouring out of it, and she wondered if she was gaining weight.

She turned sideways.

No, her figure was still trim. Only her bosom seemed larger. She smiled at herself to think that was not a bad

thing. Maybe Ryan would pay special attention to her tonight if he saw other men looking at her.

The dress was a stunning creation by virtue of its sim-
plicity. Tiny corded straps of matching red velvet cut to
the bodice, which hung in drapes before tapering to the
narrow waist. The skirt fell straight to the floor and had a
slit up one side similar to the one in the dress she had
worn to Clarice's little tea. But this time it went all the way
up her thigh, exposing most of her leg.

Diamond-and-ruby earbobs and necklace matched her
hair comb.

She stepped into red velvet slippers, then turned in front
of the mirror again, pleased with the final results.

Hesitantly, Selma murmured, "I just ain't never seen a
skirt torn like that. Are you sure you want to wear it?"

Angele laughed. "The only reason the other ladies won't
be wearing one just like it is because they haven't got here
from Paris yet. And the skirt isn't torn, Selma. It's called
a slit, it's very fashionable, and, yes, I am sure I want to
wear it."

She had eaten the toast, drunk two cups of tea, and her
stomach finally seemed to be settling. She was ready for
the evening, and it was a good thing, because Ryan
knocked on the door and told her everyone was waiting
for her.

Responding that she would be right down, her pulses
were racing.

She was about to meet Richmond society . . . *and* the
woman everyone thought Ryan would marry.

Ryan was waiting for her in the parlor. When she came
out of her room, his mouth fell open. "My God . . ." he
breathed hoarsely. "My God—" he repeated. "Angele, you
are gorgeous."

Demurely, she countered by complimenting, "And
you're quite handsome, yourself." He wore a simple dark-
blue frock coat, cut away in front, with tails. A madras cra-
vat adorned his white shirt, and his well-fitting trousers
were a few shades lighter than his coat.

He couldn't help himself. Slipping his arm about her waist, he pulled her against him as his mouth came to hers. He held tight, deepening the kiss amidst hunger and heat, passion and desire.

She clung to him, wanting more, wishing there were no party to go to, wishing there were no guests to meet . . . that they could answer the hunger that was surging like a mountain stream run wild.

Forcing himself to release her, he stood back, shaken. "We'd better join the others. Roussel is anxious to introduce you to everyone."

As he continued to ravish her with his eyes, she took his arm and they made their way to the top of the grand spiral staircase. The banister had been draped in white satin ribbons and adorned with yellow roses.

Everyone had crowded into the foyer and clustered in the doorways to the parlor and the ballroom. When Angele came into view, a murmur rippled through the air like a cresting wave.

"They think you're beautiful, too," Ryan whispered.

At the bottom of the stairs, Roussel came forward to offer his arm to Angele. Graciously she took it, and the crowd parted as he escorted her into the center of the ballroom.

At his signal, the musicians ceased to play. He then cleared his throat and declared with flourish, "I present to you the new mistress of BelleRose, my daughter-in-law, Mrs. Ryan Tremayne."

The applause was nearly deafening.

Angele glanced about shyly, appreciatively—and that was when her gaze fell on Clarice. She was standing not too far away, lovely in a demure gown of brown taffeta. Her mouth was frozen in a smile that could only be forced.

But it was the woman beside her that made little pinpricks of alarm dance up and down her spine.

It had to be Denise.

Her hair was the color of silver, swept up high and caught with a garnet-encrusted band. She wore huge diamond earrings that sparkled to compete with the glitter of the dazzling crystal chandeliers overhead. Her gown was the color of bright, spring grass, the low-cut bodice crusted in shimmering garnets.

Angele could easily see why Ryan had wanted to marry her. Not only was she lovely, but she stood poised like royalty.

And no one but Angele noticed how the corners of her lips twitched in the hint of an arrogant, confident smirk.

"My son, the proud groom," Roussel was saying, waving to Ryan to join them, then putting his arm about his shoulders.

"Now everyone in Richmond knows how I feel about my heritage, and—" he went on to boast.

"You mean everyone in the whole state of Virginia," someone shouted.

Laughter erupted.

Roussel grinned, continuing. "And I'm happy to know my grandchildren will also be French and confident they will treasure their lineage like their ancestors."

There was more applause, and then a receiving line formed as everyone pushed forward to personally be introduced to Angele. By the time the crush ended, the musicians had begun to play once more and Ryan had been swallowed by the crowd.

Clarice suddenly appeared at Angele's side. "I know you're hungry, dear," she said, drawing her away and through the archway into the formal dining room.

Angele saw the tables offering cakes, berry cobblers, fruit pies, and creamy puddings. She felt another roll of queasiness and could not bear the thought of eating anything rich and sweet. Then she saw a tray of bread and moved toward that.

Clarice stayed right beside her, and as soon as no one else was around, hissed in her ear, "You look like a whore in that dress. How dare you shame the family this way?"

Angele nearly choked on the piece of bread she had just put in her mouth and stammered, "I . . . I don't understand what you mean."

"Of course you do. That awful slit gown you wore to tea was bad enough, but this"—she gestured, nose wrinkled in disgust—"this is abominable."

Angele was swept with indignity. "Ryan and his father didn't seem to think so."

"They're too gentlemanly to say so. They don't want to hurt your feelings."

"But you don't seem to mind doing it."

"Someone has to tell you that you are an embarrassment to this family."

Before Angele could respond, Clarice turned on her heel and swept from the room.

Angele was no longer hungry. What she wanted, *needed*, was to find Ryan and see in his gaze once more that he found her pretty, appealing . . . and not at all what Clarice accused her of being.

Wandering about, she could not find him anywhere. Passing Roussel, he asked if she were enjoying herself.

"Oh, yes," she managed to sound sincere. "I was just wondering where Ryan was. I'd like him to dance with me."

"Sorry, but I haven't seen him, dear." He turned back to the man he had been talking to.

Another man standing nearby leaned toward her. "I saw him go out on the terrace a little while ago," he said.

She thanked him and moved toward the French doors that led to one of her favorite spots. By daylight, there was an inspiring view of the carefully manicured gardens with masses of daisies, zinnias, and the spectacular rose gardens. There was also a reflecting pool and a huge fountain and even a statuary.

The doors were flanked by sweeping potted palms. Angele stepped outside and glanced around. Then, in the light spilling from the floor-to-ceiling windows of the ballroom, she saw Ryan standing at the end of the terrace.

And he was not alone.

The silver-haired woman was with him.

Her first impulse was to walk right up to them. After all,

he was her husband. She had every right. But another part of her urged that she draw back into the shadows. By so doing, she might discover whether Denise was actually a threat.

"I'm so looking forward to the jumping tomorrow, Ryan. I wish you'd compete. I know you'd win that saddle."

Angele couldn't hear Ryan's response because his back was turned. Denise was standing sideways, facing him, her voice easily carrying.

"Remember when we used to ride together? You said I was the best woman rider you'd ever seen."

She was gazing up at him, making her voice soft and cooing.

Angele wrinkled her nose. She reminded her of a pigeon.

"I'll never forget that beautiful weeping willow tree by our secret pond . . . the way the fronds tickled our faces when we were laying on the ground under it. Those were such wonderful times."

Angele couldn't hear what Ryan said in response.

Then Denise gave a feathery little laugh and twirled completely around, her skirt billowing. "Ryan, I was such a fool. If I had it to do over again . . ."

Moving quietly, and as fast as she dared, Angele tiptoed closer, desperate to hear what Ryan might say. But just as he started to speak, another couple came up the steps from the rose garden. They all exchanged pleasantries for a few moments, and, finally, Ryan said he needed to get back to his guests.

Pressing tightly against the wall, Ryan didn't see Angele in the shadows as he passed. She didn't, however, return to the party after the others left. Instead, she mulled Denise's words over and over.

If I had it to do over again . . .

What had he been about to say—that he wished it were possible to turn back time?

She felt tears welling and blinked furiously.

When she had vowed never to cry again, she hadn't considered the anguish unrequited love could cause.

But dear Lord, she knew it now.

Hearing more voices, she swiped at her eyes with the back of her hand. She was trapped where she was but didn't care. If she went back inside and saw Ryan with Denise again, her heart might break so loud everyone would hear it.

If not for Clarice being so against her, probably saying terrible things to Ryan about her, Angele knew she might not feel so insecure where Denise was concerned.

Then, too, she knew she had made some foolish mistakes that caused him to doubt her. And, perhaps even worse, he might decide he had made a mistake himself— by marrying her.

Two men appeared. She remembered having met them in the receiving line. Frank Borden and Larson somebody.

They went to the end of the terrace and lit cheroots.

Lost in her own misery, she wasn't paying any attention to their conversation till one said, "That's bad about the runaway last night, Frank. Do you think your boys will find him?"

Larson sounded very angry. "I hope so, and when they do, I'm gonna have him strung up and whipped and make every slave I own watch so they'll think twice before they try to run."

"I hope you get him, but I heard Joel Winstock say a while ago that there's stronger talk about some kind of underground railroad helping slaves make it north. And I think it makes sense. I mean, think about how few have got caught lately. They just seem to drop out of sight. Even the dogs can't keep their scent."

"I've heard that talk, too," Larson said, "and I'm starting to think the same thing. I also believe we've been wrong in figuring they head straight for the James River."

"Well, that's where the dogs lose the scent," Frank pointed out.

"True, but I think that's done on purpose—to make us

think that's the way they went—to cross where the river bends below the Berkeley plantation. Actually, I believe they're going farther north, skirting up around Hopewell and then crossing inland to the York River and then making their way down to the bay area. From there, somebody is waiting to take them on up to Philadelphia, and, damn it, once they get there, they're safe."

"Yes, but don't forget the law Congress passed over twenty years ago that makes it a crime to help a runaway."

Larson's laugh was bitter. "You think those Northerners care about the Fugitive Slave Law? The Negroes up there are organized. They call themselves the Free African Society. I've even heard there's a group called the American Colonization Society that's started up a place in West Africa where freed slaves are being sent. You think they aren't going to transport runaways there, too?"

Angele was practically holding her breath so they would not know she was there. Now she believed, beyond all doubt, that the young Negro she'd seen crashing out of the woods at the compound last night was Larson's runaway. Evidently BelleRose Negroes were the first link in the underground railroad, and she needed to hear as much as possible so she could pass the information along to Selma—*if* she could get her to admit it as true.

"Anyway," Larson went on, "as soon as my boys either catch the latest runaway or lose his trail completely, we're going to start keeping an eye on the north roads and woods instead of the river due east. We're going to put a stop to it, by damn."

They tossed away their cheroots and went back inside.

Angele waited a few moments, then followed.

Entering the ballroom, she noted first that the music had become livelier. Then she saw that men and women were lined up across from each other, one couple at a time moving toward the center to join hands and then skip to the end of the line.

"It's called the reel."

Angele snapped her head about to see Clarice at her side.

Coolly, she said, "Watch carefully, and maybe you can learn the steps. Especially watch Ryan," she added with a smirk. "He and Denise are considered the best dancers in Richmond."

Angele watched as long as she could bear it, then wandered away. She wasn't feeling well and told herself it was nerves. So much had happened, and she was a maelstrom of emotions. She wished the evening would hurry and end and that Ryan would later come to her bed or ask her to his.

And she also yearned desperately to find a way to tell Selma what she had heard the men discussing on the terrace so she could warn the others.

The night wore on. Then Roussel retired upstairs and guests not spending the night began to leave.

Angele went to search for Ryan to tell him she was also going to bed.

She found him in his study. Larson, Frank, and some other men she recognized as planters were there also.

They fell silent when they noticed her standing in the doorway, but she had managed to catch a word or two before they did.

Slaves.

Runaways.

Patrols.

They were planning their strategy.

And Ryan had apparently been trying to make them understand why he did not want to be involved.

"Excuse me, everyone," she said quietly, politely. "I want to tell my husband good night."

He followed her out in the hall. "Forgive me if I don't go with you," he said, "but I have to see to the rest of the guests."

"I'll wait up," she murmured.

And she did so until she could hold her eyes open no longer.

* * *

She had curled up in Ryan's bed, but when she awoke at the first light of dawn, she saw, with heavy heart, that his side was empty.

He had been out all night.

Twenty-three

Angele awoke feeling even more nauseated than she had the night before. And when she got out of bed, she was dizzy and thought for a few seconds she was going to faint.

It did not last long, and she remembered she hadn't eaten anything and decided that was probably why she felt so bad. Then again, she might be coming down with something. But even if she were, she had no intentions of staying in bed and giving Denise free rein to flirt with Ryan.

And where was he, anyway?

She dressed quickly.

It was still quite early. Stepping into the hall, she didn't hear a sound. She went to the stairs and leaned over the railing, but all was quiet below. Everyone was still asleep and probably would not be up for a while yet.

As she crept down the steps, she was torn between looking for Ryan and finding Selma to tell her what she'd overheard last night.

Then she realized perhaps she'd be better off not knowing where Ryan had slept, because if she found him in Denise's room, she was not sure what she would do.

Slipping out the back door, she headed for the compound.

She didn't know that Roscoe was awake . . . and waiting to follow wherever she went.

* * *

"Miz Angele, what are you doin' here? It ain't even good daylight yet."

Selma was standing on the porch of her little shack, washing her face in a basin of water she'd brought up from the creek like all the other women did first thing every morning.

Angele ran up on the porch. "I have to talk to you right away. It's important."

Toby appeared in the doorway. He had just got up, but his sleepy eyes opened wide when he saw Angele.

"Both of you need to hear. Let's go inside, please."

Exchanging an anxious look with Toby, Selma said, "All right, if that's what you want."

Angele glanced about. There was only one room, and it was sparsely furnished with a rickety table, two chairs, and a mattress on the floor, which was cluttered with their few belongings.

Angele remained standing, even though Selma politely offered her a chair. "This won't take long, and I can tell you're nervous about me being here."

"It could get me and Toby in a peck of trouble," Selma said.

"I won't let that happen, and I don't intend for anybody to know I was here this morning, anyway. I have to ask you a question, and I want the truth."

Selma nodded uncertainly. "All right."

"Is this plantation the first stop for a runaway slave?"

Selma paled and cut a glance at Toby, who shook his head ever so slightly. With a thin laugh, she replied, "I don't know what you mean."

"I think you do. Last night after I left here, I heard strange noises and turned back to see what was going on. A Negro came out of the woods, and he looked out of breath and scared."

"I still don't know what—"

"Selma, stop lying," Angele snapped. "I know a slave ran away from another plantation last night, and I believe it was the boy I saw coming out of the woods."

"I'm telling the truth," Selma said, lips trembling. "I swear there ain't no runaways here."

"I didn't ask if there were any here *now*. I want to know if this is where they come first when they run away. I only want to help, and I promise your secret will be safe with me."

Selma looked to Toby again, and this time he gave his head a firm swing from side to side.

Angele saw him and cried, "Don't you understand? I want to help. I overheard some of the planters talking last night about how they think there's some kind of underground movement—a railroad, they called it—to help runaways go north. And they think they've been wrong about which direction they've been heading."

She recounted everything the men had said.

When she had finished, Toby walked over and knelt in front of her so they were eye level. "Miz Angele, now I want you to listen to me. Our people like you, but you ain't got no business gettin' mixed up in this, so it's best you just get on back to the house and forget whatever it is you think you saw last night."

She knew she was getting nowhere. They were not going to admit anything, but at least they could pass along the information she had given them.

"Very well," she sighed. "I'm sorry if I upset you." She noticed that Selma looked as though she were about to cry.

Toby went to the door with her, while Selma hung back. "We appreciate you caring about all of us, Miz Angele. We really do. But there ain't nothin' goin' on here that ought not be, and I hope you'll tell anybody that who might think otherwise."

"You don't have to worry." She looked past him to where Selma was still huddled in a chair. "Selma, do you by any chance know what time Master Ryan retired last night? He was asleep when I awoke this morning, and if the guests were terribly late leaving, I want him to sleep as long as possible so he won't be tired today."

Selma's fingers were splayed across her face, and she

peered through them at Angele. "No, ma'am. I was busy cleanin' up. I didn't see him."

The minute she was off the porch, Selma leaped up to run to the door and watch till she was out of sight, then whirled on Toby to cry, "I don't trust her. She was tryin' to get us to admit we're helpin' runaways so she can tell. I just know it."

Toby looked uncertain. "I don't know, honey. She seems like a real nice lady. Maybe she does want to help. And don't forget that runaway came last night just a minute or two after you finally got her to leave, so she probably did see him."

"Maybe she did, but she can't prove anything, and that's why she was tryin' to get us to tell her. She probably made up the whole story about hearin' those men talkin'."

"I'm still gonna pass the word along, and if any white men and dogs are where she said they'd be, we'll know she was tellin' the truth. Then we can trust her."

"Hmmph," Selma grunted, continuing to stare down the path. "Probably all she really wanted was to find out whether I saw Master Ryan with Miz Denise after everybody left."

She went back to the basin to finish washing her face.

Toby watched her in silence for a few moments, then quietly asked, "Did you?"

She wiped at her eyes with a rag, then hung the towel on a nail to dry. "All I know is, the last time I saw either one of 'em, they were together."

"And where were they?" Toby persisted.

Selma's expression turned sad. Actually, she liked Miz Angele and hated for her to be hurt. "Everybody was gone but them. I went to get the last of the glasses, like Mammy Lou tol' me to, and that's when I saw 'em—goin' into Master Ryan's study. He closed the door, and when I left the house a long time later, they were still in there."

"That don't look good," Toby said with a solemn shake of his head. "That don't look good at all."

It was still so early that Angele felt it was safe to cut through Roscoe's woods and pass his cabin to get back to the house faster.

Her heart was aching to know whether Ryan had made love to Denise. It would mean he loved her, and, if so, Angele would have no choice but to set him free.

She slowed as reason set in.

It was obvious Denise had been throwing herself at him last night, but Angele had no proof that he enjoyed it . . . no reason to assume he had bedded her. And if she went tearing into the house to search all over to try and find them together, she would look like a fool.

The thing to do, she decided, was give him the benefit of the doubt as long as possible. Meanwhile, by God, she would fight for him.

She only wished she felt more like fighting.

She still felt sick to her stomach. She was tired, and her nerves were on edge. That was not like her, and she needed to get hold of herself in order to think clearly.

What she also needed to do, she thought with determination rolling through her veins like liquid fire, was to make Ryan really sit up and take notice of her—and not by merely looking pretty. She wanted him to see that she was smart and knowledgeable.

She came to a halt as the idea struck like the mosquito she quickly slapped off her arm.

There was something she could do that would not only make him notice her but also outshine Denise.

She would show him and everyone else she could not only ride—she could beat all the men at jumping the hurdles. But she would need a horse, and—

A twig snapped, breaking the silence around her. Whirling about, she gasped in surprise to see Roscoe Fordham.

* * *

Roscoe wanted to kick himself all the way to the barn and back. He hadn't expected her to stop walking all of a sudden and just stand there. Afraid she might turn around and see him, he had managed to get into the brush without making a sound. But then, when she had started walking again, he had stepped on a stick, breaking it with a loud pop. Now he had to come up with a fast explanation as to why he was there.

She was staring at him expectantly. "Mr. Fordham? What are you doing up so early?"

"Uh . . ." He was floundering, then, out of the corner of his eye, saw a nearby blackberry bush. "Picking berries," he said. "I like berries for breakfast."

"I see."

He told himself to stop acting guilty. After all, he had a right to be in the woods where he lived, but what the hell was *she* doing there? "It's kinda early for you to be out, isn't it? Especially around here. Is something wrong?"

"Actually, I was looking for you." Angele was able to think faster than Roscoe, and, needing a horse, remembered his offer to take her riding.

She got right to the point. "Mr. Fordham, can you get me a good jumping horse and not let anyone know?"

He thought a minute, then drawled, "Well, I might could, but what do you want one for?"

"I'm going to compete against the men this afternoon, and I want it to be a surprise."

Her eyes were shining with the mischief, and Roscoe could not wait to tell Corbett about this latest development. Already he had followed her to the slave compound and watched her go inside Selma and Toby's cabin. There was something funny going on, all right.

He scratched his chin to give the impression he had to really think about it.

"Please, Mr. Fordham. You won't get in trouble. I'll tell

Ryan I got the horse myself, and I suppose I could do that, but I wouldn't know which one was the best jumper."

"Are you sure you can ride good enough?"

"Positive. Now, will you help me and keep it our secret?"

That comment made him think how there were a *lot* of things he'd like to do with her and keep secret. Finally, he said, "All right, but you've got to promise not to tell anybody."

She was bouncing up and down on her toes, she was so happy. "I won't. I swear it. When can you have him ready?"

"Right before they start jumping, you come to the back of the last stable—the one on the very end, and I'll have him ready. Don't let anybody see you, though."

"I won't," she promised. "And thank you, Mr. Fordham. You don't know how much this means to me."

Roscoe was beaming. "I'm glad to do it, Miss Angele. But remember—it's just between us."

He couldn't wait to tell Corbett.

When Angele returned to her wing of the house, she found Ryan in the parlor. He was wearing black suede riding pants and a red silk shirt, open at the neck. His hair was still damp from his bath.

Angele saw the redness in his eyes and knew it was from lack of sleep. "You look tired," she said.

"Actually, I'm exhausted. I fell asleep in my study last night."

She feigned innocence. "You didn't come upstairs?"

"No. Some of the guests staying over didn't want to go to bed, and I had to be polite and keep them company. By the time I got rid of them, I leaned back in my chair to rest a minute, and the next thing I knew, the sun was coming up."

He was on his way out. "Sorry to be in such a hurry. Some of the folks wanted to go for a morning ride. I'll see you at lunch."

* * *

Ryan felt like a hypocrite to have made Angele think there would be several people on the ride. He hated deceit and was now guilty of it himself but saw no other way. Had he told her he was going out alone with Denise, she might have got the wrong idea.

He didn't want to go, anyway, but promising he would had been the only way he had been able to get rid of her last night. Now all he wanted was to get it over with quickly. Otherwise, she would think he wanted to be with her.

And he didn't.

He had found the woman he truly wanted by his side.

The problem was—he feared that was not where she wanted to be.

Angele hated being so suspicious but felt she had to know exactly what she was up against.

She waited a few moments, then followed Ryan to the stables, careful that he would not know she was watching.

And when she saw that there was only one other person going on the ride with him and that person was Denise, the crack in her breaking heart deepened.

Somehow, she got through the morning, helping Clarice greet guests, making small talk . . . polite chat, pretending to be happy and having a wonderful time. But all the while she was fighting nausea. Sipping cool tea and nibbling Mammy Lou's soda biscuits helped a bit, but she still didn't feel at all well.

For lunch, linen-covered tables were set on the lawn beneath pastel canopies. The air was pungent with the smell of pigs roasting on hand-turned skewers over pits of smoldering hickory chips. Fish and chicken fried in big, black cauldrons over open fires. White-coated servants scurried about with trays of potato salad, coleslaw, tureens of buttered vegetables, crisp watermelon pickles, peach chutney, and corn relish.

Ryan joined Angele and led her to a table where no one else was sitting. She was grateful to be alone with him but the precious time did not last. Clarice came over, bringing Corbett and little Danny, and a few minutes later she spotted Denise in the crowd and waved her to join them.

"I hope you don't mind," she said sweetly to Angele. "She's my cousin, but if she makes you uncomfortable . . ."

"Of course not," Angele responded cordially. "I don't mind at all. If she's your family, then it makes her *my* family," she added, taking secret delight as Clarice's face flashed with annoyance.

At once, Denise monopolized the conversation, making sure to talk about things that Angele knew nothing about so she would feel left out.

Her patience wore thin. To make Ryan turn his attention from Denise, she brought up the subject of the horses he had bought in France. Then she was able to easily hold his interest by telling him things she knew about Anglo-Arabs she'd not shared with him before.

He held on to her every word, fascinated, and believing she had learned it all during the time she had spent with *relatives* in England.

It was only when Dr. Pardee came to tell Ryan it was time for the horse jumping that he and Angele realized they had been so engrossed in the topic they had become oblivious to everything else.

Ryan glanced about in surprise. Everyone had finished eating and either moved to the terrace or gone inside the house. All the tables were being cleared away except for theirs, and they were the only ones still there. The others had left, unnoticed.

"Doctor Pardee, thanks for letting me know. I'll be right there."

The doctor nodded and left.

Ryan turned to Angele. "You just continue to amaze me, and I wish you'd share everything about yourself—all the way back to when you were born," he added with a smile that washed over her like liquid sunshine.

Angele regretted that was not possible, but at least she could reveal one more thing. He was about to discover she was an excellent rider.

And so was Denise.

She went to the last stable, just as Roscoe had told her to do, and was relieved to find him waiting outside.

"I really appreciate this," she greeted him. "Is my horse ready? I can't wait to see him. Is there time for me to take him for a quick ride somewhere we won't be seen? It would give me a chance to get used to him, and . . ." She trailed off to silence to see how he was staring over her head as if he were afraid to look her in the eye.

"Is something wrong?" Anxiety nibbled.

"Well . . ." he drawled, still looking beyond her. "I've been thinking how this isn't such a good idea."

"Please don't change your mind," she groaned. "You said you'd do it."

"Yeah, I know, but if anybody found out, I'd lose my job. And what if you got hurt? You don't know nothin' about this horse, and you don't have time to try him out. You'd have to get on him and jump."

She was undaunted. "Is he well trained?"

"One of the best."

"And he's a good jumper?"

"Roussel used to jump him all the time."

Hearing that made her all the more determined, for she knew Ryan's father would have had nothing less than the finest horse on the plantation. "Then I have to ride him. Please, hurry and get him saddled."

"He already is. I took Miss Clarice's saddle from the tack room. But I still don't know. I just don't feel good about this."

Frustration was making her feel even sicker than she already did. Once the jump was over, and she had proved herself, she was going to talk to Dr. Pardee and ask him what he thought might be wrong with her. But right then, she had only one thing on her mind. "I'm begging you, Mr. Fordham. Let me have the horse. I swear to you again and again that I will never tell it was you who helped me. I'll say I picked him out and took Clarice's saddle. Your name will never be mentioned."

He scratched his chin. "Are you willing to do that no matter what happens? Even if you fall and get hurt, you won't tell I had anything to do with it?"

She held up her right hand. "I swear to God, Mr. Fordham."

He did look her in the eye then, long and hard. She began to think he really wasn't going to give in when he finally said, "All right. He's in the first stall on the left. Now I'm getting out of here. You're on your own, and I don't know nothin' about any of this."

She thanked him and ran inside the stable.

Roscoe glanced around to make sure no one could see him and then took off for the woods. He would circle around as though he had been nowhere near the stables— just as Corbett had told him to.

And, just as Corbett had also instructed, he had given her the old man's horse.

What she didn't know, however—and *would soon find out*—was that nobody had ever ridden him *but* the old man.

Angele opened the gate to the stall very slowly.

The horse was a beauty, sleek and black as midnight, with a powerful chest and strong, heavily corded and muscular legs.

He looked like a jumper, all right.

He also looked leery of her.

"Ho, boy, it's all right." She spoke softly and was careful not to make any sudden moves.

He began to prance around a bit as he watched her warily.

Stroking him gently, she continued to whisper soothing words.

When he seemed calm enough, she climbed up on the railing, then slowly lowered herself into the sidesaddle.

Careful not to jerk the reins too tight, she backed him out of the stall, then walked him out and along the back side of the row of stables.

Reaching the closest point to where the jumping was going on without anyone being able to see her, Angele waited.

The horse seemed restless, and the way he pawed the ground impatiently made her nervous. He probably hadn't been ridden in months and had too much green grass in his belly. That always made a horse a bit hard to handle, but as soon as he sensed that she wasn't afraid of him and knew what she was doing, she was confident everything would be all right.

Finally, the time had come. Everyone was cheering Dr. Pardee, who appeared to have won, but Angele laughed out loud to think how she had news for all of them.

"Go, boy!" She popped the reins over his neck. "Show them what we can do."

The great horse took off at full gallop as though he had been waiting for the moment.

Angele leaned forward, heading him straight for the line of hurdles. There were only three. She had jumped as many as five before but was grateful for a short ride on a strange horse, especially when she felt she was going to throw up any second.

She heard the cries and shouts from the crowd when they saw her. She couldn't tell what they were saying but knew they were all rushing forward to watch. Those on the porch ran down the steps, all hurrying to the impromptu track.

She was almost lying across the horse's neck, in position for the first jump. He was running wide open. She had given him full rein.

"Now, go!" she shouted, as his forelegs left the ground.

He took the first hurdle, and the crowd yelled even louder.

Then came the second, and he flew over that one.

And when he made the third, his hooves nowhere near the wooden beams, cheers went up like a tidal wave.

She straightened and began to pull back on the reins. "You did it, you wonderful horse! I'm going to feed you sugar and apples for a week . . ."

He kept on going.

She yanked harder. "Whoa, boy. It's over. Whoa, now."

He went faster, head thrown into the wind. She was having difficulty hanging on. Again and again, she jerked the reins and screamed for him to stop, but it only seemed to make him charge harder.

Suddenly he turned sharply, and Angele went sailing through the air to land with a hard smack on the ground.

She tried to breathe, but the effort sliced painfully through her like a knife. She'd had the wind knocked out of her before, knew the anguish of her lungs fighting for air. But she was also hurting terribly low in her stomach and around to her back. Feeling something warm and wet between her legs, she thought with a jolt that she must have landed on a rock and been cut somewhere and was bleeding.

Ryan was the first to reach her, having leaped on a horse to gallop after her.

He slid from the saddle and dropped to his knees beside her. "God, Angele. Are you hurt bad? Damn it, what made you do something so foolish?"

He saw she couldn't breathe and raised her head, and she managed to gasp and gulp a bit of air and the pain in her chest lessened.

"Do you think anything is broken?"

"I . . . I don't know . . ." she managed to wheeze, still fighting to fill her lungs.

Some of the other men came riding up with Dr. Pardee. He immediately knelt beside her, across from Ryan, and began running his hands up and down her arms, around her face. "Tell me where you hurt, Angele," he urged.

"We can't move you till I find out how bad it is. Any motion might make it worse."

Blackness was closing in, and there was a great roaring in her ears.

One of the men standing nearby asked of no one in particular, "Who told her she could ride Roussel's horse? It's a wonder he took the hurdles before he acted up like he did."

Another man harrumphed in disgust. "I don't know, but Ryan ought to kill the son of a bitch."

"No one . . ." Angele strained to whisper as she felt herself sinking ever deeper. "I did it myself . . ."

"Angele, I need to know where you're hurt," Dr. Pardee implored again.

"Bleeding . . . below . . . I must have hit a rock . . ."

Dr. Pardee nodded to the others to politely look away before he lifted her skirt to see what she was talking about. Then he whispered to Ryan, "We need to get her back to the house quick."

Ryan tensed.

"What's wrong? Why is she bleeding like that?"

Angele could hear him speaking from far, far away as invisible hands pulled her toward the darkness.

Then she heard Dr. Pardee say in a voice thick with pity, "She's having a miscarriage."

Ryan was having difficulty accepting what the doctor was trying to tell him. "I . . . I don't understand."

And as Angele sank into merciful oblivion, Dr. Pardee's words were like a dagger to her soul.

"I'm sorry, Ryan. It looks like she's losing her baby."

Twenty-four

Ryan and Dr. Pardee were sitting on opposite sides of Angele's bed.

It had been several hours since the accident. Shadows were drifting across the room as the sun began to slip away, and darkness was creeping across the sky.

Selma stood near the door, hands folded beneath her bosom. She was ready and willing to do whatever she could to help, but her presence seemed to have been forgotten.

Now and then tears would fill her eyes, and she dabbed at them with the corner of her apron. She felt so sorry for Miss Angele losing her baby. Bad enough she had taken such a terrible fall from the horse. Selma hadn't seen it happen, but Toby had, and he said it was a wonder she hadn't broken her neck. But her face was pale as goose down, and Selma was praying real hard she'd be all right.

Watching Master Ryan also made her eyes tear up. He hadn't moved from Miss Angele's bed since she'd been put there. He had pulled his chair so close his knees were touching the mattress. He hadn't let go of her hand the whole time, and ever so often he would reach and touch her cheek like he wanted to make sure she was still there.

She thought back to how Miss Angele had said the dumplings made her stick to her stomach. But that hadn't been the reason after all. Miss Angele had been in the family way.

Just like me. Selma almost smiled. She was past the being

sick part of it and was almost starting to show. But she was keeping it a secret for the time being, and it was just as well, because it wasn't right for her to be so happy over having a baby when Miss Angele had just lost hers.

Angele's sudden, soft moan broke the silence.

Ryan and Dr. Pardee sprang from their chairs at the same instant.

They stared at her intensely for a few moments, then sat down.

Ryan slumped against the back of his chair and stared miserably up at the ceiling. "I thought maybe she was waking up. It's been so damn long . . ."

"Not considering how much laudanum I gave her," Dr. Pardee said. "It will make her sleep, and that's what she needs right now. She lost a lot of blood. She's weak."

He began gathering his instruments and putting them in his worn leather bag. "I think I'll go see about Roussel. I'm concerned over how upset he was when we were bringing her in. I told Willard to get him to bed and try to keep him there till I could take a look at him."

"Yes, I imagine he's worried. He's grown real fond of Angele."

Dr. Pardee closed his bag. "I'll be back in a little while, but if you need me, let me know."

Ryan frowned with the need for reassurance. "And you do think she'll be all right once she's had some rest?"

"Yes, and as I've already told you—there's no reason she can't have another baby. She probably wouldn't have lost this one if she hadn't taken that fall. Next time, keep her from riding."

"And I told you," Ryan said tightly, "I didn't let her ride *this* time. I was just as surprised as everybody else when she came galloping across the lawn. Had I known what she was up to, you can bloody well believe I would have stopped her."

"And you had no idea she was pregnant?"

"She never said a word."

Dr. Pardee rounded the bed and patted his shoulder.

"Stop worrying. It was just one of those things. Let's be thankful she wasn't any farther along than she was."

"How far do you think she was?"

"I couldn't tell, and it doesn't matter, anyway. It's over. Now why don't you go downstairs for a little while and have something to eat? You can't do anything here, and you need to stretch your legs . . . get some fresh air."

Selma seized the chance to be useful. "Master Ryan, I can go fetch you some vittles."

He didn't turn as he said, "I'm not hungry, but I could use some coffee. And tell Mammy Lou to lace it with scotch, please."

"Yessir, I'll go right now."

She walked down the hall behind Dr. Pardee a little ways, then turned toward the rear and the servants' stairway.

She hoped she would be allowed to return to Miss Angele's room instead of helping with the cleaning. She liked her a lot and wished she had been nicer to her that morning when she had come to her cabin.

And she also wished she could have told her that she was right about what she saw that night.

The boy *had* been a runaway slave.

And BelleRose *was* the first stop for runaways on the way north!

Denise and Clarice were sitting on the lawn to catch the evening breeze coming from the river. It was too hot to be inside, and they had wanted to be where they could talk without the servants being able to hear.

"I still can't believe it." Denise shook her head in wonder. "Riding a horse, jumping him, when she was in the family way. No woman in her right mind would do such a thing no matter how bad she wanted to show off, which was obviously why she did it."

Clarice had thought about that very same thing again and again in the hours since it had happened. Angele would never have risked losing her baby, she had sense enough to know giving Ryan a child would bond her to him and all his wealth forevermore. She would also have been afraid that if he blamed her, it could end their marriage.

As for his confiding to Corbett he had fallen in love with her—Clarice wasn't too concerned about that. Ryan had been drinking. It might have been whiskey talk. And even if he had meant it when he said it, Angele's stupid action could change his mind—especially if he believed she *had* known she was pregnant.

Denise cleared her throat. "Excuse me, but if I'm annoying you I'll be glad to go pack my things and leave for Richmond tonight and get out of your way."

Clarice blinked back to the present. "What are you talking about?"

"You're ignoring me."

"I'm sorry. And you aren't leaving tonight *or* tomorrow. So get that silly notion out of her head."

"Well, I'm certainly not going to stay any longer than I'd planned to after what's happened. Ryan isn't going to leave her side for an instant, and it won't make any difference where I'm concerned if he does. He's made it quite clear he's no longer interested in me."

"Don't be such a ninny. Sometimes I wonder how on earth we can be kin when you never think like I do. For heaven's sake, I'd never give up as easily as you seem to be doing."

Denise flashed with resentment. "It happens to be a matter of pride, my dear cousin. I've told you he's tried to avoid me all weekend. I have literally had to chase him down like a dog after a rabbit. And when I did manage to get him off to myself and let him know in dozens of little ways that I was willing and eager to make love, he pretended not to notice. I even came right out and said if I had the chance to do it over again, I would've said yes when he proposed.

"So tell me"—she threw up her hands in defeat—"what more can I do? It's time to give up and accept the fact that he doesn't want me."

"That is hogwash."

"How can you say that? It's how it is."

"That little tart has bewitched him, because he's never been exposed to someone as carnal as she obviously is. There's no telling what filthy things she does to him in bed to drive him crazy with lust. Men can be so lewd and disgusting. He probably does fancy himself in love with her, but it's just raw, animal desire. He'll get over it. And her losing the baby will make it happen faster—especially when he thinks she knew she was pregnant before she got on that horse."

Denise stared at her sharply. "How could you ever make him believe that?"

With a sinister smile, Clarice said, "Quite easily. I'll tell him Angele confided in Selma, who's her personal maid, and Selma told me."

Hope faded. Denise thought it was a ridiculous idea and said so, pointing out, "Even if you could get Selma to lie, Angele would deny it."

"Of course she would. But that's what Ryan would expect, and that is why he'd believe Selma instead."

Denise was still not convinced. "Why don't you just show Roussel the letter Corbett received that proves she's only half French? Isn't that enough to break up their marriage? Roussel will be so furious he'll tell Ryan to either divorce her or forget about inheriting BelleRose."

"Maybe. But Corbett says we can't be sure, and he also says we can't afford to take a chance it won't matter to Ryan. She might have him under such a spell that he'll say to hell with BelleRose and take her and leave.

"Stranger things have happened," she warned, "when lust is stronger than reason in a man. But add lying about her lineage to being responsible for losing his baby, and I think that will be more than he can bear."

Denise considered it, then gave a firm nod of assent. "It might work at that. But why do you want me to stay on? Won't that look obvious?"

"No. You are family, and it's understandable you would

want to be around to offer what comfort you can in a time of sorrow. When Ryan needs a sympathetic ear, it's important that you be close by. And don't worry. He *will* turn to you. It's only natural that he would, because even though he's smitten by Angele for the moment, he can't forget how he once felt about you."

Denise wondered about that. Actually, she had never felt he was deliriously in love with her. They had more or less been drawn together by her kinship to Clarice and her French blood, and everyone in Richmond knew about Roussel Tremayne's ultimatum to his son.

She also had to admit—if only to herself—that she had never been particularly enamored with Ryan. He was a devastatingly handsome man, but she was also attracted to many others and doubted she could ever lose her heart to only one man. His main attraction had been his fortune, which was why, after quickly thinking it over, she decided to go along with Clarice's scheme.

"All right. I'll stay as long as necessary."

Clarice clapped her hands in delight. "Wonderful. And if Ryan doesn't take you to his bed, we'll make it appear that he did."

"Now you aren't making any sense at all."

"You'll understand when the time is right." Clarice gave her a hug as she rose from her chair. "Just be ready to do whatever I ask."

Denise also stood, and, as she did, swept the lush lands around her with covetous eyes. "You can count on me. I'm not going to let all this slip through my fingers again."

Selma cut a glance into the tea kitchen as she passed, hoping Mammy Lou might be there. Seeing Miss Clarice, she quickened her step, as always, wanting to avoid her at every chance.

But Clarice saw her and called shrilly, "Selma, you get right back here! Where have you been all evening? There's a lot of work to be done."

Biting back a groan, Selma turned and went back to explain. "I've been upstairs in Miz Angele's room, waitin' in case somebody wanted me to do somethin' and now Master Ryan wants some coffee, and I came to fetch it."

"Is she awake yet?"

"No, ma'am."

"Well?" Clarice scowled at her. "Aren't you going to tell me how she is, you stupid girl?"

Selma bit her lip to keep from crying. It always made Miss Clarice mad when she cried, but it hurt so bad when she called her names. "Ma'am, I don't know. Miz Angele, she just lays there. Master Ryan thought she was wakin' up one time, but she didn't, and Doctor Pardee said she needed to sleep, anyhow, 'cause she's so weak."

"She's a stupid girl, too," Clarice said crisply as she poured lemonade for herself and Denise. She added a sprig of mint before continuing. "Anyone who would get on a horse in her condition hasn't got the sense God gave a billy goat. I hope she feels like a fool when she wakes up. She ruined the weekend for everyone."

Selma swallowed hard and hoped she wasn't doing the wrong thing by defending Angele. "She didn't mean to," she said softly.

"Is that so?"

Selma desperately wanted to be on her way. "Can I go now?" she begged. "I need to get the master's coffee to him. He's waitin'."

"I most certainly do want you for something else. I want you to tell me what you know about all this."

Selma was dumbfounded. "I don't understand." The way Miss Clarice was looking at her was scary. Her eyes were shining like she was all excited about something, and the corners of her mouth twitched like she was trying not to laugh.

"I will help you to understand." Clarice clamped her hands firmly on Selma's quaking shoulders and pushed her against the wall and held her there. Leaning so close Selma could feel her harsh breath on her face, Clarice did not mince words. "I want you to tell me if Miss Angele showed any signs of being in the family way, such as being sick to her stomach. Or has she fainted? Think back, Selma. You should know—because you are her personal handmaid."

Selma bit her lip and tried to look away, but Miss Clarice gave her a vicious shake that banged her head against the wall. But still she did not want to betray Miss Angele by saying the wrong thing. "I don't know," she wailed.

Abruptly, Clarice released her. She went to close the door into the hall. Then she returned to Selma and spoke in a low, ominous tone. "How long have you and Toby been married now?"

Selma didn't know about dates and such, but Toby had said there had been three full moons since they jumped the broom. She hadn't told him yet that she hadn't had her monthly time since the second one.

"I don't rightly know," she answered finally.

Clarice's mouth curved in a smile that Selma found terrifying. "Would you like to continue to live here, at BelleRose, and be Toby's wife?"

Selma's heart almost stopped beating. "Yes'm, yes'm I would. You wouldn't sell me, would you?"

"That depends. We get fine prices for slaves farther south. I heard Mr. Fordham say those two boys he sold while Master Ryan was in France brought a handsome sum. You know the boys I'm talking about, don't you? The ones Master Ryan thinks drowned?"

Selma knew all right, but she hadn't dared admit it when Miss Angele asked her about it. Anytime one of the slaves was sold, Master Ryan thought something else had happened to them. But it didn't happen very often. Selma and Toby had talked about it . . . about how when a slave got to be lazy, or made Mr. Fordham or Master Corbett mad, they got sold. And they figured the reason they lied about it to Master Ryan was two-fold. He wouldn't allow it, and Mr. Fordham and Master Corbett were keeping the money for themselves.

Clarice was annoyed by Selma's silence. "I asked you a question, stupid girl."

Selma started crying. She couldn't help it. "Yes'm, I know all about it, but I haven't said anything to anybody and I never will."

"That's because you know if you do, you'll be sold, too, don't you?"

Selma's head bobbed up and down. She was crying too hard to talk.

"Now, then. Let's talk about you, Selma. It really would be a shame to have Mr. Fordham put you in a wagon in the middle of the night and take you down to North Carolina or maybe Georgia and put you up on a block and sell you to the highest bidder. You'd never see Toby again. And your new owner might beat you with a whip. Not all slaves are treated as kindly as here at BelleRose."

"Don't . . . don't do it . . ." Selma begged, tears streaming down her face and running off her chin. She didn't dare wipe them away with her apron. She was afraid to move at all.

Clarice was enjoying the torment, knowing Selma would eventually agree to do anything she told her to. "Just think, you would never see any of your family again. And Toby would be told you were dead. He might guess the truth, but there wouldn't be anything he could do about it."

Selma fell to her knees and clutched at her skirt. "Why are you doin' this to me, Miz Clarice? I always do what I'm told. I always do my work, and I don't sass you. Why would you want to sell me and take me away from my Toby?"

Looking down at her with amusement and contempt, Clarice murmured, "Well, it doesn't have to be that way. All I want you to do is say that you saw Miss Angele being sick, and that she told you she thought she was going to have a baby. You're also to say that she told you how she planned to ride a horse and jump him and you said it was dangerous with her thinking she was pregnant. But she said she didn't care. She was going to do it, anyway."

Selma slowly got to her feet, and she dared to rub her

face as she backed away and whispered in horror, "But she didn't say all that to me, Miz Clarice, and if I say she did, Master Ryan is going to be real mad with her, 'cause he's terribly upset over her losing the baby."

Clarice shrugged. "It's either that or you're going to find yourself on an auction block. Now, which is it to be?" Her eyes narrowed as she put her hand on Selma's shoulder and squeezed so hard her nails cut into her flesh. "And if you deny it later, Toby won't be wrong in thinking you're dead."

Selma felt a roll of nausea. She couldn't let them sell her, not when she loved Toby so much . . . not when she was going to have his baby.

She bowed her head and quickly said a prayer asking forgiveness for the sin of lying.

Clarice gave her a rough shake. "Do you want me to go and tell Mr. Fordham right now to get ready to take a stupid little girl slave to the auction block?"

Her voice breaking on a sob, Selma answered, "I'll say whatever you want me to, Miz Clarice. Just please don't sell me . . . don't take me away from my Toby."

Clarice smirked in triumph. "It seems the stupid little girl might not be as stupid as I thought.

"Now, you will listen to me," she continued gravely, "and do exactly as I say . . ."

In the light of the bedside lamp, Angele seemed to be bathed in an ethereal glow.

Ryan was keeping vigil. Dr. Pardee had left, saying there was no need for him to stay the night. The house was quiet. Everyone had apparently gone to bed. But Ryan had no intention of doing so.

Losing the baby had crushed him deeply. That was a small blow, however, compared to the pain of wondering if Angele would now leave him.

And since Clarice's visit, the fear was even greater.

She had come to ask if there was any change . . . anything she could do, then broke down and cried.

She said she couldn't help it, because she felt so bad about the baby.

And she had also said how sorry she was for Angele and only hoped, prayed, that it might make her reconsider her discontent, and plans—if she had any—to leave. After all, Clarice pointed out, Ryan and Angele had made a baby together, and even if God had taken him before he had a chance to be born, it was still a holy thing and bonded them as man and wife.

Ryan had never seen Clarice so moved over anything, and he almost thought she was going to collapse into hysteria when she grabbed him by the front of his shirt and sobbed, "Ryan, tell me she didn't know . . . tell me she wouldn't have done such a thing if she had . . ."

He had wished Corbett was there to peel her off him. He finally managed to do it, trying not to hurt her as he pulled her arms from around his neck and pushed her into a chair.

He had then assured her that he'd had no idea Angele was pregnant and was confident Angele hadn't either, or she would have told him.

Clarice had wept and thanked him for that. She said she needed to hear it . . . needed to believe Angele wasn't so homesick and miserable that she'd purposely try to have a miscarriage so she wouldn't be tied down and could go her own way.

And if that scene hadn't been enough to set his teeth on edge, Denise came not long after Clarice finally left to offer her condolences.

She said she also wanted to apologize if she had made him uncomfortable by anything she might have said or done.

"I feel absolutely wretched over this," she had avowed fervently. "Had I known she was carrying your baby, Ryan, I would never have admitted to loving you, wanting you . . . wishing things could be different. But I couldn't keep still any longer. I had to tell you how I've rued the day and hated myself ever since for teasing you like I did.

"So love her if you must," she had said, weeping as she

backed toward the door. "You have my blessings, and I'll never bother you again, I swear. But I'm here if you need me. Know that, my darling . . ."

He had locked the door after her, determined there would not be another intrusion this night.

He was, by God, going to sit by Angele's bed and hold her hand so he would be there when she awoke. And the second she did, he planned to look her straight in the eye and tell her that he loved her, and beg her, if need be, to give him a chance to prove it.

He was willing to do anything in his power to make her happy. If she wanted him to take her riding, he would, by damn. And if she didn't want to tat and sew and do all the other things she found so boring, he wouldn't ask that of her, either. He had probably been a clod to expect her to conform, anyway. She was a free spirit, and that was one of the reasons he loved her, and he knew now he had been wrong to try to change that.

He only hoped it wasn't too late.

As for whatever it was in her past she found too painful to share, he would respect her need to lock it away.

They would go forward, together, into the future.

There would be other babies, as many as they both wanted.

And nothing else would matter.

If she would only let him love her . . .

Selma had been standing rigidly outside the door to Angele's bedroom so long that her legs were numb.

Even if she could count, she wouldn't remember the number of times she had raised her hand to knock but hadn't mustered the nerve.

It was getting very late, and she knew she had to do it or Miss Clarice might make good her threat.

She could be on her way south by morning, in the back of a buckboard wagon, heading for a slave auction.

The deep breath she took seemed to come all the way from the tips of her toes.

Her arm was shaking, her hands trembling, as she finally tapped on the door.

When there was no response, she thought Master Ryan might be sleeping but knew Miss Clarice would tell her to knock louder till she roused him. So she did. And it wasn't long before the door swung open, and he was glaring down at her.

"Yes, Selma, what is it?"

She pulled her voice from somewhere deep within. "I wanted to sleep near Miz Angele. On the floor. I want to be here if she needs me . . . if you need me."

"I suppose that's a good idea." He waved her inside. "And if anybody else comes, you can be the one to tell them to go away."

Selma sat on the rug near the empty fireplace and hugged her knees to her chin. Miss Clarice had told her to wait till the right time before saying anything.

It was not long in coming.

"I'm going to stay here till she wakes up," Ryan said soberly, absently, as though talking to himself. "I want to be the one to tell her about the baby. She's going to be so hurt."

Selma tried to speak but no sound came.

Then the image of Toby's dear face swam before her tear-filled eyes.

She also thought of the tiny life growing inside her.

And she knew she had to do it for Toby's sake . . . and her baby's.

Finally, she was able to say, "I expect she's gonna be real upset, but I warned her she might lose her baby, and she wouldn't listen."

Ryan winced. "What did you say?" Dropping Angele's hand, he whipped about to stare at her, hoping he'd not heard right.

Selma drew a sharp breath. She had gone too far to stop

even if she could. "She said she was gonna ride anyway, 'cause she could jump a horse as good as any man, and—"

"Wait a minute." He reached her in a flash to grab her by her shoulders and yank her up, leaving her feet dangling inches from the floor. "Are you saying Angele knew she was going to have a baby? She *told* you that?"

Selma had never been so scared in her life as she repeated the lie Miss Clarice had coached her to say over and over till she knew it by heart. "She was sick a lot . . . throwin' up . . . and said she was afraid she was gonna have a baby."

"Afraid? She said she was *afraid?* You mean she didn't want to?"

". . . can't speak for her . . ." Selma wished he would put her down, afraid he'd go crazy and throw her across the room, because he had a scary look in his eyes.

He shook her so hard her head bobbed to and fro. "Did she say she didn't want the baby? Answer me, damn it."

"Sorta . . ." she managed despite the terrified sobs racking her body. "She sorta said she didn't want no baby . . ."

To her surprise, he suddenly, and gently, set her down on her feet and backed away.

Covering his face with shaking hands, he whispered, "I'm sorry, Selma. I shouldn't have grabbed you up like that. I didn't mean to hurt you."

"I . . . I'm not hurt," she stammered, edging toward the door. "But I think maybe I'd like to go sleep in my own bed if you don't think you need me."

"No. It's all right." He sighed. "The only thing I need is a drink."

Opening the door, Selma watched as he shuffled across the parlor to his room, head down, shoulders curled.

She knew she had never seen such a broken man.

And prayed she never would again.

She also asked God, if He could, to forgive her for what had to be the biggest sin she had ever committed.

* * *

"Now for the coup de grâce," Clarice said happily, after telling Corbett how she'd had Selma lie to Ryan about Angele. "All that's left is for him to find out she's only half French and she'll be gone as soon as she's well enough to travel.

"Maybe even sooner," she added, giggling. "He might be so angry he won't wait that long. He might make her pack her things and get out now."

It was after midnight. Clarice was sitting on the side of Corbett's bed. Too excited to wait till morning, she had awakened him as soon as Selma reported the deed was done.

But, to her surprise, he did not share her elation.

"Don't count on it." He yawned and rubbed his eyes. "It might not make any difference to him at all."

"Are you out of your mind? Of course it will. He's going to be absolutely furious that she dared do something so foolish when she knew she was going to have a baby. Haven't you heard a word I've said?"

"Yes, but you need to calm down and remember we don't want to look like we're a part of any of this. If I show him the letter right now, he's liable to get angry with me for meddling in his business."

"He'll do no such thing," she yelped. "He'll be grateful you cared enough to find out the truth about the deceiving little tramp. And that, in addition to believing her recklessness caused her to lose his baby, will make him want to be rid of her once and for all.

"And I've asked Denise to stay the week," she added. "I want her close by to offer him comfort when he needs it."

"Well, I'm not willing to take any chances. How many times do I have to tell you he loves Angele? And love makes men do foolish things sometimes."

"Then go to your uncle. Tell him the truth. Tell him how Ryan met Angele . . . how it worried you so much you hired someone to see what they could find out about her. Tell him how her uncle in England even offered a reward after she and her mother ran away, because they probably stole from him. When he hears that, he'll order Ryan to run her off."

Corbett sighed wearily. "We have already discussed this, Clarice. Angele's got the old man wrapped around her little finger. It might make him angry at me for meddling, too. I just can't take the chance. We have to look innocent in all of this."

She rolled her eyes. "Then what good is the letter if you aren't going to use it against her, for heaven's sake?"

"I plan to when the time is right."

"And when will that be?"

"After she's gone, in case Ryan wants to go after her and bring her back. I'll tell him it's for the best to let her go and then show him the letter. I'll say that after he told me he loved her, I decided not to say anything about it. Then, if he still wants her back, I'll promise to keep it a secret so the old man doesn't find out. He'll be undyingly grateful and never suspect either of us tried to do anything except help him keep his marriage together."

"Are you still asleep?" Clarice asked incredulously. "Is that why you aren't making any sense—or have you lost your mind? You mean to tell me that you'd actually help him get her back after he made her go? That you'd then try to get along with her in hopes she'd never make him tell us to leave BelleRose? You have to be crazy, Corbett, and—"

Suddenly he lunged to sit straight up and grip her shoulders and lean into her face. "Listen to me, damn it. You're the one who's crazy if you think for one minute I will ever allow that little sewer rat to stay here and take anything away from us. I have an alternate plan in case all else fails."

"And what might that be?" she asked dubiously.

"Roscoe will take her away, and I have to make sure Ryan doesn't try to go after her. Now do you understand?"

Clarice relaxed and breathed easier. It was going to be all right. Corbett was sane, after all, and what he said made good sense. "So all we do now is wait and see what happens, and if he doesn't run her off, Roscoe will take her by force. Is that it?" she asked.

"Not quite. We can't just have her disappear. It might look suspicious. It has to look as though she left of her own free will. But we can use Selma for that, if need be. But let's not get ahead of ourselves. Ryan may surprise us and toss her out on her deceitful little fanny. It would make things a lot easier that way."

"And meanwhile?" Clarice asked.

A wry smile curved Corbett's lips. "It was a good idea—your having Denise stay on a while. Just make sure she's around if he needs a shoulder to cry on . . . *or anything else.*"

Twenty-five

It had been four days since the accident, and Angele was bewildered—and hurt—that she hadn't seen Ryan.

She had awakened sometime the day after, groggy and sore all over. Selma was the only one in her room at the time and had immediately gone to tell everyone the news.

Dr. Pardee came a short while later, and, after a cursory examination, said all she needed was plenty of rest.

No one else came. Not even Clarice. Angele's only contact was with Selma, who brought her trays of food but hardly said a word. She did, however, finally mention that she thought she heard Willard tell Mammy Lou that Master Ryan had gone to Richmond for a few days.

Angele was hurt to think he could leave her that way but reasoned it might be for the best. He was probably furious over what she had done, and his anger needed time to fade.

She still couldn't dispel the notion that something was wrong. Selma was so nervous she jumped at the least little sound and also seemed to be avoiding meeting her gaze. Then there was Dr. Pardee's strange behavior. Ordinarily he was a gruff old soul, and she had expected him to chide her not only for jumping but beating him out of the saddle, as well—because she had no doubt but that she had won. Instead, he was quiet and said little except to urge her to rest as much as possible.

"Everyone must really be upset with me," she remarked

when Selma brought her supper tray that fourth day. "I would've thought Clarice would come to rail at me for borrowing her saddle without asking. Has she said anything to you?"

Again, Selma would not look directly at her. "No, ma'am. She wouldn't say nothin' to me, no how. She don't talk to none of us except to tell us what to do or fuss about something. I try to stay out of her way as much as I can."

"And Master Roussel," Angele pressed. "Have you heard whether he's angry that I rode his horse?"

"If he is, Willard didn't tell me."

Angele pushed back the tray and sat up. "Then it's time I went to see him and found out. Clarice stays peeved over something all the time, anyway, but I don't want Master Roussel irritated with me. Get my robe and slippers, please."

"You can't, missy," Selma argued. "You know the doctor said you've got to stay in bed a week, and I know it can't have been that long 'cause Sunday hasn't come yet, and I always know when it's Sunday 'cause Mammy Lou fries a chicken."

Angele lifted her chin stubbornly. "Will you hand me my robe like I asked you to?"

"No, she won't. Because you aren't going anywhere."

Angele turned to see Ryan standing in the doorway. His face was tight with anger. "I'm feeling better," she offered gingerly. "And I want to tell your father I'm sorry if he's angry at me for taking his horse."

"Don't you care that *I* am?"

His glare was blistering. Glancing away, she began to pick absently at the sheet. "I was hoping to talk to you, as well, and try to make you understand why I did it."

"I'm listening—not that anything you say will be the truth. But let me hear it, anyway. You're so creative that your lies are always entertaining, if nothing else."

Angele was fast becoming annoyed, herself, because he was not giving her a chance. She faced him again, no longer intimidated. "Did it ever occur to you that I wanted to prove to you that I can ride—jump—a horse? I happen to be quite good at it, and I've missed it. All you want me to do is stay in this house all the time. I've wanted to scream from boredom."

"That doesn't excuse what you did."

"What else could I do? You wouldn't let me ride. Now you know I can, and there's nothing to worry about. And I wouldn't have fallen," she added petulantly, "if I'd been more experienced with that particular horse."

His upper lip curled in a sneer. "That particular horse has never been ridden by anyone but my father."

"Then you see? That proves I'm a good rider, because I stayed on him long enough to make every jump. And I won, didn't I? That special saddle is mine, and that's why you're angry—because a *woman* won." She dared a smile, thinking she might be able to tease him out of his wrathful mood.

"I am angry," he said harshly, "because your recklessness caused you to lose our baby . . . a baby I wanted very much but you obviously didn't."

At that, Selma bolted by him and disappeared.

Angele reeled and gasped, "No . . . no, that's not true!"

"It's cruel to tell you this way, but, quite frankly, I think you deserve it. What you did was unforgivable."

"I . . . I didn't know," she managed to chokily deny. "Ryan, if I had, do you think I'd have done it? I swear to you—I didn't know I was going to have a baby."

He stepped on into the room to point an accusing finger and lash out, "You want to know what I think? I think you don't care about anyone but yourself. The baby, me, our marriage—none of it matters so long as you get your way, and you'll stop at nothing to do it."

"That's not true," she protested above the roaring in her ears as she tried to grasp the horror of what he was telling her about the baby. She'd had no idea she was pregnant. Miss Appleton had never discussed symptoms. Neither had her mother. She'd never been around childbearing women, so how could she have known?

"I can't believe you still have the gall to lie even now."

He ran his fingers through his hair in agitation. "Hell, I've got to get out of here . . ."

Angele scrambled to her knees, the tears she had vowed never again to shed welling in her eyes as she pleaded, "Please, Ryan. You've got to believe me. I never dreamed I might be having a baby. I'd been nauseated, but I don't know about things like that. No one ever told me, and—"

"Stop lying!" he shouted. "Damn it, I should have known you'd never appreciate what I was offering you."

"I did—and I do—and my heart is breaking, Ryan."

Suddenly he asked, "Who helped you? Damn it, I'll break the son of a bitch's neck. Who told you about my father's horse? Who helped you with him?"

Remembering her promise to Roscoe and terrified of what Ryan might do to him, she swallowed hard and lied, "No one. I chose him myself."

"And I suppose you knew my father's horse was a good jumper, because you heard someone say once upon a time what a good jumping horse looked like."

"Yes . . . that's true . . ."

"To hell with it."

"Please believe me, Ryan—"

He sneered. "You've never told the truth about anything yet. Why should I believe you now?"

"Because I—"

The door slammed on her last words.

He didn't hear her say that she loved him.

He went straight to his father's wing. He had avoided him since learning Angele had known she was pregnant before she rode. And he did not intend to tell him now, because he would be so hurt and disappointed. But Ryan knew if he continued to stay away, he would wonder why.

"I'm glad you're here," Willard greeted when he opened the door. "I've been afraid if somebody didn't tell him somethin' soon about how Miz Angele was doin', he was gonna go see about her himself."

"Well, he won't have to do that now." Ryan breezed by him and into the bedroom.

"It's about damn time!" Roussel bellowed from where he was sitting in his usual spot by the window. "How's she doing? Doc said she'd be fine, but since you haven't been to tell me yourself, I was afraid she might've taken a turn for the worse. Losing a baby can be hard on a woman, you know, and that was a hell of a fall she took.

"But she rode my horse, didn't she?" he added, grinning broadly . . . proudly. "He's never let anybody else stay on him that long. And as soon as she's able, I'm going to tell her she can ride him all she wants to. Hell, I might even give him to her, because nobody else will ever be able to control him."

"She *didn't* control him," Ryan reminded his father.

"She did for a while, and it was just her first time." Roussel noted how bitter he sounded . . . how angry he looked. "Say, what's wrong with you, anyway? She was just trying to show off in front of Denise. I figured that out, and you should have, too. Women are like that. And I saw how Denise was following you around at the party the night before. Angele was just fighting back, that's all."

"Maybe." He didn't think so but was afraid disagreeing might make him wonder if something else was wrong. "I'm just upset about her losing the baby, that's all. Don't worry about me. You just take care of yourself. Doc didn't like how upset you were."

"I couldn't help it. The truth is, I've come to love Angele, and I was scared she was seriously hurt. It's sad about the baby, but there will be others. We just have to be grateful we still have her. She could have been killed, you know."

Ryan had thought of that, again and again as he had sat beside her bed praying she would not die. And, despite what she had done, he knew he still cared about her deeply. He didn't want to lose her but, sadly, feared he already had.

Suddenly he felt the need to prepare his father for what

might happen. "It's nice you think so much of her, and I'm glad, but the fact is, she seems homesick for France."

Roussel was quick to respond. "Then for heaven's sake, take her and go back for a visit. Stay as along as she wants to. Corbett can look after things here, and I'm feeling stronger every day. We'll manage fine without you. Now, go tell her so she'll feel better."

Ryan only wished it were that simple. But he'd said all he intended to for the time being. His father didn't look as well as he would have people believe. There were deep circles under his eyes, and his hands had a slight tremor. It would not do for him to worry about Angele any more than he already did.

"Go on. Tell her you'll take her home." Roussel slapped his knees and grinned. "Who knows? You might make another baby while you're over there. And wouldn't that be something—my grandchild conceived in France?"

"Yes. Yes, that would be something." Ryan wanted to get out of there, afraid if he didn't, the pain he was trying to hide would show. "Well, I'd better be going. I have things to do."

"I'd like to see Angele as soon as she feels like having company."

"I'll let you know. She still needs to rest. Maybe in a day or so."

Roussel nodded. "Of course. But be sure to tell her that I'm thinking about her."

"Of course I will. Now, stop worrying." Ryan crossed to the door.

"Son, wait a minute."

He paused.

"Do you want to go with her?"

Ryan cocked his head to one side, not understanding.

Roussel made himself quite clear. "I'm asking if you want to go with her to France or if you'd rather let her go alone."

Ryan knew what he was getting at but didn't know how to respond.

"I'm asking you, goddamnit, if you even care if she

leaves," Roussel then irritably snapped. "Maybe you're such a fool you think you'd rather have Denise, who's nothing but a spoiled brat. I'd as soon have a goat for a daughter-in-law."

Ryan could not help laughing, then quickly sobered. "No, I don't want her to leave. I love her. I didn't when I married her, but I do now . . . with all my heart. As for Denise, I thank my lucky stars she turned me down when she did. Otherwise, I'd probably be the most miserable man on earth.

"And another thing," he said, pointing a finger. "*You'd* better thank *your* lucky stars Angele didn't hear your blasphemy just now, or she'd have told you off good."

Roussel's smile was placid. "I look forward to the day she can. And I'm glad you love her, Son, because I do, too."

Ryan went downstairs and stopped by his study only long enough to take some money from the safe. He was almost out the front door when Corbett caught up with him to ask where he was going.

"Richmond," he said tersely. "I may be gone overnight."

"But it's getting dark. You have no business riding alone. Let me get my hat and holster, and I'll go with you."

"What about Clarice? She might not like you staying out all night."

Corbett said it didn't matter. "She's got Denise to keep her company."

Hearing that, Ryan was even more anxious to be on his way. The last thing he wanted was to fend off Denise again.

Denise was reclining on the pink velvet divan in her room.

She was bored and ready to go back to Richmond, but Clarice wouldn't hear of it, promising the opportunity they were waiting for would come soon.

"Well, it better hurry up," she grumbled out loud and reached for the wine bottle again. "Or I'm leaving before all my beaux think I've dropped off the face of the earth."

Suddenly Clarice opened the door without knocking and hurried to sit down at the foot of the divan. "I've something to tell you."

"Before you do, I want you to know I'm going home tomorrow, and there's no point in arguing about it." Her voice was slurred from too many glasses of wine to remember.

"No, you aren't." Clarice flashed a coy smile. "Because tonight's the night. Ryan finally came home today, and—"

"I know, I know. I saw him from the window. I was going to meet him on the stairs to ask him to walk with me a bit, but before I could, he had already gone to see *her.*" She tossed down the rest of the wine in her glass.

"Selma eavesdropped and heard everything, just like I told her to, and I know everything that was said."

Impatiently, Denise prodded, "So tell me. I know he had said he wanted to be the one to tell her about the miscarriage when Doctor Pardee thought she was strong enough. What happened?"

"According to Selma, she denied knowing about it—just like we knew she would—and he told her she was lying. But nothing was said about a divorce, so we have to follow through on our plan."

Denise sighed, disappointed. "I might as well go home now. I just saw him leave with Corbett, and you know he won't be back tonight, so there's no chance we can have Angele find us together."

"Of course there is."

Denise was bewildered. "You aren't making sense. How can I sneak into Ryan's room after he goes to bed and have Angele find us together and think we're making love if he isn't even there?"

Clarice grinned. "It isn't important that he be there, dear cousin. It's only important that Angele *thinks* he is. And don't worry. Selma is going to take care of that little detail for us."

* * *

Selma hated what she was doing but kept telling herself over and over she had no choice. She had told Toby about the baby, and he was so happy he had cried. Then he had told her over and over how much he loved her. So she had to do what Miss Clarice told her to because she couldn't leave him. He'd die. She just knew he would.

Miss Clarice had explained exactly how she was to sit in the parlor between Miss Angele's room and Master Ryan's room and watch the big case clock. When the little hand got to a certain spot, and the chimes started, she had to say her piece, real loud, so Miss Angele would hear. And then she was supposed to get out, no matter if Miss Angele got to the door in time to see her and told her to come back. She was to keep on going, then tiptoe back and listen to see what happened. And if nothing did, if she didn't hear anything, she was to pretend to look in on Miss Angele a little while later to see what she was doing.

It all sounded strange, but even though Selma had no idea what was going on, it had to be something bad . . . something that would hurt Miss Angele. And she hated doing it, but, like she kept telling herself, loving Toby like she did and with his baby inside her, she had to do whatever it took to stay with him.

Finally, the little hand pointed where it was supposed to, and then the chimes began.

Selma rose and walked to Master Ryan's door and yelled real loud, "Master Ryan, I got the extra pillow you told me to get you, and I'm leaving it outside your door, like you said. You have a good night, sir."

And then she walked as fast as her shaking legs would carry her out of the parlor and down the hall to wait a few minutes before easing back to finish what Miss Clarice had told her to do.

Angele was not sleeping very soundly. She awoke in time to hear everything Selma said and was elated to know Ryan was back.

She sat up and reached for her robe, then went to her dresser and brushed her hair. She even used a dab of perfume, wanting to present herself as nicely as possible.

She had rehearsed the words she would say to him until she knew them by heart.

She was going to tell him how truly and deeply she loved him, and how having his baby would be the greatest gift God could ever bestow.

Maybe then he would believe she had not known about the one she had lost.

To hell with pride and everything else, Angele was bent on making her husband see this night that her heart belonged to only him.

Crossing the parlor, she saw that the door to his room was ajar, and light came from within. But before she could call out, the sound of a woman's voice turned her blood to ice. She froze where she stood, unable to move.

It was Denise.

"Oh, Ryan," she was cooing in that annoying way she had. "It's sad your father won't let you divorce Angele, but at least we've realized how we love each other."

Angele forgot to breathe, and an invisible fist closed about her chest.

Her eyes grew so wide she felt her skin tearing as she caught sight of Denise through the open door.

She was naked.

"I'll pour more champagne." She made her voice husky. "I love it when you lick it off my breasts . . ."

Angele stumbled backward, almost fell, but righted herself in time to keep from falling, making noise, letting them know she had heard.

She made it back to her room, closed the door and leaned against it, fury and heartache rolled into one as she began to tremble.

For long moments, she stood there as the shock of what she had just seen . . . heard . . . rolled over her.

At the sound of a knock on the door, she hurried back to bed. If it were Ryan, pretending to be solicitous by checking on her, she was not sure she could bear to look at him. Probably he had realized he had failed to lock his door and wanted to make sure she was still asleep and unaware of what was going on.

But it was Selma, instead, and she poked her head in to whisper, "Are you all right, missy? I was passin' by and thought I heard you call me."

"No . . ." she managed to say past the choking knot in her throat, "No, I didn't."

"Then I'll see you in the morning."

"No," Angele called sharply. "I do want you. Close the door and come here."

Selma did so, but, again, she would not look directly at her.

Angele sat up to clutch her arms and pull her closer as she tersely whispered, "Now, listen to me carefully. I know what I saw the other night. That was a runaway slave who came out of the woods near your cabin. And I think Bel-leRose actually is the first stop runaways make on their way north."

Selma's lips parted to attempt denial, but Angele gave her a rough shake.

"Don't lie to me. You can't, because I need your help. You have to help me take the same route they take, because I want to go north, too."

Selma did look at her then to cry, "What are you talkin' about, Miz Angele?"

"I'm leaving—running away—and I don't want Master Ryan to know about it, because he might try to stop me.

"After all . . ." she said brokenly, releasing Selma and falling back on the bed, *"I'm only chattel."*

Twenty-six

Selma cowered before the three of them—Miss Clarice, Master Corbett, and Mr. Fordham.

"Now, you are sure you know what to do tonight," Clarice said, keeping her voice gentle, because she did not want the girl to get nervous and make Angele wonder why. Everything had to go according to plan with no slip-ups, because there would be no second chances.

"Yes, ma'am. I know by heart. I lead Miz Angele to the old pier, down by the bend in the river, and I leave her there. Then I come back to the house and sit in Master Roussel's parlor in case he gets sick in the night and needs me."

Clarice was pleased. "That's right. Now, can you tell me why you are the one to sit in the parlor and not Willard?"

Selma nodded, confident of her role. "Because I'm the only one you trust to do it. And Willard and Mammy Lou have been askin' to sleep with their families, anyway, and you said they could take a night off to do it."

Clarice waited, then prodded, "Yes? What else?"

Selma thought a minute, then snapped her fingers. "I remember. If Master Ryan asks how come I'm the only one in the house, I'm to say Miz Angele run me off and sent me to stay with Master Roussel."

Corbett patted her on the head. "Very good. You can go now."

In a voice laced with warning, Clarice added, "Don't forget what will happen if you tell a soul about this."

Selma ducked her head as terror danced across her scalp. She knew, because Miss Clarice had repeated her threat many, many times. "I won't say anything. I swear it."

As Selma passed by Roscoe, he growled, "You say anything, I'll take the whip to your hide, girl . . ."

She took off running, his taunting laughter echoing in her ears.

Clarice whirled on Roscoe. "Are you sure you have everything taken care of?"

"Yes. As soon as Selma gets her to the pier, I'll tie and gag her and throw her in the buckboard. Someone will be waiting about an hour down the road to take her on to North Carolina."

Corbett told them Ryan would be in Richmond all night. "I made sure he got invited to a big poker game."

"Well, the way he's been drinking lately, he'd probably gamble away BelleRose if he had the deed in his name now," Clarice sarcastically remarked.

"I'll just be glad when it's over." Corbett frowned at Roscoe. "And don't forget the most important thing—how you're to make Angele think it's all Ryan's doing. We don't want her to ever come back here should she get away."

"Get away?" he guffawed. "By the time she's sold into slavery as a mulatto all the way down in Louisiana, she'd never find her way back."

"Well, we can't take any chances."

Clarice backed him up. "That's right, Roscoe. You do your job or you won't have one."

His expression turned mean. "Don't you ever threaten me, damn it. I can have you kicked out of here just like that"—he snapped his fingers under her nose—"because I know about too many graves that are empty, remember? Where slaves are supposed to be buried but actually aren't dead and got sold down South without Ryan and his old man knowing about it."

"I . . . I don't like *your* threatening me," Clarice sputtered. "Now I think it's time for everyone to go about their business." Dismissing him, she began to gather her things. "Corbett, little Danny and I are ready to go to Richmond."

Roscoe left, grinning confidently that his position was secure for as long as he wanted.

"I don't like that man," Clarice hissed when she and Corbett were alone. "He frightens me."

"It's nothing to worry about. He's getting paid extra for this."

She raised a brow. "And where did you get the money?"

His eyes were twinkling. "Out of the safe in Ryan's study. I've peeked over his shoulder when he was opening it enough times to know the combination. I took all he had in there, which was a tidy sum, to make him think Angele stole it before she ran away."

Clarice grinned and patted his cheek to congratulate him, then sobered, holding out her hand. "Give me the rest of it," she said. "You'll only throw it away."

Disappointed, Corbett knew he would never hear the end of it if he didn't.

Angele finished packing the one bag she was going to take with her. She closed it with a click of finality, then looked about the room. Leaving all the opulence meant nothing.

She went to the window and gazed out at the lush gardens and the rich, rolling land beyond.

None of it mattered without Ryan's love. And, since he did not want her and never would, she would not stand between him and Denise.

Bless Roussel, she thought with a smile despite her misery. From what she'd heard Denise say that night, she had seen her naked in Ryan's room, Ryan must have gone to him and told him he wanted to divorce her. No doubt he was using her causing the miscarriage as an excuse, his true motive being that he was still in love with Denise. But

Roussel had refused, and Angele deeply regretted not being able to tell him how she would always treasure his loyalty.

It had been a week since that night, and the only time she left her room was to visit Roussel and read to him. Always she pretended nothing was wrong, trying to be cheerful. And if he suspected she was dying inside, he didn't let on.

As for Ryan, it hadn't been a problem avoiding him, because he seemed to be in Richmond all the time. Denise had left the very next day after Angele had found them together, so obviously he was spending all his time with her.

Angele would have preferred to have left with dignity, but had Ryan objected to her going out of pride, it would only have prolonged the agony. She couldn't stay knowing he loved someone else, and the sooner she left, the quicker her heart could begin to heal—if that were possible.

She had no idea where she was going. Neither did Selma. Some people thought the runaways wound up in Philadelphia. Others said they might make it all the way to Canada. No one knew for sure, and Angele actually did not care. In the back of her mind she thought maybe she might like to live in New York. In such a busy place, surely there was work for a woman, if only cooking and washing dishes. But she wasn't concerned with the future—only the here and now and running away before her heart changed her mind.

Darkness fell, and her tension increased. Selma had said they would leave as soon as light faded.

She paced about, anxious to be on her way. If Ryan did return, she would have to postpone everything. Selma said a lot of people had gone to a lot of trouble to help her along the way, and to hope and pray that didn't happen.

If she could hate him, it would make leaving so much easier. But no matter how hard she tried, feelings of animosity were overshadowed by memories of tenderness in his arms. And though the words were never spoken, she had, if only for a little while, felt truly loved.

She also couldn't stop thinking about the way he had

begun to look at her so adoringly in the days before she had accidentally caused the loss of their baby. Looking back, she recalled how she had dwelt on every word spoken, every nuance, to ponder whether he might actually be falling in love with her.

Yet, though it was painful beyond belief, the reality was that all it took for him to turn from her completely was being around Denise once again.

Suddenly, finally, Selma was there to tell her she would meet her in the shadows off the front porch. First, she had to make sure Master Roussel was taken care of, because Miss Clarice had given all the household servants permission to sleep with their families for the night. "I'm the only one here, thank goodness."

"You were smart to arrange it that way," Angele told her. "I'll never forget how you helped me."

She wondered why Selma looked so embarrassed—almost frightened—as she scurried from the room, again without looking at her.

After waiting till she felt Selma would be finished with Roussel, Angele snatched up her bag. She took one last look around, bit down on her lower lip to hold back the tears, and hurried out.

She was almost to the steps when Roussel called out to her.

Fearfully, she turned to see him standing in the door to his wing of the house. Hiding her bag behind her skirt, she answered, "Yes, what is it? Do you need something, Uncle Roussel?"

"I can't seem to sleep tonight. I don't feel so good. Could you come and read to me?"

She groaned inwardly. She had no time to spare, but he sounded so pitiful, so lonely, and she did adore him. Besides, it would be the last time she ever saw him, so a few more minutes couldn't make any difference. He usually fell asleep quickly when she read, anyway.

"I'll be right there. Go back to bed."

She went back to her room to leave her bag, thankful he had not seen it.

She found him in bed, looking so pale and tired she was glad she had agreed to visit him.

"Why can't you sleep?" she asked as she fluffed his pillows. "It's certainly a nice, cool night for it."

"I think I napped too long this afternoon. Besides," his smile was warm, "I like to fall asleep with you reading to me."

She made her voice bright. "All right, then. What would you like to hear tonight?" She glanced around, almost wildly, looking for a book, any book. Dear God, she had to hurry, even though she didn't want to. She enjoyed being with him, and she wanted to cry to think how he would never know she was saying good-bye to him.

He looked her up and down, eyes thoughtful. "Is something wrong? You're awfully fidgety."

She laughed—a thin, tinny sound that was unnatural to her own ears. "No. Everything is fine. Now, what book—"

"Is it because you're lonely?"

"No. I was just going downstairs for a walk when you called me."

"You have to be lonely. Ryan never stays home anymore. He's always in Richmond. I can tell he's drinking a lot, too." He was watching her intensely, searching her face for a clue as to what had her so unnerved.

Walking around the room, she picked up first one book, then another, but he waved away each one. "You need to choose one, because it's getting late," she said impatiently.

"Come over here and sit down. I don't give a damn about your reading to me. That was an excuse to get you in here."

She was stunned. "What on earth for?"

"Because I've had the feeling you aren't happy, even before you lost the baby. It's got worse since. Now, let's talk."

Knowing she had no choice, she sat in a chair next to the bed. "There's really nothing to talk about." *Dear Lord, let him have his say and be done with it.* Selma had said she had to keep to a schedule. People who were going to help her on the underground railroad would be waiting at points along the way but would leave if she were not there by the appointed time.

"Ryan said you were homesick for France."

She stiffened. "He said that?"

"Yes. I told him to take you back over there for a visit and to stay as long as you wanted." He frowned. "Hasn't he said anything to you about it?"

"No, he hasn't."

He sighed. "Be patient with him. He's stubborn and headstrong. And I know all this can't have been easy for you, especially having to put up with Clarice. She can be hell to live with. And Corbett is such a toad." He screwed up his face. "I'm sure sooner or later Ryan is going to get enough of both of them and tell them to make their home elsewhere."

Angele couldn't help laughing at Roussel's description of Corbett. "But you were going to leave BelleRose to Corbett."

"No, I wasn't."

She was dumbfounded by how he had suddenly taken on such a mischievous look. "But you said—"

"I know what I said, and I also know the reason I said it—to make Ryan find a wife and settle down."

"But your ultimatum was that she had to be French."

He shrugged. "Nothing wrong with that. I preferred that she be, but do you honestly think I could disinherit my own flesh and blood?"

She breathed on a sigh, and, without thinking, spoke her mind. "So he didn't have to marry me, after all. And all of this was for nothing."

"Nothing?" he hooted. "I don't know how you feel about him, but I happen to know he loves you, and that certainly cannot be considered *nothing.*"

Angele was swept with fresh sadness. If only it were true . . .

"You look as though you don't believe me. Surely you

can tell when a man loves you. Hell, I knew it before he told me, but like I said, he's stubborn. It probably took him a while to admit it to himself."

Angele gulped, blinked. "He *told* you that he loves me?"

"He sure did. It was the same day he told you that you'd lost the baby, and also when he was worried about you wanting to go back to France."

She almost didn't say it but told herself she had nothing to lose. "You're mistaken. He loves Denise."

"No, he doesn't. But she made it obvious to everyone at the ball that she wishes he did. What you need to do is let her know she's wasting her time, because the two of you are in love, and nobody is going to change that.

"You've got to learn to fight for what you want in this life, Angele," he continued. "Because if you don't, life will fight *you*—and win."

His lashes were fluttering, eyelids growing heavy. He was falling asleep.

Angele tucked the sheet under his chin and kissed his cheek. "Thank you," she whispered, "for making me want to fight."

She left his room and skipped down the stairs and out the front door and onto the porch.

Selma emerged from the darkness. "You're late. We've got to go now . . . right this minute."

Hugging herself, Angele turned completely around, delirious in her joy.

Roussel would not lie to her.

And Ryan had no reason to lie to him.

He had said he loved her.

And now, nothing else mattered . . . except that she let him know that she loved him, too.

"I'm not going, Selma. And I'm sorry for any inconvenience I've caused. You can go tell everyone, because I'm going to bed to wait for my husband to come home."

She ran back to the house, stopping now and then to twirl and dance, because she was suddenly, delightfully, so happy.

Selma called to her, but she kept on going, thankful she had answered Roussel's call . . . thankful she was now ready to do whatever it took to claim her love . . . her life.

Twenty-seven

Roscoe grabbed Selma by the front of her dress, tearing it as he lifted her off her feet. Holding her at eye level, he screamed into her face, "What the hell do you mean, she changed her mind? If you've made a mess of this, I'll whip the skin from your hide."

"Nossir, nossir, nossir," Selma babbled, frantic to make him understand she'd had nothing to do with it. "She just said she won't be goin' after all and to say she was sorry."

"Sorry, my ass! She's going." He dropped her to the ground and as she stumbled backward, he yelled, "Don't you run from me! You're gonna show me where she is."

With Selma cowering in the rear of the wagon, Roscoe returned to the house. He reined the horses in at the back door and leaped out.

Grabbing Selma by the nape of her neck and setting her on her feet, he ordered, "Now, take me to her." The only room in the plantation he had ever seen was the study, and the house was so large he had no intentions of searching each and every room. Time was wasting, anyway. The man who was to meet him would not wait long.

Selma did as she was told.

Oil lamps kept burning through the night illuminated the way.

She stopped at the door of the north wing and pointed with a trembling finger and whispered, "In there. I don't know which bedroom she'll be sleepin' in. You'll have to look and see."

"No, you stupid little bitch," he snapped. *"You'll* look and then come tell me. If she sees me peekin' in her door, she'll start screaming."

He gave her a shove. "And you better not let her know anything is going on, either, or I'll cut your throat. And when you find out which room she's in, leave the door open.

"And put out any lamps burning," he whispered after her.

Angele was in Ryan's bed, and she was wide awake, listening for any sound of him returning. The second she heard the door open, she sat straight up in the darkness, excitement surging.

She whispered his name and was disappointed when Selma answered instead.

"It's me, Miz Angele. I just came to see if you needed anything."

"No. I'm fine. You go on to bed now." Having noticed how Selma's voice quivered, she added to comfort her, "And don't worry about anyone being angry with you because I changed my mind. They won't blame you."

"Yes, ma'am."

"Good night."

When Selma did not respond, Angele knew she had gone but wondered why she left the door open.

Angele got up to close it. If she did fall asleep, she wouldn't know when Ryan came in unless she heard the door open. And she didn't want him just to find her in his bed. She wanted to tell him right away why she was there, lest he turn around and leave.

She got out of bed and padded across the floor, annoyed that Selma had extinguished the lamp in the parlor. It was always left burning, and, again, she was puzzled by Selma's behavior.

She groped in the darkness for the doorknob.

A hand closed over her mouth, and terror surged as she frantically clawed at it. Twisting from side to side, she struggled in vain, held tight against a man's huge body.

"Relax, and you won't get hurt."

A finger slipped between her lips, and she opened her mouth and bit down—hard.

"You little bitch!" he yelped, the pain causing him to momentarily let her go. He grabbed her again, twisting her arms behind her back with one hand, slapping her face with the other. "You want me to get rough? I will if you make me, but if I mess up that pretty face, you won't bring as much money, and that'll sure make Ryan unhappy. He figures you cost him enough, and he'd like to get some of it back."

Angele recognized Roscoe's voice and momentarily froze in horror to realize what he was saying.

"That's right," Roscoe laughed in her ear as he began to drag her across the floor. "Ryan wants you sold. He says it's the only way to get rid of you. The old man won't let him get a divorce, 'cause you've got him wrapped around your little finger. What did you do to make him so crazy about you? Let him take you to bed? I wish I had time to get some of that sweet stuff myself . . ."

Angele started fighting again, her screams muffled by his beefy hand mashing down on her face. But in his attempt to hold on to her, he tripped over the bag beside the door that she had forgotten to put away. It fell open, and he struggled to keep from tripping as the contents spilled out.

She kicked her leg back, catching him in the shin. With a loud curse, he slapped her again—harder. For a moment, she went limp, and he hurriedly threw her over his shoulder.

Pain was shooting down the side of her face, her head bouncing against his back as he ran down the hall.

As they passed a table, Angele tried to grab the vase sitting on it. She missed, and it crashed to the floor.

"Damn you," Roscoe muttered, running faster.

He took the steps two at a time and finally charged out the back door.

Roussel awoke at the sound of something breaking.

"Who's there?" he mumbled groggily. "Willard? What's going on out there?"

When she had heard the vase smash on the floor, Selma had dived from the sofa where she had been sitting to huddle on the floor behind it.

Roussel shuffled to the door leading into the parlor and opened it. "Why the hell is it dark? How come the lamps are all out? I can't see where I'm going, damn it. Willard, you better be around someplace . . ."

Frightened but not wanting Master Roussel to fall, Selma came out from hiding. "Willard ain't here tonight, Master Roussel. It's me—Selma."

"Why aren't the lamps burning?" he demanded.

She could have told him it was because Roscoe had wanted the house dark but instead scurried to get a lamp going.

Then Roussel wanted to know, "Did you stumble into something and break it? Clarice will have a fit if you did."

"Nnn-n-n-no, sir," she managed. "I been right here."

"You didn't hear it?"

"No, sir," she mumbled.

"Then you must be deaf. Bring the lamp." He shuffled across the parlor. He was weak and had to move slowly. "I'm going to see what's going on around here. Where is everybody, anyway? How come nobody else heard it?"

"Everybody's gone—" She bit her tongue. Miss Angele wasn't supposed to be gone. She hoped he didn't notice what she'd said.

But he had.

"Where's Angele? I knew Corbett and Clarice were going into town, but she was just here a little while ago. She can't have gone anywhere in the dark."

Selma tried to remedy her blunder. "Uh, no, sir, I didn't mean her."

"Then why didn't she hear it?"

"I don't know."

"Let's find out. Hold that lamp up so I can see where I'm going, or I'll bump into something and fall."

He saw the fragments of the vase on the floor. "What the hell? Who did this? Let's get to Angele's room. She might have fallen and cut herself."

Selma could do nothing but obey, cringing all the while.

He saw at once that the door was open, and called, voice on the edge of panic, "Angele? Are you all right? Did you hurt yourself?"

He stepped into the parlor, and his feet became tangled in the clothing scattered on the floor. "What the—?" Glancing down, he saw the overturned bag. "How come she's packed? Get in there and find her, Selma. I can't walk so fast, and I'm feeling dizzy . . ."

Selma went through the motions of searching both bedrooms, then returned to the parlor to find Master Roussel slumped into a chair. He was breathing funny, and she was scared. "She ain't here. You look sick. I'm gonna go get Willard."

"No. Wait. Come here." He beckoned to her.

Selma stayed where she was.

He looked her up and down with wise eyes. He knew his people so well and could tell when something was wrong—and there was definitely something amiss with Selma. She was bound to have heard the noise but pretended not to. And in the lamp's glow he could see the utter terror in her eyes.

Gently, he repeated, "Come here, Selma. I've never hurt you, have I?"

She shook her head.

"And I'm not going to hurt you now. Please. Come to me, because I'm not able to go to you, and I want you to look at me while I'm talking to you."

Hesitantly, she went to stand before him.

"Put the lamp on the table."

She did so.

"Now, I want you to tell me everything you know about what has happened here tonight. You won't be punished for anything, I promise. And you've never known me to break a promise to anyone, have you?"

She shook her head.

"And I won't let anyone else punish you, either. But you have to tell me where Angele is, and why she had her clothes packed, and who broke that vase in the hall."

"I . . . I can't," she sobbed, giving way to tears. "They . . . they'll sell me."

He put his hands on her shoulders. "Who will sell you? BelleRose slaves are never sold, and you know it."

"They . . . said they'd do it, and they will." She was crying so hard her words were barely audible. "And I'm gonna have a baby. They'll sell me and tell Toby I died . . . like the others . . . and he won't never see our baby . . ."

"What others?" Roussel felt his eyes were about to pop out of his head. Surely she didn't mean what he feared. There had been unexplained accidents in the past and burials without him having seen the bodies, but he'd not thought about it till now. "Who's been selling our slaves, Selma? You must tell me so I can stop it from ever happening again."

"Can't . . . just can't . . ."

He pulled her down to sit on his lap. Slipping an arm around her, he spoke in firm yet tender tones, promising over and over that nothing would happen to her or her baby. She would live at BelleRose with her family and continue to be treated well. She didn't have to worry. He would see to it.

Finally, she broke down and told him everything, beginning with how Miss Angele had first asked her to help her run away. She explained she had agreed to do so, but then Miss Clarice made her tell her about it. After that, she was forced to betray her mistress and follow Miss Clarice's orders . . . and Mr. Fordham's, too.

As Roussel listened, he began to tremble with rage.

When Selma got to the part about Roscoe saying Angele was going to run away even though she had changed her mind, Roussel quickly set her on her feet and cried, "Get to Toby as fast as you can! Don't let anyone stop you. Tell him he's to ride to Richmond—*fast!*—and find Ryan and let him know what's happened."

Selma assured him between sobs that she would do exactly as he said. "And I'm so sorry," she whimpered as she rushed to obey. ". . . so sorry."

Roscoe had hastily bound Angele's wrists and stuffed a rag in her mouth. Then he had roughly tossed her into the buckboard and took off for the rendezvous point.

"Wish I had time to teach you a lesson, you little hell cat!" he yelled back at her as they rolled along. "At least you were smart enough to keep your mouth shut about me giving you the old man's horse"—he laughed—"even if you were so stupid you didn't figure out I did it on purpose 'cause I knew he'd throw you.

"Ryan knew it, too," he embellished, wanting to make her suffer as much as possible to get even for how his hand hurt from her bite. "Selma told him she thought you might be gonna have a baby, and he didn't want it . . . didn't want to be tied down to you anymore. And it worked, too, especially when you decided to leave after you found out about him and Denise. Only you changed your mind and put me to a whole lot of extra trouble."

Angele was no longer scared.

She was angry.

Working furiously with the ropes, they were slowly loosening. He had been in a hurry when he tied them and had not done a very good job.

He talked on, tormenting her, and with each breath she drew she despised Ryan a little bit more. To think how he had been able to deceive her made her more angry with herself than him. How could she have been so blind? And he had even fooled his father.

"It won't be long now. We're about to cross the bridge at Cooter's swamp. The old dock isn't much farther, and I might just take the time to show you what a real man is like."

At last, her hands popped free.

Feeling about in the darkness, her fingers closed on a piece of stove wood that had been overlooked the last time a load was carried to the kitchen. Rising to her knees, she crept up behind Roscoe and brought it crashing down on his head.

With a shriek of pain, he yanked back on the reins, and the horses slowed just enough that she was able to leap out of the wagon without getting hurt.

"I . . . I'll get you, bitch!" he shouted.

Angele waded into the thick cattails growing at the edge of the swamp. The cold, slimy water was waist-high, and she tried not to think about things like snakes and leeches.

Selma had said the first rendezvous point for runaways was somewhere around Cooter's swamp. But Roscoe had said he was taking her farther. So maybe, in the beginning, Selma *had* intended to help her but was forced to betray her. But that didn't matter now. Angele knew she had to concentrate on surviving, and if a contact for the underground railroad did come to the spot nightly in case a runaway showed up, then he might be around tonight and help her. There was no way of knowing, and she could only hope.

"You better come out, bitch," Roscoe's voice echoed through the stillness. Croaking frogs in the distance fell silent, and a nearby whippoorwill ceased calling for a mate.

"When I find you, I'm gonna make you wish you had, and I'm not leaving till I do."

Something brushed her arm. It was slimy . . . slick, and she ground her teeth together to keep from screaming.

It moved away, and she dared to breathe again and wondered how long she would have to endure such madness of the night.

Toby had wasted no time getting to Richmond. He knew the road well, and there was a full moon. He gave the horse the reins and let him set his own gait.

It was late when he arrived but still a little ways from midnight, he figured.

He had gone to the house before leaving to make sure what Master Roussel wanted, and he had told him where Ryan might be—in a section where there were saloons and gambling houses.

Toby knew to go around to back doors in alleys. He was polite, respectful, but made it clear that he had to find his master, because there was a crisis at home.

At the fourth place he went to, he breathed a sigh of relief when the man who responded to his frantic pounding said Mr. Tremayne was upstairs, and he would go get him right away. He was much nicer than the others had been. They had cursed and slammed the door in his face.

A few moments later, Ryan appeared, his face taut with worry. "Did you find Doctor Pardee?" he asked at once, assuming whatever Toby had come to tell him had to do with his father.

Toby alleviated that fear. "It ain't Master Roussel. It's Miz Angele. Something's happened to her, and you've got to get home fast as you can."

"What's this nonsense?" Corbett had followed Ryan and spoke from behind him. He had a stricken, worried look on his face that Ryan couldn't see.

"We've got to go home," Ryan quickly said. "Right now." He started out the door, but Corbett caught his arm.

"Wait a minute." He forced a laugh. "You can't go tearing off on the word of a stupid slave who doesn't know what he's talking about. You've got a lot of money at stake on the hand you're holding upstairs. You leave now, and they'll fold you and keep it."

Ryan jerked from his grasp. "You think I give a damn? Something's happened to Angele . . ."

"But you can't be sure of that," Corbett argued. He pushed around him to lean right into Toby's face. "Tell him you're only guessing, that you don't know anything for sure.

"Tell him"—he bit out the words so Toby would grasp his meaning—"that your wife sometimes gets the wrong idea about things. Miss Angele probably went for a walk, and she can't find her. Isn't that so?"

Toby looked him straight in the eye, not flinching. "No, sir. That ain't it at all. It was Master Roussel who told me to hurry and fetch Master Ryan, because he knows for a fact that Miss Angele's been taken away by somebody."

At that, Ryan gave Corbett a hard shove out of his way and shouted, "Let's ride, Toby!"

Twenty-eight

Selma had persuaded Roussel to return to his bed to wait for Ryan. She hoped he would fall asleep, but he was much too worried. He kept asking her to repeat over and over every detail of what had happened . . . everything that Clarice had asked her to do. That included her lying to Ryan to make him think Angele had known she was going to have a baby before she jumped the horse. And when he heard that, he was livid.

When Toby finally arrived, walking right behind Ryan, Selma had never been so glad to see anyone in her whole life. She ran into Toby's arms and asked him to take her home and send Willard back, because she was afraid to be there when Miss Clarice found out what she had done.

"You aren't going anywhere," Roussel said firmly. "And I've told you that you've got nothing to fear from anybody. Now, tell Ryan what you told me—word for word."

She quickly proceeded to do so, but Ryan did not wait for her to finish. He'd heard enough, he said grimly.

"I'm going after the son of a bitch. Where was he when you were supposed to take her to meet him?"

"The pier on the other side of Cooter's swamp."

"Then what?"

"She thought she'd be goin' north."

Ryan knew Roscoe had no intention of seeing she got there. Neither would he be involved in the plot very long himself for fear of being found out. "Where was he taking her then?"

Selma told him she honestly didn't know. She had only been told to take her to the pier. He would have to ask Master Corbett or Miss Clarice, because they were all in on it together.

"There's no time." He started out.

Roussel called to him. "Wait, Son. Let me have Toby ride for some of the neighbors to bring some men to go with you. There could be trouble."

Ryan paused at the door. "There will be trouble, all right . . . and I intend to be the one to make it."

He ran out.

"Somebody should go with him," Roussel worried out loud. "But by the time you could get some white men together, Toby, he'd be too far ahead for you to catch him."

"I could get some of my folks," Toby offered.

"No. I'd have to arm you, and a bunch of slaves out at night could get you hung if you were to be caught. We'll just have to let Ryan take care of it."

"As angry as he was," Selma said dryly, "I reckon he'll do just that."

Angele felt like she was being eaten alive by mosquitoes and gnats.

She continued to crouch in the cattails, but gave thanks that Roscoe's shouts and threats seemed to fade farther and farther away.

She didn't know how much longer she could remain where she was. Despite the heat and humidity, her teeth had begun to chatter with cold from standing in the water for so long. There would probably be leeches clinging to her legs, but she dared not look for fear of splashing water, and that might bring Roscoe straight to her.

Finally, his voice faded, and she dared to creep out of the swamp and onto dry land. She might have to dash back in, but, for the moment, could have reprieve from the misery.

Running her hands down her legs, she was horrified to feel slimy little creatures attached to her flesh. She tore them off and flung them away, then cringed to hear the gentle splash they made as they hit the water. She prayed Roscoe could not hear.

After a few moments, she began to breathe easier and started working her way up to the road. During the anguished hours standing in the swamp, she had come to the conclusion that Roussel was her only hope . . . the only person she could trust. If she could make it back to the house, surely he would be able to help her—or send her to someone who could.

The light of the full moon filtering down through the overhanging trees was not bright enough to show the way, but she finally managed to find the road.

She would not have been able to tell which direction she needed to go except for the buckboard. It was right where Roscoe had left it, which meant BelleRose would be the other way.

She didn't see the skulking shadow coming up behind her.

She was unaware of *anything* until a hand closed over her mouth for the second time that night.

Again, she was pulled back against a man's hard body, but this time he whispered, lips to her ear, "Shush now. You've no reason to be afraid. My name is Lucas, and I'm a friend. If I let you go, will you be quiet? You could get us both killed if you scream."

She nodded furiously.

He released her, and she whirled about. She could barely make out his face, but it was enough for her to know she had never seen him before. "Who are you?" she asked warily.

"I told you—my name is Lucas. I help runaways on their next leg north from Cooter's swamp. I always come here at night to see if there's anybody waiting, and tonight I saw you. I also saw the man looking for you, so even though you aren't a Negro—not a slave—I think you're in trouble."

"I am, and if you'll help me go north, I'll be so grateful. But I don't have any money to pay you."

She could see his wry smile in the moonlight. "Nobody ever does. Come along, and I'll take you back in the bushes where you can wait till I come for you. I've had word there might be a runaway tonight, so I've got to wait a while longer. Then I've got a boat hidden on the river, and I can take you to the next person who'll be waiting to help you both.

"There're some thick bushes right over here," he said taking her hand. "And a little ditch just behind. You can crawl down in it and wait."

After making sure she was settled on the ground, Lucas left her, disappearing as quietly as he had come.

Angele wondered if the waiting would ever end. She had no way of telling time but sensed a lot of it had passed. In the east, above the dark, hulking trees, she could see the first watermelon streaks of dawn.

Panic began to creep into her whole being. If Lucas did not return soon, she was afraid to stay where she was. In daylight, she might be seen. Where was he and what was taking him so long? He'd said he was waiting for a runaway, but surely if the runaway were coming, he'd have made it by now.

Cramped and aching, she struggled to stand and stretch for a moment, but just as she did, Roscoe's voice rang out again.

"I know you're around here somewhere, goddamn you, and I'll find you if it's the last thing I do. Maybe if I start shootin' in the bushes, you'll either come out or get hit."

She was about to duck down in the ditch again but suddenly tensed to hear a horse approaching, hooves striking the road hard and fast.

Then it was Ryan's voice she heard, calling Roscoe's

name, shouting threats, obscenities. No doubt he was furious she had escaped.

Never had she wanted to scream so loud, to be able to tell him how she despised him for what he had done. If he wanted to be rid of her, she'd have gladly left, even if Roussel had protested. But he had chosen not only to try to sell her into slavery but to destroy their unborn child as well.

And she also wanted to rake her nails down his face, and—

A shot rang out.

A few seconds later, she heard the horse again—this time galloping away.

Easing up, she pushed her way into the bushes to stare out in the milky morning light.

A body lay on the ground, and she could see blood soaking into the ground.

She covered her mouth with her hand to hold back a cry when she realized it was Ryan.

"What are you doing? Get back here!" Lucas grabbed her arm and tugged. "Come on. We're ready to leave. The runaway finally arrived, and we've got to get out of here before it gets any lighter."

With lips quivering, she pointed at Ryan. "He . . . he's shot," she said uncertainly. "I . . . I don't know why Roscoe did it, but he's left him to die."

"Then let him. Come on."

Lucas kept pulling at her, but Angele continued to stare down at Ryan, so still . . . so helpless.

She was hesitating, because, as much as she loved him, she also hated him.

And if Roscoe had told the trut—if Ryan had, indeed, been behind the macabre scheme and she helped him now, he would eventually do the same thing all over again.

And next time she might not be able to escape.

But despite all the arguments within, she knew she had to take that chance.

"Ma'am, I can't wait no longer," Lucas pleaded.

"And neither can I!" she cried, bolting from the bushes and into the road to run to Ryan's side.

Lucas went behind her, continuing to beg her to go with him, but she refused.

"I know you have to get the runaway to safety, but please help me get him in the wagon first."

He looked from Angele to Ryan in doubt. "I don't know if I should. Who is he, anyway?"

"He's my husband," she murmured. "And I can't leave him."

At the sight of the buckboard coming up the road, Toby ran out to meet it. When he saw Angele, he slowed, apprehension creeping.

She stood up and shifted the reins to one hand so she could frantically wave at him with the other. "Ride for Doctor Pardee, Toby. Go fast! Master Ryan's been shot."

Toby yelled to Selma, who was coming up behind him, to help Angele. Then he took off.

As soon as Angele reined to a stop at the front steps, she told Selma to run to find some men to lift Ryan from the wagon and get him inside. Then she climbed down beside him and cradled his head in her arms.

He was so pale and hardly seemed to be breathing at all, his chest rising and falling so very slowly.

After what seemed forever, two brawny field hands came tearing around the house. Gently, with Angele coaching them every step of the way, they lifted Ryan and took him inside and put him on the sofa in the parlor.

"A blanket," she said to no one in particular. "He feels so cold."

Mammy Lou came running from the back of the house, out of breath. It had taken longer for her to rally from sleep and get there. She took one look at Ryan and wailed, "Oh, Lordy, Lordy, he's done been killed!"

"No, he's still alive," Angele told her. "Toby has gone for Doctor Pardee, but until he gets here we need to try and slow the bleeding. Get towels—rags—anything to press against the wound.

"And don't let Master Roussel know anything," she called to Mammy Lou as she took off to do what she had been told.

"Master Roussel already knows."

Angele moaned to see Roussel coming into the room with the help of a cane. She knew he must have been watching from the window and divine intervention had brought him down the stairs to the side of his wounded son.

"Who did this?"

"Roscoe. I managed to get away from him earlier in the night and hide. He was in the road, about to start shooting in the bushes to try and find me when Ryan rode up. I couldn't hear what was said. Then Roscoe shot him and took off."

Selma quickly got him a chair.

In despair, Angele turned to him. "Roscoe said Ryan told him to get rid of me . . . and to give me your horse, knowing he'd throw me and make me lose the baby."

Roussel looked aghast. "That's not true. Ryan didn't know what was going on till I sent Toby to bring him back from Richmond and tell him. He took off then like a bat out of hell to find you and bring you back. And as for wanting you to lose the baby, how did he know you were that way when you didn't?"

Selma could keep still no longer. "That's right, Miz Angele, 'cause Miss Clarice didn't make me tell him you did till afterwards. He couldn't have thought that."

"But I didn't know!" Angele gasped.

Selma hung her head. "She made me lie. I'm so sorry. I've caused you so much trouble." Tears trickled down her cheek.

"It's not your fault," Angele comforted the woman, knowing she had been forced into all of it. And, at last, the pieces of the horrible puzzle were starting to come together.

And as she continued to kneel by Ryan and hold his hand, she could only hope that she had been wrong about something else, too . . . that she had been wrong in believing he didn't love her.

It was late in the day when Ryan awoke. Dr. Pardee had given him a strong dose of laudanum to help him endure the removal of the bullet from his shoulder. He had to sleep it off, he told Angele and Roussel, and then he would be fine in a few days.

When Ryan opened his eyes, Angele was there to wait fearfully for his reaction when he saw her. Then, to her delight—and in answer to her prayers—a smile spread across his face, and, with his good arm, he folded her against him.

"You're safe," he whispered huskily. "Thank God. I was afraid I wouldn't get there in time to keep Roscoe from taking you wherever he planned to. Can you forgive me for letting this happen to you?"

"But it wasn't your fault," she protested. "You didn't know . . ."

"I knew things weren't the way I wanted them to be for us, and I didn't do anything about it. Clarice told me you hated it here . . . that you wanted to leave. Then the baby—"

"Ryan . . ." she blurted then, anxious to tell him. "Selma told me how Clarice made her lie and make you think I knew I was pregnant. But I didn't. And it was Roscoe who helped me with the horse. He said you told him to—because you knew I'd be thrown, and you wanted me to lose the baby. You wanted to be free of me."

"That's not true."

He raised his head, made to get up, but she gently pushed him back. "I know that. We were victims of a diabolical scheme, but there will be time to explain all that later."

"Then it's not too late for us." All the strength of his love for her shone in his eyes. "Not if you love me as I love you."

"I do, Ryan. I do," she said fervently. "But you may not want me when I tell you how I deceived you in the worst possible way." They were alone, and she knew it was time to confide all of it . . . everything about her past.

He lifted his hand to brush a tendril of hair back from her face. "Then tell me. It can't be so awful."

"But it is." She closed her eyes for a long, heart-stopping moment, then said the words in a rush before she could lose her nerve. "I'm not pure French. I let you believe I was, but the truth is, my father was English.

"And there's more . . ." Once she began talking, all the secrets came tumbling out—how her uncle had betrayed her father, driving him to suicide, then brutally raping her and causing her and her mother to flee, destitute, to Paris.

Wincing as he shared her pain, Ryan put his finger to her lips. "It doesn't matter. I only wish you'd told me sooner, but then maybe it might have. Who's to say? The only thing I know is that I love you, and I always will, and I don't care what kind of blood flows in your veins . . . as long as your love for me flows in your heart."

"It does, my darling," she avowed, leaning closer for his kiss. "And it always will."

Epilogue

Angele was in the ballroom, making sure all the Christmas decorations were in place.

"It sure looks pretty," Selma said, marveling at the greenery intertwined with holly sprigs. "And I just hope I'll be here tonight to see all the folks dressed up in their holiday finery."

Angele pointed at Selma's very large tummy. "I can't believe you're even here now. You look like you swallowed a watermelon."

"Two watermelons," Ryan laughed as he walked through the arched doorway. "Is everything ready?"

"I think so." Angele lifted her cheek for his kiss.

"Then come outside with me. I've got a surprise for you."

He was smiling mysteriously, and Angele took his hand, excited as a child awaiting the arrival of Saint Nick. It was her first Christmas at BelleRose, and she was enjoying every minute.

He squeezed her hand. "Happy, darling?"

"Yes, but—"

"But what?" he asked, alarmed to see her sudden frown.

"I just can't help thinking about little Danny."

"Don't worry. I saw to it that lots of toys were delivered to Corbett and Clarice's house."

"Are they terribly unhappy?" she asked worriedly.

"As unhappy as they deserve to be, I suppose. They have a comfortable house in Richmond, but it's far from a mansion. You know I paid for that. And Corbett has a job tending bar in one of the saloons, and I hear Clarice is working as a maid. That has to be quite a comeuppance for them both."

They walked across the foyer and out the front door to the porch.

Angele thought of Roscoe, how he'd been caught a few days after shooting Ryan. Ryan had not wanted revenge but told him if he ever saw him again, he'd kill him. Evidently Roscoe believed he meant it—as she did—for he seemed to have disappeared.

As for Selma, Ryan had made her and all the slaves promise never to have anything to do with helping runaways again. BelleRose would remain an entity within itself, he insisted, and would not become involved with problems from the world outside.

Angele was impatient to see Ryan's surprise. "Will you please hurry?" she jabbed him playfully in his ribs. "I've got to start getting dressed for the party."

Just then, Toby came around the side of the house from the stables. He was leading the most beautiful horse Angele had ever seen.

With her lips parting in wonder, she let go of Ryan's hand and walked slowly down the steps. "He . . . he looks like Vertus," she said, awed. "Vertus was my horse in England, remember? I told you about him, and—"

She stopped walking, cocking her head to one side as she took a closer look. "It . . . it can't be." She took the last few steps. "He looks so much like him, but there is no way . . ."

And then the horse threw back his head and let out a loud whinny of greeting . . . and love.

"Dear God . . . Ryan . . . it is him. It's Vertus."

She ran to throw her arms around the horse's neck, and he tried to nuzzle her as she hugged him. "How did you ever find him? How were you able to buy him from my uncle?"

Ryan went to stand beside her as he proudly explained

how he had hired several men in Richmond to go to England—to Foxwood—and persuade Henry to give up the horse. "They were very large men," he laughed. "Henry didn't give them much of an argument.

"So, my sweet," he slipped his arms around her from behind to hold her close against him. "Merry Christmas. Now you can ride to your heart's content."

"No, I can't." She turned about, putting her hands behind his neck. "Not for a while. But I can still enjoy having Vertus, knowing he's mine . . ."

Ryan blinked, confused. "I don't understand."

"You will," she smiled. "In about six months . . . because that's when you'll receive your Christmas present from me."

With a cry of delight, Ryan grabbed her and kissed her for long, breathless moments.

Then, hand in hand, they went to tell Roussel the wonderful news, at last.

His first grandchild would be born at BelleRose in the spring . . . to parents who would love each other forever.